Als

THE CAMERA EYE

THE POWER

DAN SMITH

P.O. Box 275
Boonsboro, Maryland 21713-0275

First Edition-October 2007
ISBN 1-59133-243-5
978-1-59133-243-5

Book Design: S. A. Reilly
Cover Illustration © S. A. Reilly
Manufactured/Printed in the United States of America
2007

Dedicated to the memory of my father, Thomas W. Smith

Acknowledgements:

As always, I want to thank my wife, Teresa, for helping me find the time to complete this book, and for lending her editing skills to the manuscript. My gratitude goes out to Stephanie and Shawn from Hilliard and Harris for once again believing in my writing.

This book is a mix of fiction and historical facts, and a good amount of research was needed to get those facts correct. I had to learn about specific periods of Nazi history, the customs of Aryan groups from the past and present, details of the Amazon jungle and northern Ecuador, the Cofan Tribe of Ecuador, the eating habits of Anacondas, a small town in Germany, seaplanes, details about Eva Braun and her family, the Aryan Nation compound, and so much other information.

I didn't do all this research alone, and had help from some great people A special thanks to my friend, Jim Witowsky and his wife Kamala Kesavan for going out of their way to visit Ruhpolding, Germany, which provided me with amazing insight into that town. Thanks to David Sokolow, who helped me with the development of several different plot points, and also helped me research numerous facts throughout the book. I want to thank my TIVO for working so hard to record countless hours of documentaries on Nazi history, Eva Braun, and Aryan groups. My friend, Jim Hickey, read a portion of the manuscript and provided me with the following inspiring words: "I've read worse." I don't know if I would have found the motivation to complete this book without that rousing support.

I want to extend my gratitude to everyone who read *The Camera Eye* and shared their feedback. Thanks to everyone who came to the book signings, sent cards, and wrote me notes through my web site. Your support meant so much.

PROLOGUE

The old man awoke with a start, panting as if he had just run a marathon in his sleep. At first, he thought he was home in his bed. The thought of being on his soft mattress calmed his rapid heartbeat as he imagined a warm blanket covering his shivering body. He thought he could smell the ocean breeze drifting in through his bedroom window. He thought he could hear the seagulls flying over the marsh and searching his lawn for scraps of food.

But when he tried to sit up, his horrible reality faced him. The hard slab he lay upon. The cold. The tight ropes around his wrists and ankles. The raspy breathing of the Bald Man—somewhere near him.

He felt groggy, and rocked his head from side to side, wondering if he had been drugged. The lights came on and burned his eyes. When he could finally focus, he saw the fat white face of the Bald Man.

His jowls dangled inches from the old man as he said, "Tell me where he is."

The old man cringed at the putrid stench of the Bald Man's breath as he said, "What?"

"Where is the boy?"

"Boy? I don't know what you mean."

The Bald Man sighed with disappointment. He reached down and placed a black leather bag on the old man's chest. He opened the bag, and pulled out a pair of pliers. "It's your choice how we do this. You can tell me now, or I'll find out the hard way."

Before the old man could speak, he felt pressure on his right index finger. He screamed as his body convulsed like a fish on dry land. When the pain abruptly ended, he felt the sharp tip of a knife resting against his nose.

The Bald Man moved closer as he asked, "How far do I have to go?"

CHAPTER ONE

April 11th, 2007

When the truck lurched forward, the milk cans clanked together, almost tipping over. As it pulled away, Shannon chased it, tears rolling down her face. "Come back! Come back!" she shouted.

She stumbled and fell on the dirt road. She sobbed so hard that a violent case of the hiccups consumed her. The cloud of dust stung her eyes and made her cough. She lifted her tear-filled face as her dirty hands smeared sand and pebbles into her sweaty hair.

Then, his warm embrace engulfed her. "It's okay, baby," he whispered. "The truck has to leave so it can deliver the milk. It will be back for more in the morning." He carried her inside, gently brushing the dirt off her clothes.

Shannon's dream was interrupted as the wind snuck in through a tiny opening in the window and gently tickled her cheek. She smiled, thinking it was him. As she stirred in bed, she expected his warm breath on her neck. But when she opened her eyes, she saw only the sheets and blankets tangled around her ankles.

She sat up, kicked them away, and bounced out of bed. She took two steps to the window and opened it, welcoming the morning chill. It was a new day—a spring day—and she felt refreshed as the ocean breeze blew the long blonde hair off her face.

She looked at the calendar on her wall and saw that it was Wednesday, April eleventh—her twenty-ninth birthday. But she knew there would be no celebrating today. Not after what happened. Not so soon. Her friends were giving her space, as she requested. But today, finally, she was starting to feel like she might be ready.

It's time, she told herself as she quickly dressed in shorts and a tee shirt, and made her way down the stairs. She stepped into the kitchen and went immediately for the phone. She dialed the all too familiar number.

"Information technology. This is Gary."

"Gary. It's Shannon."

"Oh...Shannon...I didn't expect to hear from you so soon."

"I'm ready to come back."

"What? You're kidding."

"I need to come back. How about Monday?"

"Are you sure you're ready?"

"I'm calling you, aren't I?"

"It's not my place to tell you what to do," Gary stammered. "It's only been a few weeks. You can take more time. The company is behind you. They're sending someone up from Atlanta to fill in for you until you're ready."

"Well, I'm ready now. So tell central office to send my replacement back to Georgia. I'll be in Monday."

"Okay, Shannon. If you're sure."

"I'm sure." She hung up the phone.

She strolled to her front door and thought of her mail. She had spent the previous few days in the house, and never made the walk to her mailbox. As she stepped onto her front lawn, she looked out at the wide river that led to Long Island Sound. She enjoyed the feeling of the sunshine seeping into her pale skin.

She considered herself lucky to have such a fine piece of shoreline property in southern Connecticut. She and Derek couldn't believe their good fortune when their real estate agent called to tell them about the home in New Haven. When they learned the ridiculously low asking price, they purchased it before the listing ever made it into the newspapers.

It was their home for the past two years. Their quiet little sanctuary, hidden away from the rest of the world. With the river as their backyard and not a neighbor in sight, they adored the privacy.

She strolled toward her mailbox as her bare feet kicked up dust from the dirt road. She walked past the only other house on the narrow street, which belonged to a kind old man named Mr. Henry. Shannon had a soft spot for old men, and was particularly fond of her only neighbor.

After she and Derek moved in, she was touched when Mr. Henry walked down the road and brought her a basket of flowers to welcome them to the neighborhood. They had spoken only briefly, as was Mr. Henry's custom, but the thoughtful gesture endeared him to her.

She quickened her pace, reached the end of the road, and retrieved two days worth of mail from her box. A quick glance revealed lots of junk mail, some catalogues, and a few belated sympathy cards from old friends. No birthday cards, as she had requested.

She started to head back, but couldn't help noticing Mr. Henry's mailbox. It was so overstuffed with mail that the door hung open. *How odd*, Shannon thought. The man followed a predictable routine, and made a slow walk to his mailbox every afternoon.

She wondered if he was sick or injured and was unable to make the walk. *But why wouldn't he call and ask me to drop his mail off?* she wondered. She had made it clear that she was available to assist him with anything, and made sure he had her phone number.

Maybe he's too stubborn to ask for help, she thought. She walked back down the road, stopped in front of his house, and decided to check on him. She walked up his long front walkway, but froze about halfway when she saw his front steps. Her heart sank into her stomach as she focused on the sight: five rolled newspapers scattered across the steps.

They were obviously delivered, but never picked up. Her muscles tightened as the only logical explanation entered her mind. This was not a man who was young enough to take off on a vacation. And in two years, she had never seen a visitor at his house.

She prayed she was wrong as she ran up the steps and pounded on the door. She rang the bell twice, knocked some more, and waited, hopefully. Hearing nothing, she ran to the back of the house. She opened the screen door and rapped loudly on the back door.

To her surprise, the door opened a crack. At first she thought someone had opened it, but then realized the door was ajar. She knocked some more before pushing it completely open.

There was silence.

"Mr. Henry, are you home? It's Shannon from up the road."

Again, she heard nothing. She took a deep breath and slowly walked into the house. She stepped carefully through the kitchen, calling his name loudly. She looked around the cluttered but clean living room, and quickly inspected the dining room. The furnishings and decorations didn't surprise her; they were modest but tasteful—much like Mr. Henry, she thought as she made her way down the hallway.

She took a step into the bathroom, looking for some sign of life. But there was nothing. No damp towel, no moist toothbrush, no droplets of water in the tub. She walked farther down the hall and saw two doors. One was open and she could see boxes and some other debris piled on a wooden desk and a small twin bed in the corner; the other door was closed.

She swallowed hard as she faced the closed door. She assumed this was his bedroom, and imagined the worst. "Mr. Henry, are you in there?" she yelled, her face inches from the door.

There was no reply. She waited a moment, licked her dry lips, and pushed the door open. She scanned the room from the doorway, frozen in terrified anticipation. But he wasn't there. She released a pent-up breath as she took in the rest of the room. The bed was neatly made with the comforter pulled tight around it. The rest of the area contained ordinary bedroom items. Nothing shocking. Nothing unusual.

She walked back to the living room, found the basement door, and went downstairs. Again, she found no trace of him—just a musty old unfinished basement. She returned to the living room, and slumped on the couch.

Where could he be? she wondered. *Even if he did manage to travel, he would have made arrangements for his mail and newspapers. Something was wrong,* she told herself. She had heard about elderly people developing dementia and wandering away from their homes.

She saw him from time to time, but not often enough to judge his mental state. They usually just shared a wave or a few quick words. *He could have Alzheimer's and I don't know it,* Shannon thought, as she estimated his age in the late seventies or early eighties.

She couldn't leave without doing something, so she found his phone and called the police. She sat on the front steps until a police cruiser appeared in the driveway. A middle-aged cop with a billy club dangling from his hip sauntered up the walkway; his name badge read "Officer Fuller."

"Good afternoon, ma'am."

"Thank you for coming, Officer. I'm Shannon Dinardo." She paused for a moment and then launched into the complete story, including her theory that he wandered away.

"I'd like to take a look around," he said and walked inside. Shannon followed him around the house, her skinny five-foot-eight frame dwarfed by his tall blue shoulders. His radio crackled as he finished and stepped back onto the front steps.

"Do you know the gentleman well?" he asked as he jotted some information on a small notepad.

"Not very well. But I usually see him a couple of times a week. He's my only neighbor."

"Only neighbor?" Officer Fuller said, surprised, as he glanced down the road. Then, he looked back at Shannon with a newfound look of recognition. "Oh my God," he muttered as he met eyes with her. "I didn't realize."

"Excuse me?"

"You said your last name was Dinardo?"

"That's right."

"I'm very sorry. I didn't realize where I was. You're the woman whose husband was killed in the car accident last month."

"Derek was my fiancé."

"My condolences. What a horrible thing. I hope you're doing okay."

"I'm all right, Officer. Thank you for asking."

Officer Fuller exhaled a deep sigh, and flipped a page in his notepad. "Regarding your neighbor," he began, "you did the right thing to call us. But there's not much we can do right now."

"But he's missing. Aren't you going to investigate?"

"Technically, he's not missing until he's been gone for twenty-four hours."

Shannon gestured at the pile of papers on the front steps and said, "Don't you see this? He's obviously been gone for days."

"I realize that may be the case, but we can't consider him missing until twenty-four hours from the time I submit this report."

"So you'll start an investigation tomorrow?"

Officer Fuller met eyes with her, and quickly looked away. He looked at the ground when he said, "I'll file a report, and we'll keep an eye out for him...I'm sorry...I wish we were able to do more."

"I don't understand."

"To be honest, we don't have the time or manpower to investigate something like this. I'll look around the area today, and we'll keep an eye out for him. But there's not much more we can do. Do you know if his family is aware?"

"I have no idea if he has a family. I've never seen a soul coming or going from here in two years."

Officer Fuller wrote on his pad. He passed her a business card and they shook hands. "I'm sorry I couldn't be of more help. Please call us if you find him, or if you learn about any family members."

"Yeah. Thanks."

The officer left, and Shannon sat on the front steps, her chin resting on her palms. The term "family members" bothered her. *Why couldn't someone who cares about him be considered as important as a family member?*

She glanced at the front lawn, remembering her parents. They had been dead for five years now, but she still thought about them every day. They adopted her when she was three years old, and raised her as an only child. Aside from a distant uncle and a couple of cousins somewhere on the West Coast, she also had no family members to speak of, and never learned the identity of her biological parents. She only knew she had been adopted from Russia.

I know the feeling of not having family close by, she thought to herself as if she were speaking to Mr. Henry. Still, she knew she had to do the proper thing and search his house until she found a phone number of a relative.

She walked back into the house and looked through some drawers in the kitchen. There was nothing. No phone book. No number jotted down on the calendar that hung inside a cabinet. *Surely, there was a number for a relative somewhere,* she assumed.

She remembered the desk in the spare room. *Perhaps something was tucked away inside of it,* she hoped. She entered the tiny room and lifted a few boxes off of the old desk, placing them on the bed. She opened the top drawer and saw a large neatly-folded red cloth. She closed the drawer and wondered where he would store a phone book.

She started to open a side drawer, but stopped. *The cloth. What was it?* She opened the top drawer again and looked at it. *This was an odd place to store a tablecloth,* she thought. *But maybe it wasn't a tablecloth.* She touched it. It took her a moment, but then she recognized the texture. It was some sort of flag.

Maybe it's an old American flag. Perhaps he's a World War II veteran. She pulled the flag out of the drawer and let it unfurl. With outstretched arms she held the flag in either hand, anticipating the familiar sight of old glory.

But what she saw stole her breath. Her mouth fell open as her stomach tightened into a knot that nearly doubled her over. It was a flag, as she expected, but it was not the American flag.

She closed her eyes, hoping she was hallucinating. When she opened them back up she was still holding the red flag. Her eyes darted back to the large white circle in the center of it. It was still there. A horrifying symbol she had never seen outside of a book. But there was no mistaking it.

She knew she was looking at a swastika.

CHAPTER TWO

Shannon waited as the Internet search engine did its job. A moment later her computer screen was filled with links to web sites about the swastika. Just from a quick scan of the sites, she learned that the swastika did not originate with the Nazi party. One of the sites, which claimed to be the authority on the history of the swastika, said the symbol dated back 3,000 years.

She clicked on that link and anxiously waited for the site to load. There, she found a plethora of information. She learned that the swastika was an ancient symbol that was used to represent positive ideas such as the sun, life, power, strength, and good luck.

Historians found the symbol on age-old artifacts such as pottery and coins that dated back to 1,000 BC. Some believed that it even appeared on artwork in the ancient city of Troy.

The swastika was not only used in ancient times, but also throughout history. It was commonly used in the cultures of China, India, and southern Europe, and had long been a symbol of peace in the Buddhist religion.

It was utilized as recently as the early twentieth century, and could be found on cigarette cases, postcards, and even some buildings. It was used as a shoulder patch for the United States 45th Infantry Division during World War I. The Finnish airforce used it as their symbol until after World War II.

But on August 7th, 1920, the Nazi party changed the meaning of the swastika forever by adopting it as their official emblem. Adolph Hitler personally selected the swastika, thinking it was an adequate representation for the struggle of the Aryan man. Since then, it has been known as a symbol of hatred, anti-Semitism, violence, and murder.

Shannon had no idea the symbol had such a history, and always assumed the Nazis had created it. She wished what she saw in Mr. Henry's desk was something other than the Nazi flag. Maybe an ancient Chinese carpet or a Buddhist cloth. But she knew better. Still, she wanted to confirm her belief.

Back at the search engine, she typed: Nazi flag. And in a matter of seconds she was looking at a picture of the same flag she had held hours earlier. Solid red with a large white circle in the center, which contained the black swastika.

She picked up a calculator off of her desk. She put in 2007 and subtracted 1945; it answered 62. It had been over sixty years since World War II ended. If Mr. Henry were in his early twenties when the war ended, then he would be in his early eighties now. *My God,* she thought. *Could he have been a Nazi?*

The thought seemed preposterous. *He seemed like such a nice man. But what was he like sixty years ago?* She leaned against the desk, lost in her thoughts. Her imagination took over and she started to wonder if his disappearance could have something to do with his past.

If he was a Nazi, maybe someone found him. She had heard about Nazi hunters that pursued suspected Nazi war criminals all over the world. She tried to recall some details, but couldn't remember any specifics.

Once again, she returned to the search engine and decided to do some research. In an instant, she was choosing among hundreds of sites that had information about Nazi hunter groups. She started to surf.

One name that appeared on almost every site was Simon Wiesenthal. Shannon learned that he was a Holocaust survivor who was liberated from Mauthausen, Austria, by an American armored unit on May 5, 1945.

After he recovered from the war, Wiesenthal started The Jewish Documentation Center in Vienna; the organization's main purpose was to assemble evidence for the possible future trials of Nazi criminals. After Wiesenthal's work helped Israeli authorities locate and capture Adolf Eichmann, a ruthless Gestapo chief, he changed The Center's main purpose to the hunting of war criminals.

Wiesenthal and his group helped to capture dozens of Nazis who were responsible for the murder of millions of innocent people: Frances Stangl, the commandant of the Treblinka and Sobibor concentration camps; Karl Silberbauer, the Gestapo officer who arrested Anne Frank; and Klaus Barbie, head of the Gestapo in Lyon, France and known as "The Butcher of Lyon."

Shannon went on to read that Wiesenthal had finally retired a few years ago. But because his files still contained information on thousands of suspected Nazis, others carried on the hunting.

Shannon read different opinions on the current state of Nazi hunting. Some believed that it continued to be a legitimate cause, and thought tens of thousands of Nazis were still at large, living in unsuspecting communities all over the world. Others thought it was now a waste of time, thinking that all the war criminals had either been caught or died off.

Some articles on the subject accused certain groups of being overzealous in their pursuits of suspected criminals. In the worst examples, some groups took justice into their own hands, sometimes at the expense of innocent individuals.

The words she read pierced into her heart as she thought of the gentle old Mr. Henry. *Could he be a victim of some crazed Nazi hunter group?* She worried about him, but felt helpless. *Without the assistance of the police, what can I possibly do?*

She left her desk for the first time in hours, and poured herself a glass of red wine. *Another lonely night in a painfully empty house.* She looked at the clock and was surprised to see that it was two in the morning. *I surfed the web for that long?* She figured it was time to get off the Internet and pick up a novel—something to get her mind off of her neighbor.

She strolled back into the office as she took a big sip of the wine. She approached the computer and was about to shut it down, but stopped when she saw she had a new e-mail message. After a few quick clicks of the mouse, her new message appeared. It was from the screen name Altman42089, and the subject read, "Shannon, Happy Birthday!"

"Altman?" Shannon said aloud. *I don't know anyone named Altman.* When she saw there was an attachment with the e-mail, she was reluctant to open it, fearing a virus. *But it says my first name, and whoever sent it knows it's my birthday.*

With a good deal of trepidation, she opened the e-mail. She saw that the attachment would take a minute to load, so she walked across the room to her bookcase. It was time to start a new novel. She wanted something that would take her mind off of her troubles—both her fiancé's death and the disappearance of Mr. Henry. She chose a science fiction thriller as she took another sip of the wine.

She walked back to the desk and hoped her computer wasn't crashing. A quick glance revealed some sort of picture on the screen with a few words below it. As she got closer and the picture came into focus, she froze. The wineglass fell from her hand and shattered against the hardwood floor. Her face went white, as her hands grasped for something to steady herself.

The picture was of a naked blonde woman about her age. She appeared to be dead with a noose around her throat. There were three words at the bottom of the picture. It read: "STOP YOUR RESEARCH!"

CHAPTER THREE

At 7:00 AM, she decided to give up trying to sleep. Maybe she dozed a little here or there and wasn't aware of it, but she knew she couldn't have slept more than an hour. *Someone was spying on me online. Someone knew what I was reading.*

She considered the message a death threat and wanted to get help. *But who to call? Certainly not the local police. If they didn't have time to look for a missing person, what could they do about a threat over the Internet?*

She had heard that the FBI investigated crimes over the web, and thought about calling them. *But this is nothing they'll care about. Would anyone even take my call?* She wasn't sure what to do; she paced from her bedroom to her front door and back again for a half-hour.

Finally, after taking a long look at the dead woman again, she decided to call. She flipped through the phone book and found an FBI office in New Haven. She dialed the number and expected to hear a recording telling her that no one could take her call right now.

But, to her surprise, a real person answered. "FBI, how may I help you?" a female voice asked.

"I...I...my life has been threatened over the Internet."

"What's your name, ma'am?"

"Shannon Dinardo."

"What's your address?"

"One Riverside Road, New Haven."

"Hold for a moment."

Shannon paced faster now, as she pressed the cordless phone to her ear. She wondered if she made the right decision to call. *Maybe it was just a hoax. Maybe a prankster was monitoring one of the Nazi sites and wanted to scare me.*

After a couple of minutes, a man's voice came over the phone. He identified himself as an agent and asked her a series of questions. Eventually, she explained the whole story, including Mr. Henry's disappearance, her research, and the mysterious threat.

He listened patiently until she was done, and then said, "We have a division here that specializes in this sort of matter. I'm going to page another agent who will help you."

"I don't want to disturb anyone over this. It's probably nothing."

"Miss Dinardo, you're not disturbing anyone. Just give me your phone number and I'll have someone get back to you."

She reluctantly agreed, told the agent her phone number, and thanked him profusely. After hanging up the phone, she paced even harder for a few minutes, still wondering if she had done the right thing.

She walked onto her side porch and sat in a cushioned swing, which faced the river. She exhaled a worried breath as her head settled into a comfortable position. With the phone carefully cradled in her arm, she finally fell asleep.

Two hours later, the phone rang and Shannon jumped to her feet. Before she was fully awake, she was speaking to an FBI agent named Brad Palmer. Once again, she explained the entire story, and this time, included even more details.

"Do you still have the e-mail, Miss Dinardo?"

"Yes. I printed a copy, and I have it saved on my computer."

"Good. I'd like to come by and take a look at it."

"Okay."

"How about one o'clock today?"

"Today?" Shannon replied, surprised at the immediacy.

"Yes. Is that okay for you?"

"Of course. Yes. I'll be here."

Shannon gave him directions to her hard-to-find road and hung up. She looked at the clock and saw that it was 10:00 AM. She actually felt refreshed now; her two hours of sleep had done a world of good.

She was still amazed that an FBI agent would be at her house in three hours. She made sure the e-mail was still saved on her computer, and the printed version of the threat was on her desk.

Then, she thought of Mr. Henry. She had left his house so quickly that she wasn't sure if she had closed his front door. She knew she had to go back, bring in his mail and newspapers, return the flag to the desk, and close up the house properly. And she still needed to find a phone number of a relative.

She walked down the dirt road, approaching his house. She gathered the newspapers from the front steps and entered through the front door. She dropped the papers on his dining room table, and decided to return the flag to the desk before she did anything else.

As she walked down the hallway, she saw something unusual. The door to the extra bedroom was closed. She had left the house in a mad rush after finding the flag, and didn't remember closing it.

She continued to move toward the room as she searched for an explanation. *The wind, maybe? What else could it be?* She finally dismissed the anomaly and opened the door. She took a step toward the desk and looked for the flag.

But it was gone. She was absolutely sure that she dropped it on the ground in front of the desk. She looked at the exact spot where she dropped it, and saw that it wasn't there. She took a step back, knowing something was wrong.

Then, she heard a noise from the corner of the room, and whirled to face it. To her horror, she saw something in the bed—a large moving lump under the covers. Then, a head popped up, and she looked at the face of a man about her age.

She screamed in a panic as the man jumped out of the bed, landing roughly on the floor. He wore a white tee shirt and blue boxer shorts, and lost his footing as he tried to stand. Shannon continued to scream, as the man fell back into the corner.

Shannon scanned the room for a weapon. She lunged forward and grabbed a small metal lamp off the desk. She held it over her head as if she were about to strike the man.

He screamed as he raised his arms in front of his face. "Don't hit me," he yelled.

"What did you do with Mr. Henry?"

"What?"

"You heard me!" She cocked back her arm as if she were about to slam the lamp into his skull. "Where is Mr. Henry?"

The man looked at her with a puzzled expression, and said, "I am Mr. Henry."

Shannon became angry at the lie, and convinced herself that this man was not only responsible for Mr. Henry's disappearance, but maybe even the threatening e-mail. She took a step toward him, raising the lamp even higher. "Don't lie to me!"

"I'm not lying," he screamed, as he held his arms up for protection. "My name is Neil Henry. This is my Grandfather's house."

CHAPTER FOUR

The Bald Man had been to the compound many times, but had never been allowed in the Great Room. He felt uneasy at first—a bit intimidated by the cathedral ceiling, the long mahogany table, and the lit candles that circled the room. But after a few minutes, he relaxed in a wingback chair. *After all,* he thought, *I am an invited guest.*

But when he heard the footsteps approaching the room, the nervousness returned. Not many had earned the honor to meet the Supreme Leader. After years of loyal service, he was finally being rewarded.

The Bald Man studied the Leader's face as he strode across the room. He had pictured him in his mind so many times. And now, at last, he was seeing him for real. The Leader sat at the head of the table as two armed guards flanked him. He slowly shifted his eyes to the Bald Man.

"I'm told you were successful," the Leader said.

"Yes, Your Excellency."

"I commend you. You must be quite persuasive."

"I have some very effective methods, Your Excellency."

"So where is the boy?"

"Ecuador."

"Ecuador," the Leader said, surprised. "How interesting that they would choose South America." He paused, rapping his fingers on the table as he thought. "I trust you disposed of my old friend."

"No, sir, he's still alive."

"Really?" The Leader's stern gaze locked in on the Bald Man. "And why is that? I didn't take you for the type to leave a job incomplete."

"Not at all, sir. I will gladly complete the job. But I think we need him alive for a bit longer. He was not able to explain the exact location from memory. But I believe he can guide us there."

"I see. You want to employ your methods on him in Ecuador."

"I believe that's the only way, Your Excellency."

The Supreme Leader dramatically rose from the table and stepped toward the Bald Man. "I am pleased. Take two of my best men with you and carry out the rest of the plan. You are aware that we have only eight days."

"I am, sir. I will return with the boy."

"Very well, young man, be on your way."

The Bald Man stood and gently took the right hand of the Leader. He kissed the Leader's ring and said, "It is an honor to serve The Power."

CHAPTER FIVE

Shannon apologized for the umpteenth time as she sat red-faced at the dining room table. Neil moved around the kitchen barefoot, wearing his grandfather's bathrobe. His dark hair, unshaven face, and handsome eyes appealed to Shannon in a way she wasn't able to acknowledge at the time.

He poked around a cabinet as he said, "I can't seem to find any coffee except this jar of instant." He held the glass jar out for Shannon to see. "Would you like some?"

"No, thank you. Again, I'm so sorry. I owe you an explanation."

Neil opened the refrigerator and said, "How about juice? Would you like some juice?"

"Please let me try and explain. My name is Shannon Dinardo. I live at the end of the street."

"Dinardo, huh?" Neil replied, peering above the refrigerator door.

"Yes."

"I never would have guessed you were Italian."

"I'm not, at least not as far as I know. My father was Italian, but I'm adopted."

"Okay. That explains it. Cause that blonde hair and blue eyes make me think more of a Northern Europe ancestry. Maybe Swedish, or even Scandinavian."

"Yes. I've heard that before, but I was actually adopted from Russia....anyway, as I was saying, I'm your grandfather's neighbor, and I noticed the papers piled up on his front steps..."

Neil pulled out a carton of orange juice. "This OJ looks good. Can I pour you a glass?"

"That would be fine. Thank you." Neil placed two glasses and the carton of orange juice on the table. He sat down and filled the glasses as Shannon continued. "I let myself in after ringing the bell and knocking for a long time. I was worried about him. I was afraid he went missing."

"It looks like he is missing. That's why I'm here. I've been calling him for days and he didn't pick up the phone. I was worried he had a heart attack or something. I live in Boston, so I drove down to check on him."

"And you have no idea where he could be?"

"If I did, I'd be looking there right now. I thought I would stay here awhile and see if he comes back. I don't know what else to do."

Shannon thought of the Nazi flag. *Would this help him?* She wanted to ask Neil about it, and see he if he thought his grandfather's past could have something to do with his disappearance. *But how do I ask that? By the way, Neil, was your grandfather a Nazi?*

She decided to put the question off for now. For a moment, she got lost admiring his square jaw and muscular shoulders. But she composed herself and said, "I should tell you that I called the police."

Neil popped up and started looking through the refrigerator again. "Yeah, I bet that did a lot of good," he scoffed. "Did they even bother to look for him?"

"Not really. But they told me to call if I found a family member."

"Thanks. I'm not expecting them to do much, but I'll call them later. I really would like to offer you something to eat, especially since I'm starving myself. But there's nothing in this place."

"Why don't you come to my house? I can make us something."

"Really?" Neil said as he kicked the refrigerator door closed.

"It's the least I can do. After all, I almost clocked you over the head with a lamp."

As they strolled down the dirt road, Shannon tried to imagine what Neil was experiencing. His grandfather was lost with no explanation. *How helpless he must feel,* she thought.

But, surprisingly, she didn't think he appeared that upset. *Perhaps this was just his way of dealing with a crisis. He must be worried about his grandfather, otherwise why would he have driven down from Boston?*

The flag! I have to tell him about the flag.

As they stepped onto Shannon's porch she said, "Neil, I should ask you about something I found in your grandfather's house."

"Yes." He stopped and turned toward her.

"The police officer asked me to try and find a family member, so I was looking for an address book. I was going through that old desk in the spare bedroom, and...well...I found something strange."

"You mean the Nazi flag?"

Her eyes widened. Then it occurred to her. *Of course he saw the flag. I left it on the floor and it was gone when I went back. He must have put it back in the desk.* "Yes," she replied after a short pause.

"He keeps it as a memento."

"A memento?" she said with a raised eyebrow. "So he was a Nazi?"

His eyes shot up at her. "What?"

"I was wondering if you think his past might have something to do with his disappearance. You know, like if one of those Nazi hunter groups may have found him."

Neil laughed and shook his head. He looked down at the ground and seemed to be trying to regain his composure. *This is funny?*

"Shannon," he began, still trying to suppress a smile, "my grandfather was not kidnapped by a Nazi hunter."

"How can you be so sure?"

"Because he *is* a Nazi hunter."

"Oh...my...I..."

"I should say he was a Nazi hunter. He's been retired for quite some time." Shannon felt the blood rushing out of her head and took a step toward her patio furniture. "He's a Holocaust survivor."

She sat down and looked up at him. "A Holocaust survivor, but..."

"He changed our family name after the war." He strolled over and sat on the other side of the plastic table. "Our name used to be Henstein. He dropped the stein and changed it to Henry. We're Jewish."

"That's unbelievable," Shannon muttered, still in shock.

"Is it more believable that he was a Nazi? He hated the Nazis so much that he devoted his whole life to tracking them down. He worked in Austria with the most famous Nazi hunter in the world."

"Simon Wiesenthal," Shannon proudly said, perking up a bit.

"I'm impressed," Neil replied. "How do you know about him?"

"After I saw the flag yesterday I did some research on the Internet."

"Because you thought Nazi hunters took my grandfather?"

"That's right. I ended up surfing the web all night. I learned all about the Nazi hunters, but I also did a lot of reading about famous Nazis and how they escaped after the war."

"So you learned about The Odessa Organization."

"I did."

Shannon learned that when World War II ended, many Nazis escaped arrest and fled to Argentina. The Odessa Organization was thought to be a clandestine group of individuals who sympathized with the Nazi party. Many people believed this organization set up an escape route to Argentina that was used successfully by hundreds of Nazis.

Still, some thought this was a myth, a product of overactive imaginations after a couple of Nazis were found in Argentina. But when writer Frederick Forsyth published a book in 1972 entitled *The Odessa File*, a wide audience was introduced to the idea. The popularity of the book in the 1980s coupled with the 1987 arrest of Klaus Barbie, who supposedly used the Odessa ratline to escape, raised interest in the truth about the organization.

In 1992 Argentina's president, Carlos Menem, ordered that all government files related to Nazis be made open to the public. The results shocked the world. The files revealed that Nazi-sympathizing officials in the governments of Spain and Italy had indeed supported a complex escape route to Argentina. In addition, the files also contained information implicating corrupt individuals in the Red Cross and the Vatican.

"Interesting stuff, huh?" Neil said as he leaned back in the chair.

"It sure is." She swallowed hard and decided to tell him. "I want to talk to you about something that happened to me last night."

"You mean while you were surfing the web?"

"Yes. I got a strange e-mail. Actually, I consider it a threatening e-mail."

"You're kidding."

"Would you like to see it?"

"Absolutely."

Shannon led him into the house and to her office. She handed him the picture of the dead girl. "Stop your research," Neil said loudly, reading from the picture.

"Obviously, someone was spying on me online. And I don't know if this is a serious threat, or just some prankster who was trying to freak me out."

"Who sent this?"

"Some name I never heard of. I printed that too." She took a piece of paper off of her desk and looked at it. "It says Altman42089 at Cool Mail dot com."

Neil's head snapped toward her. He grabbed the paper out of her hand and looked at it with wide eyes.

Shannon said, "Cool Mail is a free ISP, so it's practically impossible to track their users. I work with computers, so I can try, but I'm not real optimistic."

"It's not necessary. I know who this is from."

"What?" Shannon felt the hair on her arms stand straight up.

"I'm sorry to say that this is not a prank."

"Who sent it?"

"A Neo-Nazi group."

"What? How the hell do you know that? I just told you that Cool Mail is a free service. Anyone can use it."

"It's not the Cool Mail address. It's the screen name. It's a code."

"A code! For what?"

"Altman is the name Klaus Barbie was living under when he was arrested in Bolivia."

"So what? Altman's not that uncommon of a name."

"The fact that the name Altman is matched with these particular numbers leave me with no doubt as to who you're dealing with."

"What can the numbers possibly mean?"

"It's a date."

"A date? What date?"

"Four is April, and 20 is the twentieth of April. The 89 is short for the year."

"So what happened on April 20th, 1989?"

"Not 1989. This refers to 1889." Neil took a deep breath and met eyes with Shannon. "It's Adolph Hitler's birthday."

CHAPTER SIX

Shannon sat at her kitchen table, her hands slightly shaking.

"Are you sure you're okay?" Neil asked from across the table.

She shook her head. "I'm a little freaked out."

"That's understandable."

"I don't know how you can be so sure about this. Couldn't it be a coincidence? They're just a bunch of numbers and a name."

"I wish that were true. But, unfortunately, I'm absolutely certain."

"Why?"

"Because I'm familiar with this particular group, and they use that number online to identify themselves to other members. That date is sacred to them. And it's their practice to use the alias names of Nazis who escaped through the Odessa ratline."

"How do you know all of this?"

"It's my job."

"Excuse me? Did you say your job?"

"That's right."

Shannon leaned her tired, tense body back against the chair. Her pale face looked at him, bewildered. "I can't even begin to imagine what you're talking about."

"It's complicated. For starters, I'm a lawyer."

"A lawyer? And it's your job to know all about Neo-Nazi groups?"

"Sort of. You see, I work for an organization called The New England Law Center. We're a small law firm that primarily works pro bono for clients who've had their civil rights violated. We survive on grants and donations, and obviously, none of us get rich. I drive a Honda, not a Mercedes."

"That's great, but what does it have to do with the Nazi groups?"

"I work in a special department in the firm called The Intelligence Division."

"Sounds very covert," Shannon said as she leaned forward, seeming interested.

"Our primary function is to monitor the activities of hate and extremist groups."

"To stop them from committing hate crimes?"

"Yes. And to gather evidence for future lawsuits."

"You've sued these groups?"

"In 1995 an African-American man in Stone Mountain, Georgia, was beaten up by a gang of KKK members. They chained him to the back of their pickup truck and dragged him along a paved road for a half-mile. He was decapitated after a quarter mile, but they kept dragging him anyway."

"That's horrible. Did they catch them?"

"Yeah, or at least most of them. They all got convicted, but when we found out they were members of the Klan, we sued on behalf of the man's widow."

"You can sue the Klan?"

"At the time, they were a registered organization with chapters in all fifty states. They called themselves The United Klans of America. They had extensive assets, so we went after them."

"Did you win?"

"We won 7.2 million dollars."

Shannon's mouth fell open. "You're kidding."

"We bankrupted the entire KKK."

"But they're still around."

"They are, but we destroyed their finances and ripped apart their organizational infrastructure."

"Good for you." Shannon smiled for the first time in a while. Neil reciprocated with a smile of his own, and, for a moment, she got lost in his eyes again.

"They haven't been the same since. But the Klan is not the group that worries us the most."

"Let me guess. With my luck it's probably this Neo-Nazi group that threatened me."

"I'm afraid so. They have incredible resources, but are smart enough to hide them. They have intelligent leaders, and they don't expose themselves in the public eye like the Klan and some of the less organized hate groups."

"What do you mean when you say they don't expose themselves?"

"We've all seen news footage of Klan rallies with beer-bellied rednecks running around in sheets and waving the confederate flag, or young, stupid skinheads getting arrested for beating someone up."

"Of course."

"This group doesn't do things like that. They don't attract attention to themselves. Their members fit in with the rest of society. And they're smart and organized."

"I don't understand. If they're so low profile then what crimes are they committing? Who are they hurting?"

"Good point. They're not hurting anyone right now. But they will."

"What do you mean?"

"They're waiting."

"Waiting for what?"

Neil leaned back in his chair and released a tired breath. His eyes wandered around the room. "It's going to take me a while to answer that."

"Don't you think I deserve to know? After all, these people threatened me," she shot back.

"Of course you deserve to know. And I'll tell you." He paused and looked at his watch. "It's just that we've been here for almost three hours, and I'm starving to death."

Her face lit up as she jumped to her feet. "Oh my God. Three hours? What time is it?"

"Almost one."

"I'm so sorry. I was supposed to make you something to eat." She took two long strides toward the refrigerator as she said, "I think I have some eggs. Do you like omelets?"

"No...I mean yes, I like omelets, but you don't have to cook. I'll go out and get something."

She turned to him with a carton of eggs in her hand. "I can make them with cheese, tomatoes…some onions if you like."

Neil stood up and stepped toward her as he said, "That would be wonderful, but please...don't go to any trouble."

She cracked an egg into a mixing bowl. "It's no trouble. Let me do this for you."

He leaned against the counter and said, "Okay. I appreciate it."

She cracked three more eggs and grabbed a frying pan from the cabinet as she said, "There's something else I should tell you."

"What is it?"

"The subject line in the e-mail I got said 'happy birthday.'"

Neil looked at her with a puzzled face. "I don't understand."

"Yesterday was my birthday. How did these people know it was my birthday?"

Neil didn't speak for a moment. "Are you sure the happy birthday was directed to you?"

"The subject line said 'happy birthday, Shannon.' Wouldn't you say that's directed to me?" She stirred the eggs into the pan and glanced at him, waiting for a response.

"That's disturbing," he said as they met eyes. He opened his mouth to speak but stopped when he heard a noise. It was the sound of car tires rolling along gravel. He looked out the kitchen window and saw a silver sedan slowly making its way down the road. "Looks like you've got a visitor."

"What?" Shannon replied, looking up from the frying pan.

"It's a silver car. Are you expecting someone?"

Shannon's eyes darted quickly toward the clock on her wall. Then, a look of surprise took over her face. "I completely forgot. It's one o'clock. That must be that FBI agent."

Neil's head snapped toward her. "What FBI agent?"

"I forgot to mention that I called the FBI. That e-mail really scared me. I had to call someone about it."

Neil looked at the window, closely examining the approaching car. "When did you call them?"

"This morning. I talked to an agent...Brad Palmer I think his name was. He told me he would be here at one. I forgot he was coming."

Neil watched the car for another moment, and as it pulled into the driveway, he snapped the shade shut. "We need to get out of here."

"What?"

Neil turned off the stove burner and took Shannon by the hand. "We have to go now."

"Why?"

Neil pulled her out the back door, and scanned the landscape. "We need to hide. Where's a good spot?"

"I don't understand why we're hiding. He's here to help me."

Neil spotted a hill with some high grass. He took Shannon by the hand and quickly guided her to the spot. "Get down." He tried to pull her over the hill but she resisted.

"No!" she screamed at him. "I want to talk to him."

The car door slammed and Neil grabbed her. He fell into the high grass and took her with him. "Please be quiet," he whispered. He held her against his chest, and for a moment, they were nose to nose.

"Why are you doing this?" she whispered.

"I can't explain now."

"Why?"

He muffled her mouth with his hand as they listened to the sound of the agent knocking on her front door. "We need to be quiet." She could barely hear him as they slithered farther behind the hill.

"You owe me an explanation," she whispered.

"You're absolutely right. When he leaves, I'll fill you in on everything." They met eyes and their lips were so close they could have kissed.

"I'm going to hold you to that," she replied.

Then, they lay motionless in the grass, listening to the agent's footsteps as he walked around the house.

CHAPTER SEVEN

The boy's pale skin and blonde hair absorbed the wickedly hot South American sun as he gripped the piece of wood and tapped the end of it against the thick green grass. He wiggled it in his hands, rotating his wrists like he had been taught. Finally, he was ready, and stepped up to the palm leaf. His blue eyes cast out at his competitor as he held the wood high behind his head.

The short, dark man stood confidently on the small hill of dirt. When he saw the boy was ready, he stepped back and then lunged himself forward, throwing the ball as hard as he could.

The boy only had a second to react, but when he did, his arms thundered forward. The big stick of wood swung violently and made perfect contact. The ball sailed off in the distance. Just as the boy was thinking it was the best hit he ever had, he saw a piece of string float to the ground. As the ball sailed through the air, the trail of string unwound behind it.

The fielders moved, amazed not only by the distance of the hit, but by the sight of the unraveling string. They gathered together as they watched the ball land and skip along the grass, stopping close to the tree line. They spoke in their native Cofan tongue, and chuckled at the unusual sight of a string stretched across the length of their village.

Curt Stillwell—an American white man—walked toward them from the outfield. He could understand only a few words of their language, but knew they were amused that yet another ball had become unraveled.

"We need a cover for Christ's sake," Curt yelled as he approached the group. The men were dressed—as all Cofan tribe members were—in tee shirts, colorful headbands, and necklaces of beads and animal teeth.

"Real baseballs are wrapped in cowhide. We need something like that. Some kind of smooth, thin leather," Curt said as he met eyes with the tribesmen. He was met by blank stares from men who did not speak a word of English.

Randy Berkman appeared from a nearby cabana, and made his way to the makeshift baseball field. He was dressed like the tribesmen, but was Caucasian and about six feet tall. "I'll be travelling to Quito next week," Randy called out to Curt. "I'll see if I can find some baseballs while I'm there."

"I still think we can make them," Curt replied. "All we need is some thin leather. These guys hunt over two hundred different kinds of mammals out of this forest. I'm sure we can find something that can cover a baseball."

"Maybe. But remember, they have no idea what a baseball is supposed to look like. Although I have to say, some of them have taken very well to your teaching of the game." Randy finally reached him.

"It's the boy I care about teaching. I think he has talent."

Randy nodded his head in agreement as he watched the boy swing the homemade bat. "I agree. He's quite an athlete."

Randy was the son of Christian missionaries, who dedicated their lives to spreading the word of Christ in South America. Although his parents were Harvard-educated Americans, Randy was born in Quito, Ecuador. He was raised there, but his parents taught him English and frequently brought him on trips to the United States.

He graduated from high school in Ecuador, but like his parents, attended Harvard University. There, he met his only long-standing American friend, Curt Stillwell. After graduation, he moved back to his native country, settling in Quito.

Not long after his return, Randy found himself swept away by the dark hair and brown eyes of a beautiful young lady. She was a member of the Cofan tribe, which made its home in an area called Dureno in northeastern Ecuador.

The Cofan people are the last remaining direct descendents of the ancient Inca civilization. They continue to live as their ancestors did, holding true to age-old customs and beliefs. They live without electricity, and hunt, gather, or grow all of their food.

Randy found himself following the love of his life to a primitive village on the outskirts of the Amazon Jungle. There, they married and lived happily—with Randy sacrificing the easier, modern life of the Ecuadorian cities for the traditional ways of the Cofan community.

Although a bit of an outcast at first, Randy's ability to speak English and knowledge of Western Culture may have saved the tribe. When an American oil company started to branch out of the nearby oil town of Lago Agrio, it moved into the Dureno area. With the support of bribed Ecuadorian officials, the oil company took over the sacred Cofan land for oil exploration.

Randy Berkman fought them every way he could. He lobbied high-ranking Ecuadorian officials, made the situation known to the media, and even reported the actions of the oil company to members of the United States Congress. In the end, the Cofan tribe was still forced out of the Dureno area, but with a nice consolation prize.

The Ecuadorian government awarded the tribe a valuable piece of land in The Cuyabeno Wildlife Reserve. The area is known as Zabalo, and is rich with fertile ground and plentiful game. Zabalo is about eighty miles east of Dureno, running along the same river.

Randy helped his fellow tribesmen relocate their families and possessions down the Aguarico River. Although the move seemed traumatic at the time, eventually they all realized they were better off in the new location, and they had a comforting guarantee from the Ecuadorian government that the new land was protected and forever belonged to the Cofan People.

Once they were settled in their new home, Randy found himself in the awkward position of being exalted to a leadership position within the tribe. After a few years of thriving in their new home of Zabalo, Randy Berkman—a six-foot white man with American parents—became the leader of the Cofan tribe.

On this day, he found himself standing next to his old college friend, trying to wrap string into a tight ball. "I don't think this is going to work," Randy said to Curt. "Your kid hits the ball so hard it won't stay together."

"I know, but that's precisely why we need to make a real ball. If he has to live out here, he should be able to do things that he likes."

"If you feel that way, then why do you have the kid out here?" Randy replied.

"I told you already, I can't talk about it."

"Talk about what?" Victoria said as she appeared behind the men. Victoria, who like Curt was white and American, wore a Cape Cod tee shirt with khaki shorts. She carried the boy's afternoon schoolbooks under her arm.

"Just the usual question," Curt answered. "You know, why me, you, and the boy are here."

"Where is the little bugger?"

"He's there," Randy replied, gesturing to the boy. He stood with several of the tribesmen. They tossed him small stones, which he whacked with the homemade wooden bat.

"The boy needs a ball," Curt said, as he held up the string, showing Victoria the unwound mess.

"He needs a lot of things," she said and walked away. She took the boy by the hand and led him into one of the cabanas to begin his afternoon lesson.

Curt and Randy watched them. "How long do you have to keep him here?" Randy asked.

"We know this isn't the ideal life for him. But right now things are bad; they're looking for him hard. We have to stay put for at least another eight days."

CHAPTER EIGHT

After peeking around the corner of the house, Neil turned back to Shannon and said, "It's okay. He's gone."

She walked toward him with an annoyed scowl. "Now, will you please tell me what the hell is going on?"

"It's going to take a while to explain everything."

"Well," Shannon began as she stepped up on her deck and fell into a chaise lounge, "I don't have to work until Monday."

Neil joined her on the deck. He sat in a lawn chair and looked her in the eye. "We believe the group that sent you that e-mail is the most dangerous terrorist organization in the world. We monitor them closely, and we have reason to believe they're preparing to make a big move."

"What are they doing?"

"Like I said before, this group is normally low profile, but lately they've been making some bold maneuvers. And I'm afraid to say that I think my grandfather missing may be one of them."

"What?" Shannon almost jumped out of her seat. "You think this group kidnapped your grandfather?"

"Yes."

"I don't understand why you didn't want to talk to the FBI then."

"Because it's not safe."

"What do you mean?"

"Given the threat on your life, we need to be extremely cautious about anything that doesn't seem right. You called the FBI about a strange e-mail, and an agent comes rushing out to your house. That wouldn't normally happen."

"You're not suggesting this group controls the FBI..."

"Of course not. But they could have someone inside."

"That seems a bit far fetched."

"Believe me, these people are capable of that, and a lot more."

"Would you please tell me who these people are?"

"Like I told you before, they're a Neo-Nazi group. But not an ordinary one. They have an incredibly long history."

"How long?"

"As long a history as a Neo-Nazi group can have. They were started by Hitler himself."

"What?" This time, Shannon did jump out of her chair. She walked across her deck, shaking her head in disbelief. "How can that be?"

"Have you ever heard of Hitler's final political testament?"

"No." She leaned against her deck's railing and folded her arms.

"On April 29th, 1945, which is the day he married his mistress, Eva Braun, and the day before he killed himself, Hitler dictated his final political testament to his personal secretary. It's famous and well documented in history books. But it didn't contain anything that he didn't say a thousand times before. Historians consider its content fairly boring."

"So what does that have to do with anything?"

"Nothing. But it wasn't the only testament he gave that day."

She walked back across the deck, placed a chair next to him, and sat down. "Tell me more."

"The second testament he dictated was much longer than the first, and ultimately, much more important. But not too many people know about it. Hitler was aware that his days were numbered, and knew his army was defeated. But he never gave up on his vision of the Aryan race ruling the world. So he set up a roadmap for a new Nazi regime. But this time, the regime would operate underground, quietly, secretly."

"And this group formed because of this testament?"

"They didn't need to form. They already existed."

"I know there were lots of Nazis around at the end of the war, but weren't they too busy running from groups like your grandfather's?"

"The high profile targets that were considered war criminals had nothing to do with the new Nazi group."

"Then who did?"

"There were thousands of Nazis and Nazi sympathizers in countries all over the world. And no country had more than the United States."

"You're kidding."

"I take it you never heard of the American Nazi Movement during World War II?"

"Absolutely not."

Neil leaned back in his chair, trying to get comfortable. "I'll give you a quick history lesson. In the thirties there were two relatively small American Nazi groups. They weren't very well organized and lacked a strong leader until a man named Heinz Spanknobel consolidated them. Although he lived in America, he was a personal friend of Hitler and commanded a tremendous amount of respect from members of the organization. He named the group 'Friends of the New Germany' and they quickly expanded from hundreds to thousands."

"Thousands?" Shannon seemed surprised.

"At their height, 'Friends' had twenty thousand members in forty-seven states."

"What happened to them?"

"They got so big that they started attracting attention. Unwanted attention. Jewish protestors started showing up at their rallies. That wasn't what Hitler wanted. You have to remember that this was all happening before Hitler invaded Poland. The last thing he wanted at the time was to be stirring up trouble in America.

"So he had Spanknobel step down and let a man named Fritz Kuhn take over the organization. The name changed to The German-American Bund, and carried on with a large number of members. But Spanknobel continued to run 'Friends' the way Hitler wanted it to be run: underground and low-profile with members that had more than just a casual interest."

"What do you mean?"

"The Bund had people who were just proud to be German and wanted to celebrate their heritage, but the underground group had only hardcore Nazis, men who believed in the superiority of the Aryan race. They remained in existence during the war, and when it was over the Bund disbanded, but Spanknobel's 'Friends' continued. And before Hitler died, he gave them a written plan to follow. A very specific mission to carry out."

"It's hard to believe that this group, that you call a terrorist organization, has existed for all of these years without doing anything. If they haven't caused any trouble by now..."

"They're planning to cause more trouble than you can imagine."

"After all this time?"

"Hitler identified a specific time when the group is supposed to rise up and take action."

"What date did he give them?"

"It's not a date."

"What? But you said—"

Neil's cell phone rang, and he jumped to his feet. He took several long strides away from Shannon as he flipped his phone open. Shannon heard him answer the phone, and watched him walk across her yard, close to the water.

He was out of her hearing range now, so she sat back in the chair and thought about the sensational information she had just received. *This couldn't possibly be true*, she thought. *How could this group survive passing on secret information across generations? What kind of action were they planning to take? And what were they waiting for?*

The questions overwhelmed her mind as she sank deeper into the lounge chair and closed her eyes. She thought about Derek and the whirlwind that had spun around her since his death. *It's hard enough to deal with him being gone without the added dread of Mr. Henry's disappearance. And now these bizarre tales of Nazis.*

She watched Neil pacing across her yard. *Is he telling the truth?* She wanted to believe him. *He seems sincere. He seems like he wants to help me.*

She still felt unsure about hiding from the FBI agent. But she would believe him for now. She would give him a chance. She opened her eyes and glanced toward her house. *The kitchen. The omelet.* She had almost forgotten that poor Neil still hadn't eaten. She stood up and decided to finish making the meal.

She took a step toward her house but stopped when she saw Neil quickly walking back to the deck. His face looked flushed and his expression tense. He bounded onto the deck with a giant stride. She was about to tell him that she would finish the omelet, but he didn't give her the chance.

"We think we know where they took my grandfather."

"You do?"

"I need to get there immediately."

Her jaw dropped as they met eyes. "But I...well...at least have something to eat here."

"I can't. I'll eat on the plane."

Plane? she thought. *Where did they take him?* "Okay," she stammered, "I hope you find him."

"Listen, Shannon." His face looked serious as he stepped closer to her. "I don't want to leave you here alone."

"What?"

"It's not safe for you to be alone. Not after that threat. For some reason they're interested in you. And I wouldn't feel right leaving you alone until I know why they've been watching you."

"But...I..." She grabbed the railing, almost losing her balance. "I have friends I can stay with."

"They can't protect you like I can. I'd feel better if you came with me."

"But I...I...have to be at work on Monday."

"If all goes well, I'll have you back in time."

"I don't know if I should."

"Listen, Shannon, I know this is crazy. We just met and I don't expect you to trust me on blind faith. But these people mean business. You're a sitting duck if you stay here by yourself."

Shannon's eyes absorbed his face, desperately searching for some sign that she should trust him. She wanted to believe him. She didn't want to be alone.

"I'm going to get my car and give you a second to think about this."

He started to walk away but stopped when she said, "Neil."

He turned to face her. "Yeah."

"Where are we going?"

Neil's tense face was overtaken by a huge smile. "Ecuador."

CHAPTER NINE

The twelve-year-old Honda emitted a high-pitched squeal when it finally reached highway speed. Shannon realized that Neil wasn't kidding when he mentioned that he didn't drive a fancy car. She leaned forward and tightly gripped the side of the seat as he weaved the noisy vehicle in and out of the heavy traffic.

She wanted to know so much more about the situation, but wasn't sure if she should ask him now. She was too afraid of distracting him while he pushed the jalopy to speeds that seemed beyond its capability. So she remained silent, and occasionally watched his tired, tense eyes straining to focus on the road.

After manipulating the roadways with the skill of a race car driver, Neil guided them into Bradley Airport in Hartford. Shannon exhaled her first relaxed breath since leaving New Haven almost an hour earlier. She looked at the various airline terminals as they bolted past them with no sign of slowing down. She finally decided to speak.

"Which airline are we taking?"

"None of them."

Shannon wasn't sure how to interpret his response, as she knew there was no doubt they were flying to Ecuador. *We're in an airport. Obviously we're taking a flight.*

"I'm sorry?" she replied, looking at him with a puzzled expression. "I asked which airline we're taking."

"I understood your question. I told you we're not taking any of them."

Shannon was starting to get angry with the game, and was about to deliver a caustic reply when the car suddenly stopped. They were at a gate, and Shannon could see a number of unmarked airplanes on the other side. She heard Neil exchange a few hurried words with a security guard. He quickly flashed the guard something in his wallet and they were on their way inside.

He turned the car immediately to the right and parked. He hoped out in a rush, but stopped abruptly, looking back at her. She was frozen, stunned by the sights around her. He waved at her, red-faced and breathing heavy. She got out of the Honda as a van squealed to a stop behind them.

"Come on," Neil called and waved at her to join him as he climbed inside. As she sat in the back of the van, she saw him smile for the first time since they left New Haven.

The van sped off down the tarmac, sailing past private planes that were lined in a row like a string of pearls on a necklace. She watched in awe as each impressive aircraft entered, and then just as quickly left her field of vision. The planes were smaller and skinnier than commercial jets, and looked sleek and sexy as the sunlight beamed off their powerful frames.

He finally spoke. "I know this must be weird for you, but you're doing the right thing by coming with me."

Her eyes were still focused on the passing planes as she asked, "Whose plane are we taking?"

"It belongs to the Center."

The van stopped, and she followed him out. There, waiting for them, was a white, high-powered flying machine—purring like a hungry tiger. "We're going in that?" she asked.

"Yes. It's a Gulfstream."

"A what?"

"Never mind. Just come aboard." He took her hand and led her up the steps. The smell of leather filled her nose as he guided her to the back of the plane. The aircraft was lined on either side with tan leather seats. She noticed the light green carpeting, and felt like she was in someone's well-decorated living room rather than a plane.

In the rear of the aircraft, they stopped in front of a set of couches near a table and television. Neil collapsed into one of the couches and his body seemed to melt into it. "Have a seat," he said without moving a muscle.

Shannon sat on another couch, facing him. There was a small, shiny table between them, which seemed to be bolted to the floor. She was unable to relax, still feeling uncomfortable in the strange environment.

Then, a middle-aged man wearing blue pants, a white shirt, and a tie appeared behind her. "Hey, Neil," the man said with a smile.

"How's it going, Rick?" Neil sat up. "This is my friend, Shannon Dinardo."

Rick took Shannon's hand and gave her a firm shake as he said, "It's a pleasure to meet you, Miss Dinardo."

"Likewise."

Rick smiled at her politely and then looked back at Neil. "I'm told we'll be flying nonstop to Quito."

"We need to get there as fast as possible."

"I'll do my best. We should be clear for takeoff in just a minute. Enjoy." Rick started to walk toward the cabin.

"Hold on, Rick. I'm starving. Please tell me there's some food on this plane," Neil said.

"I'm not sure. You'll have to check the fridge. I brought a party in from LA last night. I know no one restocked it since then. This was last minute. I was getting ready to go for a jog when I got beeped."

"It's okay. I'll survive."

"The bar is stocked if you care for a drink."

"I couldn't handle that now, but thanks anyway," Neil replied. Rick smiled and walked into the cockpit.

A moment later the sleek, white monster began to move, and then, with the ease of planetary motion, they were airborne. Shannon looked out the window in amazement as they climbed above the clouds and began a hurried journey south.

When she turned away from the window she saw Neil rummaging through a refrigerator in the front of the plane. She watched him walk back to the couch empty handed and looking miserable.

As sorry as she was that he was still hungry, she thought it was finally time to start asking some questions. She waited for him to sit down before she said, "I'm a little confused. You drive me to the airport in a death trap that barely makes it, and now we're sitting in a multimillion dollar private jet."

"It's not that complicated," he began as he settled back into the couch. "The car is mine and the plane belongs to the law firm."

"I understand that. But if the law firm can't afford to pay you enough so you can drive a decent car, then how do they afford this unbelievable airplane?"

"The firm has many wealthy supporters who donate things. Usually it's cash, but sometimes we get equipment or property so we can keep up."

"Keep up?"

"The Power has a private jet, so we need a private jet."

"Excuse me? Did you say The Power? What is The Power?" She leaned forward, excited by the idea that he may have slipped up and told her something that he shouldn't have.

"That's the name of the group that sent you the e-mail."

"I didn't realize they had a name. What does it mean?"

"Have you ever heard of George Lincoln Rockwell?"

"No. Who is he?"

"He was a member of The Power during the 1950's, but broke away and started his own movement in the early sixties. There had been no public organization in America that supported the Nazi party since The German-American Bund disbanded after the war. But Rockwell started what came to be known as the first Neo-Nazi group, and popularized an infamous phrase."

"A phrase?"

"He took credit for a phrase that he didn't create, and then made it known all over the world."

"What phrase?"

"I'm sure you've heard of White Power."

Shannon looked at him, confused. She had heard the saying many times but never thought about its origin. *White Power. The Power. Did this mean that...?"*

"The name The Power has always been an abbreviated form of White Power, and this group adopted the shorter version as their name."

"So The Power never wanted Rockwell to make that name public?"

"They didn't want anything to be public. That was part of Hitler's testament. This group was to operate underground until a specified time."

"So what happened to Rockwell?"

"He was assassinated."

"By The Power?"

"What do you think?"

Her mouth went dry as she thought about the picture of the dead blonde girl. *These people kill their own.* She swallowed hard and tried to hide her anxiety. "Did the public Nazi group disband after Rockwell was killed?"

"The Power hoped that it would, but a man named Frank Collin took it over. He wasn't a member of The Power, but just a follower of Rockwell."

"So he didn't know about The Power?"

"No. He thought he was the one and only leader of the modern Neo-Nazi party. And he did the exact opposite of what The Power wanted him to do."

"He put his group in the public eye?"

"Tremendously. He tried to arrange a march of his group, in full Nazi uniforms, in a town that was mostly populated by Holocaust survivors."

"That's terrible."

"The march never happened, but there were endless legal battles about it, which, of course, were highly publicized."

"Did they kill him too?"

"No, but he was mysteriously convicted on child molestation charges."

"They set him up?"

"We don't know that for sure, but one has to wonder."

Shannon felt chills run up her back as she imagined The Power's covert capability. *What do they want with me?* "So what happened to this big Neo-Nazi group after Collin went to jail?"

"There were too many of them to just completely disband, so they broke off into their own separate groups. Less dramatic leaders took over different factions and they lived on. The Neo-Nazi movement was alive and in action all over the country in separate groups with no centralized leadership."

"The Power must have hated that. Wasn't it counter-productive to their mission?"

"That's exactly right. But it was too far out of their control, so they had to take a different approach."

"How so?"

"They came up with a way to control all the groups without anyone realizing it."

"How is that possible?"

"They did it through a book."

"Did you say a book?"

"Have you ever heard of *The Turner Diaries*?"

"The what diaries?"

"*The Turner Diaries* is a book written by Andrew Macdonald. But, the interesting thing is, there is no Andrew Macdonald. It was a pseudonym used to conceal the identity of the real author."

"I take it that the real author was a member of The Power."

"Yes. His name was William Pierce. The book tells a story of an Aryan militia rising up against an oppressive government. Although it's fictional, it was intended to be a guide for all the Nazi groups to follow—"

"Hold on a minute," Shannon interrupted. "I want to hear more about this book, but there's one thing I need to know now."

"What's that?"

"You said that Hitler specified a certain time for The Power to take action."

"That's right."

"But then you said it wasn't a date. If it's not a date, then how does The Power know when to act?"

The question hung in the air as Neil looked at the carpet and didn't speak for a few minutes. Shannon sat at the edge of the couch, waiting. "Well," she finally said, "are you going to tell me?"

"I think it would be best if I didn't explain that right now."

"What?" She couldn't believe his words. "Why not?"

"I still have a lot to tell you about these people, and I think if I told you about the time that Hitler specified right now it might...well...it could be a little overwhelming for you."

"Overwhelming?" Shannon's face was bright red. She fought the urge to jump off the couch and pace around like a lunatic. "Let me remind you of something." She took a deep breath before continuing. "I've been grieving the death of my fiancé for the last few weeks, and then I'm horrified to find my neighbor is missing. While looking for a family member's number I come across a Nazi flag in his desk, which totally freaks me out. But, not nearly as much as an e-mail I receive that threatens my life.

"Then, you enter the picture with stories of Hitler and Neo-Nazi groups. And I find out the e-mail is from a terrorist organization. And now, I'm in some super-powered private jet speeding off to Ecuador.

"Now let me ask you this. Do you honestly believe that after going through all of this in the last two days that I'm going to be *overwhelmed*, as you put it, by something written in a testament sixty years ago?"

She stared at him, feeling satisfied that she had summarized her situation accurately. She expected him to nod his head in agreement and finally tell her what The Power was waiting for.

But, instead, he looked her in the eye and spoke three words that made her heart sink into her stomach: "Yes, I do."

CHAPTER TEN

The helicopter slowly crossed the Aguarico River, and hovered over a glade between the thick rain forest and the riverbank. The Ecuadorian pilot looked over his shoulder, meeting eyes with the Bald Man.

"Senor," the pilot yelled over the noise of the helicopter, "this is as far as I go." The Bald Man motioned his hand downward, signaling the pilot to land. The pilot carefully lowered the craft onto the recently purged area of forest.

The Bald Man handed the pilot some American currency, and climbed out. He turned and watched the two henchmen roughly escort the old man to the ground. A moment after stepping out of the helicopter, the powerful flying machine rose straight above them, disappearing over the trees.

The Bald Man was still sizing up the two henchmen that the Supreme Leader had assigned to assist him. He preferred to work alone, and didn't believe he needed the help. But for now, he was stuck with them.

One was tall with blonde hair and a sadistic look in his steely blue eyes. The Bald Man could tell that Blondie squeezed the old man's arm tighter than his shorter, brown-haired, crooked-toothed counterpart.

It doesn't matter, the Bald Man told himself. Both Blondie and Crooked Teeth were there to take orders from him. He was in charge. There was no question of that. The Bald Man knew that as sadistic as Blondie might be, he was about to see things he never imagined.

"Bring him here," the Bald Man barked and lit a cigar. They obeyed the order. At first, the old man tried to keep his feet moving, but eventually gave up and let the two brutes drag him.

When they reached the Bald Man, Blondie and Crooked Teeth leaned into either side of the old man, forcing him to stand up straight. The old man winced in pain and looked into the evil eyes staring back at him.

After a casual puff on the cigar, the Bald Man moved closer to him and said, "Bring us to him."

"I told you, I don't know exactly where he is," the old man struggled to say, seeming short of breath. "The government gave them a sanctuary in The Cuyabeno Wildlife Reserve. We're somewhere near there, but I don't know my way around that well." He cried in pain as the two goons continued to lean into him.

The Bald Man took another drag on the cigar as his eyes bored into the old man's soul. "Boys," he began, "I think you might be hurting the old guy." The henchmen looked at him, surprised.

"He's gotta be old enough to be your grandfather. Why don't you lighten up a bit?"

The men looked at one another, still surprised. They each stepped away from the old man simultaneously, but kept a hand on the back of his shoulders. The old man breathed a sigh of relief as his body relaxed. "Thank you," he said, looking at the Bald Man.

"You're very welcome. Now, are you gonna tell me where they're hiding the boy?"

"I think we need to go west down this river. But like I said, I don't know the area that well. I'll never be able to guide us to the tribe."

"That's too bad," the Bald Man said, all eyes focused on him. Then, his right arm burst forward like an attacking python and grabbed the old man by the neck. He pulled him forward and flipped him over his hip. The old man hit the ground with a loud thud as a cloud of dust rose into the air.

The Bald Man planted both knees on the old man's chest, and grabbed him under his chin. The old man tried to scream, but only produced a pitiful groan. The Bald Man held the cigar less than an inch from his forehead. "God help me," the old man managed to mutter.

"If you don't bring me to the boy, you're going to need Him." The Bald Man lowered the cigar, and pressed it into the old man's forehead, searing his flesh.

Despite the tight grip on his chin, the old man released a scream that carried down the Aguarico River, and echoed into the outskirts of the Amazon Jungle.

CHAPTER ELEVEN

Shannon felt the plane slowly descending as her eyes focused on the flickering city lights below. The Quito airport was a welcome sight after the eight-hour flight. But in a way, Shannon had enjoyed her time on the plane.

She had spent the majority of her time sipping ginger ale and watching DVDs as she reclined on the comfortable leather couch. The time had served as an unexpected respite from the turmoil in her mind. *A bit of an upgrade from coach*, she thought as she turned to look at Neil.

He had been asleep for the last four hours and continued to emit a light snoring sound from a couch on the opposite end of the plane. She was amused at the sight of his now wrinkled shirt, and thought he looked like a homeless person crashed on a park bench. She tried not to be angry that he wouldn't reveal more information about The Power—specifically what they were waiting for and what they planned to do.

I'm sure he has his reasons, she thought as her eyes widened at the sight of the runway lights. She approached Neil and gently tapped him on the knee. He sat up abruptly and opened his red eyes.

"Are we there?" he asked, shaking the sleepiness off.

"It looks like we're about to land."

He nodded his head knowingly as he sat up and glanced at his watch. "Right on time," he mumbled.

"Listen," she said as she sat next to him, "I won't ask you anymore about what The Power is waiting for, but I am curious to know some other things."

"Okay. What do you want to know?" Neil said, seeming fully awake now.

"You started talking about that book. The Turner something?"

"*The Turner Diaries.*"

"That's right. That's the book you said The Power created to try and control all the Neo-Nazi groups. But I don't understand how that could be possible."

He stretched his neck toward the windows to catch a glimpse of the approaching airport. "I think I already told you that the book was written by a man named Andrew Macdonald. But his real name was William Pierce, who was a member of The Power."

"Yes. But how does the book control the Neo-Nazi groups?"

"Have you ever heard about Hitler's fondness for wolves?"

"Wolves?"

"Yes."

"I've never heard that."

"He had a strange affection for them. He even named his dog Wolf. During the occupation of Germany after World War Two there were groups of Nazi loyalists who fought a guerilla war against the allies. The resistance group called themselves 'werewolves' in honor of Hitler."

"What does that have to do with this book?"

"*The Turner Diaries* also honors Hitler's love of wolves. But the book uses the term 'lone wolf.'"

"Lone wolf? What does that mean?"

"The Power has been well aware that there are many white supremacists in the US that are looking for action. They recruit some, but they don't want every psycho with a confederate flag hanging off the back of their truck. That wouldn't work for them. It would compromise the covert nature of the organization, and it wasn't part of Hitler's plan.

"So this book tells the stories of radical men, referred to as lone wolves, who take violent actions against the government and society on their own. The Power was hoping that this would influence the radicals to act alone, and discourage a mass organization."

"Did it work?"

"For the most part. There are still organized hate groups, but the most radical racists have bought into the ideas of *The Diaries*, and have acted alone."

"What kind of things did they do?"

"There've been a lot of lone wolves inspired by *The Turner Diaries* who did some crazy things. Eric Rudolph is the man the FBI believed bombed the 1996 Atlanta Olympics. He also bombed abortion clinics and gay bars."

"I've heard of him. He was a lone wolf?" Shannon crept forward, almost slipping off the edge of the couch.

"He was. There was also a man named Benjamin Smith who randomly shot innocent people. And Joseph Franklin, who killed inter-racial couples after becoming a believer in *The Turner Diaries*."

"That's terrible."

"Those guys all made news, but the most well known follower of the book is Timothy McVeigh."

"The guy who bombed the building in Oklahoma City?"

"That's him."

"That's unbelievable."

"They found a copy of it in his car when he was arrested. They used it as evidence in his trial. He was a classic student of *The Diaries*."

Shannon leaned back and glanced out the window, seeing the bright lights of the airport illuminating the windows. Neil's words seemed beyond belief, *but why would he lie?* She trusted him, or so she thought.

They didn't speak for a moment as they listened to the groaning engine of the plane. She looked back at him and said, "Anyone else I may know that was a part of this?"

"I'm sure you've heard of the shootings at Columbine High School."

"Those boys were lone wolves?" Shannon leapt back to the edge of the couch.

"Absolutely."

"But if that were true, it would have been more publicized. The media picked apart and reported on every little detail of the Columbine massacre."

"Some of the media outlets did report the story from that angle. But there were so many angles, that I think it got lost in the shuffle. But if you know what to look for, there's no doubt what influenced those boys."

"What kind of things did you look for?"

"Well, we can start with the date it happened. Do you remember?"

"It happened in 1999. The spring, I think."

"It was April twentieth."

They stared at each other intensely. Shannon knew the date meant something, but her brain wasn't producing the answer.

"Don't you remember?" Neil said softly. "That's Hitler's birthday."

Chills ran up Shannon's spin as she listened to his words. "That can't be," she muttered without thinking.

"It's true. Look up the date if you want."

The plane's wheels screeched as they made contact with the landing strip. Both Shannon and Neil sat back in their respective couches as the plane decelerated and eventually stopped.

She followed Neil to the front of the plane, thanked and said good-bye to Rick, and stepped out of the door. Her body calmly moved down the stairs, but her mind spun like a tempest.

The information Neil had told her terrified her. The fact that this group had some interest in her was incomprehensible. She wanted to grasp on to something familiar—something to comfort her. But she was standing on a dark tarmac next to a man she had met just hours earlier.

What the hell am I doing in Quito, Ecuador?

After entering the airport and rushing their way through customs, they went back outside near the plane. She watched Neil struggle to communicate with a swarm of Spanish-speaking men. "New England Law Center. Helicopter," she heard him repeat several times.

As the various men pointed and guided him away from the plane, Shannon followed. Although the airport was much smaller than most in America, it looked impossibly confusing—dark and loud. Shannon sucked in the wickedly humid air as her legs plodded forward, robotically following

Neil and the wave of confusion he was creating.

"English. Does anyone speak English?" Neil loudly asked. After at least ten minutes of repeating the same question, a young man approached them.

"Senor," the young man said to Neil, "you are from the Law Center?"

"Yes, I am," Neil replied.

"I am Pedro. I welcome you."

"There's supposed to be a helicopter here for me."

"No helicopter, Senor. Small plane will take you to Lago Agrio."

"No," Neil replied forcefully. "I need to get to Zabalo. That's about ninety miles west of Lago Agrio."

"The closest landing strip is in Lago Agrio. That's as far as we take you."

"What about a helicopter?"

"No where for helicopter to land. Near Zabalo it is nothing but river and jungle. No one knows the area well enough to take helicopter in there."

Neil turned away, looking annoyed. Shannon moved next to him and said, "Why don't we take the plane to where the landing strip is, and in the morning we'll see if someone can drive us to where we need to go."

"That'll take too long. We need to get there tonight." A look of revelation took over Neil's face. He turned toward the young man and said, "A seaplane. Do you have a seaplane here?"

"A what, Senor?"

"A seaplane. A plane that can land on the water, so you can get us to Zabalo tonight."

Pedro looked perplexed. "Land on the water, Senor?"

"Yes. They're called seaplanes."

"Let me find out."

Pedro wandered away, but Neil and Shannon followed him closely. A wave of fast-spoken Spanish filled their ears as they tried to understand a few words. They heard him say "Avion de mar," many times and to over a dozen different employees. Finally, someone seemed to respond positively, and they were whisked off to a golf cart.

Neil and Shannon sat in the back as Pedro sat in the front with the other man behind the wheel. They drove to the opposite end of the airport, and stopped in front of a hangar. The two Ecuadorian men exchanged quick words that Neil and Shannon could not understand.

They got out of the cart and approached the hangar as another man appeared from a door in the front of the structure. A frenzy of Spanish ensued, but this time Shannon could understand the gist of what the new man was saying. He pointed to the hangar and emphatically said, "No. Mantenimiento. Areglar."

Shannon whispered in Neil's ear. "I think he's saying that the plane needs repair. I don't think we should push it. If he doesn't think it's safe then—"

Neil quickly walked toward the men and took out a wad of cash from his pocket. He waved the money in the air and said, "I need that plane to get us to the Aguarico River near Zabalo tonight. Fix it up, get it running, and find me a pilot."

The Ecuadorian men looked at him with their mouths hanging open. Pedro translated Neil's request to the others. The men conversed amongst themselves again, but this time with increased vigor. After a minute, Pedro approached Neil.

"Senor, the plane needs major repairs. He doesn't think he can fix it tonight. And to find a pilot this late—"

Neil slapped the cash into Pedro's hand, and flashed another wad of bills from his pocket. "Make it happen tonight. I need it as soon as possible. I'll make it worthwhile for everyone involved."

Pedro looked at the money, at Neil, and back at the money. He slowly approached his coworkers, displaying the US currency. Their speech was hurried, almost manic, and then they split up. Pedro returned to Neil. "We will do our best. Julio will get to work on the plane. I will search for a pilot."

"Thank you very much."

The men went in different directions. Neil and Shannon followed Julio to the hangar. Neil turned to watch a plane appear out of the night sky and smoothly touch down. Shannon watched Julio open the main door of the hangar.

When it was fully open and she could see what was inside, her heart skipped a beat. She was looking at a small, blue and white, single-engine seaplane. It rested on two large landing bars, which were meant to keep it afloat in the water. But one of the landing bars looked cracked, which made the craft tilt horribly to one side. Sections of the exterior were rusted, one of the windows was broken, and there was a large dent in the nose.

"Neil," Shannon called loudly to get his attention over the noise of nearby jets. "Please tell me we're not going to fly in that."

Neil turned and looked at the old plane. He was poker-faced, but Shannon knew he could not possibly be pleased by the sight of the decrepit thing. He looked at her and said, "I know this may be a little risky, but we have to get there right away."

CHAPTER TWELVE

The engine started with some reluctance, and the battered aircraft barely sputtered its way out of the hangar. Shannon stared at the ancient single-engine seaplane in horror. As she tried to force herself into believing that the trip would be safe, she thought she spotted something dripping from underneath the engine compartment.

She turned to point this out to Neil, but his attention was on Pedro, who was quickly approaching. Another man in his mid-thirties trailed a step behind as they reached Neil and Shannon.

Pedro was slightly out of breath as he spoke. "Senor, this man," he gestured to the man behind him, "has flown before. He has many children and very much needs money. His name is Magglio."

Neil took a step toward Magglio and took out a wad of cash. "Can you fly this?" Neil pointed to the plane.

Magglio nodded. Neil paused, waiting for him to speak, but he did not. He repeated the question, and Magglio nodded again.

"He speak little English," Pedro interjected.

"Can he fly the plane?" Neil asked.

"He says he can. If you pay him."

Neil stuck the wad of cash in Magglio's face. "You fly?" Neil yelled.

"Yes, Senor," Magglio spoke. "Fly. Plane."

"You can land on the water?" Neil asked.

Magglio looked confused and looked at his English-speaking friend. "He told me that he has flown this kind of plane before," Pedro said.

"Does he know where we need to go? The Aguarico River near Zabalo."

"Yes, Senor, he told me he knows where that is."

Magglio said, "Yes. Aguarico. Zabalo."

Neil nodded his head, seeming satisfied. He slapped the cash into the pilot's hand. "Take us away, Magglio."

Magglio looked at the money, and Shannon thought his eyes were going to burst out of their sockets. His face broke into a wide smile as he ran toward the seaplane. "You have made him very happy," Pedro said. "He has many children, and you have given him over a year's salary."

Shannon's knees slightly buckled when she heard the statement. *A year's salary?* The concept frightened her. *Does he really know how to fly this thing? He would probably try to fly the space shuttle for a year's salary.*

And then there was the dripping. Her eyes darted back to the spot, and to her dismay, it was still leaking. When she looked at the ground, she saw a small puddle starting to form. She didn't know anything about engines but...*could that be oil?*

Neil took her by the hand and guided her toward the plane. "Don't worry about a thing," he said. "We'll be there before you know it."

"Wait, Neil," she said as he pulled her along. "I think there's something wrong with the plane."

"Of course there's something wrong with the plane. There's all kinds of things wrong with the plane. But we have a very short flight. Just a hop, skip, and a jump away." Neil shook hands with Julio, who smiled widely back at him. "The plane is fixed?" Neil asked loudly.

Julio continued to smile and nod. Shannon was convinced that he didn't understand a word Neil was saying. She only hoped the pilot knew what he was doing.

Neil and Shannon climbed into the back seat of the aircraft. They barely fit into the cramped space—their thighs touched when they finally sat on the cloth seats. They watched as Magglio settled himself in the cockpit.

Once again, Shannon thought she should say something about the dripping oil, but she thought again. *Is a little dripping oil really going to matter in this wreck?* She took a deep breath and tried to relax. It felt as hot as an oven, and although they had only been in the plane a minute or two, her shirt was already stuck to the back of her seat.

They started a bumpy ride toward the runway as Magglio gave them a thumbs up. Shannon saw their English-speaking guide and Julio waving as they taxied away. It was a far cry from the cool, comfortable trip in The Gulfstream. *And just a little scarier.*

When they hit the runway, the plane sped up, and surprisingly got off the ground without a problem. They were airborne, and before Shannon knew it, she was once again admiring the flickering lights of the Quito airport below her.

The aircraft rocked violently from side to side and they listened to the sputtering sounds of the engine, but they continued to climb higher. They leveled off at about five thousand feet and sluggishly made their way toward the northeastern corner of Ecuador. Shannon noticed that Neil's body had finally relaxed a bit, so she felt more at ease. But then she thought about where they were going.

We're going to land on a river, and then somehow climb into a pitch-dark jungle.

"Where exactly are you taking me?" she asked, her eyes burning.

"I know this must be scary for you," he began, "but it really won't be that bad. If the pilot can get us to Zabalo, I promise you'll be sleeping in a comfortable bed tonight."

"A comfortable bed? In the middle of the jungle? Should I expect room service in the morning?"

"Very funny. But seriously, I know a tribe of people in Zabalo. They'll welcome us into their village. They're good people."

"I thought we were looking for your grandfather. Is he in this village?"

"No. Unfortunately, he won't be there."

"Then why are we going there?"

"It's a bit complicated."

"Complicated!" Shannon's face turned beet-red again as her nostrils flared. "You drag me away from my house, fly me halfway across the world, and now you have me in this deathtrap heading toward the middle of a dark jungle. I thought we were trying to find your grandfather. If we're not looking for him, then I want to know what the hell we're doing!"

"Okay. Okay." Neil held his hands up, gesturing for her to calm down. "I already told you that my grandfather was kidnapped."

"Yeah."

"He was kidnapped because The Power wants information from him."

"What kind of information?"

"They're looking for someone, and my grandfather knows where he is."

"This person is with this tribe in Zabalo?"

"That's right."

"Do you think your grandfather told them where he is?"

"Not willingly."

"What does that mean?"

"I think they may have tortured him."

Shannon flinched, horrified by the idea. She imagined the kind old eyes of Mr. Henry, and could not imagine him being tortured. "So you think he told them where to go?"

"My grandfather is a scholar. He's an academic man, a professor. He's not a soldier. He's never been trained to endure torture. Besides, he's too old. He could never withstand the things this group is capable of."

"Where do you think he is? Why aren't we trying to find him?"

Neil shook his head, sadly. "I don't think there's any hope. They would never let him live."

The plane bucked violently, sending Neil and Shannon flying forward. They quickly bounced back into their seats and began scrambling to find their seatbelts. They both dug into the ripped cushions but found nothing.

Suddenly, the plane seemed to stop in midair—and drop straight down. But a moment later, they were moving forward again. The plane rocked from side to side, and then it took a sharp turn.

Neil tumbled out of his seat as Shannon avoided joining him by wrapping her arm around her headrest. As Neil struggled to his feet, he fell forward, and yelled to Magglio, "What the hell is going on?"

The plane turned sharply again as the engine sputtered some more. But Magglio was all smiles when he turned his head to the backseat. He pointed straight ahead and said, "Aguarico."

Shannon could see a wide river below them, and realized that Magglio must know where he's going. His confident smile relaxed her nerves. *Just turbulence. Any plane can be jostled by turbulence.*

As Neil settled back into his seat, Shannon said, "Who's in this village that they're looking for?"

"Umm...I don't think we should get into that now."

"Aren't you keeping enough secrets from me?"

Neil frowned as the plane bounced and rumbled as if it were being dragged over jagged rocks. "I'll make a deal with you. You'll meet him in the morning, and then I'll explain who he is."

"Okay. But in the morning I want to know."

Neil smiled at her, and for a moment, his eyes made her forget she was in a rattling tin can thousands of feet over an Ecuadorian rainforest. He opened his mouth to say something, but never got the chance.

At first, Shannon assumed it was just more turbulence, and wasn't worried when a big bump almost knocked her out of her seat. But then she found herself being thrashed back and forth like she was strapped to the back of a bucking bronco. She tried to grab onto Neil, but couldn't find him in the whirling chaos.

But then everything suddenly stopped, and once again, she felt the plane dropping. She knew, when this occurred just minutes earlier, that it was most likely due to a harmless air pocket. But this time it was different.

Something was missing; something had suddenly changed. It took a moment before the horrible realization came. She could no longer hear the sound of the engine.

Her panic-stricken eyes shot forward, and found Neil just inches from her, struggling to his knees. She froze in anticipation, waiting to hear the sound of the engine again—waiting to feel the plane move forward. But instead, she focused on Neil's face, which was white with fear.

She heard Magglio yelling Spanish words she did not understand. But she didn't need an English translation. She knew that he was just as terrified as she was. "What's happening?" she screamed as she managed to sit up.

She braced herself by grabbing onto the back of Magglio's seat, and could see nothing but blackness out of the windows. She realized that the temporary drop had now evolved into a full nosedive. She watched in complete terror as Magglio frantically grabbed and pulled at every instrument in his reach.

"The engine died!" Neil yelled into Shannon's ear. "I'm so sorry. I was just trying to protect you."

"Don't talk like we're going to die. He can get it started again, can't he?"

Neil reached out and grabbed her elbow. He pulled her into his chest and wrapped his strong arms around her. "I'm sorry, Shannon. I'm so sorry," he whispered in her ear.

She knew then that death was just seconds away. She felt his heart racing against her cheek. She thought her life should have been flashing before her. She thought she would have been thinking about Derek and her parents—wondering if she was about to see them again.

But one question danced in her brain, and then unexpectedly, came out of her mouth. "Who is hiding in the village?"

Neil pulled his head back and looked at her, surprised. After a moment his look of shock slowly faded, and he answered. "It's a boy."

"A boy? How old?"

"He's thirteen."

"What do they want with him?"

"Why do you care about this now? Don't you realize that we're about to—"

"Just tell me!" she interrupted him. "Why do they care about a boy?"

"Well, for starters, he's not an ordinary boy."

"What's so special about him?"

Just as Neil was about to answer, they heard a sound that they were convinced they would never hear again. It was the engine. They listened to Magglio scream as he struggled to right the aircraft.

When it seemed he was successful, Shannon felt a wave of unprecedented relief sweep over her body. Neil still held her, but now he was laughing as a tear of joy rolled down his cheek.

Magglio, however, did not seem as relaxed. He still fought with the controls like he was trying to wrestle a five-hundred-pound bear to the ground. As Shannon and Neil broke their embrace and settled back into their seats, they looked out the windows.

And then, they heard an unusual noise—like machine gun fire peppering the side of the plane. When Shannon focused on the sight outside of the plane, her heart sank like a stone. They were flying just above the trees.

The wing of the plane whacked against the top of tree branches as Magglio fought to steady the craft. "We're in the trees!" Neil yelled.

"I can see that." The engine sputtered horribly, and the plane once again bucked ferociously.

Neil screamed into her ear again. "Put your head between your knees, and cover the top of your head!"

"Why?"

"I think we're going to crash."

"He just has to get us above the tree line, and get us back to the river," Shannon replied, hopefully.

But then, they listened to the engine spit a few more times, and once again, it died. This time they knew it would not be restarting. They only descended a few feet before an ear-deafening crash made them jump.

The left wing had been completely torn off after impact with a tree. Just as Shannon realized what had occurred, they were upside down, swirling through dark madness.

She tried to cover her head as she was wildly tossed in random directions. The one moment when she was able to open her eyes and look forward, she saw the horrific sight of the windows shattering.

She covered her head again, and screamed with what she was convinced was her last breath.

CHAPTER THIRTEEN

The Bald Man's feet sunk in the mud as he marched closer to the riverbank. Blondie and Crooked Teeth trailed him, dragging the old man by a rope that bound his wrists together. As they made their way out of the jungle, the sun brought a welcome warmth to their skin after a long night.

The Bald Man stopped when he saw a boy about sixteen years old, pulling a canoe onto shore. "Looks like our ride is here, boys," he said over his shoulder. He stopped, turned, and took a step toward the old man. "This is your chance to save your life."

The old man gasped for air as the fetid breath of the Bald Man engulfed his face. The Bald Man grabbed his shirt and pulled him even closer as he said, "I know you speak Spanish, so don't try and pretend that you don't. You're going to talk to that kid and find out where we need to go. What's the name of the place?"

"I heard he was in the Cuyabeno Wildlife Reserve," he replied with quivering lips.

"Good. Then you ask the kid where that reserve is. Then, I'll gut him like a pig, and we'll take his canoe." The Bald Man grabbed the old man by the back of the neck and squeezed. "And if you give me any trouble, I'll gut you too."

He released the old man, almost knocking him over. The Bald Man started waving his arms in the air, and when the boy looked at him, he motioned for him to come.

After he pulled the canoe completely on dry land, he took a few cautious steps toward the strange white men in the distance. The boy, obviously indigenous to the area, looked curiously as he slowly approached. The Bald Man whispered in the old man's ear. "You do the talking. And remember, if I hear anything I don't like, you'll pay."

The boy slowed his approach for a moment, and the Bald Man began walking toward him with a wide, welcoming smile as if he were about to greet a dear friend. The other three followed; the old man looked at the ground, with a worried, tense face.

When they reached each other, the Bald Man stepped aside, the fake smile still pasted across his face. He looked at the old man, shooting him commands with the glare in his eyes. The old man stepped forward and spoke Spanish to the boy. "Are you of the Cofan tribe?"

"Yes," the boy answered, looking confused.

The others could not understand what was being said, but the Bald Man was interpreting their inflexion, facial expressions, and body language. He locked eyes with the old man, breathing heavily with balled fists.

The old man had to make the most difficult decision of his long life. He didn't expect to live much longer regardless of whether he led them to the boy or not. But he couldn't bear the thought of such a young, innocent life being wasted.

He decided that he would rather die here on the riverbank than watch the Bald Man kill the youngster. And he was all too aware of the horrific consequences if they found the boy hiding in the village. He would not make it easy for them. He wouldn't go down without a fight.

The old man lunged forward and spoke hurried Spanish, knowing his words might be his last. "These are bad men. They are here to take the white boy in your village, and kill your people. Go. Run. Tell Randy bad men are coming for the boy."

The young man didn't pause for a second. The message was clear, and before the Bald Man could comprehend the nature of what was said, the young Cofan tribe member was sprinting back to his canoe.

The Bald Man was flooded with rage as he charged at the old man like a wild bull. He struck him with a powerful roundhouse right to the side of the head. The old man collapsed like a boneless slab of meat. "Stay with him!" the Bald Man shouted to Blondie. He turned to Crooked Teeth and ordered, "Come with me."

The Bald Man and Crooked Teeth ran as fast as they could, but their middle-aged, fat bodies were no match for the lean, fleet-footed young man. He was boarding the canoe after only a few strides from his pursuers. He dashed off down the river, paddling frantically.

The men slowed to a trot as the boy disappeared around a corner. Knowing they had no hope to catch him, the Bald Man lumbered to a stop, bending over to suck in the humid, thick air. Crooked Teeth tripped over his own feet and lay on the ground, panting like a wounded dog.

The Bald Man slowly turned back to the old man and Blondie, who were about a hundred yards behind him. At first, he couldn't believe what he was seeing, and after squinting to confirm the unbelievable sight, he ran like mad. "No! Don't do it!"

The old man expected to die soon, and assumed it would be at the hands of the Bald Man. But when he struggled up to his knees, his head still pounding from the ferocious blow to his skull, he was surprised by the sight of a gun barrel less than an inch from his forehead.

His mouth opened, and he started to form a word. But what could be said? He knew there was nothing left to do but die as he focused on the soulless eyes of his murderer. He heard the click, and then it was over—painlessly.

The Bald Man cursed loudly as he witnessed the act. He charged toward Blondie, who was putting the gun back into his pants. "What did you do?" the Bald Man yelled. When he reached them, he dropped to his knees and examined the body of the old man. He had hoped to resuscitate him somehow, but when he saw that the back of his skull was blown away, he knew that would not be possible.

As Crooked Teeth barely stumbled into the area, horribly out of breath, the Bald Man approached Blondie. "What the hell did you do?"

"What do you mean? He screwed us. I knew you were gonna cap him. I just saved you the trouble."

"You stupid fool," the Bald Man screamed in Blondie's face. "Don't you realize that he was our only hope of finding the boy?"

Blondie looked at the dead old man and then back at the Bald Man. "But you couldn't trust him."

"And now I can't trust you," the Bald Man said as he whipped a pistol out of his side pocket and held it to Blondie's head. The thug opened his mouth, trying to speak, but no words came out. The Bald Man pulled the trigger, and didn't break his impassive stare as Blondie's head exploded.

The Bald Man turned toward Crooked Teeth who was slowly backpedaling away—sweating like he was in a sauna. "Don't kill me," he pleaded, nervously.

"It's your choice," the Bald Man said, pointing the gun at him. "You're with me or you're against me."

"I'm with you. I swear I'm with you," he replied, with his hands raised in the air.

"I hope that's true," the Bald Man said as he lowered his gun.

They were interrupted by the sound of splashing from the river. They turned and saw two men paddling a canoe down the river. "I hope you're ready to go," the Bald Man said as he slipped the pistol back into his pocket. "Cause it looks like we found another ride."

They looked at the men casually paddling their way along the river. "I'm ready, boss," Crooked Teeth answered.

The Bald Man nodded his head in the direction of the river, and they started walking toward it. The Bald Man yelled and waved his arms to the men in the canoe. When they saw him, they changed direction, and guided their canoe to the shore, happily waving back.

CHAPTER FOURTEEN

Light danced in front of her eyes and she felt sweat on her arms. She decided to get out of bed and open the window. *The ocean breeze is usually so nice in the morning.*

She lifted her head slowly, and then an unexpected pain stabbed her in the ribs. She groaned as her head fell back. Her eyes, fully open now, focused on the sights above her. *Where the hell am I?*

As she realized she wasn't in her bedroom, pain shot out of her ribs, down her legs, and back again. Then she remembered it all. The plane crash. The jungle.

But it was daylight now. And to her surprise, she was still alive. She endured the pain and leaned forward. The plane was in pieces all around her, but she was stretched across the back seat of the aircraft, which seemed undamaged. Then she realized that a large portion of the roof was above her. After a closer examination, she saw that it was wedged between two trees.

Someone put me here, and made me a shelter. Neil! He must be alive.

The thought comforted her as she shifted to a seated position. The pain attacked her and she froze—her eyes closed tight, waiting for the discomfort to subside. Her hands gently probed her body, trying to evaluate her injuries. She was happy to realize there were no cuts, and nothing seemed to be broken. Her temples pounded and she wondered if she had a concussion.

I'm just a little banged up; nothing but a few bruises, she told herself.

She decided to stand, shake off the pain, and find Neil. But when she opened her eyes and looked at the ground, she saw it move. *Shit,* she cursed in her mind, *I'm in worse shape than I thought.*

She looked up at the makeshift shelter, and at the thick patch of trees that surrounded her. Nothing else was moving. She thought she was all right then, and looked down. But again, the earth seemed to shift below her.

She leaned back against the seat, unsure of what to do. She prayed for Neil to show up, but knew she had to be strong on her own. *I'm all right,* she told herself. *I have to be all right.*

As she was preparing to get to her feet, she heard an unusual sound. Hissing. Then, she thought she felt something touch her foot. Her muscles stiffened as she imagined what it might be.

She looked down again, but this time more than just a quick glance. She stared at the ground, and once again saw movement. But now she knew it wasn't because of her head injury. What she was looking at was real.

She had never seen a real anaconda before, but immediately recognized the creature from photographs and television. Her first reaction was to run, but the sight of the thick, black, twenty-foot beast crawling under the seat paralyzed her.

She searched her brain for an escape plan. *Should I run? Or should I remain still? Are they poisonous? Will it attack me?*

She watched the sun sparkle off of the snake's scaly dark skin as it poked its head out from under the seat. When it started to move away, she felt a little better. *Maybe it's just passing by. Maybe it wants nothing to do with me.*

But then she saw something that brought back the paralyzing fear in an instant. Once again, the anaconda's head appeared from under the seat, and was just inches from her leg. It moved more, and slid its coarse skin against her thigh.

Then, to her horror, the reptile sprang forward and wrapped itself around her leg. Although her adrenaline had temporarily blocked the agony from her previous injuries, this pain hit her like a tidal wave. She didn't think it was possible that her leg could be squeezed so hard and not pop off her body.

Without realizing it, she was screaming bloody murder. She felt the beast yank her forward as it continued to constrict around her leg. She desperately wrapped her arms around the back of the seat, hoping for a miracle.

Then, she thought her miracle had arrived. He appeared out of nowhere—stealthily from a patch of trees. It was Neil. But he didn't leap forward and rescue her like she hoped. He just stood there, apparently as shocked as she had been when she first saw the evil thing.

She clung to the seat, as she continued to scream in agony. Her eyes pleaded with him for help while the anaconda relentlessly squeezed and pulled. She knew he would do something. He would have to do something. *He'll get me out of this. Somehow he'll get it off of me.*

She watched him hopefully, knowing he would dash forward at any moment and save her. But then she saw his eyes turn dark, and drift away like stones sinking into a murky pond. Unbelievably, he was gone—back into the jungle.

Alone again, she lost her will to fight, and was ripped from the seat. Her head thumped against the ground as she realized the anaconda had plans for her, and didn't intend to waste time.

The grip around her leg grew even tighter as she felt herself being dragged across the ground. She frantically reached for the base of the seat, but it was just out of her grasp. Her arms flailed in both directions, trying to clutch on to anything.

He's left me for dead.

She was distracted from facing her deadly predicament only by the blood-boiling fury she felt toward Neil. *How could he leave me to die like this?*

The thing continued to pull her, and before she knew it, she was in a patch of trees. She looked behind her; the makeshift bed and shelter seemed miles away. She was able to grab on to the base of a tree and held on for her life. The pulling continued, and it felt like her leg was about to be separated from her body.

Her ears hurt from her own screaming as she contemplated letting go of the tree. Her leg felt detached from her body now as she started to lose hope that she would survive. It was too powerful, too determined, and with no one to help her, what chance did she have?

She looked at it closely for the first time—shifting its slimy body across her skin and pulling, forever pulling. She tried to reach for it, but her desperate attempt was worthless. With her hands off the tree now she was being pulled again—surely, to her death.

He leapt into the area as if dropped from the sky. Before she even had the chance to comprehend he was there, he thrust a long object into the anaconda. She felt instant relief from the squeezing around her leg as she saw the creature flail. He stood over it and thrust downward several times until it finally stopped moving.

She lay on the ground, stunned. Her lungs sucked in and expelled the humid air, wheezing like a deflating balloon. He knelt next to her and took her hand. She saw then that he was holding a long stick with a blade on the end of it.

So many thoughts and questions raced through her mind, but she asked him something that she didn't have time to think about. "Where the hell did you get a spear?"

He looked at the weapon, smiled, and looked back at her. "I don't know if you would call it a spear. But when I saw the anaconda, I went to find a good stick. Fortunately, I found this one pretty quick, and tied the knife to it with my bootlace."

Her eyes darted downward and saw his lace-less boot. Then she focused on the long, sharp knife at the end of the stick. "Where did you get that knife?"

He looked down for a moment and then said, "I got it off the pilot."

Magglio! She had forgotten all about him. "Where is he?" she said and sat up, turning her head from side to side.

He didn't answer right away, but took a slow breath. She knew immediately that the news was not good. "He didn't make it," he said softly.

"What happened to him?"

"I don't know if you remember the crash or not, but we smacked into a tree last night. The cockpit was crushed. It's a miracle we survived, but Magglio wasn't so lucky. That's why I was gone. I buried his body."

"You buried his body?"

"Well, I didn't actually bury him. I covered him with heavy rocks as best I could. I was hoping to protect him from the wildlife until we can get word to his family."

She stood up and stepped back—still cautiously—from the giant dead snake. "What the hell are we going to do, Neil? We're in the middle of a damn jungle. Without Magglio, how are we going to find our way out of here?"

"Don't panic. We'll get out."

"How can you tell me not to panic? This thing," she raised her voice as she pointed to the severed anaconda, "almost squeezed my leg off!"

"Actually, the fact that we came across an anaconda is a good sign."

"A good sign? It was trying to kill me! How could there be anything good about this thing?"

"They live in the river. They come up on dry land to look for food, but they never wander too far from the water."

"So what? How is the river going to help us?"

"We need to go down the river to get to the Cofan tribe."

"But how are we going to get down the river? Is the noon ferry going to show up and give us a ride? And I hope you don't think I'm swimming with these things in the water."

"We'll figure something out. I'll just feel better if we're at the river. At least we'll know where we are."

She looked at the motionless snake carcass and kicked the scaly body to ensure it was dead. "Why was this thing dragging me, anyway?"

"I was surprised it attacked you because they usually don't go after humans. It must have sensed your body heat, and because you weren't moving much it was probably confused and thought you were its prey."

"I don't understand why it didn't bite me."

"Believe it or not, they're not poisonous. They kill their prey by suffocating them, or by drowning them."

"So it was going to drag me to the river and drown me?"

Neil shrugged his shoulders. "At least we know what direction to walk."

"That's real comforting, Neil," she shot back with an irate glare. She angrily stomped through the jungle and tried to not think about how the snake would have dragged her through the area where she was now walking.

Neil caught up with her, stepped in front of her, and led the way. "Let me go first; I have the spear," he said over his shoulder.

Shannon didn't respond, but followed him silently. After a few minutes of walking, she said, "What about cell phones? I have one, but I'm assuming it won't work out here."

"No chance. You need cellular towers nearby for those to work. We don't have anything close to us."

They walked for a little longer, and saw the river just ahead. *Great.*

Closer to more snakes, she thought as they drew nearer. Then, they heard something in the distance. They both stopped to listen. It was familiar, yet hard to identify.

They looked at each other, puzzled. The sounds became a little clearer, and Shannon heard a few Spanish words. "People," she said, hopefully to Neil.

She watched Neil's eyes scan the area like a hawk. The voices became louder and they heard footsteps. "Maybe they can get us out of here," she said, excited.

She started to move in the direction of the voices, but Neil interrupted by saying, "Hold on."

"What is it? Don't you want to see if they can help us?"

"Yes, but I want to make sure they're not the wrong kind of people."

"Wrong kind of people," she scoffed. "I was almost dragged to my death by a snake. Do you think I'm going to worry about the wrong kind of people?" She started to walk toward the voices, waved her arms, and yelled, "Hey! Over here!"

"Shannon, wait!" Neil said.

She looked over her shoulder at him but kept walking. "Relax, we need their help." Neil followed her, and just as he was about to grab her shoulder to pull her back, they appeared.

They were three rough-looking Ecuadorian men. They were bare-chested with bandanas wrapped around their heads. But Shannon didn't notice their appearance; she was consumed with the sight of their guns.

Oh shit! She thought as she realized they weren't ordinary guns, but automatic rifles—machine guns. Shannon and Neil stood motionless as the men pointed their weapons and shouted commands in Spanish that they did not understand. When one of them stepped forward and snatched Neil's spear, Shannon knew they were in big trouble.

She watched in horror as two of them turned Neil around, unraveled some rope, and began to tie his wrists. The other one came at her and grasped her arm. He shouted at her in Spanish as she tried to recoil from his foul-smelling breath. But before she knew it, he spun her around and she felt the rope tighten around her wrists.

After she was tied, he patted her down, confiscating her cell phone. He pushed her forward, and she struggled to not tumble to the ground. She looked to her left and saw that Neil was also being pushed in the same direction.

He looked back at her, stone-faced and said, "Looks like it's going to be a long day."

CHAPTER FIFTEEN

The old pickup truck bounced over the uneven terrain. Shannon and Neil struggled to keep their balance in the back of the dirty, rusted bed. With their hands still bound behind their backs, they were flung from side to side, bruising their bodies and turning their stomachs.

Shannon's sore, possibly broken ribs sent unrelenting surges of pain up and down her torso. Every bump was like a sharp knife being stuck into her ribcage. But as uncomfortable as her ribs were, the nausea from the violent movement was worse.

Just as Shannon felt ready to vomit, the jostling subsided. She was finally able to focus on her surroundings, and saw the jungle behind them. They were in an open plain now, speeding along a narrow, dusty path.

"Where are they taking us?" she asked Neil, who looked miserable leaning against the back end of the truck.

"Columbia," he shouted back over the noise of the vehicle.

"What?" she replied with surprise, not actually expecting him to know their destination.

"We're in northern Ecuador, near the Columbian border."

"I know that, but how do you know they're taking us over the border?"

"Because I know how these kidnapping operations work. These guys are just a small-time band of thugs. They're going to try and sell us to FARC."

"FARC? What the hell is FARC?"

"They're a Columbian guerilla group. They call themselves the Revolutionary Armed Forces of Columbia. They have about 20,000 members and are very well organized. They're in the business of kidnapping tourists, and holding them in prison camps until they get a ransom."

"How do you know these guys aren't part of FARC?"

"It's easy to tell the difference. FARC soldiers wear specific uniforms."

"They wear uniforms?"

"Think of an American street gang in the jungle. But instead of gang colors, they wear black masks from the nose down, and camouflage pants and shirts. Believe me, these guys know what they're doing. If these thugs sell us to them, we'll have no chance of getting away. It will definitely be over."

"What do you mean, over? They're not going to kill us. You said they would hold us for a ransom. Won't your law center pay?"

"Of course they'll pay. But by the time they make contact, negotiate, and get the money, it will be too late."

"Too late? Too late for what?"

"We have to stop The Power from finding the boy. If they get him, then we're in big trouble."

"In bigger trouble than we're in now?"

"I don't mean just me and you. I mean everyone."

"Who's everyone?"

"Everyone in civilization." He paused and gulped hard as Shannon stared at him in confusion. "I'm sorry. I know you don't understand."

"I don't understand because you won't tell me anything that's going on," she shouted, red-faced.

He looked down as he pensively shook his head. "I need to apologize to you for being so elusive about all the details. But you should know that it's for your own safety."

"What?"

"Just in case the unthinkable happens, and somehow they get you."

"You mean The Power?"

"I'm not saying that will happen. But if for some reason it does, the less you know the better off you'll be."

"I don't care about that. I want to know what's going on."

"I don't think that's a good idea."

"If you don't want to tell me who the boy is, then at least tell me how this group is planning to end civilization."

"They're not going to end it. They plan to take it over."

The truck suddenly screeched to a halt, sending Neil tumbling forward. He crashed into the back window, his head landing in Shannon's lap. Their thoughts of the awkward position lasted only a moment as they realized the truck was at a complete stop.

Neil rolled to his side and sat up on his knees. Shannon looked around the empty plain, and spotted two small houses nearby. "What's going on?" she asked.

"This could be a very good thing. We're not at the border yet, so this must be their base. If they're stopping here for a while, then we might have a chance to escape."

Shannon was about to reply but stopped when the thugs approached. They gestured with their guns for them to step out of the truck. They complied as the machine guns stayed aimed at their torsos. One thug roughly pushed them in the direction of one of the structures, and Shannon felt the barrel of the gun jabbing her in the back as they traipsed along the dusty plain.

Shannon and Neil stopped walking when they reached the front of the small, decrepit house. One of the kidnappers stepped forward holding a long knife, and cut both of them free. He opened the front door, and waved Shannon and Neil inside, frantically yelling something in Spanish. Shannon looked at Neil, and he slightly shrugged his shoulders and stepped into the house. She reluctantly followed.

The door slammed against the backs of her heels as it closed tight. Before she could even focus on their new environment, the stale, humid air poured over her like molasses. "It's like a sauna in here," she said as they both scanned the space.

They stood in the largest room in the tiny house, which was empty, save a discolored mattress in the corner. The walls had cracks and holes with plaster spilling over to the floor as if it had endured a bombing raid. What appeared to be a small kitchen area was on the left; it was gutted with no appliances and just a few cabinets. There was one other room on the right, which was a smaller version of the main room.

Shannon gestured to the mattress as she said, "I hope we're not spending the night."

"Actually, the longer we stay here, the better off we'll be."

"That's not exactly what I was thinking."

"The longer we're here, the more possible opportunities we'll have to escape."

There were two windows, one next to the front door and the other on the opposite wall across the main room. Neil checked them both and pointed out that they were both nailed shut. Shannon felt a layer of sweat oozing out of her skin.

They heard the hurried voices of their kidnappers, and looked out the window. They saw two of them walking away toward the other house. The third man approached the door, machine gun slung over one shoulder and a bag in his hand.

The door pushed open violently as the thug stepped inside. He dropped the bag, and aimed the gun at them. He barked at them authoritatively, and quickly exited. Neil continued to gaze out of the window as Shannon picked up the bag.

Neil watched the thug move away from the house as he said, "It looks like just that one guy is going to guard us. His buddies went into that other house. We have to think of a way to get out of here fast because we may not be here long."

"I have good news," Shannon said as Neil turned to face her. In one hand she held a bottle of water, and the other a bunch of bananas. "At least you finally get to eat."

CHAPTER SIXTEEN

Shannon leaned against the crumbling wall, feeling hopeless and hot as hell. His legs passed her field of vision every thirty seconds or so as he bounced from one window to the other. She didn't bother looking up at him, listening only to his heavy strides squeaking the shoddy floorboards. But she knew he was staring out the windows, desperately searching for an idea.

Finally, after stuffing the remainder of his fourth and last banana in his mouth, he crouched beside her and asked, "Do you hear that?"

"Hear what?"

He took her by the hand, helped her to her feet, and led her to the window by the front door. "Look at the house next door. There's a generator running."

Shannon heard the sound of the generator now but was unenthusiastic. "Yeah. So what? They have electricity and we don't."

"If we can hear it from this distance and bottled up as tight as we are in here, then imagine how loud it must be for the guys inside that house."

She looked at him, still not understanding his point. "Yeah, I guess it must be pretty loud."

"That works to our advantage."

"How?"

"Two of the three guys are in there. If they can't hear, then all we have to do is get by that one guard."

"But that one guard has a machine gun. How do you plan to get by him?"

"We have to think of something. But we have a better chance now thanks to that generator."

Shannon strolled across the room, looking for anything that might spark a thought. She stepped around a discarded banana peel, and almost tripped on a loose floorboard.

Neil walked to the loose piece of wood and jabbed at it with his boot.

"What are you doing?" she asked.

He snatched the end of the board with his fingers and started to pull it up. "I think I can rip this out."

"Why? Do you want to dig a tunnel?"

"Very funny. I was thinking more of using it as a weapon."

"Oh yeah. I'm sure that would hold up well against a machine gun," she shot back.

He yanked the board completely out, and held it in his hands like a baseball bat. "We need to distract him. If I can nail him in the back of the head with this, then we'll have a chance to get away."

"And how do you think we'll accomplish that?"

"I don't know. You're a college graduate. Think of something."

She readied a caustic reply, but stopped suddenly. *College graduate?* "How do you know I went to college?"

"Umm...you mentioned it yesterday."

"I did not."

"Yeah you did. On the plane, I think."

"I'm positive that I didn't tell you that."

"What's the big deal? You told me you worked with computers. Maybe I just assumed."

She frowned, not entirely pleased with his explanation, but she didn't have the mindset to be overly suspicious. "Speaking of things we talked about on the plane, you said that you would tell me what The Power plans to do if they find the boy."

"Did I say that?"

"You promised you would tell me."

"All right," he replied as he released an annoyed sigh. He leaned against the front door and began. "The majority of the plot is actually spelled out in the same book that I told you about before."

"*The Turner Diaries*?"

"That's right."

"But you said that book was to make the radicals that The Power didn't want to be associated with act as Lone Wolves."

"It was. But it also told the story of a militia group called The Order. In the book, this group rises up against a fictional government."

"But in real life The Order is The Power."

"You got it. And I bet you can guess who the fictional government is."

"The United States."

"Bingo."

She sat on the floor next to him, intrigued by his every word. "But why the U.S.?"

"Actually, it's not so much personal as it is strategic."

"What do you mean?"

"They can only sneak attack one government. After that, too much attention will be on them. So, if you wanted to take over the world, what military would you want to control?"

"I see. They want to control the U.S. so they can use the military power to take over the rest of the world."

"You got it."

"But if the U.S. has the strongest military in the world, then wouldn't we be the hardest to take over?"

"In a conventional war, yes. But this will be nothing like America has ever seen before. This will be a sneak attack that will make Pearl Harbor and Nine-Eleven look like child's play."

"And this part is in the book too?"

"Yes. In the book, The Order launches a series of attacks on the government until they take it over."

"What kind of attacks?"

"The Power has a detailed plan. Much of it they've already done; like expanding their group with the right kind of members and keeping things organized, raising funds, planting operatives in key government positions, and training their soldiers for later work."

"And then what?"

"The actual attacks will occur in stages. The first phase would be assassinations."

"Assassinations of whom?"

"They plan to take out as many high level officials as they can in one day."

"How high?"

"They won't implement that stage of the plan unless they're reasonably sure they can take out the President and Vice President."

Shannon didn't speak but her eyes widened with surprise. "But that's not all," Neil continued before she had the chance to speak. "They'll go after members of the President's cabinet, and leaders of his opposing party, influential senators, high-profile governors, anyone who might be looked at as a potential leader."

"But I don't understand how they can do that. What about the Secret Service and other security?"

"They know it won't be easy, and they may not get all their targets. But they plan and train every day. As far as the Secret Service, they have men inside there too. And they're not only supplying The Power with information, but we think they may actually carry out some of the assassinations."

She inched closer to him, their legs now touching. "But how can that be? The Secret Service must screen their applicants incredibly well."

"That's why The Power doesn't want crazy radicals joining their group. They want young men and women with college degrees and no criminal records. They want the boys and girls next door. The Secret Service, CIA, and FBI can screen them all they want, but if there's nothing suspicious there, then there's no reason to exclude them."

"But can't the authorities figure out that these men are a part of this terrorist group?"

"Not when the terrorist group has lain dormant since the late forties. We've tried to enlist the help of the FBI and CIA and inform them of The Power's plan, but they don't have the resources to really investigate it. To them, it's just a far-fetched idea that they take as seriously as a UFO invasion."

"So what are they going to do after the assassinations?"

"The next phase is to bomb government buildings, public utilities, and communications systems. And most importantly, they'll move teams into the nuclear weapons operation centers."

"To start bombing other countries?"

"No. That'll come later. First, they'll nuke U.S. cities."

"What? Why?"

"They know that the assassinations and small-scale bombings of some buildings will not topple the government. They know there will still be some body of government to deal with it. Some third string team buried in a bunker somewhere. But still, this team will have some degree of power and will certainly have a strong influence over the American population. So they'll keep nuking U.S. cities until the remaining government formally surrenders and instructs its citizens that a new regime has taken over."

"But the people won't accept that."

"If you've just survived a month with no power or water, and your best friend and sister just died in a nuclear attack, how strong do you think you'll be? If a new government comes in and tells you they'll turn your water and power back on, and there'll be no more bombs, you'd probably go along with them. Even if you don't like it, you'll accept it; otherwise, you're looking at death."

Shannon swallowed hard, trying to imagine this unbelievable concept. "I understand that since The Power has never done any actual terrorist activity that the FBI would ignore any warnings from you about them, especially with all of the other threats they have to deal with. But I don't get one thing. If the FBI doesn't know much about The Power, then how does your law center?"

"You have to remember that the Jewish roots of my law center are from 1940's Europe. Our center is a modern version of Simon Wiesenthal's mission. As long as the Nazi movement is alive, we'll be there to try and stop it. And now, we're faced with the biggest risk since Hitler's Third Reich. We've been watching them when no one else has. And we succeeded at something that they've been doing to the U.S. government for years."

Shannon leaned forward. "What?"

"We've got someone inside."

"You've got a member of your law center in The Power."

"Yes, we do. But that's all I can say. I've already told you more than I should."

They didn't speak for a minute as Neil walked to the window. He glared out at the guard, anxiously squeezing the floorboard. She watched him, still trying to process the information he had just shared. It seemed unbelievable to her, but even if some of it were true, then she understood his urgency to get to the village.

"So you really want to attack the guard with that board?" she asked.

"Unless you have a better idea."

"If we're going to do it, we have to distract him somehow. And there's no way we can approach him. We'll have to get him in here."

Neil turned to face her and said, "We know it's important to them that we stay alive."

"Right. They can't sell us to FARC if we're dead."

"So let's pretend to have a big fight. We'll scream like crazy at each other, and then I'll smash the back window with the board. The guard will be concerned and come inside to investigate. You lay by the window like you're knocked out. He'll walk toward you and I'll clock him from behind."

"What about the other two?"

"They shouldn't hear any of it. Not with that generator."

"But what if the guard goes to get them when he hears the yelling and the glass smash?"

"I'll only hit him if he comes in alone. If he gets the others, we'll play it cool. I think it's worth a shot. We have to try something."

"Okay," she said, nodding her head in agreement. "So we have to yell at each other?"

"Yeah. For about a minute or so, and then I'll smash the window. After that, lay down near the window and pretend you're unconscious."

"Just be absolutely sure he's alone before you swing that board."

"I will."

They looked at each other tensely. And then, Neil exploded into a loud verbal tirade. Shannon jumped back in shock. He paused, and coaxed her with his eyes to return the yelling. Without thinking, a barrage of obscenities poured out of her mouth.

It had been so long since she screamed at anyone that it felt odd, but she also sort of enjoyed the release. She continued and even surpassed Neil's volume at times. He didn't seem to be paying much attention to her. He crouched in front of the window, and watched the guard intensely.

The guard stared at the house, obviously alarmed by the yelling. Neil continued to watch him as he fidgeted and paced, but didn't approach the house. Neil held his hand up to Shannon and whispered, "Okay." He ran toward the back window and swung the board into it, shattering the glass.

They stood motionless for a moment, staring at the now broken window. Neil waved for her to get into position. She carefully lowered herself, and laid her head onto the dirty floor.

Neil moved to the door. He gripped the board firmly and cocked it back. He heard the door rattle, and saw the doorknob move. As he prepared to strike, he realized that he had neglected to look out the window to see if the guard was alone or not.

But he knew it was too late. He would swing at the first thing he saw.

CHAPTER SEVENTEEN

Curt was helping one of the tribesmen untangle fishing net when he heard the frantic splashing. He recognized it as the sound of an approaching canoe, but the hurried paddling was unusual. The Cofan people normally took their time when completing everyday tasks. They only seemed to rush in the face of danger. *Was there danger?* Curt wondered.

Curt and the tribesman watched curiously as the canoe came into view from around a corner. The sixteen-year-old's face looked tense, almost panicked. At first, Curt hoped it was the result of an encounter with some of the area's wildlife—maybe an anaconda. But then he thought better.

A sixteen-year-old boy was considered a man in the Cofan Tribe. And this particular young man was one of the tribe's best hunters. Curt realized that he wouldn't be spooked by an anaconda—or anything else. Something must have happened. Something bad.

The young man bounded out of the canoe as it hit the dirt. He ran to Curt and the tribesman and said one of the few words he knew in English. "Randy!" He rested his hands on his knees as he repeated their leader's name. Then, he broke into a hurried speech in the Cofan language.

The tribesman dropped the net and ran off. Curt leaned close to the young man and said, "What happened? Please tell me!"

The young man caught his breath, as he stood upright. He looked at Curt and spoke two English words: "Bad men." He pointed to the ground, and Curt understood the meaning.

Bad men are coming here.

Curt dashed toward the main area of the village, and saw Randy running toward him. "What the hell is going on?" Randy said as they reached each other.

"One of your young men says bad men are on the way."

"I have to talk with him." Randy ran to the riverbank and listened to the young man's story. He turned back to Curt, who was just reaching them.

"He said there were four white men. One of them was older, and warned him in Spanish that the other three are on their way here. He said they are bad men, and are coming to take the white boy."

Curt staggered backward a step after listening to the words of his friend. "Curt," Randy continued, "do you know who these men are?"

Curt nodded his head yes, and tried to speak, but it took him a moment. "I believe these are the men I told you about. The ones we are hiding the boy from."

"I thought you said they would never know he was here."

"I'm sorry, Randy. I've put your tribe in serious danger. I need to get the boy out of here now, and get to my satellite phone. But first, I need to know something. I know you wouldn't allow me or Victoria to bring any guns here, and we didn't. But if you have something hidden, an old shotgun—anything—it's time to get it out."

"I told you that my tribe forbids firearms. We don't have anything."

"Please get your women and children to a safe place. Then get your best bowmen and spearmen to the riverbank."

"What? Why?"

"They may come in shooting."

Curt ran off toward Victoria's hut. They would have to implement the emergency escape plan that they had practiced. Only this time it was all too real. This time she would have to take him to the secret location up the river.

He burst into Victoria's hut and quickly explained the situation. She was in the middle of giving the boy a math lesson. But after hearing the news, they dropped the books and ran toward the river. Curt helped her drag a canoe into the water.

The boy looked frightened, but neither of them had time to console him. Curt knew Victoria would have plenty of time in the secret spot to calm him down—hopefully.

Victoria and the boy set off up the river, her toned arms pushing the paddle forcefully into the water. "We'll follow the plan as we practiced," she said, looking at Curt to confirm her statement.

"You know what to do," he said, and watched them paddle away. He glanced down the river nervously. He was relieved to see no sign of the men yet. He sprinted toward his hut, intent to dig out his satellite phone, and prayed that it would work.

He saw that the village was in an uproar with Randy trying to organize the women and children to make an escape into the jungle. Many of the men were running around with bows and spears, but there was no coordination to their efforts.

Curt intended to call the Law Center. He hoped they had anticipated The Power moving in on the boy and had help on the way. As he frantically searched his hut for the phone, he thought of one more thing.

Did Randy know the where the secret location was? The answer was of the utmost importance, and he had to know right away. He forgot about the satellite phone for the moment, and ran to find Randy.

He knew his answer to the question was a matter of life or death.

CHAPTER EIGHTEEN

Neil's white knuckles clutched the end of the board as the figure stepped into the room. Neil saw the back of a head and swung the board with all of his strength. He heard the loud thud of wood striking a human skull, and then lost his balance after the impact.

He stumbled forward, tripped over the feet of the man he had just struck, and crashed to the ground. He immediately lifted his head and looked to his left. The man he had struck was indeed the guard. He was face down—apparently unconscious—with blood dribbling out of the back of his head.

Neil rolled to his side and realized he was still clutching the board. But when he held it up, he saw that it was broken in half. His weapon was no longer as powerful, and he thought of the doorway behind him.

He still didn't have a chance to see if the other guards had accompanied their friend into the house. It was possible that two men, armed with automatic rifles, were standing right behind him. If this were true, he knew it was over. Neil believed fury would overtake the kidnappers, and they would gun him down.

Neil could see Shannon still on the floor across the room. She lifted her head up and looked toward the doorway behind him. He knew he wouldn't need to look at the doorway to know; her reaction would tell him if anyone was there.

Her face was frozen for a moment; her eyes locked on something in the doorway. Neil expected to hear the explosion of gunfire. He tightened his muscles, waiting to die. But then, Shannon's eyes looked back at him. Without expression she said, "Let's get the hell out of here. I think you killed him."

Neil jumped to his feet and spun around toward the door. He staggered back, almost tripping over the motionless guard, and saw no one in the doorway. Shannon grabbed his shoulders, helping him to regain his balance.

Shannon stepped carefully around the guard's blood, and picked up the machine gun. She held it out to Neil, who was still calming his breathing. "Do you know how to use this?"

He looked at her and replied, "I'm a lawyer."

She slapped the gun in his hands. "Well, I think we should take it with us anyway. We'll figure out how to work it."

Neil took the weapon and dashed to the window. He looked out at the neighboring house. "I don't see anything going on over there. We have to go now. But quietly."

"Lead the way," Shannon replied, and followed Neil outside. They quickly ran to the side of the house, and Neil peeked around the corner.

"What do you think we should do?" Neil asked.

"That's a stupid question. Let's get the hell out of here."

"No," Neil said, gesturing to the pickup truck, which was about twenty yards away, "do you think we should take that, or go on foot."

"Won't they hear us, if we start that up?"

"Probably. But it's a long walk to the river. If we go on foot, we'll never beat The Power to the village."

"But if they hear us start that, they may come out shooting. We're not going to get to the village at all if we're dead."

"I'm sorry, but I think we have to take the chance."

"I'm glad you're so willing to take chances with my life," she shot back.

"I already explained what The Power is capable of doing if they get that boy."

"I know," Shannon replied with a sigh, as if she were conceding to his request.

"Listen, there's no reason for those men to rush out shooting just because they hear the truck start. They'll probably think it's the other guard starting it for some reason. Most likely, they'll just look outside when they hear it. There's no other vehicle here for them to chase us in, so as long as we get away fast, we should be okay."

"How are we going to get it started? I hope you don't think we have time to hot wire it."

"Like I said before, I'm a lawyer. I don't know how to use a machine gun, and I sure as hell don't know to hot wire a truck. I'm hoping they left the keys in the ignition. If not, the guard I knocked out was the one driving, so he probably has them on him."

"And what if that's not the case?"

"I'll make a deal with you. If we find the keys in the vehicle or on the guard, then we take the truck. If not, then we'll sneak away on foot."

"Fine."

"I'll check the truck, you check the guard."

Shannon nodded her head in agreement. Neil got on his hands and knees, awkwardly tucked the machine gun under his arm, and quickly crawled toward the truck. Shannon moved back to the front door, her eyes fixed on the neighboring house.

She jumped through the doorway, and almost tripped over the guard on the floor. She was relieved to see him in the same position, and realized he was alive when she heard the sounds of his breathing.

She wanted to be careful—in case he might wake up—but knew there was no time. She roughly patted his shorts, and was surprised to hear the jangle of keys. The man did not move as she reached her hand in his pocket and pulled out the set of keys.

As she exited the house, she thought about crawling, as Neil did, to stay out of sight. But when she saw the truck just a few yards away, she decided to make a mad dash. Neil sat in the driver's seat, and looked alarmed when he saw Shannon sprinting toward the vehicle.

She hopped in the passenger seat and tossed him the keys. He caught them, but still looked shocked. "Let's go!" she screamed. He fumbled with them for a moment, but then inserted the proper key and turned the ignition.

The engine started much louder than they would have liked. Neil struggled with the stick shift, trying to find first gear. When he finally did, the truck lurched forward. Neil hammered the gas until the big, clumsy vehicle moved forward steadily. Shannon cringed as the loud engine rumbled, metal parts clanked, and belts squealed.

Neil's muscles flexed as he fought with the steering wheel, finally pulling it all the way to the left. The truck thundered across the dirt surface, spitting out a tremendous cloud of dust and dirt. Shannon thought they would be less inconspicuous if they launched a mortar shell through the window.

When the truck was finally heading in the right direction, Shannon looked over her shoulder. She was alarmed—yet not surprised—to see the door of the house open. Both men appeared; each of them held their machine guns.

She saw the machine gun they took from the guard resting near her feet. She leaned forward to pick it up, but the truck bounced over a bump, sending her head into the dashboard. She sat back with a yell as she continued to be jostled around in her seat.

"What are you doing?" Neil yelled.

"I was getting the gun. They're out of the house."

Neil looked in the rear window and yelled, "Shit!"

Shannon heard a popping sound, and then the sound of bullets striking the bed of the truck.

"Get down!" Neil screamed as he pushed her forward. Bullets peppered all areas of the truck with the back and front windshields cracking. Neil floored the accelerator, sending the truck rumbling forward—almost out of control. He sank in his seat to avoid the ricocheting bullets as he tried to keep the truck on a path toward the jungle.

His arm draped over her shoulder and chest. She held onto him, afraid to open her eyes. When the sound of the gunfire finally subsided, she popped her head up, and saw Neil breathing heavily and creeping back to an upright position.

The truck was rapidly approaching the jungle. Shannon said: "Is this where we came out?"

"I have no idea. But I'm not driving around to find the exact spot. That looks like a path up ahead," Neil said as he pointed to an opening at the edge of the jungle.

Shannon looked over her shoulder through the cracked rear windshield. She saw their two pursuers still after them, but fading—and hopefully out of range. Neil guided the truck through the opening in the woods, and soon, their pursuers could no longer be seen.

Neil stepped on the brakes for the first time since he started the truck, but kept the vehicle moving at a fast pace for fear the thugs could someone still follow them. The truck bounced up and down and rocked from side to side. Shannon held her arms over her head to protect her from the vicious thrusts into the roof.

She scanned the area as they raced though it, and said, "I don't think this is the way we came. I don't recognize any of it."

"We have to get as far away from them as possible. We'll figure out our way to the river."

"How? It's not like we can ask directions at the next gas station."

"Don't worry. I'll get us there."

They drove for a while in silence. Shannon was finally convinced they were a safe enough distance away from the thugs. But she worried about what they would encounter next, and if she would ever see civilization again.

The path was smooth for stretches, but then they bounded over a tree stump, sending Shannon's head into the roof again. As they continued to speed along, they noticed that the path narrowed a bit, and they noticed several more tree stumps.

Then, the tree stumps seemed to be all around them, and Neil struggled to weave the lumbering truck between them. The path seemed to be gone now, and was replaced by a maze of tree stumps. Finally, Neil could not avoid one, and they bounced over it hard. As Neil attempted to regain control of the vehicle, another stump was in their path.

The stump was higher than the others, and the front end rammed into it. The truck could not endure the impact and rolled over on its side. It tumbled over a few times until a full tree stopped it.

Shannon and Neil were still cursing as the sound of rumbling metal faded, the truck finally coming to a rest. Despite aggravating Shannon's earlier rib injury, they escaped unharmed. "Are you okay?" Neil asked, out of breath.

"I'm all right. What the hell are all these tree stumps doing in the middle of the jungle?"

Neil kicked his door open as he said, "Loggers I guess." He crawled out and extended his hand to Shannon. "Give me your hand." He pulled her out, and they took a moment to look at the battered vehicle. "Let's try and roll it back over."

With their hips slightly touching, they strained to lift the truck. It rocked forward but they failed to flip it. They took a moment to catch their breath, and Neil said, "Let's give it another try."

They got back into position, determined to roll it over this time. But before they had the chance, Shannon felt something poke her in the back. She let go of the truck and froze with a shocked expression. Neil saw her and also let go of the truck.

Before either of them had a chance to speak, a voice came from behind them. It was a loud male voice that spoke in perfect English. "Put your hands in the air and don't move."

CHAPTER NINETEEN

Curt found the village no more organized than when he left it, but he was happy to see most of the women and children out of sight. The men of the tribe wandered around looking lost, loosely clutching their bows and spears. Curt knew these men never had a reason to take up their arms against other people. They were skilled hunters, but Curt understood that to fire upon another man was an entirely different thing.

He saw Randy running back from the woods and approached him. "Randy," Curt called out, "I need to know something very important."

"What is it?" Randy said, terribly out of breath.

"Do you know where Victoria took the boy?"

"What? What does that matter now?"

"Believe me. It matters."

"You made it very clear that no one was to know that. Victoria never said a word."

"I know Victoria would never tell you. But the boy knew. You two are very close. I need to know if he ever told you about the location."

They looked at each other, and Curt became worried by the odd look in his friend's eyes—like he was about to tell a lie. "I don't know the location," Randy said, impassively. Curt wanted to believe him, but wasn't sure. "Why is it so important that you know this now?"

Curt moved closer to him and said, "I hope you're telling the truth. But in case you're not, I should tell you—"

The tribesmen erupted into a loud chatter as the splashing of a canoe could be heard. Curt and Randy ran to the river as the tribesmen rushed around in a panic, drawing their bows and brandishing their spears.

The Bald Man guided the canoe to the riverbank until it stuck in the mud. He was apparently unfazed by the bows and spears pointing at him as he stepped onto shore. He held his arms high in the air as his companion sheepishly crouched behind him.

"We come in peace," the Bald Man yelled.

"What should we do?" Randy said as they sprinted to the river.

"I'm not sure," Curt replied, "I don't recognize these men. I'm not a hundred percent sure they're the men I spoke of."

They slowed to a jog as they reached the tribesmen, who were still aiming their weapons. "We should hear what they have to say then," Randy said.

Curt and Randy stopped, standing next to the Cofan tribesmen. The Bald Man took a cautious step forward with his arms still raised. His partner now stepped to the Bald Man's side, his arms trembling in the air.

"We mean you no harm," the Bald Man said loudly, flashing a toothy smile to everyone. "We're with a tour. We got separated from our group and are lost. Can you help us?"

Curt thought it was possible that they were being truthful. Tour groups from Quito frequently brought curious travelers into the area. The Cofan Tribe was a popular attraction because of their primitive lifestyle. Randy had deals with several tour groups to bring people into the village from time to time, and used the money to purchase certain supplies in the city.

"There's no group due to come here this week," Randy whispered into Curt's ear.

Curt stepped forward and said, "We're not expecting anyone this week. Who are you with?"

"A travel agency in Quito," the Bald Man replied. "We came to see the wildlife reserve. Me and my friend wandered off a bit in the canoe, and the next thing we knew our group was gone. We have to get back; our wives are going to kill us."

Curt and Randy looked at each other, both knowing this story was possible. There were many groups that went to different parts of the reserve and didn't stop at the village. Some of them did travel in canoes, and getting lost was not impossible.

Curt believed the young man that warned them of invading bad men, but thought that maybe these were not the men. He said there were four men, and one of them was old. Here, there were two middle-aged men. Perhaps they were just a couple of stupid guys that strayed away from their tour group. Maybe the men from The Power were still on their way.

Curt wanted to believe the strangers, but was still skeptical. He scanned the area for the boy who had given them the warning, but didn't see him. He was about to ask Randy where he was, but his friend started speaking to the tribesmen.

He spoke in the Cofan language, and the hunters immediately relaxed after hearing his words. Curt recognized the Cofan word for tour, and knew that Randy told them to no longer fear the men. The tribesmen lowered their weapons, and began to chatter, obviously relieved.

As Randy started to move toward the visitors, Curt noticed the sixteen-year-old boy, who arrived with the frantic warning, emerging from the jungle. Curt assumed he was returning from securing the women and children to a safe spot. He immediately started walking toward the young man, anxious to know more about the men he had encountered.

The young man walked toward the river as Curt approached him.

As they drew closer, Curt saw a frightened look in the young man's eyes. The young man stopped dead in his tracks, and raised his trembling arm in the direction of the strangers.

As Curt realized the young man had spotted the same men he warned them about, he heard what sounded like a firecracker. Then another and another. He whirled around, and to his horror, saw the Bald Man and his partner holding pistols.

They fired repeatedly, systematically shifting their position with each shot. The Cofan tribesmen fell like dominoes, completely surprised by the attack. In just a few minutes, the two gunmen took out more than half the tribe.

As they screamed and rushed to help their fallen brothers, the tribesmen didn't fire back as the two gunmen expelled their spent cartridges and loaded full clips. After only a brief pause, they were back to firing their automatic weapons on the scrambling tribesmen.

Curt pushed the young man back toward the jungle, and told him to hide with the women and children. He then turned and raced toward the chaos. As he grew nearer, he saw the gunmen load another round. They fired upon the last of the living tribe members, and soon, none of the scattered bodies moved.

Curt saw a river of blood seeping into the dirt. The men of the Cofan Tribe—all fifty of them or so—had been wiped out in a matter of minutes. Their lifeless bodies leaned against each other in a massive, bloody mound.

Curt slowed his pace—unsure of what to do—and then saw something move from within the carnage. It was Randy, crawling away from the bloody mess. The gunmen could obviously see him, but for some reason didn't fire.

Curt looked at the Bald Man, and saw his slight smirk. He knew then what he had to do. He lunged forward and grabbed Randy's hands. "I'm so sorry, my friend. I never meant for this to happen. Please forgive me. I have to run now."

Randy wouldn't let go of his hands as he said, "Don't run. They'll kill you."

Curt glanced up at the Bald Man, who was rapidly approaching, and then back at Randy. "No they won't," Curt said, dropped Randy's hands, and ran off toward the jungle.

The Bald Man raised his gun at the fleeing Curt, and seemed to be taking aim. But then he lowered it, and turned to Crooked Teeth. "Stay with him." He gestured toward Randy on the ground. "I'll be back in a minute."

The Bald Man took off, moving fast for a man his size. Curt only had a few yards on him as they disappeared into the thick jungle.

CHAPTER TWENTY

Shannon and Neil held their arms in the air, and did their best to not move a muscle. Shannon could not imagine the source of the American-sounding male voice.

We're in the middle of the Amazon jungle. What American is out here?

Then, they heard the voice again. "Keep your hands in the air and turn around slowly."

They did as the voice instructed. Shannon focused on the man in front of them, but couldn't believe what she saw. He was about six-two with a wide girth. His arms and shoulders had bulging muscles, and he carried a fat belly. He wore a baseball cap backward with no sign of hair protruding out of it. A neatly trimmed goatee with dark sunglasses finished his face.

Once again, they found themselves staring down the barrel of a machine gun. But Shannon did not find the machine gun as shocking as the man's white skin.

He must be American, she thought. When she realized he was wearing a New England Patriot's football jersey, she knew for sure. *He's definitely American. But what the hell is he doing here?*

At first, the man aimed the gun at them as if he were about to shoot at any moment. But then, he lowered it a little and took a step back. His shoulders relaxed as he asked, "Are you two Americans?"

"I'm from Connecticut," Shannon blurted out with a smile.

"And I'm from Boston," Neil added.

"Boston?" the man said loudly. He completely lowered the gun, took off his baseball cap, and flashed the front of it to Neil. There was a large B on the front, the baseball hat of the Boston Red Sox.

The man stepped close to Neil and firmly shook his hand. "Born and raised in Medford, bro."

"I work in the city," Neil replied. "My law firm is on Comm Ave."

"No shit," the man replied. He looked at Shannon. "And you're a New Englander too, huh?"

"New Haven, Connecticut," she answered.

"I'm Frank." He shook her hand and put the hat back on his bald head. "What are the odds of three New Englanders meeting way the hell out here? What are you two doing here, anyway?"

"It's a long story," Neil began. "We're trying to get to the Cofan tribe in Zabalo."

"Oh yeah, the Cofan people in The Cuyabeno Reserve. I know exactly where that is. But you're pretty far from there."

"We were kidnapped by a band of thugs who held us in a little house about twenty miles north of here."

"No shit," Frank said. "That's the reason I'm here."

"Excuse me?" Neil replied, confused.

"My security company has a contract with Dalaco Oil. We're guarding the oil workers."

Shannon asked, "Is that why there's so many tree stumps around here?"

"Yeah. The tree guys have started to clear this area, but the bulk of the work right now is a few miles south. They have a bunch of us stationed in different areas to circle the workers. That Goddamn FARC would come down here and pick off the workers right and left if it wasn't for us."

Shannon and Neil looked at each other with hopeful eyes, both wondering if Frank could be their ticket out of the jungle. Frank circled the overturned truck and said, "This baby's not looking too good." He leaned close to the engine, carefully inspecting something. "Oh, shit!"

"What is it?" Neil said as he moved next to Frank.

"Looks like you got a cracked axle."

"Are you sure?" Neil asked.

"Oh yeah. Not only that, but it looks like the oil pan got ripped off. You won't be driving this thing out of here."

"Listen, Frank," Neil began, looking the hulking security guard directly in the eye, "it is extremely important that we get to Zabalo as soon as possible. Can you help us?"

"Sure. At then end of the day we'll pack up and head back to Lago Agrio. You can come along with us. You can probably buy yourself a ride down the river tomorrow."

Neil and Shannon shot each other a quick, desperate look. "I appreciate the offer," Neil replied. "The only problem is that we have to get there today."

"Today?" Frank said, surprised. "There's nothing I can do for you until my shift ends. Why is it so important that you get there today?"

"It's a long story that I can't get into right now. I'll just say it's a matter of life and death."

"Jesus Christ. Someone's going to die if you don't get there today?"

"Many people will die if we don't get there today."

Frank shook his head, looking distressed. "I can try and call my supervisor," Frank said as he pulled a two-way radio from his hip. "But I don't know what he'll say."

"Is your supervisor from Boston too?"

"Yeah. We all are. Our company's based in Mass."

"Is he a Red Sox's fan?"

"Diehard."

"My law firm has season tickets. Box seats. Five rows behind the Sox's dugout."

"That's cool. But what does that have to do with anything?"

"If your supervisor can free you up to get us to Zabalo right now, I'll get you those tickets for any weekend series you want."

Frank looked at him, puzzled by the concept. "You're serious?"

"We have four seats. The Yankees will be at Fenway over the July fourth weekend. All three games are yours."

Frank's eyes widened. "And what do you want me to do exactly?"

"Do you have a boat at the river?"

"Of course."

"Drive us to the river, and then take us to Zabalo in the boat."

Frank looked at Shannon and then back to Neil. "That's it. And you can really get us those tickets?"

"You have my word."

"All right. Hang on. Let me call my boss."

Frank stepped away with the crackling noise of the radio. Shannon moved next to Neil and said, "I hope this works."

"If it doesn't, we're screwed."

They stood in silence, listening to Frank reiterating the terms of the proposed deal to his supervisor and reassuring him that the strangers seemed honest. After several minutes, he put the radio away and returned.

"Okay. He'll be here in a few minutes with a Jeep. He's going to relieve me, and I'll take you where you need to go."

"Thank you, Frank," Neil said. "You don't know how much this means."

CHAPTER TWENTY-ONE

Curt's legs plodded forward like well-greased machine parts. The uphill climb burned his quadriceps and strained his hamstrings. But he could hear the sounds of the Bald Man behind him, and he knew he had to keep going.

He weaved in and out of countless trees, and maneuvered around large boulders. He tried to ignore the stabbing cramp in his side and kept climbing—and climbing. He glanced over his shoulder and saw that he had gained no ground on his relentless pursuer. The Bald Man kept after him, apparently unfazed by the arduous hill.

Finally, the ground leveled off, and Curt found himself at the apex of the small mountain. He wanted to drop to the ground and suck in as much of the air that he could, but he knew he didn't have time.

He could see the edge of the cliff, and dug deep for one last burst of energy. As he drew closer, he heard the Bald Man's voice behind him. "Stop running or I'll shoot." Curt ignored the command, and knew it was almost over.

Then, he heard a gunshot, and an instant later, a bullet sailed past his head. It was close, but Curt knew that was the intention. The Bald Man wouldn't kill him; he needed him.

But then there was another blast, and Curt felt a sharp pain in the back of his left leg. He tried to keep moving, but his leg gave out and he found himself rolling in the dirt, his leg burning as if it were over an open flame.

He looked behind him and saw the Bald Man closing fast. He looked forward and saw the cliff just a few yards away, calling him. It seemed like an impossible feat, but he was aware what was at stake. He felt like a supernatural force invaded his body, lifted him, and propelled him forward. Somehow he was running again.

Just a few steps from the edge, he heard the Bald Man yell, "No! Wait! Wait just a minute!"

Curt stopped just inches shy of the cliff, and looked down at the perilous drop. He turned back to the Bald Man, who stood still with his hands raised in the air. "You don't have to do this. I'll let you live. I promise."

"You're a liar," Curt fired back.

"Just tell me what I need to know, and I'll let you go."

Curt and the Bald Man locked in a stare, and Curt said, "You mean that?"

"I promise. You know the information I need. Just tell me, and I'll be on my way." Curt continued to stare at the Bald Man as his breathing slowed. "Step away from the cliff and come over here with me." The Bald Man stepped back, and gestured to a few large boulders behind him. "We'll sit here and talk."

"Fine," Curt said.

The Bald Man smiled and slowly turned. He stowed his gun back in its holster, but felt for the knife in his pocket. He was so close he could almost feel the boy's presence. He knew the Supreme Leader would exalt him as a hero within The Power. He would make history.

And now, he had a very simple task to complete. He started to carefully pull the knife out of his pocket as he stepped toward the boulders. *It will be like taking candy from a baby*, he thought as his smile widened.

He hid the knife in his palm as he turned toward Curt. He thought his eyes were playing tricks on him for a moment. But when he refocused his vision, there was no doubt of what he was seeing. Curt was gone.

He didn't think it was possible, but then realized what had happened. He charged to the edge of the cliff, stopping just a step away from the straight drop to the jagged rocks below. When he looked down, he could see Curt's body falling, vanishing from sight like a pebble into the ocean.

He kicked the dirt in frustration, and yelled—his voice echoing through the rocky valley below. He stormed away from the cliff, muttering and cursing to himself. But he knew hope was not completely lost. There was one last person.

He ran back down the hill, coasting easily compared to the grueling climb up. He hoped that Crooked Teeth hadn't done anything stupid like Blondie had done. He needed this last man alive.

He quickly reached the base of the mountain and returned to the area of the massacre. There, he found the carnage as he had left it. The lifeless, bloody bodies were strewn about the area. Crooked Teeth was still milling about. Then he saw the white American on the ground, motionless.

He thought the worst, but then he saw Randy move. Relief flooded through his body as he released a tense breath.

Crooked Teeth ran to him and said, "What happened? Did you catch the guy?"

"He threw himself off a cliff," the Bald Man answered as he looked at Randy. "Any trouble from this one?"

"Not yet."

"Good. Go stand by the river and keep lookout. I need to spend some time with him."

"Okay, boss," Crooked Teeth replied and did what he was told.

The Bald Man slowly sauntered his way to Randy, who was lying on the ground in shock and covered with the blood of his fellow tribesmen. "Leave me alone," Randy moaned. "I don't know anything."

The Bald Man took the knife out of his pocket and unfolded it. "That's too bad," The Bald Man said and slammed his knee into Randy's chest. Randy groaned in pain as the Bald Man pushed down on his ribcage.

He rested the point of the knife against Randy's cheekbone. "Cause if you don't have anything to tell me, this is gonna hurt a lot."

CHAPTER TWENTY-TWO

Technically speaking, the place was a cave. A natural aperture in the earth made of rock. It was not on a trail or path of any sort, but could be found deep in the jungle—about a mile hike east of the Aguarico River.

The mouth of the cave was eight feet wide and four feet high. There was a little more room inside—but not much—and it only extended about fifty feet into the mountain. A powerful waterfall thundered about two hundred feet in front of it—providing a magnificent landmark for the secret place.

It was stocked with two sleeping bags, a flashlight, bottled water, insect repellant, and extra batteries. There were two important items hidden in the back of the cave in a hard leather case: a satellite phone and a loaded .22 caliber pistol. After Curt stocked it, he secured mesh netting over the entrance to prevent any wildlife from disturbing the supplies.

Victoria and the boy had been there only once—during a practice drill. She was worried about her ability to find it again, but realized they were in the right place when she saw the waterfall. As they approached the secret spot, she was relieved to see the mesh netting still in place.

She tore the netting down and turned to the boy. "Okay, we have to hide inside here."

"Why do we have to go in there? It's too dark and small in there. Can't we just wait out here?"

"I told you that we have to hide. There are bad men looking for you. They'll see us if we stay out here."

The boy sat down angrily. He rested his chin on his hands as his eyes filled with tears. "I don't care if they find me. I don't want to go in there."

Victoria sat next to him and gently patted his back. "I know you don't want to do this. But if these men find us, they will hurt us and take you away."

"I want to go home," the boy said, fighting back more tears.

"I'm doing everything I can to get you home as soon as possible. But this is where we need to be for now. I promise that I'll get you home soon."

The boy looked at the cave and back at Victoria. "It looks scary in there."

Victoria stood up and moved toward the cave. "It's actually not scary at all. Come see." She waved for him to join her. He reluctantly inched over. She reached in the cave, pulled out the flashlight, turned it on, and pointed it inside. They saw that the supplies were as Curt left them. "See, that's not so bad."

The boy shrugged his shoulders. "I guess it's okay." The hard leather case caught his eye and he pointed at it. "What's in there?"

Victoria wasn't thrilled about the idea of letting a young boy play with a gun, but if she unloaded it...why not? She needed to get him out of sight. "Come inside and I'll show you."

They both crawled into the small space, and Victoria opened the case. She immediately expelled the ammunition clip, and checked the gun several times to be absolutely sure it was empty. Then, she held it up for the boy to see.

"Wow!" His eyes lit up like he was looking at a roomful of gifts on Christmas morning. "Can I hold it?"

"You sure can. But you have to promise to keep it in here."

"Okay."

She handed him the unloaded gun, and watched him examine it with eager eyes. She went back into the case, took out the satellite phone, found the portable battery charger, and attached the phone to it. She hopefully turned the hand crank for several minutes, sending the needed juice into the phone's battery. She held the power button down with her thumb and waited. After a moment, the little red light came on—it had power.

She crawled to the front of the cave as she watched the boy shoot at imaginary bad guys. She held the phone out of the cave, angling it to the open sky. She entered the number to the Law Center and pressed the send button, silently praying that someone was there.

CHAPTER TWENTY-THREE

Shannon and Neil sat in the front of the boat and looked back at Frank. The muscular security guard held the handle of the outboard motor, and had it running at full power. The fifteen-foot craft's wake spilt the river in half as they sped toward their destination.

Shannon was too nervous to enjoy the scenery of the rich green landscape. Neil's tense face reminded her that they might be too late. And she couldn't imagine what that truly meant—or what they might find in the village. One thing was for certain: she was anxious to see this boy—and find out who he was.

Neil yelled to Frank, "Are you sure we didn't pass it?"

"Positive," Frank yelled back over the roaring motor. "I was just down here last week. You can see some of the huts from the river. I think it's up around that bend." Frank pointed forward to a spot ahead where the river curved.

"Cross your fingers," Neil said to Shannon. "As soon as we see the village, we'll know if we're too late."

"What do you mean?"

"These aren't nice men, Shannon. They think they're the superior race. They would just as soon kill these Cofan people as you or I would kill a cockroach. To them, they're not even human."

The boat approached the bend as Shannon said, "But why would they bother with the people in the tribe? If they just want the boy, wouldn't they just take him and leave?"

"Let's hope so," he solemnly replied.

Shannon was looking at Neil's face as they rounded the bend. She was about to speak, but stopped when she saw his expression. Immediately, she knew something was terribly wrong.

When she turned to look toward the riverbank, she thought she saw a group of people huddled together. But a moment later, she realized what was actually there. The bodies of the dead men leaned against each other—bloody and lifeless. A few screaming women dragged some of the bodies through puddles of blood—desperately pulling them away from the massacre site.

Young children ran around the area unsupervised, wailing and slipping in the gore. The pitiful crying and moans of agony stabbed at Shannon's heart as she tried to process the horrific scene. Suddenly, she gagged, and felt bile rise up her throat. She leaned her head out of the boat and vomited into the river.

She leaned back into the boat, gasping for air. She saw that Neil looked no better—white as a bed sheet and clutching onto the side of the boat. She heard Frank yell from behind them, "What the hell! What the hell!"

Frank beached the boat and Neil immediately leapt out of it. Some of the women ran at him and began yelling. They threw stones, and one chucked a spear, which barely missed him and hit the side of the boat. Shannon was about to step out, but stopped when she saw the hostility.

Neil, with his arms raised in the air, pleaded with them, but it was obvious they did not understand. They continued to scream and hurl rocks, some of which were hitting the now cowering Neil.

"Get down!" Frank yelled to Shannon as he grabbed her and lowered her below the side of the boat. Frank jumped out and began speaking loudly in Spanish. Shannon couldn't understand what he was saying, but the commotion gradually subsided.

When she peeked over the boat, she saw Frank hugging one of the women. They were still crying loudly, but the aggression seemed to be over. Neil stepped to the boat and took Shannon's hand. "Come on."

Neil helped her out, and they carefully approached the distraught women as if they were walking on broken glass. Frank pointed at them as he explained something to the women in Spanish. "These people have their own language," Neil whispered to Shannon as they walked closer. "But some of them speak Spanish, which is what Frank is speaking."

"Thank God for Frank."

"You can say that again," Neil replied as they reached their new friend and the hysterical women. "Frank, it's very important that we know where the men who did this went."

Frank communicated with one of the women and then turned back to Neil. "They say they saw them take a canoe up the river."

"Please ask them if they had the white boy with them."

Frank asked and then told Neil, "They say no. The boy went up the river with a white lady before the killers got here."

"Okay," Neil replied, "there may still be a chance. Please ask them if Curt or Randy is here."

Frank asked them. "They say Curt ran off into the jungle and hasn't come back. They say Randy is in the hut over there," Frank said as he pointed to a nearby hut.

"Good," Neil said. "We have to see him now."

Neil and Frank walked quickly—almost running to the hut—as Shannon followed a few steps behind. Neil and Frank entered, and Shannon planned to follow them inside. But when she reached the entrance, Neil suddenly jumped in front of her.

His face looked paler than a corpse. He extended his arm and guided Shannon back a few steps. "What's wrong?" she asked.

Then, Frank rushed out of the hut and vomited in the dirt. Neil could only shake his head, and gesture for her to back up. "What is it? Is the man dead?"

"Dead?" Frank loudly responded, "He's cut up like a jigsaw puzzle."

"What? Why?"

"They obviously tortured him before he died," Neil answered. "He's badly mutilated."

"But I don't understand why they would do that. I thought you said they only wanted the boy."

"It sounds like the boy escaped with a woman who lived here with him. She would have taken him to a secret location to hide until it was safe. The men from The Power must have tortured this poor man, thinking he knew where they went to hide."

"Do you think the man knew?" Shannon asked.

"I have no idea. But I sure as hell hope not. No one could have endured that amount of pain."

Shannon saw wetness in Neil's eyes, and thought of Mr. Henry. She assumed Neil was thinking of his grandfather, knowing he most likely met a similar fate. She took his hand and gave him a tight hug.

"I'm so sorry," she whispered in his ear.

"Thank you," he whispered back and returned the hug. They held their embrace for a few moments as they listened to Frank yelling frantically into his two-way radio. They heard him explain where he was and what he had found. He demanded that the authorities be alerted right away.

They broke their embrace and Neil approached Frank. "Thank you so much for bringing us here, and calling for help for these people. But I need some more help."

"What do you need?"

"The men who did this are looking for a boy. I think the boy is still alive and hiding up the river somewhere. The men are looking for him now. But we have to find him first."

"Then let's go," Frank said with anger and started to move toward the boat.

"But there's a problem," Neil continued, stopping Frank in his tracks. "I don't know where the boy is hidden."

"Do the killers know?" Frank asked.

"I'm not sure. But I know they were trying to find out from the man in the hut."

"Jesus Christ!" Frank said, shaking his head in disgust.

"Listen," Neil began, "there was a man living here named Curt. I need you to ask the women which hut was his."

"What for?" Shannon asked.

"He had a satellite phone, and hopefully, it's still in his hut. I can call the Law Center."

"What good is that going to do?" Shannon replied.

"The woman who's with the boy should have her own satellite phone stashed in the hiding spot. Part of the emergency protocol is for her to call the Center and request rescue from her location."

"So she would have explained to someone at your center exactly where they are?" Shannon asked.

"I hope so," Neil answered.

"Whatever we got to do, bro. Let's just do it now!" Frank said, and ran off toward the women. Shannon and Neil watched him anxiously communicate with some of them. One of the women started to walk away and pointed toward a hut. "She says this is the one."

Once Neil realized what hut she was identifying, he ran inside of it and started searching. Shannon joined him, and without speaking, they tore the contents of the hut apart. Finally, Shannon held up a small black phone.

"Good job," Neil said as he grabbed the phone, dashed outside, pointed the phone to the sky, and hurriedly entered a number. Shannon sat quietly in the doorway of the hut, anxiously staring at Neil. A wave of relief engulfed her when he started talking with someone. She felt even better as she realized he was getting directions. "Let's go," he said to Shannon as he turned off the phone.

They rushed back to the boat and found Frank waiting for them. "You know where we gotta go?"

"I think so," Neil said and climbed into the boat with Frank and Shannon close behind. When they were all in the boat, he turned to Frank. "Do you still have your gun?"

"Hell yeah!" Frank said and reached down, pulling out the AK-47. "Don't worry, Chief, if we see anyone, I'll be shooting first and you can ask questions later."

"Great. Let's go," Neil said, but Frank hesitated, noticing one of the women.

He spoke with her for a moment and then climbed out of the boat. "She doesn't want us to leave. They're afraid the killers are going to come back."

"Did you tell her that you called for help?" Neil asked.

"I did. I just feel like hell leaving these people like this."

"You understand that we have a chance to save two people that these killers are after."

"I know. I know. I'm not saying I'm going to stay. It's just..." Frank tearfully scanned the area and then looked back at Neil. "Why don't we say a quick prayer for these people before we leave? I'd feel better then."

"Every second is critical right now—"

Shannon took Neil's hand and squeezed it. "Come on, Neil. It will only take a minute. Look at these poor people." She gestured to the horrendous chaos in the village. They watched the crying women and children as they tried to sort through the bodies of their fallen loved ones.

"Okay," he said softly. "But quickly."

They climbed out of the boat and joined hands with Frank. The three of them looked down and silently prayed as the agonizing cries hung in the air, mixing with the smell of death.

CHAPTER TWENTY-FOUR

When Neil believed they reached the landmark—an old fallen tree protruding out of the riverbank—he signaled for Frank to stop the boat. When the engine abruptly cut, Neil said, "I think this is the spot. We have to go on foot from here."

"Gotcha, Chief," Frank said and started to row the boat to shore.

"Listen," Neil said, looking at both Frank and Shannon, "we have to be extremely quiet. I'd prefer if we only spoke when absolutely necessary. And we have to keep our eyes open for any movement."

"Why?" Shannon asked.

"The men from The Power could be looking for the boy in this area. If we see them before they see us, that'll give us a huge advantage. And unfortunately, if they see us before we see them…well…we could be in trouble."

The boat slid into the mud of the riverbank, and they all climbed out. Frank slung the gun over his shoulder as he said, "All right then, we'll keep our yaps shut, and our eyes open."

"I'll lead the way," Neil said and walked into the jungle. Shannon and Frank followed him closely, their eyes scanning the area for any sign of danger. They walked slowly and quietly for a while, and jumped the first few times they heard the squawking of various birds.

After about a quarter of a mile into the jungle, they became accustomed to the ordinary noises, and were able quicken their pace. They continued to search the rich green surroundings as they crept along, but saw nothing of concern.

Shannon tried to forget her encounter with the anaconda, but couldn't help paying extra attention to anything moving along the ground. She felt better the farther they got away from the river, but knew the real danger was not the wildlife but men with guns.

Suddenly, they heard rustling through the bushes behind them. Whatever it was, it was much louder than anything they had heard thus far—definitely not a bird.

Shit! Shannon thought as she froze in place. *It's them!*

They all spun to face the noise as a few errant shots burst out of Frank's gun. Neil leapt toward him and pushed his arms down as he yelled,

"Don't shoot!" Another round exploded out of the gun, but Frank quickly gained control of the weapon.

When Shannon focused on the sight in front of her, she jumped back in fright. But she instantly became relieved when she realized it was not the men. She never thought she would be so relieved to be face to face with an enormous cat. The creature growled once and disappeared as quickly as it had appeared.

"What was that?" she asked.

"A hell of a big cat," Frank answered.

"I think it was a jaguar," Neil explained. "Don't worry, it won't bother with us. He was probably resting here and we disturbed him."

"Sorry about the gun. I didn't mean to fire it," Frank said.

"Speaking of that," Neil interjected, "you have to be careful. Even if we see people, we have to be sure it's okay to shoot. Victoria and the boy could be walking around. Or even if we do find the men, they may have the boy with them."

"I gotcha, Chief," Frank replied and the group was back on their way.

Their stealthy trek continued without incident for another quarter mile. Neil knew he had to start looking for the next landmark. He whispered to Shannon, "We're looking for a waterfall."

"A waterfall?" Shannon replied quietly and with surprise. "How big?"

"I have no idea."

"Did you say a waterfall?" Frank interjected, as they continued to march along.

"Yes," Neil answered.

"Hold on a second," Frank said, and they stopped. Shannon and Neil stared at the large man as his face strained like he was trying to concentrate on something.

"What are you doing?" Shannon asked.

"I thought I heard something before. I was thinking it sounded like running water." He continued to focus, and his face broke into a wide smile. "I got it."

"You hear the waterfall?" Neil asked, surprised.

"I'm pretty sure it sounds like water. It's coming from there." His muscular arm pointed left of the direction they were walking.

"Are you sure?" Neil asked.

"I hear something, Chief."

"Okay. Let's go see." They changed direction, moving to where Frank pointed. They crept along quieter than ever. Their heads bobbed up and down, and from side to side like owls, as they were prepared to react to the slightest noise.

They walked for a while, and then they saw it. A modest waterfall, dribbling a stream over a small rock cliff. They stopped walking, crouched behind some trees, and examined the area. After seeing nothing unusual, they moved forward.

They carefully inspected their surroundings until they agreed that it appeared safe. "Where's the boy supposed to be hidden?" Frank asked.

"In a small cave," Neil answered.

Frank looked around the area and said, "It don't look like there's any caves around here, Chief."

Shannon was about to agree, but then something caught her eye. At first, she didn't think it was a cave, but after a second look, she thought it looked like some type of opening in a rock ledge behind the waterfall. It was small...*but maybe.*

"There," she said, louder than they had previously been speaking. She pointed to the spot as her two companions strained to see.

"Let's check it out," Neil said, and they moved quickly to the rock ledge. As they walked closer, it became obvious that there was indeed an opening. They approached it cautiously, their eyes centered on the dark opening.

They stopped in front of it, and for a moment, no one spoke or moved. Neil broke the silence. "Victoria, are you in there?" There was no reply. "This isn't it. Let's keep looking."

Neil started to move away, but Shannon interrupted him. "Hold on," she began, "don't you think we should at least look inside? This does fit the description of the spot, right?"

"It does, but they're obviously not in there."

Shannon and Frank shared a sober expression as they looked at Neil. His eyes widened as he realized what they were thinking. Frank took a flashlight off his hip and held it up. "Let's have a look," he said.

He turned the light on and moved to the mouth of the cave. He shined the light into the darkness, and cautiously leaned against the ledge, peering inside. At first, he had no reaction as his head shifted from right to left. But then, his impassive face was overtaken by a rush of redness.

"What the hell is that?" he exclaimed.

"Is someone in there?" Neil asked, excited.

"No, but that's fucked up!"

"What is it?" Neil took the flashlight. Shannon moved into Frank's spot as he backed away, looking distressed.

Neil aimed the light inside, and they both saw it. There were some scattered supplies on the ground, which told them Victoria and the boy were once in the cave. But that wasn't what drew their attention.

On the back wall of the cave, they saw blood. The dark streaks were formed into some type of symbol. It took them a moment to realize they were looking at the ancient symbol for peace and good fortune: the swastika.

CHAPTER TWENTY-FIVE

Shannon sat perched on the end of the couch, hovering over the leftovers from an earlier corporate flight that Rick had left for them. She wished she had an appetite. But after leaving the massacre and discovering the boy had been taken, her stomach was twisted tighter than a knot.

She knew Neil felt the same because after two days of hardly eating anything, he didn't even glance at the food. She rested her head against the comfortable couch as she watched Neil pace the floor of the Gulfstream, anxiously talking with someone from his law center.

She knew he had reason to be nervous since The Power had the boy. But now, he seemed more concerned about the innocent lives lost in Ecuador. She listened to him describe the massacre of the Cofan Tribe, and now he was trying to describe the deceased pilot.

"His name was Magglio...Magglio. No, I don't know the last name. Ask the workers at the Quito airport about Magglio. He's been missing for the last couple of days. They'll know who you mean. This guy gave us a ride because he had a big family to take care of. We need to find his family and do the proper thing.... You can find them; just ask around, for God's sake.

"Listen," Neil continued, "I buried him in the jungle. I can let you know exactly where if I can look at a map...a map! Are you there? God dammit!"

Neil threw the phone against the wall. "Friggin' satellite phones are supposed to wok anywhere."

"We're 30,000 feet," Shannon commented.

"It doesn't matter; it should still work." He sat on a couch, his sharp breaths revealing his frustration.

Shannon strolled to the bar and clanked some bottles as she looked for something she liked. "What do you drink?" she asked Neil.

"I don't need anything."

She pulled out a bottle of Macallan Scotch. She filled two rocks glasses with ice, and carried the glasses and bottle over to Neil. "This is good stuff. Have you ever had it?"

He glared at the label. "How did you know that I drink that?"

"I guess we have more in common than we thought." She filled the glasses and passed him one.

"You really drink Scotch?"

"Really," she answered as they clanged glasses. She took a big sip.

"Why don't you put that bottle in a bag, and we'll finish it when we get to Chicago."

"Chicago?"

"Oh shit," Neil nervously replied. "Didn't I tell you that was our next stop?"

"Next stop?" she said angrily and slammed the glass on a table in front of her. "I thought we were flying back to Hartford. Why the hell are we going to Chicago?"

"I need to meet with an associate there."

"But why the hell do I need to go? I'm supposed to be back at work this morning."

"Your job is willing to give you more time off if you want it."

"What?" Shannon replied, shocked.

Neil looked surprised. "I mean...after what we just went through...you deserve some time off."

"How did you know that my job is willing to give me more time off?"

"You mentioned it."

"I absolutely did not."

"Yes, you did. When I was at your house—"

"I'm getting the impression that you've looked into my background a bit."

"What? Don't be ridiculous."

"You seem to know things about me that I haven't shared," she fired back with a raised voice.

Neil looked down with a defeated expression. "Listen, Shannon, my grandfather was a very important man. When you and your boyfriend moved in, I had to make sure you didn't mean him any harm."

"Derek was my fiancé."

"I'm very sorry about what happened to him."

She shook her glass slightly, stirring the ice cubes, and took a big sip. "Yeah, me too." She leaned back in the couch. "So what do you know about me?"

"Just where you went to school...and where you work. I promise. That's it."

"Then how do you know my company is willing to give me more time off?"

"I don't for sure. I just assumed. A big corporation like that usually gives a generous amount of bereavement time, and you would most likely have plenty of sick time since you've been there awhile. It hasn't been that long since Derek's death. It just seemed like you were going back a little early."

"Yeah. They think that too."

"So come to Chicago with me. You can call your job when we land. I'm sure they won't be surprised if you tell them you want more time."

"I want to go home. I want to get back to my normal life."

"I still don't think you're safe there."

"Why not?" She leaned forward and placed her drink on the table. "Your grandfather is gone, and they have the boy. What would they want with me?"

"I'm not sure. But they showed a serious interest in you by sending that e-mail. I'd prefer if you stayed with me for now. It's safer."

"You almost got me killed. Multiple times, in fact."

"I know. I'm very sorry that all happened the way it did. But when we get to Chicago, I promise we'll be safe. When my associate and I leave for Idaho, we'll leave you in his apartment with a guard. You'll be safe there."

"Idaho? What's in Idaho?"

"The Aryan Nation compound is in Hayden Lake, Idaho."

"You've got to be kidding me."

"We believe they'll take the boy there."

"But how are you going to get into the compound?"

"Remember when I told you we had a person inside The Power?"

"Yeah," she answered, taking a big slug of the scotch.

"That's the person we're meeting in Chicago. He's going to get me in too, and then we'll rescue the boy." Shannon shook her head in disbelief. Neil leaned forward and also took a large swig of his cocktail. He swallowed hard and said, "If you feel that strongly about going home, then when we land I'll have our pilot take you back to Hartford. But I really think you should stay with me. I promise we'll protect you."

There was silence as they both rattled their ice cubes and looked at the floor, the jet engine humming in the background. After a few minutes, Neil asked, "So what are you going to do?"

"I'm not sure yet," she replied. She finished her drink, dropped it on the table, and leaned back in the couch. She shot Neil an intense glare.

"What is it?" he asked.

"I'll make a deal with you."

"What kind of deal?"

"I'll come to the apartment in Chicago with you under one condition."

"What's that?"

"You tell me who the boy is, and why The Power wants him."

Neil returned her serious stare. He finished his drink, and immediately grabbed the bottle, refilling his glass. He poured more scotch into Shannon's glass as he said, "I suppose you deserve to know after all this."

"You'll tell me?" she said, almost jumping off the couch.

"It's less dangerous for you to know now that The Power has the boy. So, yes, I'll take that deal."

"Okay," Shannon replied, obviously pleased with his decision. She stared at him and leaned closer, as if she were about to pounce on him. She waited, and watched Neil slump against the couch, sipping his drink. "Well?"

He looked at her, surprised. "What?"

"Tell me," she almost yelled.

"Oh," he popped up, and strode across the plane. He retrieved a small bucket of ice and returned to the couch as he said, "You want me to tell you now?"

"Yes. Now."

"I think it would be better if I told you when we get to my associate's place."

"Why?"

He added ice to both their drinks. "Well, to be honest with you, you may find what I say hard to believe. When we're in Chicago, my associate can verify what I tell you. Besides, when we're there, I can show you the video."

"There's a video?"

CHAPTER TWENTY-SIX

The city of Coeur d'Alene is located in northern Idaho, not far from the Canadian border. It has a population of about 35,000 people, and is situated several miles south of the small town of Hayden Lake. The quiet little town, which contains a serene lake of the same name, has a population of about 500. The residents of the town are all Caucasian—with twenty-five percent being of German ancestry.

When The Power's private jet landed in the Coeur d'Alene airport, there was a helicopter waiting. The Bald Man and Crooked Teeth walked down the stairs of the plane with the boy tightly situated between them. As they approached the helicopter, Crooked Teeth looked at it with surprise.

"We're taking a helicopter?" he asked the Bald Man over the deafening rotors.

"You catch on quick," the Bald Man replied, keeping them on a quick pace.

"But it's only a ten minute drive."

The Bald Man opened a door to the helicopter, and gently guided the boy into the front seat. He closed that door, and slid open the back door. He looked at Crooked Teeth and said, "Just get in." The Bald Man climbed in first, and Crooked Teeth sat next to him.

"Now close the door," the Bald Man barked at Crooked Teeth. The confused man did as he was told, and sat back uneasily.

"All set?" the pilot asked, looking to the backseat. The Bald Man flashed a thumbs up and they were airborne.

"Now we need to talk," the Bald Man said, turning to Crooked Teeth.

"About what?"

"About your blonde friend."

"Listen," Crooked Teeth said, "he had it coming. He had no business shooting that old man. I'll explain everything that happened to the Supreme Leader."

"What if I don't want you to explain everything?"

Crooked Teeth stared blankly for a moment, but then a look of understanding overcame his face. "Okay. I can tell him whatever you want, if you don't want me to mention that you shot him."

"How do I know I can trust you?"

"I'm giving you my word."

"But I don't know you."

"I helped you get the boy, didn't I? We're gonna be famous for this. People are gonna look up to you and me. We made history." He stopped talking and looked out the window when he noticed the helicopter was starting to descend.

They were hovering over an area of wilderness along the shore of Hayden Lake. The pilot stopped the descent about five hundred feet over a rocky landscape. "What the hell are we doing?" Crooked Teeth asked loudly.

The pilot looked to the backseat and said, "I think something is caught in the back door."

"What?" Crooked Teeth replied.

"We're dragging something. I think it's caught in the back door," the pilot said.

"I don't see anything," Crooked Teeth said, peering out the window.

"Open the door, you idiot," The Bald Man barked.

"Open the door?" Crooked Teeth responded, nervously. "That's a long drop."

"You're not gonna fall. Just open the door," the Bald Man ordered.

Crooked Teeth reluctantly lifted the handle and carefully slid the door open. He shifted away from the opening as he pretended to inspect the outside of the craft. "I don't see anything," he said as he turned to the pilot.

He looked at the Bald Man, who had a strange smirk on his face. "What?" Crooked Teeth asked, puzzled.

Then, the Bald Man lifted his leg and hit Crooked Teeth in the face with the bottom of his boot. The stunned man fell back, out of the helicopter. The thundering rotors drowned out his screams as he dropped.

The Bald Man watched him make impact with the rocky terrain, and continued to gaze down at the motionless body. "Don't worry," the pilot said, "in a couple of hours, the mountain lions will get rid of him."

"Good job," the Bald Man said, smiling at the pilot. The boy sat shaking in his seat. The Bald Man patted him on the shoulder. "Don't worry, young man. In a few minutes, you'll finally be home." The boy looked back at him with confused, teary eyes.

Then, the helicopter roared forward, and within a minute, they were looking down upon the four hundred acres of the Aryan Nation Compound.

CHAPTER TWENTY-SEVEN

Shannon stood behind Peter Barnett as he unlocked the door to his apartment. He pushed it open, smiled at her, and gestured for her to enter. Shannon took a few steps into the modestly decorated space, and Neil followed a few steps behind her.

As nice as Peter seemed, she felt awkward being in his home, especially since the plan was for her to stay after the men left for Idaho. Peter was in his early thirties, with a lean frame and short black hair. Shannon found him to be polite, but the conversation during the ride from the airport was limited to formal pleasantries and small talk. Now, she felt obligated to get to know him, but was too consumed by the mystery of the boy's identity.

Peter closed the door behind him and invited his guests to have a seat in the living room. Shannon and Neil sat down on a comfortable couch as Peter sat in a chair facing them. Neil had filled Peter in on the basic details of what had occurred in Ecuador, so Shannon hoped they wouldn't linger on the topic for long. There was only one thing she wanted to discuss.

She had given Neil a number of impatient glares since Peter picked them up, and was confident he was aware of her desire. And she wanted to know now. She delivered one more look in Neil's direction, and it was obvious that he understood.

"I know we need to catch up on several issues," Neil said to Peter. "But I promised Shannon we would explain some things to her first."

"That's fine, but there's something I need to tell you right away," Peter interrupted, his face suddenly looking serious.

Neil's body immediately became tense as he leaned forward. "What is it?" he asked.

"As you know, we dispatched a team to Ecuador to provide assistance to the victims there." Peter swallowed hard and continued, "On the way down the river that leads to the Cofan Tribe, they found a couple of bodies."

Peter paused. His words hung in the air like a balloon that was about to burst. Shannon knew what he was about to say. She slid her hand into Neil's as Peter resumed. "One body was not identified, but they believe the other is your grandfather."

Neil shook his head slowly as if he were expecting the news and said, "Are they sure?"

"No. But he appears to be the same age and matches his general description. Given the fact that he was missing, and presumed to be in that area, it seems likely that it's him."

"I agree with the assumption," Neil replied stoically. "Did they report the cause of death?"

"There was a gunshot wound to his head."

Neil looked curiously at his associate. "Only one wound to the head? Are you sure there were no other injuries. No mutilation? No signs of torture?"

"They said he appeared to be unharmed with the exception of the gunshot wound."

Neil and Shannon looked at each other, surprised. She hugged him and whispered into his ear. "This is great news. He didn't suffer."

They slowly broke their embrace as they fought back tears. "He must have died quickly then," Neil said with a relieved smile.

"I would say he died instantly. He probably didn't feel a thing," Peter added.

Shannon kept her arm around Neil as she said, "We know they can't hurt him anymore. He's at peace now." Neil and Peter nodded their heads in agreement.

They were silent for a moment, picturing the scene of the old man lying dead by the river. "It doesn't make a lot of sense," Neil said.

"What doesn't?" Peter asked.

"It's strange that they would shoot him in the head. And even stranger that they would leave him out in the open," Neil said. "That tells me they killed him in a hurry, and didn't have time to hide the body. I don't understand why they would have to do that. And who was the person they found with him?"

"They said it was a man in his forties with blonde hair. They have no idea who he is, but he also had one gun shot wound to the head."

"Very strange," Neil said as he anxiously tapped his knee. "Don't get me wrong, if he had to die, I'm glad it was quick, but the scenario is suspicious. Not normal behavior for The Power. The poor soul we found cut up in that hut is more similar to The Power's M.O."

"Where is he now?" Shannon asked.

"The team has his body with them in Ecuador. They're waiting to hear Neil's wishes."

"I think it would be best to send him back to Boston," Neil said soberly. "I'll get there as soon as I can to identify him. But I think our business in Idaho takes priority right now."

Peter nodded in agreement. "Unfortunately, that can't wait for anything."

"I think that brings us to our next topic," Neil said as he patted

Shannon's leg. "Shannon has been unbelievably patient, waiting for a complete explanation of what's going on, and I promised I would tell her everything when we got here."

"Everything?" Peter asked. "You mean, even about the—"

"Everything about who the boy is, and why The Power needs him."

"Okay," Peter said, restraining his disbelief. "We can do that."

Neil pulled a paper bag out of his pocket and took out the bottle of Macallan Scotch from the plane. "If you wouldn't mind," Neil said to Peter.

Peter took the bottle and gave it an approving nod. "For the conversation we're about to have, I think we'll need this."

CHAPTER TWENTY-EIGHT

"So where do we begin?" Peter said as he took a sip of the Scotch.

"Well," Neil said, "I've already told Shannon some things."

Shannon sat comfortably on the couch and swallowed a large mouthful of the amber liquid. She hoped it would sooth her nerves. She was aware that outwardly she appeared perfectly relaxed, but her stomach churned like a tempest.

"What does she know so far?" Peter asked.

"I told her about Hitler's political testament, but I didn't get into the details of it."

"I suppose we should start there," Peter said, and pulled a folder out of a drawer in the coffee table. He took out a document and showed it to Shannon. "I assume you're familiar with this?"

Shannon strained to see it. The top of it said: "Adolph Hitler's Final Political Testament—April 29th, 1945."

"I'm not sure. Should I be?" Shannon said.

"This is the testament that I told you about," Neil interjected. "This is the one that's well known."

"Okay. Yes. I do remember you telling me. But you said it didn't contain anything that Hitler hadn't said before."

"That's right," Peter said, still holding the document in front of Shannon. "He dictated this to his personal secretary, Traudl Junge, on April 29th, 1945, which is the day he married Eva Braun, and the day before he killed himself. This document can be found in any history book."

"But isn't there another testament?" Shannon asked, her head bouncing between the two men. "Neil told me about one that's been kept a secret. And it started the whole Neo-Nazi movement." Her eyes fixed on Neil. "You said it was like a plan for the Neo-Nazis to follow."

"That's it exactly," Neil said and then nodded in the direction of Peter. Shannon turned her attention back to Peter and watched him put the document back in the folder and pull out another one. Once again, he held it front of Shannon.

She squinted, trying to read it, but there was no large title like the other paper had. "Is that the testament?" she asked.

"This is a copy of the original," Peter answered.

"I want to read it, but first, I'd like to know something. What does this have to do with the boy? Neil told me that the testament gave instructions for future Nazi groups on when to rise up against the governments of the world to try and take over." She turned to Neil with a look of recognition. "You said it outlined a specific timeframe, but it wasn't a date. That's always confused me. How can it specify a time, but not give a date."

"It gives part of a date," Peter replied.

"Part of a date?" Shannon said, looking at both of them, confused.

"It gives the month and day of when to start the revolution, but not the year," Neil explained.

"That's right. The month is April and the day is the 20th," Peter added.

"Hitler's birthday," Shannon said.

"Very good," Peter said with a smile.

"And is this the year?" Shannon asked.

"Yes," Peter answered. "They plan to start their revolution in fifteen days."

"But if the testament doesn't specify the year, how do the Nazis know this is it?"

Neil and Peter shared a long look. They shifted their attention to Shannon, who shot back an expression of complete bewilderment.

Peter cleared his throat and spoke. "The testament says that the Neo-Nazi revolution will begin on April 20th in the year that Hitler's first male heir is thirteen years old."

There was silence as Peter placed the testament on the table and slid it near Shannon. Her eyes darted down to the document and then back up at Peter and Neil. "I don't understand," she said. "If those are the instructions, then there's nothing to worry about. How can Hitler have a male heir? He had no children."

Shannon studied their blank faces, her thoughts tethered to a hundred different tidbits of history regarding Hitler. *Am I mistaken?* she wondered. *Hitler never had children, did he?*

She was confident that she was correct, yet their looks told her she was wrong. "I've never heard of Hitler having any children," she said.

"Of course you haven't," Peter replied. "A lot of people went to a great deal of trouble to ensure that you never heard that."

As the concept danced through her brain, she spoke. "That can't be. It just can't be. The boy is thirteen years old. How can he be Hitler's child?"

"The boy is Hitler's grandchild," Neil explained. "The testament says the first male heir to turn thirteen."

Shannon looked confused as she tried to grasp the information.

"When Hitler dictated this testament, he knew he only had a daughter," Peter said. "He was relying on the fact that she would reproduce, and that he would eventually have a male heir."

She sucked down a huge gulp of Scotch. "How could that be?"

"You're aware of his mistress, Eva Braun?" Peter asked.

"Yes. I know she was his mistress. But if they had a child, why would they keep it a secret?"

"Good question," Peter said and took a slug from his drink. "Would you like to answer?" he asked, gesturing to Neil.

Neil leaned forward and said: "It was important for Hitler to maintain an image that he was committed to Germany and Germany alone. This is why most scholars believed he didn't marry Eva Braun until their final days together. He wanted it to be clear that he dedicated all of his time to the Third Reich.

"As crazy as Hitler seems to us today, he was actually a very skilled politician. He played to the masses like an accomplished musician. He was acutely aware of the importance of his public image, and did tireless work to shape it in the way he thought best."

"And he didn't want people to know he loved Eva Braun?" Shannon asked.

"No," Neil continued. "He thought that would make him look weak and distracted from his job. There are theories that Hitler was gay or asexual, but the truth is that he loved Eva Braun very much, and she adored him."

"How do you know this?"

"It's easy to figure out," Peter interjected. "Just look at their behavior. Her father was dead set against her being with Hitler. And even though she was a good Catholic girl from a stable family, she defied her father. But the most telling fact of all is that even though Eva could have easily hidden with her family at the end of World War II, she chose to be with Hitler. It's important to know that Hitler pleaded with her to flee for her life, but she made the decision to stay. And she had to know that she would die with him, but she still chose to stay.

"And Hitler had a will, in which he left all his worldly possessions to her. But the most obvious evidence is their marriage. When Hitler was faced with the destruction of his empire, the end of his dreams, and his own death, he still felt it was important enough to marry her. Despite the macabre circumstances, one could look at it as a touching romantic moment. Hitler and Eva could have been pulled right off the pages of a Shakespearean tragedy—madly in love, yet destined to die."

"I'm sorry," Shannon said. "It's hard to imagine a man who killed millions of people as a sweet romantic."

"We're not arguing the fact that he was probably the most evil person to ever walk the earth," Neil said. "We're just saying that their love was real, and so was their daughter."

"All right. Even if I accept your psychological profile, you're talking like you know for a fact that they had a daughter. Like you have proof."

"We *do* have proof," Peter said.

Shannon was about to speak, but hesitated when she realized what Peter had said. *Proof? How can you possibly have proof?* She cleared her throat, and took a swig of her drink. "What type of proof?"

"We've learned that Eva gave birth to her child in Hitler's Alpine retreat in January of 1945," Peter explained. "Her sister, Gretl, visited her there, and stayed with her during the delivery and for some time after. This fact has been something we've overheard when eavesdropping on high-ranking members of The Power. But we also have some documentation to back it up. A couple of handwritten letters from the sister to her mother reporting on the birth of the child."

"You're kidding?" Shannon said, amazed at the idea. Then, she saw Peter sorting through some papers in the folder. *He couldn't possibly have the...*

Peter held another piece of paper in front of Shannon. She moved her face close to the document and saw that it was handwritten in a language she didn't recognize. The paper looked weathered—slightly yellow and deteriorating at the corners.

"Is that it?" she asked, mesmerized by the letter.

"This is an original letter," Peter proudly stated.

Shannon studied it, desperately trying to read some words of the foreign language. Peter pulled another document from the folder. "This is the English translation if you care to read it."

Shannon took the typed letter. She read:

Mother,

The baby is beautiful. Eva is well and happy. A doctor and nurse have attended to her through the birth. We will all be home with you soon.

With Love,
Gretl

"This letter is from Eva Braun's sister?" Shannon asked as she placed the translated letter on the coffee table.

"That's right. Gretl Braun was Eva's younger sister." Peter replied.

"She says in the letter that we'll all be home soon," Shannon said as she handed the letter back to Peter. "What did she mean by that?"

As Peter carefully returned the folder of documents to the drawer, Neil answered, "The plan was for Eva, her sister, and the baby to return to a small town called Ruhpolding to live with their mother. But Eva made the decision to go to Berlin."

"She left her baby to be with Hitler?" Shannon said.

"To die by Hitler's side," Neil corrected her. "But her sister brought the baby to their mother's. They raised the baby there, and gave her a peaceful, happy life."

Shannon was awestruck by the information, yet she still had some doubt. She decided to share her skepticism. "This is amazing if it's true. But are you sure this letter is authentic? If the letter is real, then it would make sense for you to have some other evidence to back it up."

Shannon noticed Peter fumbling with a VCR below the television. "Okay," he said as he stood up. "The tape is ready to go."

Shannon looked baffled as she watched Peter and then turned to Neil. "You have a tape?"

"You want other evidence," Neil said as he gestured toward the television, "and here you have it."

CHAPTER TWENTY-NINE

The Supreme Leader leaned on the windowsill as his eyes fixed on the sights outside. He watched the assassins aim their automatic weapons and pepper the bull's eyes of their targets. After emptying their magazines, the drill sergeant bellowed orders and the men promptly hid their weapons in duffel bags.

The Supreme Leader walked onto the balcony as he observed the assassins start the drill again. The killers walked casually with their bags, and then, on their drill sergeant's order, pulled out their guns in a smooth motion and started to fire.

"A thing of beauty," the Supreme Leader whispered to himself as he imagined the possibilities. If events unfolded as he hoped, these same assassins would be unleashing their bullets on real targets—the leaders of the United States government. But he needed his people to believe. And there was only one way to achieve that.

He wandered across the balcony and stared across the vast open land of the Aryan Nation compound. The guns popped in the background as he wondered about the boy. He had been on edge for days, waiting for his arrival. His assassins were trained, his moles planted, and his teams ready to invade key facilities. The Aryan Nation was perched on a ledge, anxious to jump. But the Supreme Leader knew they had to be patient.

Randolph stepped onto the balcony, his skinny, pale body casting a sliver of a shadow across the deck. The Supreme Leader heard his assistant's labored breaths, and hoped for good news. He turned to face Randolph, looking at his weathered, jagged face. The sickly man took a step forward as a piece of his jet-black hair fell over his small beady eyes.

"Your Excellency," Randolph struggled to say, his lungs still recovering from the walk upstairs. "They have arrived."

The Supreme Leader jumped forward. "Who has arrived?"

"The bald gentlemen and the young man you have been expecting."

"Where are they?"

"In the great room downstairs. They are waiting for you, Your Excellency."

"How does the boy look?"

"He seems afraid, Your Excellency." Randolph coughed roughly, seeming to dislodge a clog of mucus.

"Dr. Kuhn," the Supreme Leader said loudly. "I need Dr. Kuhn."

"I anticipated your desire and took the liberty of summoning her."

The Supreme Leader shook his head in approval. "Very good, Randolph. I am pleased with you. Now go and tell our guests I will join them shortly." Randolph bowed, acknowledging his master's order, and left the balcony, his raspy breathing fading as he closed the door behind him.

The Supreme Leader looked back to his assassins, who continued to fastidiously run the drill. He released a slow breath that seemed to be pent up for years. At last, it was time for The Power to take action.

CHAPTER THIRTY

After only a few seconds of the video, Shannon found herself awestruck by the beauty of Eva Braun. In the past, the name of Hitler's mistress had always evoked an image of an uptight German shrew. A pale faced hag, who obediently succumbed to the orders of the most evil man in the world. But as she watched the video, she realized that wasn't true.

The video showed some sort of social gathering on an outdoor, stone balcony with magnificent mountains in the background. The balcony was crowded with German officers and a few women pasted in the background, barely moving a muscle.

But there was one woman who moved about quite a bit. She had medium-length, bouncy blonde hair and bright, soulful eyes. She sprang between the partygoers like a pinball—smiling, talking, and laughing. Shannon didn't need anyone to tell her that this vivacious young woman was Eva Braun.

"I never realized she was so pretty—so lively," Shannon said.

"That's a common response when people see this," Peter replied.

"Was this taken at Hitler's Alpine retreat that you mentioned?" she asked.

"Yes," Neil answered. "This footage is from an elaborate fortress that Hitler kept in the mountains of southern Germany. It's well known that Eva Braun lived there for some time with only a couple of Hitler's people to watch after her.

"Previously, she lived in a villa that Hitler owned in a Munich suburb. He also gave her a Mercedes and a chauffeur while she was in Munich. We think she liked that much better since she was from Munich, and as you can see from this video, she was quite social."

Shannon's eyes toggled between the images of the beautiful woman in the video and Peter and Neil. "I can only imagine how exciting that must have been for her: to be dating the leader of her country, and to have her own villa and chauffeured Mercedes. She must have felt like a queen."

"She was only twenty-three years old when Hitler first put her up in that villa," Peter said. "She was a photographer's assistant when she first met him. Her father was a school teacher. Can you imagine going from that modest lifestyle to being Hitler's mistress?"

"So, if she was as social as she seems in this video, and had a nice villa and car in a town where she must have had lots of family and friends, why did she want to move to some fortress in the mountains?"

"We don't think she wanted to move there," Neil answered.

"I don't understand," Shannon said.

Peter said, "We think Hitler put her there when she got pregnant."

"Oh," Shannon said. "You mean Hitler hid her there so no one would know she was pregnant?"

"That's right," Peter replied. "We understand that she lived there with one of Hitler's personal physicians and a nurse. Hitler completely isolated her from anyone except those two."

"She must have been miserable," Shannon said.

"It would be safe to assume that," Neil commented.

"But isn't this video from the Alpine retreat?" Shannon pointed to the television. "She doesn't look unhappy there."

"This was before she had to move there," Peter said. "This is a video of a party when she was still living in Munich. When she was probably a lot happier."

"Okay...but I don't understand how this video proves that she gave birth to Hitler's baby."

"This one doesn't," Peter said as he picked up the remote control. "But I want you to take a close look at her." He hit a button on the remote as the image on the screen froze.

Shannon fixed her eyes on the television, staring at the fresh face of Eva Braun, her breezy hair dancing in front of the distant mountains behind her.

"Look at her body," Peter said.

"What?"

"Her body," Peter repeated. "Take a good look at her body."

Shannon focused on the young woman's slim frame. "What about it?"

"I just want you to remember it," Peter said and shut off the video.

Shannon watched in silence as Peter inserted a new video into the VCR. He pressed play and sat back on the couch. This video was of the same stone balcony, and although the camera was on a slightly different angle, the same mountains were visible in the background.

But as the video played, the stark differences became obvious. Although there were Nazi officers milling about, these men did not look happy and relaxed as they did in the other video. In fact, the whole scene had a different look to it. The faces of the officers looked serious and stressed in front of the grey sky and barren trees behind them.

Shannon squinted, trying to understand the significance of the video. "What is this?"

"Look there," Peter said, pointing at the screen.

Shannon saw someone in the background that she didn't notice at first. It was a woman leaning against the brick parapet bordering the balcony. It wasn't obvious at first, but as she studied the woman's face, she realized it was Eva Braun.

But this was not the animated woman from the previous video. This version of Eva Braun sat in the background, looking at the ground—almost brooding. "She doesn't look very happy," Shannon commented.

"We learned that this video was taken in 1944," Peter said, "after The Nazis started meeting fierce resistance from the allies. They gathered at the retreat, not to party like they were in the first video, but to have a meeting about their dire situation."

"This is when she was living at the retreat?" Shannon asked.

"That's right," Peter answered.

"So she was pregnant here?" Shannon asked, studying the screen.

Neil leaned forward and said, "She was."

"She looks very different, but she doesn't look pregnant," Shannon said, her eyes still fixed on the screen.

"Wait just a minute," Peter said, aiming the remote at the television. Shannon watched intensely, and then she saw Eva Braun step forward and turn to her right. Peter emphatically pressed a button on the remote. "Here!"

The image was frozen on the screen. Shannon examined the profile of Hitler's mistress. And then she saw it. The swelling in her stomach was subtle, but it was definitely there.

"My God," Shannon muttered, "I see it."

"She's only showing slightly," Neil said. "If her pregnancy was more obvious, then Hitler probably wouldn't have let her around his men. But if you look at her, especially after watching her in the last video, you can clearly see the shape in her belly. She was pregnant here."

"That's amazing," Shannon said, finally turning away from the television. "You said that her sister took the baby to some small town. What happened after the baby grew up? Did she ever find out who her parents were?"

There was a pause as Neil and Peter shared an uncomfortable look. "We should probably leave that for another time," Peter said.

"Why?" Shannon shot back.

"Well," Peter began, "it's two in the morning, and Neil and I have to catch an eight AM flight."

"What are you talking about?" Shannon asked, surprised. "You have a private jet."

"Unfortunately, tomorrow we have to fly commercial," Peter replied.

"Why?"

"I'm undercover in Idaho. They know I'm coming back tomorrow, and they're picking me up at the airport. They may get a little suspicious if they see me land in a Gulfstream."

"I see," Shannon said. "But won't they be suspicious of Neil?"

"I don't think so. I'm going to say he's an old friend, and try to get him in."

Neil said, "Another thing we have to do is get someone to stay here with you."

"Yes, Shannon," Peter interjected, "you don't have to worry. I'm going to have someone I trust here watching you. He'll be armed, just in case."

"I appreciate that," Shannon said. "But I've decided I want to go with you."

"What?" Neil said.

"I don't think that's a good idea," Peter added.

"Listen," Shannon replied, forcefully, "I know I said that I didn't want to be a part of this. But now that I've seen everything, I've changed my mind. Let me come along. I'm sure I can provide some help somewhere along the way."

Neil nervously finished his Scotch as he locked eyes with Peter. Peter leaned forward, shaking his head and said, "There's a good deal of risk with this mission. I'm not comfortable with you getting involved."

"I'm already involved. There was a lot of risk in Ecuador too, but I made it." Shannon turned to Neil. "Tell him, Neil. Tell him what we went through in Ecuador."

"That was different," Neil responded. "There were a lot of unexpected things that happened when we were in Ecuador. But this will be a different kind of danger. We're going undercover into the heart of the enemy camp. It's incredibly dangerous."

"Okay, guys," Shannon exhaled, and stood in frustration. "If you want to go without me, I understand. But I'm not sitting holed up in this apartment. If I'm not going to Idaho, then have Rick fly me back to Hartford."

Shannon stood awkwardly—the buzz from the Scotch making her a little unsteady on her feet—as she glared down at the two men. They looked at the floor, and then looked up, their glassy eyes dancing. Neil released a heavy sigh and said, "All right then, let's pull out this couch and get some sleep."

"Does that mean I'm going to Idaho?"

"Well," Peter said, "we're not letting you go back to Hartford, so I guess we have no choice."

"You won't regret it. I promise. You can tell them I'm Neil's girlfriend."

Neil pulled the couch out into a bed as Peter moved the coffee table across the room. "I suppose I'll do that," Peter said as he retrieved some linen from a nearby closet. He handed them to Neil as he said, "This means there's one more thing we have to do before we crash for the night."

"What's that?" Shannon asked as Neil made the bed.

"I'm going to have to go out and find some hair dye."

"Hair dye?" Shannon repeated, confused. She looked at both of them, noticing their troubled expressions. "Oh," Shannon said, thinking she understood. "You mean to disguise Neil because The Power knows what he looks like."

"Not exactly," Peter replied.

She tried to understand his meaning, but her foggy, alcohol-filled brain wasn't cooperating. "Then why do we need it?"

"We need it for you."

CHAPTER THIRTY-ONE

Her hair was finally dry and although she knew Neil was waiting anxiously for her, she couldn't stop looking in the mirror. Her jet-black hair looked bizarre after spending her first twenty-nine years as a blonde—and nothing but a blonde.

Would I have done this if I were sober? she wondered as she took another slug of Scotch.

She ran her fingers through her new hair one last time, and decided that it was time to leave the bathroom. Not only was Neil waiting for her, but he was waiting with scissors. *Let's get this over with.*

When she walked out of the bathroom, she saw a sheet spread out on the floor with a chair in the center of it. "It's about time," Neil said, the scissors in his right hand. "Sit down. We have to be on a plane in five hours."

Shannon reluctantly sat. "Have you ever done this before?"

"Of course not. Do I look like a hairdresser?"

"Maybe I can find a place in the morning that can cut it."

"There's no way we'll have time for that," Neil said as he moved behind her. "Listen, we don't have to do this. You can stay here until I get back."

"All right," she said with a disgusted sigh, "just cut it." She drained the rest of her drink, placed the glass on the floor, and tried to get comfortable in the chair. "But don't hack me. Try to keep it somewhat straight."

"Don't worry." Neil started to cut.

"Where's Peter?"

"He went to bed."

"So why does he think The Power knows what I look like? Didn't you tell him I'm just your grandfather's neighbor?"

"I told him about the e-mail you got from Altman42089. Since they're interested in you, he thinks someone may have seen you while they were spying on my grandfather."

"It seems a bit extreme to do this just based on that."

"Hey, if he's right, then you could blow our whole operation. Better to be safe."

Shannon looked down and saw clumps of black hair littering the sheet. She closed her eyes and tried to forget that a drunken man, who had never cut hair before, was behind her snipping away like Edward Scissorhands. "What about you? Don't they know what you look like from court or something?"

"Because I'm in the Intelligence Division of our firm, I've been kept out of sight—especially with anything having to with The Power. I've been preparing to go undercover for a long time. And unfortunately, circumstances are forcing me to do it now."

The scissors stopped clicking and Shannon opened her eyes. She saw Neil standing in front of her, sizing her up like a piece of art. "Are you done?" she asked.

"Just a couple more snips." Neil snapped the scissors a few more times on either side of her head.

"How do I look?"

"Gorgeous."

"I think you've had too much to drink."

"That may true," Neil said as he stepped away and placed the scissors on a table, "but you really do look great."

"You know what?" Shannon said, popping up and brushing hair off her legs, "I can't even bear to look now." She fell into the pullout bed and rolled to the right side of it. "I'm going to sleep."

"Good idea." Neil folded up the hair-covered sheet and put it in the corner with the chair. He spread out a blanket on the floor and threw a pillow on top of it. "Peter will be waking us up in a couple of hours." Neil lay down, groaning as his exhausted body hit the ground. "Would you kill that light?" Neil said, pointing at a lamp on the end table next to Shannon.

"What?" Shannon replied as she looked up from her pillow.

"The lamp. Turn off the lamp," Neil said from the floor.

She saw him curled up on the floor—a pitiful looking lump under an old ratty blanket. A wave of guilt overtook her as she looked over the unused space of her bed. "What are you doing?"

"I'm going to sleep."

"Down there?"

"Yeah."

"This bed is huge. You can sleep up here with me."

"Are you sure? I don't want to make you feel uncomfortable. We just met yesterday morning."

"After what we've been through together, I feel like I've known you for years."

"Okay. Thanks," Neil said as he sprang up to the bed, taking the blanket and pillow with him. He lay down and adjusted the blanket and pillow until he positioned himself on the far left side of the bed.

She shut off the light and they said good night. Her sleep the previous night had occurred after the shock of the plane crash, and she realized she hadn't closed her eyes to rest since everything had begun.

Her brain automatically began to take inventory of the spectacular events from the last two days. She remembered the frightful news that a Neo-Nazi group was watching her, and the sadness she felt for the death of kind, old Mr. Henry. She relived the terrifying plane crash, and kidnapping in the jungle. She pictured the horrifying massacre in the village, and the bloody message scrolled on the cave wall.

As she lay in the darkness, she felt completely awake. She realized she had pushed her body beyond its limit, and was aware of her exhausted muscles and sore ribs. Yet her mind spun wildly with images she could not control. Although her two bizarre days with Neil were in her thoughts, there was something else keeping her awake.

She couldn't stop thinking about Eva Braun: her deep eyes, her vibrant smile. She thought about her giving birth in a deserted mountain resort and then leaving her newborn to face a certain death. Shannon imagined the desperation of the woman—the turmoil inside while making that decision.

Then, unexpectedly, a wave of emotion overtook her. Her upper body jutted forward as if she had been kicked. She gasped like she was choking and one loud sob burst out of her mouth. She fought to regain control and held back a storm of tears.

Neil popped up and was beside her in an instant. His arm wrapped around her back as he asked, "What's wrong?"

Embarrassed by her outburst, she said, "Nothing. It's nothing...I don't know what happened to me."

Neil began to gently rub her back and the wonderful feeling paralyzed her with pleasure. "It's okay," he said softly, "It's been an incredibly tough two days."

"It's just that my mind is racing—"

"Of course it is. Don't fight it. You have to process everything we went through."

As his hands continued to massage her back, her head fell onto his shoulder. At first, she wanted to pull back—afraid of where it might lead. But his gentle hands and the warmth of his chest squelched her anxiety.

Before she knew it, they were laying down. Now, both his arms were around her as her face nestled against his chest. *What the hell am I doing?* she thought. But she couldn't move. His hands ran up and down her back like a bow on a violin.

He whispered in her ear, "Let all those horrible images go through your mind. It's better to think about them now than fight them and let them fester. You have to deal with everything you saw, as bad as that might be. But you're strong. You can get over all of that. We did the best we could to help those people. And we'll rescue this boy and get him back to his home."

She found his words as soothing as his hands. Her body transformed from a tight knot of nervousness to a relaxed mass, melting into his chest. She raised her chin and focused on his eyes through the darkness.

"Thank you," she whispered. "You've made me feel so much better."

Their eyes met, and she could no longer fight the earlier attraction she felt for him. Without thinking, her lips fell into his.

CHAPTER THIRTY-TWO

The Supreme Leader heard the labored breaths of Randolph as he reached the bottom of the stairs. He saw his assistant grasping the door to the Great Room, poised to open it.

"Randolph, when Dr. Kuhn arrives, please let her in."

"Yes, Your Excellency." Randolph opened the door, and the Supreme Leader slowly walked into the room. His eyes immediately fixed on the two people seated at the large mahogany table. The Bald Man sat with his arms crossed—confident and comfortable with his purpose in the room. But as the Supreme Leader moved closer, he noticed that the boy looked terrified.

He sat at the edge of his seat and his eyes darted in all directions. He glared at the Supreme Leader as if he were there to kill him. But the Leader understood why the boy was afraid.

After all, he thought, *the boy doesn't know where he is, or who I am. In fact, he doesn't even know who he really is.*

He reached the table and cast a kindly face upon the boy. "Welcome, young man. I'm very happy you're here."

The boy fearfully inched away and almost fell off the side of the chair. He started to stand, but froze when he saw the sneering face of the Bald Man. He cowered away from him as he sank back into his chair.

The Supreme Leader suddenly realized that the Bald Man was there alone. "Where are your two colleagues?"

"They met a tragic end, Your Excellency. The tribesmen, who guarded the boy, fought fiercely. Unfortunately, they were struck down by arrows and spears from the savages. I was lucky to escape with the boy."

The Supreme Leader looked over the Bald Man carefully as he gave his explanation. He had no reason to not believe the story, so he nodded his head in acceptance.

"We will honor their bravery when we hold the grand celebration." He looked at the boy with an eerie smile. His eyes darted back to the Bald Man as he said, "Your work here will not go unrecognized. I will acknowledge your accomplishment at the ceremony. You will be promoted to an important position within The Power. And you will lead many of our men through the first phase of our attack."

The Bald Man sat up with pride. "Thank you, Your Excellency. I will be proud to serve The Power."

The Supreme Leader looked at the boy and then back at the Bald Man. "Have you and the boy discussed his true identity?"

"No sir," the Bald Man replied. "I thought it would be best to wait, since he doesn't seem to know."

The Supreme Leader released a slow sigh as he sat on the edge of the table. "That is true. Such a great injustice that a fine young man would be lied to his whole life." He looked deeply into the boy's eyes. "But now, we have the difficult challenge of educating you on who you really are."

"What do you mean?" the boy blurted out. "I know who I am."

"I'm sorry to tell you, young man, but you only think you know who you are."

The boy jumped to his feet. "He's a bad man," he yelled, pointing at the Bald Man. "He killed Victoria, and I saw him push the other man out of the helicopter. I want to go home."

"Relax, young man. Sit back down," the Supreme Leader said in a soothing voice. "You'll soon realize that this has been your home all along."

The boy reluctantly sat down at the edge of the chair as if it were coated with sharp glass. His teary eyes locked on the Bald Man. "I don't want to be near him anymore."

"Don't worry," the Supreme Leader said with a smile. "I have important work that's going to keep him busy. And I have someone special to spend time with you."

"What do you mean?" the boy asked, his lower lip quivering.

Before the Leader could respond, the door behind him rattled. A moment later, they heard the unmistakable sounds of Randolph's strained breathing. The Supreme Leader watched the curious eyes of the boy as he examined the skinny wraith-like man struggle to hold open the heavy door. But then, the boy's eyes suddenly widened with surprise as the Leader heard a new noise in the room.

The clicking of her heels drowned out even the horrific sounds coming from Randolph. When she stopped walking, the Leader could see the end of her long shadow just reaching the table. Still focused on the boy's eyes, he watched them change from surprise to a curious delight.

The Supreme Leader turned and was pleased to see the six-foot woman standing there—her short blond hair and green eyes barely noticeable over her long lascivious legs.

"Gentlemen," the Supreme Leader said as he noticed the rapt faces of the boy and the Bald Man, "allow me to introduce Doctor Kuhn."

CHAPTER THIRTY-THREE

As the jet engine rumbled, Shannon felt like there was a bass drum wedged inside her skull that kept time with a speed-metal tune. She leaned her head back, closed her eyes, and moaned in agony. She massaged her temples, but a wave of nausea interrupted her.

When she opened her eyes, she saw Neil next to her, propping his head against the seat in front of him. He turned toward her and looked like an exhumed corpse—deathly pale with bags under his eyes that were as black as scorched wood.

He grunted in her direction, and for a moment, his misery made her feel better by comparison. But then she remembered what they did last night: the kissing, the touching, the sex.

What the hell was I thinking? A sharp pain ricocheted across the top of her head, reminding her that she did more drinking than thinking. As she reached to rub her forehead, her hand grazed the stubble that was now her hair.

Shit! she thought, but then tried to put it out of her mind. She still hadn't looked in a mirror, but knew it could not be a pretty sight. *Could I possibly look any worse right now?*

Before she had a chance to answer herself, Peter sat down in the aisle seat next to Neil. "Here, I just picked this up in the airport." Peter said as he handed her a black baseball cap with a NASCAR emblem.

"Does my hair look so bad that wearing this thing would be an improvement?"

"Your hair looks fine," he replied as he passed her a pair of black sunglasses. "I just don't want anyone recognizing you."

"What are the chances of that?"

"You're a good looking woman, Shannon. You have the kind of face a guy might remember."

The plane accelerated down the tarmac, shaking their seats. "Flattery will get you everywhere." She put on the hat and sunglasses as the plane left the ground. "How do I look?"

"Stunning," Peter replied as a flight attendant asked him to buckle his seatbelt.

"And what do you think?" she asked, aiming a goofy smile at Neil.

Neil gagged and thrust his upper body forward. "Are there barf bags in here?" He rifled through the compartment on the back of the seat in front of him, tossing a couple of magazines to the floor.

"That's real nice," she said and punched him lightly in the arm.

He pulled out the paper bag, opened it, and held it in front of his mouth. He gagged again but did not vomit. He took a few slow breaths and looked at Shannon. "You know this isn't because of you."

Peter patted him on the shoulder and said, "Pretty hung over, huh?"

"Hung over?" Neil shot back. "I'm still drunk."

"What the hell did you two do after I went to bed?" Peter asked innocently.

Shannon and Neil shot him an uncomfortable look, causing him to sink in his seat and look away. "We stayed up for a bit and finished that bottle of Scotch," Neil said as he stuffed the paper bag back in the seat compartment.

"Well," Peter began, "we're airborne for the next few hours so why don't you two get some rest. I'll wake you up when we get close."

"Thanks, buddy," Neil said as he settled back into his seat and closed his eyes.

Shannon did the same, and felt the pain subside a little. She thought she might actually get some sleep. But then her mind began to race. If sex with Neil was the only thing pressing her mind, she could have slept easily. But thoughts of Eva Braun and her child kept creeping into her brain.

She thought about the details of the situation. If Eva Braun gave birth to her daughter in 1945, then the daughter would be sixty-two today. And the boy, who is the son of Eva Braun's daughter, is thirteen. Something didn't seem right with this equation. Shannon did the math in her head.

That means that Eva Braun's daughter would have given birth to the boy when she was forty-nine years old.

She sprang forward and blurted out, "Something is wrong." She was surprised to see both Neil and Peter sleeping. Neil grumbled a bit when she spoke, but Peter opened his eyes and looked at her.

"Are you okay, Shannon?" Peter asked.

"Something is wrong," she repeated.

"Relax," Peter replied in a gentle voice. "Everything is okay. We're going to land in about twenty minutes."

"What?"

"There's nothing wrong with the plane. Everything is fine. The captain just announced that we'll be landing in Idaho in about twenty minutes."

"How can that be?" Shannon asked. Neil was awake now and looking at her with red eyes, trying to understand the conversation. "We just took off a minute ago."

Peter chuckled and said, "Shannon, you've been asleep for hours. The flight is almost over."

"Oh," she said, surprised. She then took inventory of her thoughts—now unsure of her math calculation. But after a moment, she realized she was correct—asleep or not. "I thought of something."

"What is it?" Peter asked.

"If Eva Braun gave birth to her daughter in 1945, then the daughter would now be sixty-two. And if the boy is thirteen, then Eva Braun's daughter would have been forty-nine when she gave birth to him."

Peter and Neil looked at each other and nodded their heads in agreement. "I suppose that's correct," Peter said.

"Don't you see anything wrong with that?"

Again, Peter and Neil looked at each other. Neil asked, "What do you mean?"

"Forty-nine is a bit old to be having a baby."

"Oh," Peter said, now understanding her point. "I never thought of that before."

"But you're absolutely right," Neil added. "I don't think any of us ever bothered to figure out her age."

"Let me ask you something," Shannon said, now leaning against the seat in front of her. "Hitler's testament is very specific that this revolution cannot begin until his first male heir reaches the age of thirteen, correct?"

"That's right," Peter answered.

"So that means that if he never had a male heir, then there would never be a revolution?"

"I believe that's true," Neil began. "Our investigative work tells us that the true members of The Power all have one thing in common. And that is a devout belief in the work of Hitler. They think of him as a God, and would do absolutely anything he told them to do. And now, the only way Hitler is able to instruct them is through his final testament. I believe that true Power members would follow the testament to the word. And if that meant no revolution without a male heir, then there would be no revolution."

"Okay," Shannon said as she licked her dry lips and felt her headache creeping back. "This could be an act of desperation."

"What do you mean?" Peter asked.

"What if the leaders of The Power realized that Hitler's daughter was getting too old to have a baby and did something desperate?"

"Like what?" Neil asked.

"I can imagine two different scenarios. The first is that The Power forced her to have a baby, maybe with the help of a fertility doctor."

"That's possible," Peter said.

"The second is that they fabricated the idea. They may have found a boy—somehow, somewhere—and declared that he's the grandson of Hitler."

"That's certainly possible," Neil said. "We never had a great deal of information about the boy. When we learned of his existence, one of our undercover agents picked him up in a little town in southern Germany called Ruhpolding. At the time he was living with Eva Braun's daughter. We've had no reason to believe that he wasn't the real deal, but you make a good point about the daughter's age."

"This is all fascinating," Peter interjected, "but there's one thing we're forgetting. It doesn't matter if the boy is the real deal or not. If The Power thinks he's Hitler's grandson, then they'll start their revolution. And that's the only thing that should concern us now."

"True," Neil said. "But what if we were able to prove that this boy is not Hitler's grandchild? It could derail their plans tremendously. Do you know of anyone within The Power that could let all the soldiers know of the truth about the boy, if we're able to prove it?"

"I don't know anyone that important yet. I'm considered a very low-ranking member, just barely in, actually." Peter turned toward Shannon as he continued. "The amount of information you get and the people you're allowed to meet are based on your ranking within the organization. My main sponsor is a mid-level member, but nowhere near powerful enough to impact the leadership. He still hasn't seen the Supreme Leader, although we've both heard a lot about him."

"The Supreme Leader?" Shannon said, frowning with confusion.

Neil explained. "There's one central leader of The Power. His title is the Supreme Leader. They keep his identity top secret. Only high-ranking people in The Power have seen him. We know that he calls all the shots—like a dictator. It shouldn't surprise you that Hitler believed an organization ran more efficiently with an autocratic leader. And he stated that he wanted The Power to be run that way."

"So if we can prove the boy is not the real heir, then we would need to find someone to communicate this to the Supreme Leader?" Shannon said.

"Yes," Peter replied. "Unless, of course, it was the Supreme Leader who fabricated the identity of the boy."

"Good point," Shannon said. "Then what do we do?"

"I think we may be getting ahead of ourselves," Peter said. "But this is something we should definitely work on. We need to think of a way to prove or disprove that the boy is the son of Hitler's daughter."

They all looked at each other blankly for a moment. Neil said, "I suppose we would have to do some type of DNA test."

"Yes. We need to get DNA from the boy and also from Hitler's daughter in Germany," Peter said.

"How are we going to get DNA from the boy?" Shannon asked.

"Well," Neil began, "our mission is to try and find him. If we succeed, then we can get a DNA sample."

The plane began a sharp descent as the seatbelt sign lit up. They all glanced out the window and saw the airport below. "Looks like we're here,"

Shannon said.

Peter sighed and said, “This should be interesting.”

CHAPTER THIRTY-FOUR

Shannon felt better as they walked down the tunnel—the ugliest part of her hangover now behind her. She struggled to keep up with the long strides of Neil and Peter, and needed to continually push the clumsy sunglasses back up the bridge of her nose.

When they entered the terminal, Neil and Peter stopped and turned toward her. Peter said, "We're meeting a man named Ron Hale. He's my main contact in The Power, and the one that got me in. I'm not sure how much he knows about the inner workings because he's selective with what he shares. But he seems to be trusting me more and more."

"Okay," Shannon said as she glanced around the busy airport.

"I'm going to tell him that you two are married."

"Where are we supposed to be from?" Shannon asked.

"I haven't told him anything yet. Where do you want to be from?"

Shannon and Neil looked at each other, unsure of how to respond. Shannon said, "I guess we should say we're from somewhere in New England since we're both really from there."

"That's not a good idea," Peter replied. "There are not many members from the Northeast. That would make you stand out, and we don't want that."

"The south would be the most likely location," Neil said.

"I'll tell people you're from Georgia," Peter said. Neil nodded in agreement and they resumed their walk across the terminal.

"But wait," Shannon said. Neil and Peter slowed down and looked back at her. "We don't sound like we're from Georgia. We should have accents."

"You're right," Peter replied as they stopped completely, and looked around the terminal. "Well, I don't see him yet, so you have a few minutes to come up with something."

"Great," Shannon said, feigning a smile.

"Just act cool and natural, and don't talk unless you have to," Peter said.

"You won't have to worry about that," she said, pushing the glasses back up her nose. "So do you know if the boy has arrived here?"

"I don't know for sure but it seems like it."

"What do you mean?" Neil said.

"Well, I was getting deeper and deeper into the group. It seemed like they trusted me more every day. But it's been different the last couple of days. Everyone is suddenly real uptight, like they have to be careful what they say. Something is definitely going on."

"Have you heard anyone mention the boy?" Neil asked.

"No one has come right out and told me about him, but I think somebody slipped up yesterday."

"What happened?" Neil asked.

"Before I left to meet you two in Chicago, I was hanging out with a few guys on the grounds of the compound when we saw this woman. She must have been six feet tall and had incredible legs that seemed like they stretched to her chin. She was pretty far away, but you couldn't miss her.

"So we were checking her out, and this other guy comes over. He's a more senior member and he joked with us about staring at her. Then he said that she was a psychologist and the Supreme Leader brought her here to work with the boy. As soon as he said it, he looked at me and kind of cringed—like he screwed up. Then he walked away, and no one said a word about it."

"A tall, leggy psychologist?" Shannon said with a raised eyebrow as she looked at Neil and Peter.

"It doesn't surprise me," Neil began. "They need to convert the boy to their way of thinking. This woman is obviously going to try and brainwash him."

"But why do they need to brainwash him?" Shannon asked. "I thought they just needed him to start the revolution. Does it matter what he thinks?"

Peter quickly glanced over each shoulder and said, "Unfortunately for the boy, it does matter. Hitler's final testament not only says that the boy has to be thirteen for the revolution to start, but he will then lead the new Nazi party."

"What?" Shannon said as her eyes widened. "But he won't know how to lead this Neo-Nazi group."

"We have a theory about what they plan to do," Neil said. "We think the high ranking members of The Power will try and brainwash the boy but still keep him in their control. They'll need him to make some appearances before the members, and probably make some speeches. But I doubt they would let a boy make any important decisions."

"I don't understand," Shannon said, confused. "Why do they have to bother with all of this? Why can't they just tell everyone that they have the boy and start the revolution?"

"They would probably like to do that, but they can't," Peter explained. "You see, all the members of The Power know the testament. It's their bible, and they're completely devoted to it."

"That's right," Neil interjected. "To get in The Power you have to be insane about Hitler's testament. If you're not, then you have no chance of getting in. They think Hitler is speaking to them from the grave through this piece of paper. And he was very specific. He wanted to take over and rule the world, and although he wasn't able to do it, he held on to a fantasy that his grandson, or whatever male descendant would do it."

"So," Peter continued, "if they want all the members to wholeheartedly embrace and participate in the uprising, they need the boy to at least appear to be leading them. If the members of The Power don't passionately believe in the cause, then the revolution won't work."

"You have to remember," Neil added, "many of these people will be giving up their lives for this cause. They have to believe. And seeing and listening to Hitler's progeny is the only way they will."

A short, stocky, man wearing blue jeans and a white tee-shirt suddenly appeared. "Hey there," he said loudly and shared a hug with Peter—his mullet bouncing off his shoulders as they embraced. He then politely shook hands with Neil as he said, "It's good to meet you, man." He turned toward Shannon and looked surprised to see her.

"Ron, this is my friend Alan that I told you about. I may have forgotten to mention that he was bringing his wife. This is Betty."

"Hi," Ron said, looking at her curiously.

"Nice to meet you," she heard herself say in an obviously fake southern accent. She cleared her throat and silently vowed that she would sound more natural for her next utterance.

"So, Ron," Peter began, "Alan and his wife are real anxious to join the group. I was hoping to introduce them to some people tonight."

"Tonight's a bad night. I have guard duty."

"Guard duty?" Peter asked, confused.

"Normally, I don't have to do it. But the compound has been put on code red. I'd rather hang out with you three, but I have to do my job. And it's probably not a good idea for them to be meeting anyone tonight. Security is at its highest right now."

"What about me?" Peter asked. "I'd like to help out with guard duty if I can."

"I don't know. Maybe. I'll have to check if they would let you do that."

"We're all committed to the cause," Peter said as he gestured to Neil and Shannon. "We all want to be made full members some day. You can trust me."

"I know I can. And I'm sure your friends are fine too, but like I said, right now is a bad time. I might be able to get you some guard duty because you've been around, but I can't bring your friends in now. Maybe in few months if things calm down."

A few months! Shannon knew this was bad news as she traded quick glances with Neil and Peter.

"That's a shame," Peter said. "My friends are good people, and would be great members."

"I'm sure they are. Don't get me wrong, this is nothing personal. It's just that there's something going on right now. I can't get into the details, but security is real tight."

"We understand," Neil said in a fairly good southern accent. "But if there's anything we can do to prove ourselves, we'd be anxious to do it. We came a long way, and really believe in your cause."

"I appreciate that," Ron said. "I'll ask around and see if there's any way."

They followed Ron out the exit to his pickup truck. Peter sat in the cab with Ron as Neil and Shannon climbed in the back bed. The vast open land captivated Shannon's attention during the ride, and she and Neil did not share a word. The ten minute drive seemed like only a minute.

Ron stopped his truck at the foot of a driveway that led to a trailer park. Peter got out and leaned over the bed, holding a set of keys in his hand. He whispered, "This is where I'm staying. My truck is about fifty yards up on the right. It's a brown Chevy; you'll see it." He slapped the keys into Neil's hand and checked that Ron was not paying attention.

He continued in a quiet voice: "The Aryan Nation Compound is about three miles up this road." He pointed to a road behind them. "Take my truck up there. You can't miss the compound. Drive past it, and then park my truck in the woods so you're out of sight. Wait there until I call you."

Peter dropped a cell phone in Neil's lap. "Make sure you wait in a spot where you're getting a good signal. I'm hoping I get guard duty with Ron. That will give me a chance to figure out where they're keeping the boy. I'll let you know, and hopefully, we can figure out a plan."

Neil and Shannon hopped out of the truck and watched it pull away. Neil put the keys and the phone into his pocket and looked at Shannon. "Ready, Betty?"

"Ready as I'll ever be, Al."

Shannon's stomach was in a nervous knot as they walked up the road, the loose gravel under their shoes making the only sound within earshot.

CHAPTER THIRTY-FIVE

he boy sat upright in the wooden chair—his spine stiff as a pole. He touched his face with his spongy palms to make sure he wasn't dreaming. The house amazed him. The mahogany furniture. The deep cushy carpet. All the wall hangings precisely placed.

And then there was the painting. It was surrounded by a thick gold frame that looked like it was hand carved with painstaking accuracy. It was twice his height, he presumed. And it hung on the wall like a crucifix in a catholic church—the centerpiece of everything.

The man in the painting looked familiar, but the boy couldn't remember his name. He was a man from history, he knew. The small moustache. The stern face. He was a bad man. Evil. But here, he looked like he belonged—like he was worshipped.

He heard her in the other room, and knew she would be back soon. Again, he touched his face, trying to fight off the swirling confusion that invaded his brain. He desperately searched for something normal—something familiar. In his mind, he took inventory of the things he knew. And the things he could remember.

He knew his name was John Keller, and that he grew up in the small town of Houton, located in northern Maine. His parents explained that they had adopted him from Russia when he was six years old. He remembered bits and pieces of his early childhood. He remembered the tiny house and farm. And he remembered the women who cared for him—one young and one old. He could see their faces if he tried hard enough.

He grew up peacefully and happily in Maine with his parents. Everything was normal until his parents' friends, Curt and Victoria, said they wanted to take him away on a trip. Then, he was in South America with the tribe, and now, here in this place, looking at the giant portrait of the evil man.

He heard her shoes clicking against the linoleum surface in the kitchen. He knew this meant she was coming back. His heart began to race as he anticipated her return. He believed she was somehow associated with the bad man in the picture, yet he yearned to see her again.

She strutted into the room and stopped in front of him; her statuesque legs stole his attention. His groin tingled with excitement as he tried to look away—tried to focus back on the things he knew and remembered.

But her stunning green eyes overpowered him as she leaned close. Her short blonde hair stuck up like a porcupine's quills, and glistened like diamonds. "Why are you sitting in this uncomfortable chair?" Her lips moved in slow motion—to seduce him, he thought.

"Sit over here." She motioned to the plush couch and love seat under the giant portrait. "You should be comfortable. After all, this is your home."

My home? he thought as she stood upright. The high seam of her skirt clung to her smooth legs just inches from his face. He bit his lower lip as his heart tried to pound out of his chest. He robotically followed her command and sat on the couch.

She sat next to him, her thigh brushing against his. "See," she spoke in a deep, sexy voice, "isn't this better?" Her sweet breath dripped down his face. His whole body tingled now as he tried to think of something to say. But he could only stare, her strong green eyes pulling him closer.

"Okay, John, we must begin."

Begin? Begin what? He swallowed hard as his lips quivered in fear.

"I know you must be confused." She patted his leg, her long red fingernails tickling him. "I'm going to help you understand what's been happening to you."

He wanted to ask what she meant, but he only looked at her, his bewildered countenance asking the question.

"The people in your life haven't been truthful to you. But I will be. I will show you all the things they've been hiding from you."

His mouth fell open and he finally spoke. "What?"

"I'll begin with some very basic facts. Like who you really are."

"I'm John Keller."

She smiled before she responded. "That's just your name, John. But you don't know who you really are."

"But..." he stammered, "I know who I am."

"I'm sorry to tell you this, John. But you don't know. People have lied to you ever since you were kidnapped in Germany and brought to the United States."

Kidnapped! "I wasn't kidnapped. My parents adopted me from Russia."

She shook her head with a sympathetic smile. "I'm so sorry to tell you that's not true."

He stared at her in shock. She patted his leg again. "I know this is overwhelming, but you need to know the truth now. I'm going to tell you everything. But first, I want to tell you about your grandparents."

"My grandparents?" he asked in a shaky voice.

"They were famous people, and you may have heard of them."

"Who are they?"

She stood up and walked to a cabinet. She opened the door, revealing a large television. She turned it on and inserted a tape into the VCR. She picked up a remote control and returned to the couch.

"You may have been taught that they were bad people, but that's also a lie. I will tell you the truth about them." She paused, looking closely at his frightened face. "Are you ready?"

He nodded his head, and she pressed a button on the remote. He swallowed hard as his eyes fixed on the television.

CHAPTER THIRTY-SIX

Neil jangled the keys in his hand as they examined the dilapidated truck. "What a piece of shit," Shannon muttered.

"It was smart of him to get something like this," Neil said. He kicked the rusted door to make sure it wouldn't fall off. "He's got to fit in with everyone else. It's not like we're in Beverly Hills."

"Yeah, but, do you trust this thing?"

"Of course not. But it's better than walking." Neil sat behind the wheel, and Shannon climbed into the passenger seat. He turned the ignition and the engine roared like a blast of thunder. As it began to idle, they could hear the unmistakable sound of metal clanking against metal. The deafening noise filled their ears like a round of machine gun fire. Neil winced as he forced the stick shift into first gear. The truck lurched forward and stalled, throwing Shannon into the dashboard.

"You okay?"

"Fine," she answered as she sat back in the seat.

"That truck in Ecuador was easier to drive than this thing," Neil commented.

"Who would think a band of thugs in a third-world country would have a nicer ride than a lawyer from your firm?"

"I don't think he would drive this around Boston, but it's the right choice for this area. Peter's our best undercover operative; he knows what he's doing in situations like this. We have to make sure we don't blow his cover."

"I'll do my best, but remember that I'm no pro at this sort of thing."

Neil stopped fighting with the stick shift and he gave her a long look. "Listen, Shannon, maybe we should talk."

"You mean about last night?"

"I didn't plan on that happening. I swear. I know you were a little drunk, and I don't want you to think that I took advantage of you."

"We both were. And I didn't mean for it to happen either, but it did. I don't think you took advantage of me."

"I'm glad. So we can move on, and put that behind us."

"Let's go," she said and gestured for him to drive the truck.

Neil nodded with a satisfied smile. "Here we go." He returned to struggling with the stick shift until he finally got the vehicle to creep forward. He guided the tank down the narrow road, leaving a trail of displaced gravel in their wake.

They drove up the road that Peter had pointed out. Shannon enjoyed the sights of the green rolling hills, tall trees, and farmland. "This is such beautiful country," she said as her eyes looked longingly at the peaceful countryside around them. "I can't believe that such an evil place is in the middle of this paradise."

"Well, believe it," Neil said as he pointed ahead. Shannon followed his finger and saw the row of flagpoles along the side of the road. At first, she couldn't make out the flags, but as they drove closer they became clear.

The first one was a Nazi flag, exactly the kind she found in Mr. Henry's house. The second was a Confederate flag, and the third was a US flag flying upside down. As the lumbering truck carried them noisily down the road, she saw that the same pattern of three flags continued for the remainder of the stretch.

They approached what appeared to be the entrance: a simple dirt road bordered by two flagpoles that were twice the size of the others. Shannon looked up and saw one flying a Confederate flag and the other a Nazi flag.

"Is this the main entrance?" Shannon asked.

"I would assume so."

"I can't believe its wide open. I thought this place would be sealed up tighter than Fort Knox. There's not even a gate."

"I don't think they need much protection," Neil yelled over the deafening engine. "From what I've heard, people are either terrified of this place or are supporters. Who would they need to protect themselves from?"

"But what's up with the guard duty that Peter has to do?"

"That's because the boy is here now. Those guards are protecting the compound from me and you."

"I see." As they made their way past the entrance, Shannon caught a glimpse of the sprawling green hills that were hidden behind the deep layers of trees.

"I heard about an incident here a couple of years ago," Neil began. "There was a Native-American couple driving down this road. Apparently, something fell out of their truck, and they stopped to look for it. They were wandering around the front of the entrance when a bunch of Aryans charged out at them."

"What? Why?"

"I guess they saw them and thought they were a threat. So they chased them for a while, caught them, and gave them a real bad beating."

"That's horrible."

"I know. But you can understand why people around here would rather avoid this place."

"I want to avoid this place too."

"I know, but we have a purpose. A mission."

"Right. To rescue the boy and save civilization."

"I guess you could put it that way." The flagpoles ended and they found themselves driving in a wooded area. "I'm going to pull over here."

Neil guided the truck off the road and parked it out of sight. When he shut off the ignition, the engine sputtered loudly and backfired. It died with a thud of heavy metal like it would never start again.

Shannon was happy to get out of the rusted monstrosity and enjoyed the feel of the country air. Neil joined her as he made sure the cell phone was still working. "I'm getting a good signal here. Hopefully, Peter will call soon."

"What do we do in the meantime?"

Neil glanced around the area as he said, "Let's see if we can get a better look at the compound."

They walked in silence out of the wooded area and across the street. They could barely see the main entrance, but realized that they were now walking on the compound's property. "So we're in," Shannon said with a smile as her feet gently grazed the soft grass.

"Yeah, but this place is four hundred acres, and we have no idea where they're holding the boy."

"Should we back off or keep going?"

They stopped walking as they considered the question. "I'm not sure," Neil replied as he glanced at the open land ahead of them. "I guess it would make sense to keep walking while we have the chance. What do you think?"

"Didn't Peter say to stay at the truck until he called us?" Shannon asked.

"I'm not sure. Did he say that?"

"I thought he did. I don't want to end up like that Native-American couple."

"I know, but there's obviously no one around for miles. It seems safe."

"All right then, let's go," Shannon said as her stomach tightened in a nervous knot. They walked in silence for a while, the cool crisp air keeping them alert. A half-hour and a mile of walking passed as they saw nothing but nature.

As they reached the apex of a small hill, they saw a structure in the distance. It was a one-story, circular, brick building. They noticed some other buildings behind it, but couldn't clearly make out what was there.

They ran to a patch of trees and crouched behind one. As they studied the building, the cell phone rang. Neil answered, "Hello."

"Al, it's Grey Wolfe." Neil knew it was Peter.

"What's going on?"

"A lot. Where are you?"

"We drove to the end of the road and left the truck in the woods.

We walked onto the property."

"You did what?"

"It's no big deal. There's no one around."

"How far have you walked?"

"We didn't measure."

"Can you still see where you parked the truck?"

Neil glanced back in that direction. He squinted as he said, "Not really, but there's a building in front of us."

"A building? What kind?"

"It's just one floor. Kind of round, but not a perfect circle—like the Pentagon."

"Oh my God!" Peter's voice bellowed out of the phone. "That sounds like Aryan Hall. You walked that far?"

Shannon put her ear close to the phone to hear Peter.

"I don't know. We just walked for a bit. Should we go back?"

"Listen to me. This is of the utmost importance." Peter's voice was serious, and Neil and Shannon looked at each other, concerned. "Do not go back the way you came."

"Why?"

"I'm with the guard unit right now. We're being deployed around the perimeter of the entire compound. Which means that there will be armed guards stationed close to that area any minute."

"So what should we do? Right now we're hiding in a little patch of trees."

"Aryan Hall is usually unlocked. You might be able to take cover in there for a while."

"Go into the hall?" Neil asked, surprised.

"I think that's your best bet," Peter replied. "It's a recreation hall. No one should be doing anything there now. Find a spot inside and lay low."

"Okay." Neil started to walk as Shannon followed, still holding the phone close to their ears. "So what's the plan if we're trapped in the compound tonight? Do we know where the boy is being held?"

"I'm still not sure. That information is top secret. But based on how they're arranging the guard units, I have a guess."

"Oh yeah? Where do you think he is?"

"They've placed a lot of guards around a building on grounds called the Fuhrer's House. It looks like a regular house, but inside is a shrine to Hitler. They keep all the original Nazi artifacts in there. I think they use it as a meeting place for the upper level members. It seems odd that they would guard it so heavily if the boy wasn't in there."

"How can we check it out?" Neil asked as he and Shannon neared the entrance to the building.

"There's a large bunker underneath the firing range. I know they store weapons and ammunition in there. I've heard that there are underground tunnels from there that connect to some important buildings. Now I don't know for sure, but it's something to try."

"You mean to see if there's a tunnel that connects to the Fuhrer's House?"

"Exactly."

Shannon walked ahead of Neil and could no longer hear Peter's voice. She looked at the wide doors in the front of the building, and saw an engraving in the concrete above them. It read "Aryan Hall."

Looks like this is the place she thought as they approached the doors. She could still hear Neil talking into the phone a few strides behind her, but was no longer paying attention. She saw no signs of activity inside and decided to try the door.

As Peter believed, the door was unlocked and swung open in Shannon's hand. She held it as she turned to look at Neil, hoping he would see her waiting and hurry inside. But before she could make eye contact with him, a deep growl came from within the building.

What the hell was that?

As Shannon turned to look inside, she saw them coming. The two largest Rottweilers she had ever seen were charging in her direction like a freight train.

Shit!

She let go of the door and ran. But after only a few strides, she heard the door crash and looked over her shoulder. The beasts had slammed into the door before it swung shut and were out of the building.

As she ran, she saw Neil standing near her with the phone still against his ear. "Run!" she screamed. He turned toward her as his terrified face became as white as the moon. He took a trembling step backward as the phone slipped out of his hand.

"Go!" she screamed and flew past him. After a moment she saw him next to her as they desperately fled the Aryan-trained hellhounds.

CHAPTER THIRTY-SEVEN

Shannon's legs carried her to the patch of trees faster than she thought possible. She could almost feel the heat of the beasts' breath on her heels as their ferocious snarling propelled her forward. Neil was still next to her, sprinting like an Olympic athlete. She was surprised that she could keep up with her physically fit companion, but then, he suddenly burst ahead of her.

Would he leave me to be mauled? She tried to concentrate on running. Then, he did a baseball slide in front of the first tree. He sat up on one knee and held his hands together to provide a boost.

She wanted to tell him to just climb the tree and save himself; that it was too dangerous to sit on the ground in the face of charging dogs. But she had neither the time nor the air in her lungs to deliver such a message. So she continued to run like mad, and hurdled herself into his waiting arms.

Before she realized what was happening, he cupped her foot and threw her upward like a spring board. She reached up before the branch collided with her forehead and held onto it for her life. She used all her strength to haul herself on top of the branch.

When she looked down, she saw the horrific sight of the dogs closing in on Neil. She steadied herself on the branch, reached her right arm down, and let loose an unintelligible scream. He clutched her hand as he planted his feet on the trunk of the tree.

She pulled as he took a large step up the tree. As he drew closer, she saw a wince of pain on his face. The dogs' horrendous barking drowned out his agonized moans as she saw them snapping at his ankle.

She yanked him upward, barely lifting him from the reach of the blood-thirsty creatures. He grabbed onto the same branch and as she released him, she lost her balance.

The relief of rescuing him didn't last long as she felt herself toppling off the branch. As she fell, she reached up in a desperate attempt to grab anything. But something grabbed her.

It sunk its teeth into her ankle. She kicked with her free foot and temporarily stunned the evil thing. Then she realized she was hanging off the tree. But she wasn't holding anything; Neil was holding her. As he tried to pull her up, her body bumped the trunk and she started to shimmy upward with his help.

The dogs jumped up and their teeth made contact with her feet several times. The stabbing pain ended when she finally climbed out of their range. She settled on another branch next to Neil, and caught her breath.

"Holy shit!" she managed to say. "They almost killed us."

"We have to climb higher," Neil replied, examining the branches above them.

"Why?"

"The dogs may not have killed us, but their owners will."

The relentless barking hammered her brain as she realized what he meant. *The dogs weren't in the hall by themselves.* "Let's go," she said and started the precarious climb.

She stepped carefully onto each branch as she gradually neared the top. She paused, looked down, and saw Neil behind her. When she stopped, he moved next to her, their faces inches apart.

"Is this high enough?" she asked.

He quickly lifted his index finger to his lips and whispered, "Quiet." She looked at him, confused. He nodded his head downward. She looked below and saw two men milling about.

The dogs continued to bark incessantly, until one man gave each animal a mighty kick. "What the hell are you barking at?" he screamed. "Stop chasing damn squirrels and git back in the hall!" He kicked them again, and they reluctantly moved back to the building, still shouting a bark or two as they went.

Shannon and Neil watched the men glance around the grounds before they walked back to the hall. Then the men and dogs disappeared through the entrance, and Shannon's heart finally slowed its rapid beating. "So," she began, looking at Neil, "what the hell do we do now?"

"We gotta get out of here. And fast. If those guys are setting up for some kind of event in that hall, then other people might be showing up soon. I don't think we can take a whole night of being propped up in this tree."

"Let's go then," Shannon said. "Just make sure you don't go anywhere near that entrance." They slowly made their way down the tree, their eyes darting in all directions. As they descended, Shannon noticed a golf cart on the side of the building. "I bet those guys took that cart to get here. Maybe we can use it to get away."

"Good idea. Hopefully they're too busy to notice."

They hit the ground, and gingerly stepped toward the golf cart. They were almost there when Neil stopped. "What is it?" Shannon asked.

"The cell phone," he said, looking back.

"Where is it?"

"I think I dropped it when I first saw the dogs. Which was right in front of the main entrance."

"Forget it then."

"No," Neil insisted, "that phone is important."

"Those dogs almost killed us."

"I know, but how are we going to get out of here if we can't speak with Peter?"

Neil dropped to all fours and began crawling along the side of the building. Shannon grudgingly followed, ready to retreat at the slightest sound of a dog. They stopped at the end of the building with the main entrance just around the corner.

Neil pointed in front of him and whispered, "There it is." Shannon saw the phone on the ground. It was positioned perfectly in front of the door. "I'll crawl over and get it. You wait here."

"Are you crazy?" Shannon replied in a quiet voice. "They might see you. It's not worth it."

Neil ignored her and started to slowly crawl toward the phone. Shannon watched nervously. Her heart stopped when she heard the sound of growling. She called Neil's name and he stopped, looking back at her. The growling got louder and she heard footsteps that seemed to be right on top of her. She noticed a window above her, and spotted a figure moving past it.

"Get back," she desperately called in a hushed voice. Neil reversed his crawl as she saw one of the men step near the door. When Neil was back to the side of the building, she put her hand on his back. "Stay still."

They didn't move a muscle until they heard the footsteps return and then fade away. Without a word they crawled back to the golf cart. "The dogs must have smelled you," Shannon said as she sat in the passenger seat.

Neil sat behind the wheel and said, "I can't risk trying to get the phone. I guess we have to play it by ear." He turned the key to the on position and lifted the emergency brake. The cart started to roll forward. Neil pressed the accelerator and they made their escape from Aryan Hall with only a low hum from their getaway vehicle.

"Where are we going?" Shannon asked.

"I don't know. We can't go back the way we came because Peter said the perimeter would be guarded. I guess we have to find a place to hide."

"I heard Peter over the phone telling you about the underground bunker at the firing range."

"Right. That might be our best bet. But how are we going to find the firing range?" Just as Neil finished the sentence, they heard a pooping noise in the distance. "Is that what I think it is?"

"Sounds like we just found it."

Neil pointed the cart in the direction of the noise. The bumpy terrain jostled them in their seats from time to time, but otherwise, the drive was uneventful. Shannon thought the surroundings looked more like a state park than the home of the most dangerous terrorist organization in the country.

The grounds were filled with beautiful green hills and an occasional patch of trees. They passed a picturesque pond with ducks and saw a large horse stable. *Evil in paradise,* Shannon thought.

The origin of the gunfire came into view, a long one-story structure with white peeling paint. Some other structures were partially visible beyond it, and Shannon assumed they were housing or offices.

"It sounds like the range is on the other side of that building," Neil said as he applied the brake.

"So what do we do?"

"Well, we can't drive up to the front door. We have to stash this somewhere."

Shannon noticed a few trees to the right of the building. She pointed at the area and said, "Maybe there."

Neil slowed the cart even more as he sized up the trees. "It's not the best hiding spot in the world, but I guess it'll have to do." He punched the accelerator and they arrived in no time. He did his best to position the vehicle behind the largest tree. They both realized the cart could easily be seen—if anyone was looking for it—but they had no other option.

They looked at the building and then at each other. The fear and uncertainty were impossible to hide as they studied each other. "I know this isn't an easy question, but what will happen if we get caught?" Shannon said, breaking the awkward silence.

The sound of gunfire returned, startling them enough to jump. "That's actually a very easy question," Neil replied. "They'll kill us."

CHAPTER THIRTY-EIGHT

The assassins ran, dropped to the ground, and rolled before springing to their feet with a blast of gunfire. They peppered their targets with amazing accuracy, expelled the empty clips, popped new ones in, pivoted to their right, and began spraying bullets at a new target with the grace of a dance troupe.

"This is Red Wolf One," the Supreme Leader proudly exclaimed as he traipsed across the deck. "They are our top assassination team. All our best men have been assembled into this one group. And you, my friend, have earned the right to lead them."

The Bald Man stuck out his chest as he kept pace with the Leader. "I am honored to lead such a fine team, Your Excellency. If I may ask, are they preparing for a certain target?"

"Oh yes, my friend. Indeed they are. They are preparing for the primary target, and the assassination that will begin our revolution."

They stopped walking and stood shoulder to shoulder, surveying the team's drill. "Ah, yes, Your Excellency, you mean the top target that the Fuhrer wrote about in his testament?"

"The Fuhrer had an amazing vision for the future. Even in 1945 he knew that the primary target for a future revolution would be the president of the United Sates."

"And the vice president as well?"

"That's right. Red Wolf Two has been training to take him out. On April 20th, when our glorious revolution begins, we'll kill both of them. The president will be speaking that day at his alma mater. Yale University is opening a new auditorium that they're naming after the president. He'll be there at noon, and so will you and Red Wolf One. They'll have their weapons hidden in backpacks. The team will hang around outside the auditorium, posing as students. And on your signal, they'll storm one door, pull their weapons, and start firing."

"But the Secret Service will be all over the place. How are we going to get in?"

"See that man there?" the Supreme Leader asked, pointing to a tall man shooting at a target. "He's our man in the Secret Service. He'll be guarding the president that day. He will see to it that he's responsible for one exit near where the president will be speaking. The two of you will establish a system for him to signal you. When he does, your team will infiltrate the building and begin our destiny."

"You can count on me, sir. But what about number two?"

"The vice president is scheduled to be in California that day. He, and the California governor, will be addressing an environmental group that's been interrupting the logging industry out there. They're meeting outdoors in a park that borders a forest. We have snipers who specialize in long-range targets getting ready for this. They'll be tucked away in a far-off hill, but they'll be in range to make the hit."

"But when we take the first target out, won't the other cancel their appearance?"

"They're both scheduled to speak at noon Eastern Time. We'll drop them at the same time."

"And then what?"

"The next day will be chaos for the government. And we will take advantage. We have selective smaller teams assigned to take out congressman, senators, members of the president's cabinet, and high-profile governors. They'll all be doing press conferences that day, and we'll pick them off like flies.

"Once the assassinations are completed, we'll begin with the bombings. We have separate teams preparing for that. We can't hit every government building, but we'll get enough to scare the country so badly no one will leave their house. While this is occurring, you and Red Wolf One will invade NORAD. We'll have other teams infiltrating different nuclear control sites. Once we have them, then the country is ours."

"And then we can proceed with the rest of the Fuhrer's plan."

"Indeed we will, my friend."

"How will the boy be involved?"

They resumed their casual stroll across the deck. "When the boy is ready, we will hold the grand celebration. This will be to welcome and celebrate him as our new leader. He will speak to the members, and we'll make it known that the revolution will begin on the 20th."

"How do you know he'll cooperate?"

"Believe me, Doctor Kuhn is the best there is. By the time she's done with him, the boy will believe in our cause as much as we do. And finally, the Fuhrer's testament will come to fruition."

"Heil, Hitler!" The Bald Man shouted, thrusting his arm upward.

The Supreme Leader smiled and returned the salute. "Soon our Aryan brothers will openly salute the Fuhrer on the streets of America."

"I've been waiting for the day, Your Excellency. What can I do to help prepare for the grand celebration?"

"Actually, I have quite an interesting job in mind for you." The Leader paused as his eyes closed in on the Bald Man. "I want you to arrange for a human sacrifice at the celebration."

The Bald Man's eyes popped with the delight of a child on Christmas morning. "You want me to kill someone?"

"I want you to do a bit more than that. I have a specific person that I want you to kidnap and hold here. I want you to sacrifice this person during the grand celebration. I will leave the details of the kidnapping and sacrifice to you. So long as it occurs during the grand celebration."

The Bald Man fought to contain his excitement. "It would be my pleasure, Your Excellency." His fists were balled as he rocked from leg to leg. "Who would you like me to kill?"

"A self-proclaimed enemy of our organization. An annoying man who has delivered an unprovoked verbal attack on The Power. That Jewish DJ from Coeur d'Alene."

The Bald Man's face lit up with recognition. "Yes, Your Excellency. I know the man. I heard he organized some type of protest in front of the compound."

"He most certainly did. And he has chosen to speak against us on the radio almost daily. He's nothing but a nuisance and no real threat, but if we must sacrifice someone, why not have it be this filthy Jew that thinks it's entertaining to mock us. You may pick him up at any time, and in any way, that you see fit."

"Consider it done, Your Excellency." The Bald Man licked his lips in anticipation of the kill. "Consider it done."

CHAPTER THIRTY-NINE

Neil and Shannon tried not to breathe as they listened to the footsteps of the men above them. They had approached the firing range and had seen an opening underneath the deck. When they had heard people coming, they dashed into it.

Now, they lay quietly, watching the assassins through the slits in the wooden barrier in front of them. But they couldn't see above them, relying only on the sounds of footsteps and muffled voices to know someone was there.

When they heard the footsteps fade and a door close, Shannon thought it was safe to move. "I think they're gone."

"Quiet," Neil whispered. "Stay still. We have to be absolutely sure."

They were motionless for several minutes as the sounds of the nearby gunfire rattled their nerves. Neil turned to her and said, "It sounds like whoever was on the deck is not coming back, so we can talk. But very quietly."

"Don't worry...I'm not really in the mood to chat. But I would like to have an idea of what the hell we're going to do."

"We have to find the entrance to the underground bunker."

"And how are we supposed to find the bunker while we're lying underneath this deck?"

"We watch."

"Watch what? A bunch of Nazis shooting at targets?"

"Peter said that they store weapons underground. These guys have some serious firepower out here. When they're done, they'll probably store them in the bunker. So we watch where they go. And after they leave, we sneak in."

"Okay," she said, nodding her head in agreement. "Sorry for getting snippy with you. It's just that this is a little stressful."

"I know. Let's just lay here and chill out for a while. We'll get out of this situation eventually."

"Yeah, but alive?"

"Yes, alive. I promise."

Shannon smiled and felt better after seeing Neil's confident eyes.

She rested her head against her arms and stared out at the range. She didn't understand why—at this bizarre moment—she would think about the night Derek died. But her brain—despite her objections—replayed that horrible night.

She was home relaxing in front of the television. She went to their bedroom to check her e-mail, and when she was done, she noticed it was one in the morning. He had promised to be home by ten. She couldn't recall a time since they had been together that he had been more than a half hour late—ever, for anything.

Something was wrong.

She knew he was supposed to meet some friends for dinner. Even though it was late and she didn't want to disturb him, she decided to call his friend, Greg. The phone rang four times before the sleepy voice of Greg's wife answered.

Shannon fumbled through her words, but eventually spit out her reason for calling. When Greg got on the phone, he explained they had parted company around nine forty-five. He said everything seemed normal, and as far as he knew, Derek was on his way home.

A knot of nervousness clenched her throat as she forced a quick apology and hung up the phone. She knew what she had to do. She walked to the kitchen and found the number for their local police department. She dialed with a trembling hand and choked out her concern to the dispatcher.

When she stopped stammering, she knew she had conveyed her basic message. There was a strange silence before the dispatcher politely informed her he had to put her on hold. She waited an agonizing two minutes. He returned to the line, and after taking some basic information about her and Derek, informed her that someone would call her back soon.

She sat in her living room, shaking like a scared child. She clutched the cordless phone tightly and checked several times to make sure it was working properly.

She wasn't sure how long she waited, but when she looked at the clock she saw it was 1:45. She turned on the phone with an angry stab from her finger and prepared a verbal tirade in her head. She didn't understand why—after sounding as shaky and scared as she was—the police would blow her off. She knew they probably had more important things to do but...

She heard the wonderful sound of gravel under moving tires. He was home. She turned the phone off and ran to the window. She would be pissed at him for being so late without calling, but for the moment, she would hug and kiss him like she never had before.

It took her a moment to focus on the shape in her driveway, but she immediately knew it was not Derek's car. As her eyes adjusted to the darkness, she realized what she was looking at: a police cruiser.

At first, she didn't understand why the police would show up at her house when they could have just returned her call. But when the solemn face of the officer came into view, she knew.

He stared directly at the ground as he explained what they knew about the accident. He looked up, and after a hard swallow, told her Derek was dead. She didn't remember falling, but knew that she ended up on the ground somehow. The officer held her hand, and propped her head up, protecting her from the hard doorway.

She heard Neil say something, and his voice startled her. It took her a moment to realize that she wasn't lying in her doorway with a strange cop hovering over her, but underneath the deck of a firing range inside the Aryan Nation Compound.

She looked at Neil, bewildered. "Are you okay?" he repeated.

"Yeah. Why do you ask?" she replied, shaking off her daze.

"It didn't look like you were paying attention," he said and pointed to the range. "They're done. We have to watch where they take the weapons."

"Okay." She squinted and focused through one slit that gave her the best view of the moving men. As Neil predicted, they all entered one door with their weapons. After a minute or so, each man exited the same door empty-handed.

Shannon and Neil didn't make a sound as they watched them leave one by one. After a couple of minutes of not seeing any activity, they crept backward. "Do you think it's safe to move out of here?" Shannon asked.

"The place looks deserted. Let's go."

She followed him to the front corner of the deck. He picked up a rock—about the size of his hand—and smashed it against the wooden barrier in front of them. A few nails popped out, creating a gap. He pushed on it and expanded the opening until it was large enough to wriggle through.

"We have to stay low in case someone is keeping an eye on the area. Let's crawl along the perimeter until we get to the door," Neil said.

Shannon's heart was beating like a jackhammer as she followed him through the small space. The wood rubbed against her buttocks as she squeezed her way into the open air. She quickly glanced around the range as she stayed on Neil's tail.

They hurried around the periphery of the range, brushing against the structure that bordered the area. They paused when they reached the door that the men had entered. Neil grabbed the doorknob and cursed when he realized it was locked.

Shannon noticed a rock protruding out of the ground near her foot. She yanked it out of the dirt and extended it to Neil. He took it and nodded in thanks. "Is the coast clear?"

They both glanced around the area. The building that wrapped around the open area of the shooting rage was vast—certainly too large to examine every crevice. But Shannon could not detect any sign of movement anywhere. As far as she could tell, no one was there.

"Go for it," she said. He nodded in agreement and raised the rock above his head. He pounded it on the doorknob, shattering it from its wooden frame. They froze in terrified anticipation, expecting someone to come charging at them. But there was nothing.

They looked at each other and smiled. "Looks like we're going in," Neil said. "Let's hope there's no one in there."

She moved behind him as he pushed the door open.

CHAPTER FORTY

As she propped the doorknob back into place—hoping it would look normal from a distance—Neil was already on his way down the steep concrete steps. She followed him through the pitch black, feeling the wall as she descended.

"Neil," she whispered.

"I'm here." His voice came from the darkness. Then she heard the sound of a wooden door creak, and light suddenly filled the area.

The room was the size of a football field with wood paneling lining the entire length of one side. The paneling contained hundreds of shelves, each containing various types of ammunition: bullets, shells, crude-looking bombs, and grenades.

They hastily fumbled through various cabinets and drawers, finding an assortment of firearms. They examined different types of automatic rifles and handguns. "Looks like they're ready for a war," Shannon commented.

"They are." Neil held an AK-47 in his hands. "And I have a feeling this is just the stuff they use regularly on the range. I bet they have even bigger guns holed away somewhere in here."

Shannon noticed the other side of the room. There was a rack of shirts that stretched for about half of the wall. The other half contained trunks of other clothing: camouflage pants, boots, and ski masks. "We can play dress up," Shannon said, leading Neil across the room.

The shirts varied in size but were otherwise identical: a short-sleeve, light blue, button-down shirt with a collar, each adorned with a swastika on the left sleeve. "Find your size," Neil said as he rifled through the rack.

"Really?"

"Why not? This uniform could save us if we're seen."

Shannon found a shirt in a small size and she noticed Neil changing into one. She doffed the tee shirt Peter had given her earlier and buttoned up the strange garment. "Should we change into the pants and boots too?"

"Sure." They put on the rest of the uniform, and inspected each other.

Shannon straightened his shirt as she said, "You look just like the guys on the range. But do they let women wear these outfits?"

"I don't think so. But with that short hair and with your cap low, you might be able to pass for a guy." He pulled the hat down the front of her face.

"Gee, thanks. I'm getting a little overwhelmed with all these compliments today."

"Don't worry. You look great. Let's grab a gun and get out of here." They returned to the other side of the room and Neil picked up two Glock M21s.

"What's next?"

"We're going to the Fuhrer's house." Neil handed her one of the Glocks, and she awkwardly held the handgun as if it were a fragile piece of glass.

She looked at the weapon with a perplexed expression and then back at him. "But how are we going to get there? We don't know where it is."

"I haven't figured that part out yet." He unbuttoned a side pocket on his pants and stowed the gun inside. "Put your gun in this pocket."

"Is it loaded?"

"Of course it's loaded. What good would it be if it wasn't loaded?"

She opened the pocket and dropped it inside. "I don't know if it's going to do me much good, loaded or not. I've never fired one before."

"You will if you have to," he replied as he looked around the room.

Shannon heard a noise outside. As she strained to listen, she thought she heard a voice. "Oh shit!" she said in a panicked voice. "I think someone's out there!"

"Let's take a look." They ran up the steps to the broken door. Neil carefully pulled it open about an inch, and they peered outside. They saw a man in his early sixties walking across the range and holding the bullet-riddled paper targets. There was a large green trash barrel sitting in the firing area. The man dropped the targets into the barrel, and started to sweep the area.

"He's sweeping up the used casings," Neil whispered. "He must be some type of janitor." Shannon nodded her head in agreement as they watched the man clean up the area. "I'm going to talk to him."

"What? Are you crazy?"

"This could be our chance to get information about the Fuhrer's house. Stay here and wait for me."

Neil opened the door just enough to slip through. Shannon grabbed the loose doorknob before it fell, and quietly moved the door to its earlier position. She remained crouched on the top step like a baseball catcher, one eye intensely watching him through the tiny opening.

"Hey, buddy," Neil said, nonchalantly strolling toward the man.

The man turned around, surprised. "Oh, sorry. I thought you guys were all done for the day."

"It's okay. We're done. I just had a question." Neil reached the man as they faced each other.

"What is it?" The man looked at Neil, curiously.

"I have guard duty at the Fuhrer's house. Someone told me there's a shortcut to get there through an underground passage that starts over here. Do you know where that is?"

The man looked puzzled as his eyes scanned Neil from head to toe. "You want to go to the Fuhrer's house?"

"That's right. I have guard duty there."

"Well, why don't you just walk there? It's not even a half-mile away." The man pointed north.

"I know that," Neil responded as casually as he could. "I just wanted to walk through the underground tunnel. I never went that way before."

The man glared at Neil as if he had three heads. "Go through that door down to the storage room." Shannon saw the man pointing directly at her. "Then go through the door at the far end of the room, and then take a left and another left. Then just walk straight till you get there."

"Thanks so much." Neil turned and stepped quickly toward the door.

"Hold on a minute," the man called, loudly. Neil froze, and Shannon noticed the two-way radio hanging off his hip. Neil glanced back over his shoulder as the man said, "That door should be locked." The man jangled a set of keys in his hand.

"That's okay," Neil replied with a smile. "I have my own key." Neil took a few large strides, trying to move as fast as he could without actually running.

"Hey, mister," the man called. Once again, Neil stopped and slowly turned, his body tense as an actor waiting for the curtain to rise. "What's your name?"

"I'm Al."

"How come I haven't seen you before, Al?" Shannon watched the man's fingers dangling over the radio like a gunfighter poised for a draw.

"Not sure. I guess we just never bumped into each other before. Thanks again for the directions."

Neil's strides were even longer now as he bounded to the door in an instant. He paused and briefly pantomimed using a key before pulling the door open a crack. He slithered through the small space and shut the door.

"Do you think he's on to me?"

Before Shannon could reply, the knob fell out of its hole and landed outside the door. "If he wasn't before, he sure is now."

"Run!" Neil said, and they bolted down the steps. They dashed across the room, found the door the man described, and were relieved to find it open. "Go left." Neil led the way through a dimly lit tunnel until they reached an intersection.

"He said another left and then straight for a while."

They took the turn and sprinted down the empty passageway.

"How are we going to know when we're there?" Shannon asked.

"He said it was about a half mile. How long will it take us to run a half mile?"

"At this pace about five minutes."

"Okay, then in about five minutes we slow down and start looking for an entrance."

"And then what?"

"Then we rescue the boy."

"Is that all?" Shannon quipped as she gasped for breath.

"Just shut up and run."

They were silent for the next five minutes, listening only to the soles of their boots slapping against the cement floor. After rounding a corner, they slowed down and eventually stopped. They struggled to suck in the stale air as they scanned the area for signs of an entrance.

After catching her breath, Shannon said, "I don't see anything."

"There's another bend up there. Maybe around that corner we'll see something." They walked around the bend and immediately saw it. The tunnel came to an end about twenty yards in front of them, and at the end was an ordinary wooden door.

They froze and stared at the entrance in shock. "The boy is most likely on the other side of that door," Neil said, his gaze still fixed on the end of the tunnel.

"Yeah, but how are we going to get him out?"

"We can do this one of three ways. We can try and sneak inside, and hide from whoever might be in there and then slip away with the boy. Or we can go inside and pretend we're there to guard the house and then take the boy when we have an opportunity. Or we burst in shooting."

"Burst in shooting?" Shannon's eyes widened.

"We shoot anything that moves except for the boy of course. Then we grab him and go."

"I don't like that idea. Let's do one of the first two."

"Okay. Which one?"

"I don't know," she replied with a frustrated sigh. "I can't think straight right now."

Neil opened his mouth to say something, but stopped when they heard something. Their frightened expressions locked on each other as they realized what the noise was.

The hurried sound of footsteps came from behind them, drawing closer each second. "Shit!" Neil yelled. "Let's get inside!"

They dashed to the door, and Neil yanked on the knob. Surprisingly, the door swung open easily, but as they took a step inside they were forced to stop. Just inches in front of them were two automatic rifles aimed at their chest

CHAPTER FORTY-ONE

The Supreme Leader sat on the edge of the leather recliner, peering over the railing like he had balcony seats at the opera. He was confident that the boy did not know he was being watched. He had entered the house quietly, and stepped lightly up the stairs to the hidden loft. As the Leader watched, the young man remained on the couch and did not lift his nose out of the book in his lap.

Doctor Kuhn moved in front of him and handed him a brandy snifter. The Leader took the glass and looked at her curiously. She moved her other hand from behind her back, and presented a bottle of liquor. As he read the label, his eyes widened with surprise.

"Asbach Uralt," she said with a sultry smile. "If I remember correctly, you like it neat."

"Indeed I do, my dear." She poured a generous amount into his snifter. "I hope you're joining me."

She chose another glass from a hutch and poured some brandy into it. "I wouldn't let you drink alone." She sat and placed the bottle on a table between them.

"And to what do I owe this wonderful surprise?"

"I want to thank you for selecting me for this assignment. It's an honor to serve The Power at this momentous time."

"You're more than qualified, my dear." The Leader delicately sipped the brandy, savoring the exceptional flavor. After the glass separated from his lips, he looked at it as if it were a long lost lover. "Ahh, this brings back such fond memories. Did you know that I shared a bottle of this with the Fuhrer himself?"

"That's fascinating. When did you have the privilege?"

"I attended a gathering at his Berghof at Berchtesgaden in 1940. Me and a few other young officers had a drink with him on the terrace, overlooking the Untersberg Mountains. It was a beautiful sight, and a wonderful moment."

"You are blessed to have been in the presence of The Great One."

"I am fortunate to have those memories, but we will all benefit from his vision of our future."

"Well said." They clinked glasses and took a sip.

"Speaking of our future," the Leader said as he gestured toward the boy, "how are things with the young man?"

"We have a long way to go, but we've made a good start."

"How long do you expect?"

She lowered her voice to a whisper as she glanced down at the boy. "I have to earn his trust before he'll truly start to accept his destiny. This is a tremendous challenge after what he's been through. As you know, he was taken away from the only life he knew, and had to live in a primitive place with no electricity, running water, or proper shelter."

"I know what they did to the poor boy."

"Your bald henchman did not make matters any easier. The boy told me that the brute slaughtered a woman he knew right in front of him. And then he said the animal kicked one of his own men out of a helicopter, and the boy watched him fall to his death. He did these things right in front of the boy."

"I wasn't aware of this. I will address it."

"The boy has suffered severe psychological damage since he was taken from his home. And now, I've been forced to tell him the truth that's been hidden from him his whole life."

"How did he handle it?"

"He didn't have much of a reaction. Fortunately, I don't think he's old enough to have been completely poisoned by lies about the Fuhrer. He seemed to recognize his picture, but only vaguely. I showed him Eva Braun's home movies from the Berghof and Kehlsteinhaus. I told him how wonderful and misunderstood his grandparents were, and now I have him looking over some things that cast a more positive light on them."

"Do you think it's helping?" The Supreme Leader finished his drink as he glanced down at the boy.

Doctor Kuhn leaned forward, her tight dress creeping up her leg, and grabbed the bottle. She poured more liquor into his glass as she said, "Honestly, I have no idea. It's too early to tell. But I sense him becoming more comfortable in my presence. After some time, when I have earned his trust, I believe he will come to accept the truth."

"And take the position in The Power that is his destiny?"

"I hope so, Your Excellency. I will do the best I can."

"I know that, and I understand the incredible challenge that you face. But I must remind you of our plans for April 20th. And our need to have the grand celebration before then, when the boy must speak."

"I am well aware of the limited time we have. Otherwise, I would never have told the boy about his grandparents so soon. I'll work to prepare him as soon as I possibly can."

"I know you will, my dear." The Leader picked up his glass as Doctor Kuhn did the same. Once again, they clinked their snifters together. "I can think of no one else with the talent to succeed at this task."

She flashed him a seductive smile as they each took a sip. "Thank you, Your Excellency."

CHAPTER FORTY-TWO

Shannon and Neil leaned back against the concrete wall with their hands trembling in the air. They were afraid to even twitch a muscle as the two men in front of them waved their AK-47s anxiously.

"What are you doing here?" one of the men snarled.

Shannon and Neil didn't speak, each of them completely lost for a believable explanation. One of the men patted them down and immediately found the two Glocks. "Ah ha!" the man yelled as he held the handguns in the air. The other man waved his weapon even more excitedly now, and Shannon was convinced he was going to kill them.

As she pressed her back against the cold wall, she heard the once-faint sound of footsteps becoming louder. She diverted her eyes away from the gyrating gun inches from her torso, and looked down the hall.

Two men, also holding AK-47s, bounded around the corner. Gasping for air, they angrily approached. Shannon realized that one of the men looked familiar. As she focused on the man's face, she realized she was looking at Peter's contact, Ron Hale.

Ron's mouth fell open as he looked at them. "Al? Betty? Is that you?"

The other three gunmen looked at Ron, bewildered. "You know these people?" one of the guards asked.

"I sure do," Ron said as he lowered his weapon. "Put your guns down, boys. They don't mean any harm. They're just wannabes."

They all lowered their guns and one of the asked, "What do you mean?"

"They want to join," Ron explained. "I had to turn them down earlier today."

"That's right," Neil announced in his fake southern accent. "We want to be part of The Power."

"But you were trying to break in here," one of the guards said as he pointed at the door.

"Yeah," the other guard chimed in, "the janitor at the range radioed that someone was on their way here through the tunnel."

"We heard the same message," the one with Ron said. "How do you explain that?"

"We wanted to see the Fuhrer's house," Neil blurted out.

There was a moment of silence, and Shannon knew she had to say something. "We used the last of our money to get here from Georgia," she said, thinking her accent sounded a little more believable. "We couldn't go back without seeing the Fuhrer's house."

"It's our dream," Neil lied.

"You stole uniforms?" Ron asked gesturing to their clothing.

"We thought maybe we could sneak in. We just wanted to look around the house a bit, and then we were going to leave," Shannon said.

Ron shook his head in frustration as he said, "You picked the worst possible time to do this. You're lucky you didn't get yourselves killed."

"We're sorry," Neil said.

"If y'all just drive us to the front gate, we promise to disappear and y'all never see us again," Shannon said.

"I'm afraid we can't do that," Ron replied.

"Why not?" Neil asked.

"A lot of people heard that old man on the radio. We have to bring you to an officer," Ron explained.

Shannon and Neil looked at each other fearfully. "What'll he do to us?" Shannon asked.

Ron and the other three studied one another as if they were searching for the answer. "I'm not sure," Ron finally said. "Like I said, you picked a real bad time to do this. But I'll do what I can for you."

There was silence as they all looked down in thought. Shannon stared at the door as a surge of frustration overtook her. *He's somewhere behind that door.* She took a deep breath, trying to hide her anger, and said, "So what now?"

"We have to take you to a holding area. I'll talk with an officer and then he'll come talk to you," Ron explained. "But first, let's get you back into your regular clothes."

Ron and his fellow guard escorted Shannon and Neil back down the hall, leaving the other two men at the entrance to the Fuhrer's house. They walked in silence until they reached the gun storage room. "Our clothes are over there," Neil said, pointing behind a trunk.

"Go ahead and change," Ron said. The two guards politely looked away as Shannon slipped back into her outfit. When they were done, Ron waved for them to follow him.

They walked out of the underground bunker and through the empty firing range. Shannon and Neil were led into the backseat of a black SUV. Ron drove for about a mile down a narrow paved road. He stopped the vehicle in front of a group of brick buildings. As they all got out, Ron said, "Pete is gonna shit when he hears what you two did."

"I know he will," Neil said as they walked toward the buildings. "I hope your officers understand that our intentions were innocent."

Ron's face turned serious. "Like I said, I'll do what I can."

They entered a building and were brought to a small, windowless room, which contained nothing but a table and four chairs. "Just wait here," Ron said after they stepped inside. Then, the door slammed shut, and they heard a deadbolt latch from the outside.

They sat at the table in silence. Neil tapped the tabletop with his thumb as Shannon stared at the empty, white walls. After a few minutes, she said, "So how are we going to get out of this?"

Neil glared at her intensely, his index finger straight in front of his lips. "We need to be careful what we say." His eyes darted from side to side. "We don't want to give anyone the wrong impression."

She realized that he believed the room was bugged, and that they could not talk freely. "I'm sure they'll understand that we're telling the truth," she said with a nod and a quick wink.

He smiled to acknowledge her understanding. "I'm sure they're reasonable people and will understand that we meant no harm."

With the unspoken agreement that they would not talk about their situation, they sat and stared at the table, floor, and walls. Neither of them had a watch and with no clock in the room, they were unable to measure the slow, unbearable crawl of time.

When the door finally opened, Shannon jumped to her feet as she saw Ron walk into the room.

"Sorry to be so long." Ron said as he approached them. "I have to transport you."

"What? Where are we going?" Neil asked.

"Can't tell you that right now, my friend. But unfortunately, I have orders to put these on you." Rom dangled two sets of handcuffs.

"But why?" Neil argued. "We haven't done anything wrong. And we've been completely cooperative with you."

"I know that," Ron said with a sympathetic smile. "But things aren't working out like I hoped they would."

Shannon's muscles tensed as she broke into a sweat. "What's going to happen?" she asked in a shaky voice.

"Well," Ron began, looking at the floor, "I'm not really sure. I was explaining the situation to an officer, and I made sure he understood that we met earlier today, and that I thought you two were just real fanatical about joining. But when I was explaining, another officer overheard. This guy is a real high-ranking member; he has direct contact with the Supreme Leader. Anyway, he got involved and gave me the orders to bring you to him."

"Should we be worried?" Neil asked as Ron cuffed his hands behind his back.

"I don't know. This guy was real intense when he gave me the orders." Ron moved behind Shannon and slipped her wrists into the handcuffs. "I already explained to him that I thought you two were okay. But I don't know what he's thinking."

Ron led them outside and into the same black SUV. It was dark and

Shannon had trouble figuring out where he was driving in relation to the places they had been. He drove for about ten minutes and stopped the vehicle next to an area of dark woods.

Ron guided them out as Shannon scanned the area, trying to recognize something in the gloomy surroundings. She expected to be brought into another building, but only saw trees. Ron gently pushed them forward as Shannon asked, "Where are you bringing us? There's nothing here."

"I'm just following orders," Ron replied as they continued to walk through the dark, wooded area. After a few minutes, Shannon spotted two figures in the distance. When they got closer, she saw that it was another Aryan guard with a gun slung over his shoulder. And next to him was a man in handcuffs.

They stepped closer and Shannon focused on the face of the other prisoner. She lost her breath when she recognized Peter. *We've blown his cover and killed him,* she thought as they met eyes.

"Peter! What happened?" Neil said.

"There's been a misunderstanding," Peter replied. "Hopefully, we'll clear this up."

"Shut up," the guard next to Peter yelled.

They stood in silence for a moment and then heard movement in the darkness. After a moment, they saw a figure appear and move toward them.

"Officer approaching!" the guard next to Peter yelled. The guard and Ron snapped to attention and raised their right arms in a Nazi salute.

The officer stopped walking a few feet in front of them. Only a sliver of moonlight shone through the trees, but it was just enough to illuminate the face of the Bald Man.

CHAPTER FORTY-THREE

The Bald Man paced in front of the three handcuffed strangers, inspecting them like a drill sergeant on the first day of boot camp. He was aware that Ron Hale had vouched for them, but he wasn't going to take his word. He was told that one of the men had already been accepted into The Power. But when he looked at the two men, neither of them was familiar.

He took a step toward the girl and noticed her sunglasses. *Sunglasses at night,* he thought. *What's she trying to hide?* But he liked the rest of her, especially the way her jeans clung to her hips. If nothing else, he might be able to have some fun with her.

He decided that he would not listen to their explanation. What good were words? If they wanted to convince him that they were genuine followers of The Power, then they would need to show him. And he had the perfect task.

"You claim to desire entry into our organization," he bellowed.

"Yes sir," Peter said. "I can explain—"

"Shut up," he yelled into Peter's face. "I didn't give you permission to speak." Complete silence followed and the Bald Man resumed his pacing. "If you want me to believe that your purpose on this property was innocent, then you have to prove it."

He stopped in front of Neil and Peter. He pointed at them as he said, "You two will leave the compound tonight, and apprehend an enemy of The Power. You'll deliver this man to me as soon as possible. Do you know that loud-mouthed Jew that speaks against us on the radio? The one that had the balls to organize a protest in front of this compound?"

The Bald Man drew closer, trying to detect the slightest sign of fear. But the men were stoic, and stared straight ahead, impassively. "Well?" the Bald Man continued, inches in front of their faces. "Do you know the man?"

"I know of him, sir," Peter said.

"Then find him and bring him to me. And I want him alive. I'll leave his killing to someone else." The Bald Man snapped his head toward Shannon and broke into a wide grin. Now, he could sense fear.

"Wait a minute," she said. "You don't mean that I have to kill him?"

The Bald Man stepped in front of her. "Is that going to be a problem, sweetheart?"

"I...I...no," she stammered. "It's just that I don't know this man."

"If you want to be in our organization, then you do what your superior officer orders you to do. After they bring this loud-mouthed Jew here, I'm going to order you to kill him. If you want to be one of us, like you say you do, then you'll follow my order."

The Bald Man stepped back, now satisfied that he had completely terrified the young woman. He turned his attention back to the men. "So, are we clear on your assignment?"

"May I ask a question, sir?" Neil asked.

"Go ahead."

"Can my wife come with us to kidnap this man? She would be of great help."

The Bald Man laughed. He grabbed Shannon's arm and pulled her to him. He held her next to him as he said, "I don't think so. But don't worry. I'll keep a real close eye on her." He laughed again, feeling her tense body rubbing against his.

Neil took a step toward the Bald Man with an angry face. The Bald Man immediately stuck out his arm and Neil stopped. "Listen, buddy," the Bald Man began, "you do what I told you to do, and nothing will happen to her. But she stays here."

Neil's angry countenance continued as he locked eyes with the Bald Man. "So does everyone understand what they need to do?" the Bald Man asked, still staring at Neil.

Peter stepped forward and said, "We understand. We'll bring the Jew here as soon as we can, sir."

The Bald Man nodded his head, seeming satisfied. "All right then, uncuff them." Ron took the handcuffs off Neil, and the other guard uncuffed Peter. They stretched their free arms as they looked around the pitch-black surroundings.

"What are you waiting for?" the Bald Man said loudly. He pointed one arm into the darkness as he continued to hold Shannon with the other. "Get going."

Neil anxiously watched the Bald Man's hand on Shannon until Peter pulled him by the elbow. "Thank you, sir," Peter said, and Neil finally looked away from her. Then, they trudged off into the darkness.

After a moment, the Bald Man leaned closer to Shannon. "I thought they would never leave," he said with a toothy grin. "I have special plans for the two of us."

CHAPTER FORTY-FOUR

Carl Fineman sat behind the microphone as comfortable as if he were born there. His crisp words rolled off his tongue like water over a fall. The fact that his voice was now being broadcasted on a 50,000-watt signal didn't faze him. It was just another night's work.

KBIS-FM paid him well for his services, and he believed that he deserved it. After all, he blew away the competition in his time slot, helping to launch his station to number one in its market. The vast majority of people in Northern Idaho, who listened to the radio between eight PM and midnight, listened to old Carl's nightly rant.

The format of his show was simple: Carl Fineman—and Carl Fineman only—talking about issues that people in the Coeur d'Alene area cared about. He beat the music programs, the news programs, the sports programs, and whatever syndicated show dared to challenge him.

As he passionately delivered a tirade about a corrupt local politician, he saw Artie waving to him from the booth. Carl knew what the signal meant; it was ten of midnight, and time to change topics. He talked about one topic that was far more popular than any other: the presence of the Aryan Nation Compound in Hayden Lake. He always opened the show with the topic, made sure to discuss it at the midpoint, and closed his show with it.

"I want to remind everyone of the latest event I'm planning. Next Friday night I'll be asking you to join me for a midnight vigil in front of the Aryan Nation Compound. As you know, we usually end this show at midnight, but next Friday we'll extend our broadcast time for this vigil.

"We'll march with lit candles to honor those killed by the Aryans, the Klan, and extremist hate groups all over our country. We'll remember the dead, and at the same time let those Aryan bastards know that they're not welcome here in Idaho. The rally we held last month brought hundreds of you to the main entrance of their evil compound. Let's do it again and be even bigger and louder this time.

"It's time for the Neo-Nazis to pack up and leave town, and we have to show them the way out. We need to take Hayden Lake back, and allow peaceful, law-abiding citizens to live in this area without fear."

He rambled on for a few minutes until he saw Artie waving again.

"Okay, folks, save that date for next Friday. This is straight talk with Carl Fineman signing off. Peace." He stripped the headphones off as he watched Artie turning knobs on the control panel.

He opened the door to Artie's booth and took a step inside. His gangly arms hung off his six-four, skinny frame like low-hanging branches off an oak tree. "Good night, my friend," he waved to his bearded producer.

"Hold up," Artie said as he jumped up from the chair. The next show's producer slid behind him, and Artie quickly stepped into the hallway. He and Carl walked toward the back door as he said, "Hey, how about grabbing a beer?"

"Sorry, buddy. I reached my carb limit for the day." Carl patted his flat stomach.

"You gotta be kidding me?" his pudgy companion scoffed.

"Maybe tomorrow night if I skip the baked potato at dinner."

"Yeah right." Artie frowned and made a sudden turn toward the bathroom. "I'll catch you tomorrow."

Carl gave a quick wave to his friend, without breaking his stride, and was in the parking lot in an instant. He strode toward his Chevy Blazer with the satisfaction of another good night's work.

He was truthful about his disdain for the Aryans, but in a way, he was almost grateful for their presence here. By becoming the leading voice against them, his popularity had soared to heights he had never imagined. He thought the Aryans were just a bunch of ignorant rednecks, but their existence tripled his paycheck.

He pulled open his unlocked door, which always made him think of his previous home in Los Angeles. There, every car was equipped with a sophisticated alarm system. But in Northern Idaho, it was silly to even lock your vehicle.

As he settled into the soft leather seat, he brushed his long, curly black hair off his brow. His tired body ached for his bed, which was just ten minutes away. He inserted the key into the ignition, but before he could turn it, something stopped him.

There was an object around his neck that pulled him against the seat. His hand was paralyzed—just inches from the ignition—as he felt his throat constrict. The terrifying moment of no air abruptly ended when the truck door opened.

The stranger yanked his legs out of the vehicle, and when he thought he might tumble out, the restraint against his neck held him in place. He gasped for air as he saw the long metal rod in his face.

When he recognized the weapon as the tire iron from his truck, the stranger thrust his angry face forward. "Don't move or I'll bust your kneecaps!" His two attackers wrestled him into the backseat. One of them held him face down into the leather seat as he heard the truck start.

He lay motionless—feeling the tire iron digging into his back. Carl felt his truck moving now, but he didn't dare lift his head. Although he had never seen either of these men before, he knew where they were taking him.

CHAPTER FORTY-FIVE

Shannon paced nervously in the tiny space. The windowless room had nothing but a bed and an open toilet—a prison cell without the bars. After he had closed the door behind him, she heard the lock click, announcing that there was no hope of escape.

Her body was so desperate for rest that even the unkempt, scrawny bed looked inviting. But sleep was impossible now. Not when she knew he would be back. He had said nothing before he left, but his soulless eyes forecasted something gruesome. She had no doubt of his intent—and knew it would happen tonight.

She sat on the end of the bed and made a futile attempt to think about something else. But what could soothe her mind? An innocent, confused boy being held in captivity? A radio disc jockey who was about to be abducted and hauled off to this terrible place? Or a kind old man who was kidnapped from his home, forced to South America, and slaughtered like an animal?

Unfortunately, she couldn't even find peace from any thoughts prior to meeting Neil. For years she lived with the sadness of the passing of her parents, and now, scenes of Derek's accident constantly ran through her mind. She realized that the misery she carried with her every day was no worse than waiting for the return of this Aryan brute. So she would fight him—and fight him hard.

She ignored her fear and tried to think of a way to stave him off. She wanted a weapon, but she would have to be creative in her sparse surroundings. She had nothing on her she could use, save a skinny leather belt.

She lifted up the mattress and tugged on the metal box spring. She hoped a sharp piece would snap off, but the sturdy frame was unbreakable. Her last hope was the toilet. She lifted the ceramic tank top and looked inside. The frail chain was unimpressive, but she still tried to think of a way to use it.

But then, it was too late. The Bald Man stepped inside and slammed the door with a mule-kick. She stared at him—still holding the tank top—and was sickened by his disgusting smirk.

"You ready to have some fun, baby?"

She lunged at him, letting loose a primal scream, and swung the tank top with all her strength. The awkward weapon slipped out of her hand as he pushed it away, redirecting it into the wall. It cracked in half and fell harmlessly to the floor.

He caught her in his evil gaze, his nostrils flaring like an enraged bull. "So you want to have it rough?" Before she could even think about pulling away, his powerful paws grabbed her elbows and pushed them into her torso.

He lifted her off her feet, and slammed her onto the mattress. He fell on top of her, completely restraining her. Their faces almost touched as his fetid breath soaked into her skin. He snatched the cap off her head and tossed it across the room.

He looked down at her with a satisfied grin as he said, "Now let me see those pretty eyes."

She had forgotten that she was still wearing the sunglasses that Peter had given her on the plane. They seemed to become a part of her face. Maybe she liked the fact that the big black lenses disguised her—like this wasn't really happening to her.

But whatever comfort they provided ended abruptly when the beast ripped them from her face, and snapped them in half. The cheap plastic fell out of his hand like dust as his sick smile widened. "Now, I can finally see you."

He repositioned himself on top of her, crushing her already sore ribs. She gasped in pain as his face drew even closer. "Quiet now," he whispered. "Get ready for the ride of your life."

He stared at her like he was about to eat her alive. When she saw his lips start to pucker, she closed her eyes and cringed. She froze, waiting for his awful mouth to devour her. But she felt nothing.

When she opened her eyes he was still staring at her, but something was different. His eyes looked puzzled, and his mouth hung open—like he had seen a ghost. Then, to her surprise, he jumped off of her.

He stood in the middle of the room, still as a statue. He looked at her with a bewildered gaze that sent chills up her spine. Her brain formed a question. *What's wrong? What did I do?* But she stopped herself before she asked either.

This animal was about to rape her, and she should be happy that he had stopped—whatever the reason. But she had to know what was going through his mind. *What the hell happened?*

She sat up, knowing her face must have looked as shocked as his. She stared back at him, lost for words. After a moment, he raised his arm, pointing at her with a trembling hand.

"Who are you?"

"I'm Betty. I live in Georgia." The words spewed out of her mouth automatically. She did a mental check to ensure that she gave the proper information. She was satisfied with her response, but worried because she and Neil had not developed an elaborate identity. Betty from Georgia was all she had to offer.

Why is he asking me this?

A scowl took over his face as he stepped forward, angrily. "You're lying to me!"

"I don't know what you're talking about!" she yelled back without thinking.

His face turned as red as an apple as he took another step toward her and waved his arm furiously. "This is fucked up!" he screamed, and stormed out of the room.

She jumped to her feet as the door slammed. She looked at it in complete bewilderment. She dropped to her knees, lightly feeling her head and face with the tips of her fingers. Without the hat, she could feel the unfamiliar short hair on her head. She caressed her nose and the area around her eyes. She only had one question for the Bald Man.

Who did you see?

CHAPTER FORTY-SIX

Shannon rolled over, feeling the hard lumps in the bed stabbing at her spine. As she rubbed her heavy eyelids, she wondered if she had slept at all. She remembered the feeling of drifting off on a few occasions, but each time the sound of the door unlocking woke her. She realized now that the door had never opened. But knowing it eventually would was enough to stave off any real sleep.

She no longer feared rape, but now lived with the agonizing terror of the unknown. Whatever was going to happen, she knew that it wasn't going to involve her being allowed to leave the compound. Someone here had plans for her.

As her feet touched the white linoleum floor, she wondered if it was morning yet. *Did Neil and Peter really kidnap that DJ? Or will they try to rescue me some other way?* It pained her to not know where they were. Her mind needed something to focus on, something to hope for.

She paced from wall to wall, trying to loosen her muscles. She replayed every event and every conversation she had since she met Neil to sharpen her brain. But her physical and mental exercise was interrupted by the sound of the metal latch on the door. Only this time it was real.

As the door opened, she braced herself for the revolting face of the Bald Man. But it wasn't him. A large unfamiliar man with a face like a bulldog stood there, glaring at her with beady suspicious eyes. He took a set of handcuffs out of his pocket. "I have to transport you."

"I know the drill," Shannon said, and turned around, placing her hands behind her back. He cuffed her and led her to the back of a different black SUV. As they drove away she asked, "Do you guys have a fleet of these?" Her attempt to lighten the mood between them failed when he didn't respond.

They drove in silence for about five minutes, finally stopping in front of a modest looking one-story house. Shannon immediately thought of the Fuhrer's house, but realized they were not near the firing range. *Besides, why would they bring me there?*

The guard led her inside and uncuffed her. She stood in a simple living room, which was sparsely but neatly decorated. "I've been told to offer you breakfast," he said with the compassion of a robot. He gestured to the adjoining room. Shannon saw a table with a spread of breakfast food: bagels, sausages, melon, orange juice and a pan of scrambled eggs.

"This is very nice," Shannon said as she approached the table. "Are you sure it's okay?"

"It was prepared for you, ma'am."

Shannon raised an eyebrow as she glanced at the guard. "Do you always treat your prisoners so well?"

The guard turned away and sat on the couch. "Eat what you want."

She put a little of everything on a plate and poured herself a tall glass of juice. She sat in an armchair across from the Bulldog, and placed her plate and glass on a coffee table. She ate without attempting any further communication with her stony companion. About halfway through her meal, she heard a vehicle stop in the front of the house.

As she looked outside, she was convinced she would see another black SUV. But to her surprise, it was a small red sports car. "Is that a Porsche?" she asked aloud, straining her neck to get a better angle out the window. As expected, no answer came, but a moment later the front door opened.

Shannon found herself looking at the longest pair of legs she had ever seen. Wrapped tightly in black fishnets that matched a pair of Stilettos, the sight was memorable if not a bit intimidating. She looked at the woman's striking green eyes and short spiked blonde hair.

Then, she remembered. *The tall leggy psychologist, who was here to work with the boy.*

"How are my eggs?"

Shannon stared at the six-foot woman, lost for a response.

"The eggs," she repeated. "They must be cold. I made them a half an hour ago. Did you heat them?"

Struggling to shake off the shock of the imposing woman's sudden arrival, she could only shake her head no.

"There's a microwave in the kitchen," she said, scooping the plate off the table. "Let me heat it for you." Before Shannon could tell her not to bother, she was on the way to the kitchen. "Ben, I'd prefer if you waited outside now."

The Bulldog's name is Ben, Shannon realized as the muscular man silently exited the house. She then turned her attention to the kitchen, where her new hostess was punching the keypad on a microwave.

"Did you sleep okay?" she asked as the microwave hummed.

"What?" Shannon replied, dumbfounded by the bizarre woman's politeness.

"I know you slept in one of the holding rooms. Not the most comfortable accommodations in the world. I was just wondering if you were able to sleep all right."

"Actually," Shannon cleared her throat, "I didn't sleep well at all."

The microwave rang, and the blonde woman traipsed across the kitchen with Shannon's plate, her high heels clicking against the linoleum like a horse's hooves. "I'm sorry you had a bad night. If you like, you can stay here tonight."

Shannon watched in amazement as she slid the plate in front of her and sat back in the couch, crossing her curvaceous legs. "Where is here?"

"This is just a guest house. There's not much to it, but it's better than where you stayed last night. I'm staying in one just like it on the other end of the property."

"Why are you being so nice to me?" Shannon asked, red-faced and too flustered to look at the food.

"I don't know what you mean. I'm treating you like I would treat any guest."

"Guest?" Shannon blurted out in a raised voice. "Yesterday I was captured at gunpoint and handcuffed. Now I'm a guest?"

"That's right. You see, yesterday, we didn't know who you were."

Shannon stared at the blonde woman's smiling face as chills ran up and down her body. *How could you know me?* she thought. She searched her brain for a time she may have seen this woman, or the Bald Man, or the Bulldog. But there was nothing. They were all memorable people in their own way, and she was positive she had never encountered any of them.

After an awkward moment, she said, "I don't know you."

The blonde woman leaned forward over the coffee table. "You're absolutely right. You don't know me. And I've been rude to not introduce myself. I'm Doctor Grace Kuhn." She extended her hand, and Shannon took a moment before taking it.

They lightly shook as Dr. Kuhn said, "It's nice to meet you, Shannon."

CHAPTER FORTY-SEVEN

Shannon withdrew her hand, gasped for air, and had to stop herself from springing to her feet. She felt the earth move beneath her as a rush of adrenaline almost overwhelmed her. She closed her eyes, struggling to maintain composure.

Then, she heard Dr. Kuhn's voice, "I didn't mean to startle you, Shannon. I suppose I should explain."

Suddenly, Shannon opened her eyes, and with a determined voice said, "My name is not Shannon. It's Betty."

Dr. Kuhn sat back in the couch, trying to hide a smirk. "Betty, you say?"

"That's right. Me and my husband live in Georgia. We came to join The Power, but we're told they're not accepting new members now. So we snuck into the compound to see the Fuhrer's house. We just wanted to have a quick look inside, and then we were going to leave. But we got caught and now I'm here. I don't know who Shannon is."

"That's very interesting. Were you born and raised in Georgia?"

"Yes, I was." Shannon froze, realizing what she had done—or not done. She had completely forgotten about the accent, and was speaking to this woman in her normal voice. And now, she just admitted to being raised in Georgia.

She bit her lip, and looked at Dr. Kuhn, defeated. "That's amazing how you were able to develop a northern accent while living in the south your whole life."

"I...I...I forgot to mention that I went to college in Boston and lived in New England for a long time. I only recently moved back to Georgia."

"Of course you did," Dr. Kuhn said with a sardonic smile. "It's also interesting how you turned five shades of red and almost jumped out of your skin when I called you Shannon. Kind of strange behavior for a woman named Betty, don't you think?"

Shannon abruptly stood, unable to hide her exasperation, and said, "Look, my name is not Shannon. I told you, I'm Betty."

Dr. Kuhn also stood, her eyes swallowed up with anger. "I'm trying to be fair with you. But you're making it very difficult."

Shannon thought about giving up the lie and coming clean. If not for anything else, because she needed to know how this woman—and probably the Bald Man—knew who she was. But she couldn't because of Neil. For all she knew they had a knife to his throat somewhere, and were waiting for her to give up his identity before killing him.

No, she told herself. *No matter how obvious it is that I'm lying, I won't admit to it until I know Neil is safe.* "I'm telling the truth," she lied.

"Very well, then," Dr. Kuhn said as she strolled toward the front door. "We'll have to do what my colleague suggested."

"And what is that?"

"If you insist on saying that you came to join The Power, then we want you to prove it."

Shannon remembered the Bald Man's threat that she would have to kill the Jewish DJ. "Your bald friend already told me about that. And I'm not going to kill anyone."

"It's not quite that severe," she said as she opened the door. "Just follow me." Dr. Kuhn strutted to her Porsche as Shannon trailed a step behind. Ben stood by the SUV, but immediately strode toward Shannon after seeing her. "She'll ride with me, Ben."

"Are you sure?" Ben asked, looking puzzled as Shannon walked around the front of the car.

"She's fine. Just follow us."

Ben returned to his vehicle as Shannon settled into the passenger seat. She thought about running away, but knew the Bulldog would relentlessly track her down. Now wasn't the time.

As they pulled away, Shannon decided to try something. "So, who's this Shannon you think I am?"

Dr. Kuhn smiled so widely she almost giggled. "Are you trying to insult my intelligence?"

"What do you mean?"

"I know you're probably dying to know how I know you. But I won't be honest with you until you're honest with me." She glared at Shannon, as if she were waiting for a confession.

"I am being honest."

"Sure you are." After a few minutes, Dr. Kuhn stopped the car in front of a familiar sight: Aryan Hall. She turned off the car and smiled at Shannon. "Okay, honey, it's time to put up or shut up." Shannon watched the tall woman climb out of the tiny car. Before Shannon joined her, she noticed that the keys were left dangling from the ignition.

The moment she stepped out of the vehicle, Ben was by her side. Her heart raced as they approached the entrance, remembering the dogs. But they walked past the building, quickly making their way toward a much smaller grey-stone structure behind it.

Dr. Kuhn pushed open a heavy wooden door and was immediately confronted by a guard. She smiled at him and asked, "Where is he?"

"Right down those stairs, ma'am," the guard answered, pointing to another wooden door.

"Thank you," Dr. Kuhn replied and walked toward the door.

Shannon followed as she heard Ben speak to the guard. "You can take a break if you want. I'll be here for a little while."

"Thanks, buddy. I'll be back in fifteen."

Shannon heard Ben's footsteps behind her as she followed Dr. Kuhn down the steep stone staircase. The light got dimmer as they descended. When the stairs finally ended, they were in complete darkness.

Shannon heard a doorknob rattle, and then light was all around her. She saw Dr. Kuhn standing in a doorway, waving her inside. She stepped into the room, feeling the Bulldog's breath on the back of her neck. Inside the room, Kuhn stood there with her arms dramatically pointed at a wooden platform.

When Shannon saw what Kuhn was so playfully pointing at, her heart almost stopped. The wooden platform looked like an archaic operating table, about three feet off the ground with a dusty, old light fixture hanging above it. But what was on the platform was the sight that stole her breath.

The man was tall—at least six-foot three—and was so skinny that his ribs dented his naked torso. Shannon couldn't see his face until Dr. Kuhn spun the platform, rotating the man until he was facing her. Then, she stepped on the end of the platform, propping the poor soul up as if he were a side of beef being shown to a prospective buyer.

Now, Shannon could see his long black hair, gagged mouth, and terrified eyes. Dressed in only a pair of boxer shorts, his bony body trembled like a bed sheet on a breezy clothesline. His wrists and ankles were restrained to the platform by leather straps that seemed to be connected underneath the wooden structure.

Dr. Kuhn's eyes burned into Shannon as she flashed a sadistic smile. Shannon thought the wicked woman was trying to gauge her reaction to this horrific scene, so she bit her lip, balled her fists, and tried her best to not seem disturbed. But it got difficult when he started to moan. When Shannon focused on his face, he moaned louder, like he was desperately trying to say something through his gag.

"Quiet!" Dr. Kuhn said, authoritatively. But the man moaned louder, his neck protruding off the platform in Shannon's direction. Shannon fought the urge to help him, hoping he would quiet down and that they would leave the bizarre dungeon. But, then, things got worse.

Dr. Kuhn released the platform, snapping it back to its original position. "Shut up!" she yelled as the platform vibrated. But the man continued to moan as he squirmed in his tight restraints.

Then, to Shannon's horror, Kuhn lifted her right leg and planted her pointy Stiletto heel into the man's throat. Horrible choking sounds emitted from his gagged mouth, and his body convulsed as if he were being electrocuted.

Shannon sprang to the balls of her feet, but stopped herself before moving forward. She hoped it would be over before she had time to debate her actions. But when she saw the domineering woman's leg muscles flexing inside the black stocking, she thought his windpipe was about to collapse.

Shannon took a step forward and was about to speak when Dr. Kuhn mercifully lifted her heel off of his throat. She returned her foot to the ground as he gasped for air like a drowning man. Shannon froze, trying to hide the fact that she had stepped toward the table, as Dr. Kuhn flashed her green eyes at her.

Then, Kuhn turned away from her and leaned over the platform. Her nose almost touched his as she said, "Not another word." The man fell silent and his body stopped squirming as if he fell asleep—or died.

Dr. Kuhn turned away with a look of satisfaction. She reached under the platform and pulled out a wooden board and some rope. She turned her attention back to Shannon. "I bet you didn't think you were going to have this much fun today."

Shannon didn't know how to respond, and before she had the chance, Kuhn tossed the board and rope to Ben. "You know what to do."

Shannon turned toward Ben as he caught the board and rope. He walked to the wall and grabbed a key that hung off a nail. He inserted the key into the lock on the man's ankle restraints. After freeing his legs, he wedged the board between his ankles, and tied his ankles to either end of the board.

Ben returned the key to the wall, leaving the man's feet dangling over the board. After a couple of threatening glares from Dr. Kuhn, the man did not move. Then, Kuhn walked to the corner of the room and returned with an object that Shannon could not make out at first.

As Kuhn walked closer, she held the object out, and Shannon saw that it was a sledgehammer. *What do you want me to do with this?* she thought as she awkwardly took the rusty piece of metal.

"It's your lucky day," Dr. Kuhn said. "You get to show the Jew what you think of him."

The Jew? she said to herself, her sweaty palms gripping the weapon. "Is this the DJ?" she asked.

Kuhn smiled as she leaned on the platform. "Indeed it is. And I'm sure Betty from Georgia would love to break his ankles."

"What?"

"Ben was kind enough to put the Jew's ankles against the board. All you have to do is give each ankle a good solid hit."

Shannon understood what Kuhn said, but her mind was consumed by another thought. *If this is the Jewish DJ, then Neil and Peter have returned to the compound.* The realization that Neil was here somewhere made her muscles constrict.

She almost asked Kuhn where her friends were, but realized that the evil woman was not there to help her. She was only trying to coax her into a confession—probably because they wanted a rationale to kill Neil. But she would not give it to them—no matter what.

"So, Betty," Kuhn playfully pranced around the platform, "a girl who wants to join The Power should be thrilled to have this chance. You get to break the bones of one of The Power's worst enemies. A hell of a lot better than just getting to see the Fuhrer's house, don't you think?"

Shannon held the sledgehammer loosely in her sweaty palms. The idea of striking the heavy piece of steel into this poor man's ankles seemed unreal. But she knew it was being expected of her—or of Betty.

Ben put his big work boot on the end of the platform, propping up the DJ again. He leaned his leg across the DJ's knees, holding him in place. Kuhn strolled to Shannon's side. "Okay, Betty, give him your best shot."

Shannon felt the anxiety rising in her as she looked at the DJ's pitiful face. He was being quiet now, but she could see that he was screaming inside. There was an awkward moment of silence as she stood frozen with the hammer—all eyes studying her.

"What's wrong, Betty? This is a filthy Jew. You should take pleasure in this. Unless, of course, you're not really Betty from Georgia."

Shannon finally gripped the hammer tightly. Dr. Kuhn was practically breathing in her ear, taking pleasure in her obvious turmoil. Ben's huge body was clumsily stretched across the DJ's legs as the poor man's feet hung off the end of the board like snagged fish on a hook.

"Shannon," Kuhn's voice stabbed her soul. "Why don't you give up the façade? Tell me the truth, put the hammer down, and we'll go back to the guesthouse and talk. We'll forget this ever happened. You can finish your breakfast, and I'll tell you what you're dying to know."

She lowered the hammer, picturing the scene Kuhn described. She would much rather be on the couch of the guesthouse chewing on cold scrambled eggs than here, poised to break the ankles of an innocent man. Besides, she needed to know how this woman knew her name.

As she lowered the hammer, she remembered Neil. He was somewhere in the compound. Most likely under heavy guard—probably holed up in the same room she stayed in last night. She thought of the Bald Man going near him, holding a sharp knife to his throat, waiting to cut, waiting to get the word from Kuhn that she had cracked and spilled her guts.

The lower the hammer dropped, the wider Dr. Kuhn's smile expanded. As it was about to touch the floor, Shannon suddenly pulled it back up. She knew this was a trap. They were holding Neil, and were going to hurt him the moment she admitted who she was.

I won't give them what they want!

With a deep grunt, she snatched the powerful hammer above her head. Kuhn took a sudden step back, Ben tightened his grip on the legs, and the DJ released a loud moan. She paused for a moment, balancing the weighty metal above her head.

She looked down at the long, bony feet. "I'm sorry," she whispered.

In a moment that didn't seem real, she brought the hammer down.

CHAPTER FORTY-EIGHT

The boy didn't particularly like *People* magazine, but he was so happy to not be reading Nazi literature that he found himself enjoying the countless photos of pretty celebrities. He had a rare moment alone in the house, save the guards positioned outside each door. He took advantage of his privacy by sprawling across the couch, something that was normally not allowed.

When he put the magazine down, he looked up at the wall that held the gigantic framed painting of Adolph Hitler, the man they said was his grandfather. He looked at another wall and saw a framed photo of Hitler with Eva Braun, the woman they said was his grandmother. He thought she was pretty, and wondered if she were alive now—instead of back then—would she be pretty enough to be in *People*.

He tossed the magazine on the floor and thought of his home in Maine. He missed his parents, but also burned to know why they never told him about his grandparents. He knew some people thought they were bad, but Dr. Kuhn explained how they were just misunderstood. He felt like he should tell his parents about them, that he should tell them the things that Dr. Kuhn had taught him.

His thoughts did not stray from Dr. Kuhn when he heard the back door open. He hoped it was her. He hadn't seen her yet today, and he missed the fun of trying to peer up her short skirts. But when he sat up, the noises coming from the rear of the house let him know that it wasn't her.

The boy detested the wheezing and gasping that the strange, skinny man made. He always sounded like he was choking on his own phlegm. He had always been nice to the odd man, but now the disgusting noises were getting on his nerves.

"Your cheeseburger, french fries, and chocolate milkshake as you requested," Randolph said between long, labored breaths. He placed the boy's lunch on the coffee table and staggered away, trying to recover from the long walk inside.

"Why do you make those noises?" the boy asked as he started to rifle through his bag of fast food.

Randolph turned slowly, his pale, bony face now staring at the boy. "Do you really want to know?"

The boy chomped on his burger. "Yeah…I mean…it's

weird...those sounds that you make."

Randolph walked toward the boy and sat on the couch across from him. "Young man, do you know how old I am?"

"I have no idea."

"I am seventy-eight years old. But in 1939, I was ten."

"So what happened in 1939?"

"For a boy growing up in Berlin, Germany, a lot was happening."

The boy beamed with excitement. "Germany...1939? Did you know my grandparents?"

"Indeed I did, young man. Adolph Hitler saved my life."

The boy's mouth fell open, ketchup dripping off his lip. "He did? How?"

"Well, you see, I fell into an unfortunate set of circumstances at the time. My parents were friendly with two Jewish families, and I played with their children. Although we didn't know it at the time, Nazi guards were secretly abducting Jewish children."

"What? Why?"

"At the time, all the Jews in Berlin were being persecuted, and they were taking some Jewish children and giving them to the scientists."

"Giving them to scientists? For what?" He placed the burger down on the crinkled white bag.

"The Nazi scientists conducted experiments on live humans. The Jews, homosexuals, and the retarded were their main subjects. I was mistaken for a Jew, and taken to one of these experimental labs."

The boy was too intrigued to even glance down at his food as he asked, "What did they do to you?"

"We didn't know it at the time, but they were testing gas on us."

"Gas?"

"Noxious fumes, as they're known. They tested different types of gas and different doses."

"But didn't that kill the kids they tested it on?"

"It most certainty did. In fact, most of the children held in my camp died after the first round of experiments. I must have received a low dose because I lived. But as you can see and hear, I suffered serious pulmonary damage. It's gotten progressively worse as I've grown older, and I'm afraid that I'm near the end."

"But how did my grandfather save you?"

"I first saw the Fuhrer one afternoon when he was touring the testing facility. I had received my morning dose of test gas, and sat outside in the play yard. He walked through the yard, and for some reason, stopped to look at me. I told him, in my soft pathetic voice, that I was not a Jew and was taken by mistake. I was sure he would ignore me and walk away. But he didn't.

"He looked at me closely, and then called over the guards who brought me there. He questioned them for some time, and when he realized they were unsure of my identity, he began to scream at them. They scrambled and some of them brought him papers, but nothing satisfied him.

"It wasn't long before I was led away. And, to my surprise, I left in the Fuhrer's car. We drove for a long while and went into the mountains. He brought me to his famous home, which was called the Berghof. There, I met a wonderful woman named Eva Braun."

The boy's body tensed up as he leaned closer to Randolph. "My grandmother?" he said as if he were looking for confirmation that he actually was her grandson.

"Yes, indeed," he replied, folding his bony fingers in his lap. "Eva Braun was one of the loveliest people I've ever known. She took me into her home and made me comfortable. After a few days of being there, she gave me the news that my parents were also mistaken for Jews, and she did not know their whereabouts. It was years before I received confirmation of their death.

"As horrible as it was, I didn't blame Hitler or his mistress for my parents' deaths. They helped me as best they could. Eventually, I moved in with Martin Borman. He was the Fuhrer's private secretary, and had a fine home in the same mountain complex.

"After the war I escaped with him, and lived in South America. Later, as an adult, I made my way to America. But I never forgot what the Fuhrer did for me. I vowed my life to him.

"And when I met the courageous man who now runs The Power, I felt like I had stumbled upon Adolph Hitler all over again. A brave man, who also had the honor of being in the Fuhrer's presence. And that is how I ended up here, in complete servitude to the Fuhrer's vision."

"That's wild," the boy said, perched at the very end of the couch.

"But there's something I need to tell you," Randolph said as he leaned forward, his wide, dark eyes sticking into the boy like shards of glass. "They haven't told you everything."

The boy couldn't move. He stared at the sickly man, who gasped for air like a deflating tire. "What do you mean?" he asked in a shaky voice.

"It is not my place to say this." The boy could see that Randolph was shaking, his white hands trembling as if he were on a frozen tundra. "But I must speak the truth. Adolph Hitler saved my life and I am forever in his debt. I intend to do all I can to bring his ultimate vision to fruition. And that is why I must ask you to come downstairs with me."

"Go downstairs? For what?"

"Young man, I implore you to not discuss this with the others. But there is something that you and I must do."

CHAPTER FORTY-NINE

Shannon focused on her target as the sledgehammer came down. And as it skimmed over the DJ's ankle, she realized that her aim was perfect. The head of the hammer landed so squarely in the Bulldog's groin that the impact knocked Shannon off balance, sending her sprawling to the ground.

But, even as she fell, she watched the heat rise to his face, swarming him with red blotches. When his mouth opened, Shannon only heard an abrupt exhale of air before he collapsed to the ground like a boneless slab of flesh.

She popped back to her feet with the verve of a boxer who was embarrassed to be knocked down, and grabbed the hammer. She saw that Dr. Kuhn was standing motionless, her mouth hanging open in disbelief. Knowing the opportunity to strike the frozen woman was fleeting, she reared back and nailed her in the center of the chest.

Kuhn's feet came out from under her, her spiked heels flying into the air as she hit the ground. Shannon spun around, fearing the Bulldog was back on his feet. Her adrenaline caused her to scream as she wielded the hammer like a crazed Samurai. But the large man was still on the ground, harmlessly curled up in the fetal position.

She heard the now familiar moaning emitting from Carl's gagged mouth. She stepped in front of him and raised the hammer over her head. He moaned at a pitch she had not previously heard as she dropped the hammer.

She connected with the center of the wood, splitting it into two. With his legs now free, she dropped the hammer and grabbed the key that was hanging on the wall. She quickly unlocked his wrists, and then ripped the gag out of his mouth.

Surprisingly, he continued to scream, his pale body trembling like a leaf in a strong wind. "We have to get out of here!" Shannon yelled at him as she glanced at their two enemies, who still lay injured on the floor.

But Carl didn't move; he continued to scream in a frenzied panic. Lost for another solution, Shannon grabbed the hysterical man by his wrist. She started to pull him off the table, but he squirmed free. He slumped back against the table, apparently not following Shannon's cue that they should leave immediately.

Wearing nothing but boxer shorts, she knew his hair was the only reliable thing to grab onto. She grabbed a fistful of his curly black mane and dragged him to the exit. Still screaming, he followed with a slow trot that barely kept up with her pace.

She rushed them up the stairs and into the atrium of the stone building. Shannon was happy to see that the guard the Bulldog relieved was not back yet. With the rope and broken pieces of wood dragging behind him, Shannon continued to haul the frantic man out of the building.

When they reached the Porsche, Shannon opened the passenger door with one hand and shoved the lanky man inside with the other. She slammed the door shut, ran around the car, and jumped inside. Carl was still screaming, a tangled mess of bony legs and arms.

"Would you shut up!" she screamed. She was happy to see the keys still in the ignition and started the car.

Finally, he was quiet. He stared at her with a confused face. "Who are you?"

"I'm saving you, asshole!" She punched the accelerator, and they were off. Unsure of where the road led, Shannon decided to go out the same way they came in, albeit over a hilly unpaved terrain.

Shannon and Carl bounced up and down like they were strapped to the back of a bucking bronco. She let up a little on the gas when she had to dodge patches of trees, but kept them moving so fast that she avoided eyeing the speedometer, afraid of what she might see.

A small boulder appeared too quickly for Shannon to steer around, and one side of the car became airborne as they sailed over it.

"Slow down, you crazy bitch!" Carl yelled, his near-naked body squirming with anxiety in the leather seat.

Shannon's angry eyes attacked him. "Would you rather go back into that dungeon?"

"Watch it!" Carl's screamed in terror as they soared over a hill. The hard landing convinced Shannon to slow down a bit. But as she did, the sudden appearance of the road ahead exhilarated her. With no apparent obstacles in their path, Shannon slammed the accelerator again.

As their speed reached a new high, Carl pointed ahead with a trembling hand. "Slow down," he muttered, mesmerized by the sight in front of them.

Shannon saw a group of people in the distance, and as they drew closer, she realized they were Aryan guards stationed at the border of the compound. "They have guns," Carl pointed out in a terrified voice.

She studied the men, confirming that they indeed had weapons. The few possible options danced through Shannon's brain. But she knew there was only one choice.

"Hang on," she said as she glanced at Carl, his eyes wide as a lake. "We're going through them."

"What?" he screamed. As she steered the car toward the center of the group, he tried to duck below the dashboard, his knees and elbows awkwardly jutting out in all directions.

As they sped closer, Shannon saw some of the men training their rifles at the vehicle—a deadly game of chicken was underway. Shannon gambled that they wouldn't fire and held her course.

Just as the details of their faces came into view, they scattered like field mice in front of a tractor. The Porsche zipped past them and glided over the small hill at the end of the property. As Shannon tried to turn the vehicle onto the road, she realized they were traveling too fast and smacked against a stone wall across the street.

The car rebounded back into the street, and Shannon was able to regain control. She realized that the vehicle had sustained some damage when she heard the sound of metal scraping against concrete.

Aware she was dragging something, she punched the accelerator anyway, desperate to get away from the compound. "Something's wrong with the car," Carl said, finally sticking his head above the dash.

"Don't worry about the car," she yelled, anxiously glaring into the rear view window. "They may come after us."

Then, out of nowhere, a police siren blared, and there was a car behind them. Shannon saw that it was an unmarked vehicle with a siren on the dash. Skeptical for a moment, she thought about outrunning the car, but the dragging metal and hope that it was a legitimate officer convinced her to pull over.

She pulled the car to the side of the road, listening to Carl pant like a dog on a hundred-degree day. They turned and saw a man in a blue suit approaching the Porsche. "Who is that?" Carl asked.

"Hell if I know," Shannon answered.

The man stopped in front of Shannon's door and said, "Step out of the car, please."

Shannon froze, unsure if it was safe. A few seconds passed, and then she heard something she could not believe: her name.

"Shannon," the voice said. The man leaned close to the window. "Please get out of the car."

Shannon looked at the man's face in shock. Then, he opened a thin leather wallet, revealing an ID. The words "Federal Bureau of Investigation" jumped out at her. She looked at the man again, and realized he looked familiar.

Her eyes darted back to the ID, and then back to his face.

The FBI?

She remembered the day she got the threatening e-mail, and called the FBI. She studied his face again to be sure. But then she knew. This man was Brad Palmer, the FBI agent who had come to her house.

CHAPTER FIFTY

The office was empty save a desk with a laptop computer and a black briefcase leaning against it. Shannon sat in the only chair—a leather swivel type—and rolled it over to the window. She strained her neck, trying to see the Coeur D'Alene street below.

She wanted to see if Brad was handing Carl over to the local police, like he had told her. But there was no sign of them. She thought about Neil's frantic warnings the day Brad showed up at her door. He believed Brad was with The Power. She knew if that were true, then Carl was not with the police but on his way back to the Aryan compound.

Her suspicions deepened as she glanced around the empty room. *Why would the FBI have an empty office?* She could think of only one thing: *This may be my only chance to get away.*

She sprang to her feet and decided to run. She moved quickly to the room's only door and opened it. But before she could step out, she heard footsteps coming up the stairs. She closed the door and stepped back; a moment later Brad was in the room.

"You can rest easy now," he said, catching his breath. "Mr. Fineman is in the hands of the Coeur D'Alene police department."

"I was looking out the window. I didn't see a police car."

"We were in the front of the building. You can only see the side out this window."

Shannon's eyes darted toward the window and then back at Brad as she contemplated the possibility of what he said. "I need to ask you something, Brad."

"Fire away." His hands folded innocently in front of him.

"Do you honestly expect me to believe this is an FBI office? There's nothing here."

"I never said this was an FBI office. I said this is where I was working."

"So you're not really with the FBI?"

"What?" His face crinkled into a worried expression. "What are you talking about? Our closest field office is in Spokane. We're just renting this place so I have a place to work while I'm here."

"I don't understand. If you have no field office around here, then why are you here?"

He stared at her with a puzzled look. "Shannon, I've been looking for you."

"What? Why?"

"Why?" he shot back as if it were the most ridiculous question he had ever heard. "You were kidnapped from your home and held prisoner in the compound of a terrorist organization."

"Wait. That's not entirely true. I was held against my will in the compound, but I wasn't kidnapped from my home. I left of my own free will."

"Listen, Shannon..."

"In fact, the man I left with is also being held in the compound. I'm very worried about him, so you should start working on a way to rescue him too."

"Shannon—"

"His name is Neil Henry. He's the grandson of my only neighbor on my street. His grandfather was kidnapped by The Power, and they killed him in Ecuador—"

"Shannon, please stop."

She started at him impassively, her eyes soaking in his confounded face. "What is it?"

"There are many things you don't understand."

"It seems to me there are many things that *you* don't understand. That's why I'm trying to get you up to speed."

He sighed as if he regretted what he was about to say. "Believe me, Shannon, I'm up to speed. Listen, I've got to tell you something. Why don't you have a seat?"

He walked to the window, and swung the chair in her direction. She swallowed hard, her dry throat in need of water as she sat in the chair.

"I'm not really sure how to tell you this," he said softly and leaned against the window sill.

"Tell me what?"

"The one unknown to us in this case was what you were thinking. We had no way of knowing what you were aware of and what you weren't."

"What do you mean by that?"

"Well, I see now that you're very fond of Neil."

"We've become very close since we met."

"That's why it's difficult to tell you this."

"Please just tell me."

"Okay." He paused, focusing on her eyes. "Neil is a high ranking member in The Power."

CHAPTER FIFTY-ONE

Shannon's feet plowed through the green grass, the dew wetting her sneakers and tickling her ankles. As she ran, she looked up at the towering mountains that circled the green pasture, a rocky ring of protection from the outside world. Ensuring that this little piece of earth was Shannon's. And she designated it only for play.

She dove into the cushy ground as if it were a swimming pool, and took delight in skimming across the surface. When she rolled over, the sunbeam—sharp as a splinter—forced her to squint. With her eyes half closed, she let the smell engulf her, the smell of childhood.

She could hear them in the distance, but the sun prevented her from seeing anything more than two figures moving toward her. Behind them was some sort of house, surrounded by the wonderful greenness of the land. But beyond that, she could not see.

The jolt of the plane making contact with the tarmac interrupted her dream, and the sound of the squealing brakes instantly returned her to consciousness. Confused, she looked around but saw nothing but the seatbacks in front of her and Brad's face, studying her.

"You okay?" he asked with a half smile.

"I was dreaming."

"Oh yeah? Something good I hope."

"It's just this dream that I've had before...it's nothing."

"Feel good to be back on the east coast?" he asked as the plane came to a complete stop.

"I'm not sure," she replied, glancing around the crowded plane. The hurried voices mixed together like the buzz of an angry beehive. A bell rang, an unintelligible voice said something over the speaker, and the crowd jumped to their feet. As Shannon was still rubbing the sleep out of her eyes, the herd thundered past her toward the exit.

"Good thing we didn't check any bags," Brad said as he elbowed his way to the overhead compartment. "We'll be out of here in a flash." He grabbed his bag and stepped into their row to avoid the swarming crowd.

A few minutes later, the plane was empty. Brad extended his hand to Shannon. She took it and he helped her out of her seat. "Where are we going again?" she asked, stepping into the aisle.

"First thing in the morning we're going to my office."

"You mean the FBI office?"

"That's right."

"But what about tonight? Where are we going now?"

"We can make a pit stop at my place."

"Your place?" They made their way through the tunnel.

"That's right. I have an apartment in the city. You can crash in the spare room...if you want."

"Is this what the FBI normally does?"

"Of course not. I just thought you'd be more comfortable there instead of a hotel room, especially after what you've been through. But if you'd prefer..."

"That's all right, Brad. We'll go to your place." She wasn't crazy about the idea of sleeping in Brad's apartment, but she didn't care enough to insist on a hotel. Besides, she preferred that Brad make all her decisions, as she couldn't concentrate on anything except Neil's betrayal.

Her heart spun like a top as she pictured his face, and heard his lies. *How could I have believed him?*

Brad was all smiles as he led her to his car. They were silent during the ride, the low jazzy music faintly coming through the speakers the only sound. Brad aggressively drove with the confidence of a local, and got them to his neighborhood in downtown Boston in just a few minutes.

They parked on the street, walked two blocks to the brick building, thumped up three flights, and entered his apartment. "It's not the Taj Mahal," he said and flicked on a light, revealing a modest but neat two-bedroom apartment. "But hopefully it will do for the night."

"Thanks," she said as she collapsed on the couch. Still, she could think only of Neil. She hadn't questioned Brad much after he dropped the bombshell on her. But now that she had a chance to think about it, she wanted to know details.

"How do you know that Neil is in The Power?"

He stepped out of the kitchen and walked toward her. He held a tall, skinny bottle of Grey Goose vodka in one hand and a glass with ice in the other. "I'm going to have some of this on the rocks. Do you want any?"

"No thanks. But I really want you to tell me what you know about Neil."

He poured a couple of shots into the glass as he said, "I'll tell you everything. I just thought a drink might make it easier for you to handle."

"All right, then. I'll have a little, but with a mixer."

"Orange juice okay?"

"That's fine."

Brad left his glass on the coffee table and disappeared into the kitchen for a moment. When he returned, he held her drink and a file of paperwork. He sat across from her, handed her the drink, and opened the file.

"First off," he said and then paused to take a slug of the vodka, "he told you that he was the grandson of your elderly neighbor?"

"Yes."

"Well, he's not."

"But he was in his house. He was worried about him. He was there to look for him."

"Efran Heinman, or Mr. Henry as you knew him, was involved with a Nazi hunter group in Austria. He was an enemy of The Power. They were looking for him, found him, and murdered him. That's why Neil was in his house. He's probably the one that did it."

"But Neil has the same last name as him."

"You sure about that?" Brad slid a document in front of her. She picked it up and saw a photocopy of a driver's license. The picture on it was Neil's. But the name read Neil Franklin.

Her heart skipped a beat as she gasped. "That can't be."

He handed her photocopies of other documentation that identified Neil as Neil Franklin. "He lied to you about everything. Even his name."

"But what about the New England Law Center?"

Brad chortled and said, "There's no such thing."

"But what about the lawsuits he told me about? The KKK being sued and everything else."

"That may be true, but he didn't have anything to do with that. And neither did the New England Law Center because they don't exist."

"I don't understand...this can't be true. He had a plane and a pilot and—"

"All that belongs to The Power. I know this is hard to believe." Brad paused and reached under the coffee table. He pulled out a thick phone book. "You said that Neil told you the New England Law Center was located in Boston, right?"

"Yes."

"Well, we're in Boston now. And this is a Boston phone book. So if this law firm exists, then it should have a listing in here, right?"

"I suppose so."

Brad handed her the phone book. "All right, then. Look it up."

Shannon held the book in her sweaty palms. She placed it on the table and thumbed through the yellow pages until she found the listings for law firms. Her eyes scanned the pages until she found the Ns. She placed her finger on the page to hold her place as she looked away.

It had better be here, she thought to herself as she exhaled a nervous breath and took a long sip of her drink.

CHAPTER FIFTY-TWO

After finishing her third drink, she finally felt like she could sleep. Brad, who drank twice as much as her, was now snoring in the recliner. When she couldn't find the listing for the New England Law Center in the phone book, he allowed her to poke through the file he kept on Neil.

She found documents and a few pictures all relating to Neil Franklin and his suspected criminal activity. The contents of the file told her that the FBI believed he was a member of The Power—and a high ranking one. They suspected he was involved in several hate crimes, and even investigated him in connection with the Oklahoma City bombing.

Shannon remembered Neil telling her about some well-known white supremacists, as some of these names jumped off the pages at her. Richard Butler. Robert Matthews. Matt Hale. According to the documents in front of her, Neil knew, and in some cases learned from, these infamous men. She read the name of the book he had told her about, *The Turner Diaries,* and its author William Pierce. The page she read explained that Neil Franklin was a student of Pierce and a devout follower of his book.

The shock of her friend's betrayal was starting to subside as a wave of rage engulfed her. *I was so stupid!* She slammed the file onto the table and angrily thrust herself against the back of the couch.

Various memories flashed through her brain and increased her rage. Forcing her to hide from the FBI should have been enough to tip her off. Haphazardly rushing into the Aryan Nation Compound with no plan, and quickly getting caught was suspicious as well. But she should have known for sure when she saw the DJ. Who but a hardened criminal could kidnap an innocent man?

A sensation of nausea consumed her as she pictured his face. He was charming, believable, and handsome. Yet, still, she should have seen through him, she thought. She should have been smarter. She knew now that his ultimate plan was to deliver her to the Aryan Compound while maintaining his cover. Their separation after being abducted was just a rehearsed production.

But still, she needed to know why. *How do they know me? And what do they want from me?* She wondered if Brad knew these answers as she looked at her snoring host. He had quaffed his six vodkas and passed out before she had the chance to ask him these questions.

His sleep seemed far too deep to hope that their conversation would continue tonight. She stretched out on the couch and fluffed the pillow under her head. She knew she needed a good night's sleep, and hoped the alcohol had numbed her brain enough to allow her some rest.

She adjusted her position on the couch until she was comfortable. She lay motionless, her tense muscles slowly relaxing. As she stared ahead, she saw something in the corner of the room that she had not noticed previously. It was a computer on a small table. She thought of her e-mail and how wonderful it would be to connect with a part of her normal world, if only for a few minutes.

She sat up and saw that Brad was no closer to consciousness. She assumed he had an internet connection, and knew that was all she needed to check her mail. *I'm sure he wouldn't mind,* she thought and bounced off the couch.

She sat in the rickety wooden chair, positioned herself in front of the computer, and hit the power button. The familiar booting-up sound was like the comforting voice of an old friend. She smiled, sat back in the chair, and waited for the machine to load its operating system.

As she leaned back, her foot bumped against a box under the table. Curious, she pulled the box out and looked inside. She saw a smaller box that read: "Spy Tool Phone Tapper." She opened the box and found a tiny black chip with two minuscule wires coming out of it.

She was surprised he would keep such a device in his home, thinking government property would have to be kept at the FBI office. Then she saw another box that read: "Spy Tool Phone Manager." She read the back of the box and saw that the equipment could be attached to a phone and allow the user to monitor incoming and outgoing calls from a remote location.

She pulled out a third box, which read: "Spy Tool Phone Call Redirector." Again, she read the back of the box and learned that this device worked as an accessory to the Phone Manager and would automatically redirect outgoing phone calls to a different phone when certain numbers were dialed. *Amazing technology,* she thought as she placed the equipment back into the box and slid it back under the table with her foot.

She looked at the monitor and saw that the computer was now ready to go. She was pleased to see that he had a high-speed Internet connection and knew it would be easy to check her mail. She would have to simply open his web browser, go to her ISP's web site, and sign into her e-mail account.

When she clicked on the browser's icon, Brad's e-mail screen automatically loaded. "Woops," she said quietly, "I didn't mean to do that." She tried to close the screen but had to wait for it to fully load.

Again, she sat back and waited. A few seconds later Brad's e-mail inbox was on the screen. She moved the cursor to the black X in the upper right hand corner. She was about to close the screen when something caught her eye.

She saw some of the e-mails he had waiting for him, but this isn't what drew her attention. At the top of the screen was the word "Welcome" followed by Brad's e-mail address. At first it meant nothing to her, but then, the small black letters screamed the truth.

It read: "Altman42089."

CHAPTER FIFTY-THREE

As the sight of Brad's e-mail burned into her brain, she tried to move but her feet were stuck to the ground like a deep-rooted plant. Even if she could move, she couldn't take her eyes off the computer screen. *Brad sent me that e-mail!*

Just as she was starting to accept the idea of Neil's betrayal, everything changed—again. Or did it? *What does this actually mean?* she wondered. *Does this mean Brad is in The Power? And if so, what about Neil?*

She glanced over her shoulder and saw that he was still in an alcohol-induced coma. She tried to come to terms with her predicament, but not everything made sense. *If Brad is in The Power, why didn't he return me to the compound?* She saw documentation that proved Neil had lied to her. And it appeared that the New England Law Center didn't really exist. *What does all this mean?*

She considered waking up Brad and demanding an explanation. But then she remembered the fear that consumed her when she read the threatening e-mail that apparently came from him. She could finally move her feet, and swung her legs over the side of the chair. As she did, she grazed the box under the table.

She thought of the equipment inside of it, and then realized what had happened. She knew he probably had tapped her phone, monitored her calls, and programmed her outgoing calls to any law enforcement agency to be redirected to his phone. After he received her call, he pretended to be with the FBI and came to her house.

This realization was enough to make her jump up in a panic. Despite his drunken sleep, she felt in immediate danger. *I have to get out of here now!* Suddenly, her once immobile feet now scurried to the door as quickly as if the apartment were on fire.

She bounded down the stairs and burst through the double glass doors, her knees buckling as she staggered onto the dark street. As her naked feet hit the concrete, she remembered kicking off her shoes before sprawling on the couch. But it didn't matter. She wasn't going back.

She took off down the moonless street, the occasional streetlight her only guide in the residential neighborhood. She had no destination in mind; just a need to get as far away from Brad Palmer's apartment as possible.

After running awhile, she slowed down to a quick walk and started to think about her situation. She needed to find a phone. She assumed she would eventually stumble upon an open business. Maybe a bar, an all-night diner, an early morning bakery. She was in a big city, and knew it wouldn't be long before she found something.

The perplexing question was: who would she call? Who could help her? She thought of Neil, and her head swam in confusion. Before she could do anything else, she had to know the truth about him. She knew this would not be easy, but since she was in Boston, she planned to at least find out if the New England Law Center existed or not.

The street came to an end, and she looked both ways down the intersecting road. She saw some lights flickering from one of the buildings and thought it would be worth investigating. So she set off in the direction of the lights as the cool April air started to numb her naked toes.

As she drew almost close enough to see the source of the lights, something rumbled behind her. She turned with a start and saw a black sedan moving up the road. At first, she thought nothing of it, moved to the sidewalk, and returned her attention to the lights.

But the vehicle slowed as it crept behind her. As Shannon glanced back at it, she felt eyes studying her. It couldn't be Brad, she knew, but it seemed someone was interested in her. She hoped she was wrong, and knew there was only one way to find out.

As she passed a brick building—probably apartments, she thought—she dashed down the alley alongside it. Her feet stung as she hustled over the pavement, sand, and sharp little pebbles that bit into the bottom of her feet. At the end of the alley was a chain link fence, which she dove over like an athlete finishing an obstacle course.

She landed on her right shoulder and rolled over on her stomach, suddenly motionless as an opossum. As she lay there, watching the black sedan slowly move by, she thought she was probably overreacting. Most likely this vehicle was just looking for an address, and didn't even notice her. If this were true, then the car would soon be on its way down the road.

As it passed, she breathed a sigh of relief. *I'm just being paranoid.* She was reassured that no one was looking for her, except maybe Brad, but he would be out for several more hours. She stood up and brushed herself off, and realized she was in the small backyard of an apartment complex.

She looked around, hoping no one was spying on her foolish behavior, and put one foot on the fence. *Stop being stupid and find a phone,* she told herself as she prepared to hop the fence. But before she pulled herself over, she saw motion on the street.

Both feet were back on the pavement as she crouched behind the fence. She saw a car slowly moving in reverse. Trying not to be paranoid, she told herself it wasn't the black sedan. No one was looking for her. It was just a car backing into a driveway.

Suddenly, the car stopped, and in a split second she could tell it was indeed the same black sedan. Then, the entire alleyway lit up. Someone was shining a powerful spotlight, and Shannon was caught in the middle of it.

She dashed out of the light like a nimble animal escaping its prey, and ran across the small yard. She hopped over the fence and into the yard of the neighboring apartment building. After landing, she stumbled a few steps and collapsed onto the grass.

She looked up another alley and saw the car move up the road, the spotlight dancing just above her. Whoever was there had seen her, and seemed intent on finding her. As the light steadied on the alley that led to her new location, she knew it was now time to run.

She charged ahead, hopping fences and scampering behind buildings in a blind panic. She darted between children's toys and garbage cans, ran through vegetable gardens, and ducked under low-hanging branches. She didn't look at the road. She didn't need to; she knew they were trying to track her.

Her furious effort halted when she came upon a tall brick wall. She leaned against it, doubled over, desperately gasping in the cold night air. She finally looked around and saw the row of apartment buildings that she had just run behind. For now, she felt safe as she saw no sign of the black sedan.

Seeing no easy way over the wall, she considered sneaking up the alley and taking off down the road. She took two slow steps toward the alley, her feet now screaming in pain. The neighborhood was still silent with no activity. She wasn't sure how far she had run, but maybe it was far enough to lose the car for good.

As her breathing returned to normal, she stood up straight and moved toward the alley, ignoring the agonizing pain emitting from her feet. Just as she reached the end of the alley, she heard tires screech. The black sedan flew by the road in reverse, and suddenly slammed on its brakes.

Did they see me again? she wondered as she dove for the ground and rolled against the side of the building. Once again, the alley was illuminated. But this time Shannon lay motionless, possibly in clear view. She knew if she jumped up and ran they would see her for sure, so she stayed—and prayed they wouldn't spot her.

She could only see the light, not daring to turn her head to get a look at the car. She knew if the light went off, then she would be in the clear. But if it didn't, how long should she wait? A few seconds passed that seemed like hours as the light stayed on.

Finally, she heard a car door slam. It was enough of a signal; she had to get away. She jumped to her feet, and without looking back, ran back to the yard. She heard footsteps behind her, and wondered how many were chasing her.

She could run back the way she came, but wanted to get over the wall, hoping the other side would lead her to safety. She ran toward it with no plan. She desperately scanned the area for anything that might help launch her over the high barrier. Then she saw it: a swing set.

She shimmied up one of the poles until she reached the top. She stood on it and tried to calculate the length of the jump to the wall. But as the rushing footsteps closed in on her, she knew she had no choice. She would either make it or not.

She used all her strength to propel herself through the air, and almost cleared the wall entirely. She landed squarely on the top of it, gasping in pain as her torso made contact with the brick structure. She rolled to her right, falling over the other side.

Her landing was less painful than she'd expected. She realized she had landed on something soft. She opened her eyes, but it was her nose that told her what she landed on: a pile of garbage.

She saw the Dumpster a few feet in front of her, and the overflowing mess that spilled out of it. As she stood up on her knees, she realized she was in the center of the disgusting refuse. Then, she felt something move beneath her feet, heard a squeak, and saw a small furry thing scurry away.

She screamed in horror and jumped away from the Dumpster in an instant. Her giant strides carried her into some sort of parking lot as her hands furiously brushed her body as if she were swatting away an army of attacking insects. She lost her balance and toppled forward onto the concrete—her knees taking the brunt of the impact. She bounced back to her feet, and noticed her now ripped jeans.

She looked around and saw the back of a building—most likely the building giving off the lights, she assumed. It took her only a moment to realize that it was some sort of restaurant. She dashed toward the back entrance, sneaking a peek over her shoulder at the wall, but saw no sign of her pursuers.

She burst through the door faster than she intended, and once again fell forward. When she looked up, she a small barroom with about twenty men. They were all white, in their fifties and sixties, and had matching beer bellies. Their mouths hung open as they stared at her in disbelief.

The bartender pushed up the swing gate and cautiously moved near her. "Lady, are you all right? Do you want me to call a cop?"

She looked at the twenty bewildered faces, and wished Neil was with her. She had to know the truth. "No," she said as she stood up, noticing her bloody feet and knees. "I need a lawyer."

CHAPTER FIFTY-FOUR

Shannon's hand was trembling as she brought the rocks glass to her lips. As soon as the Scotch made contact with her tongue, she recognized it as Johnny Walker Black. "That okay, miss?" the bartender said, hovering over her. "It's the best we have."

Her hand slid down to her right pants pocket and felt for her wallet. After not finding it in any of her pockets, she remembered the Aryan guards confiscating it when she was taken prisoner in the compound. *Oh shit!*

"I don't have any money to pay for this. I lost my wallet."

"Don't worry about it, miss," the bartender said. "It's on the house. We're just glad you're okay. You look like you been through some trouble."

The bartender's eyes darted down to the trickling blood collecting around her naked feet. "I'm so sorry," she blurted out and stood up. "I'm making a mess of your place."

"Don't worry. Please. Sit down." He gently put his hand on her shoulder and guided her back into the chair. "We got a mop bucket. We'll take care of it."

The back door opened and a stocky, gray-haired man stepped inside, slightly out of breath. He held up a cell phone in his right hand and said with a smile, "My son-in-law will be here in five minutes."

"Louie's son-in-law is a lawyer. You want to see a lawyer, right?" the bartender asked.

"That's right. Yes. Thank you for calling."

"You sure you want a lawyer and not a cop?" the bartender asked.

"I know this must seem very unusual. But I need to talk to someone who's familiar with the law firms here in Boston."

Louie stepped forward. "My son-in-law has worked for one of the biggest firms in the city for almost five years. Tyler, Reed, and Stevens, or something like that. I bet he'll be able to help you."

"I appreciate you calling him."

The bartender slipped back behind the bar as the patrons stood in a half-circle, gawking at Shannon as if she were on display in a zoo. She looked back at them with an uncomfortable smile and sipped her drink.

The bartender returned with a dust-encrusted first aid kit. He handed the hard plastic case to Shannon. "Here. There might be something in there for your cuts."

"Thank you."

Shannon pried open the ancient case and thumbed through the contents. She used some gauze to soak up the blood from her knees, and cleaned her feet. As she applied some antibiotic ointment and Band-Aids, she was surprised to see that the men had not moved an inch.

She saw two dartboards, which appeared to have games in progress, a few tables with scattered playing cards and poker chips, and many half-drunk mugs of beers strewn around the room. Yet, still, they stood motionless as trees.

As each second passed, the eyeballs of her beer-bellied onlookers crawled over her like ants. She was about to say something when the door opened, and in strode a short skinny man in his late forties. He wore leather boots, jeans, and a long overcoat, which was buttoned snuggly.

"Okay, who's in trouble?" he said as he slapped his gloved hands together and looked around the crowd.

"This is my son-in-law, Christopher," Louie said, smiling at Shannon.

Christopher immediately looked at her, realizing she was the reason he was here. He glanced around the bar with a confused face. "What's going on? Is she being arrested?"

"Arrested?" Louie said, surprised.

"You told me someone needed legal help. Usually that means someone is in trouble with the law." His eyes scanned her from top to bottom. "She looks like she needs a nurse, not a lawyer."

"I'm sorry," Shannon offered, meeting eyes with Christopher. "I need some information about a law firm here in Boston."

Christopher's eyes widened as if he had been kicked in the groin. "You what?" he said loudly, his nostrils flaring. Shannon didn't answer, but simply stared back at him. "It's midnight. I was home with my family, getting ready for bed." His angry eyes bounced between Shannon and Louie. "You called me down here at this hour because some law student is looking for a job?"

"I'm not a law student."

Christopher's head snapped in her direction. "Then what do you want from me?"

"It's extremely important that I get some information right away."

"Information?" he scoffed. "If you're not about to be busted, then this could have waited till tomorrow."

"No, it couldn't," she shot back. The men toggled their heads between the two as if they were watching a tennis match.

"What could be so important?" Christopher asked as he threw his arms up in frustration.

"Do you know the New England Law Center?" Shannon asked.

Christopher's face changed from anger to shock. He studied

Shannon with a much more inquisitive glare. His eyes darted toward Louie and the bartender as he asked, "Who is this girl?"

"We don't know," Louie said, defensively. "She just walked in off the street."

Shannon sprang to her feet. "You've heard of them," she said excitedly, pointing at Christopher. "You know the firm."

"Hold on," Christopher said, raising his hand. He looked at the bartender. "Is there a place I can talk with her in private?"

"Sure thing," the bartender replied. "There's the office."

"Let's go."

A moment later, Shannon found herself in a small, cluttered office, sitting in a wobbly metal chair. Christopher simultaneously kicked the door closed and snapped open a folding chair, which he promptly sat on. He settled in the chair before he spoke. "Who are you?"

"My name is Shannon Dinardo. I live in Connecticut."

There was an awkward pause as Christopher gestured at her, expecting more. "And...why are you asking about the New England Law Center?"

"It would take me a while to explain everything. I really just need to know if they exist. And if they do, I'd like a phone number or an address."

Christopher rubbed his temples as if he had a migraine headache. His now blood-shot eyes focused on her. "What organization are you with?"

"Organization?" she shot back, puzzled. "I'm not with an organization. I just need to know for myself."

He drew in a slow breath, leaned forward, and said, "What do you know about them?"

Shannon popped up from her chair. "That means they exist. You know who they are," she said as her feet almost left the ground.

"Yes. Yes. They exist. But please, sit." He gestured for her to return to her seat and she did. "I really don't know much about them. Except for the nature of their work. Which is why I'd like to know your reason for asking."

"Oh," Shannon replied with a sudden look of realization. "You want to make sure I'm not a member of the KKK or something."

Christopher closely examined her and then nodded. "I guess you could say that."

"Let me reassure you that I'm not a white supremacist. In fact, my friend Neil and I were trying to stop the plans of an Aryan group called The Power."

Christopher's body shivered and his face lit up as if a block of ice had slid down the back of his pants. "You've been trying to stop the plans of The Power? Then you must mean...you mean Neil Franklin."

Shannon's heart turned over. The name Neil Franklin stung with betrayal. "Have you ever heard of anyone named Neil Henry?" she asked.

"Henry? No, I don't know anyone by that name. But Neil Franklin is very well known in the Boston legal community. And so is the New England Law Center."

She had the basic information that she wanted. For the most part, she felt tremendously relieved, but the fact that Neil was not known as Neil Henry disturbed her. "I need to find their office immediately. Can you help me? They're not in the phone book."

"The phone book?" He held back a laugh. "You're not going to find them in the phone book."

"Why not?"

"I should mention that I don't know any of this first hand, but the NELC is a bit of a legend here in Boston. They've been battling the white supremacist groups as long as those groups have been around. I've heard that they once had a building on Comm Ave, but the building was bombed in the seventies.

"Now, I've heard they have a mobile office that they move from site to site. They keep on the move, so they can't be located by the wrong people. You have to be in their inner circle to know how to find them. So, I don't know if I can be of much help getting you an address."

"I don't understand something," Shannon said. "How can a law firm get clients if no one can find them?"

"They don't take clients who walk in off the street. They usually only handle civil rights cases and high-profile ones. They hear about potential cases and they contact the clients if they're interested. But their main purpose is to thwart the efforts of white supremacist groups. That's what made them famous."

"What do you know about Neil Franklin?"

"Not much. I've never met him, just heard about him. I think he's the head of the NELC, or is at least one of the top guys. I think I heard that his father—or maybe it was his grandfather—founded the firm and he took it over. But didn't you say you know Neil?"

"I spent the last several days with him."

"Then why are you asking me about him? I don't know the guy from Adam."

"We were taken prisoner in the Aryan Nation compound and then got separated."

"What?" Christopher almost fell off the end of his chair.

"I managed to escape and a man saying he was an FBI agent picked me up and flew me here. But I figured out that he wasn't really with the FBI. He told me some things about Neil, and I just needed to find out if they were true or not."

"Listen, I'm no expert. Don't go by what I have to say."

"But you are positive that the New England Law Center exists, right?"

"Yes. That I do know."

"That's the most important fact that I needed. I'll figure out a way to find their office." Shannon stood up. "Thank you, Christopher. You've been a great help. I'll let you get back to your family."

He stood and shook her hand. "Hold on. You said this guy pretending to be an FBI agent flew you here. Do you have a place to stay? Or a car?"

"No."

"Then where are you going to go?"

"I haven't figured that out yet."

"Let me give you a ride downtown. There are a few decent hotels there. Get a good night's sleep and take a cab to the train station in the morning. Fortunately, Connecticut is not that far."

"The Aryans took my wallet. I have no cash or credit cards."

"Oh my God." Christopher rubbed his temples.

"Don't worry about it, Christopher. You gave me the information I was looking for. I'm a big girl. I'll be okay."

"No. I'm not leaving you in this predicament. I'll drive you to a hotel and pay for your room—"

"That's very kind, but I—"

"And I'll give you some cash for a train ticket."

"I'm not leaving Boston until I find the NELC office."

Christopher sighed and slouched his shoulders. "At least let me put you up in a room."

"Okay. But I want your address. I'll send you the money when I get back home."

"It's a deal."

When they left the office Shannon was amazed to see that the men had still not returned to their games and beer, but remained in a similar half-circle, all eyes fixed on the office door. After quickly thanking the bartender and waving goodbye to her mesmerized spectators, she was sitting in the comfortable leather seat of Christopher's Lexus.

"Listen," he began as they pulled away, "I can't make any promises, but I'll make some calls in the morning and see if I can find anyone who might have an idea about the location of the NELC office."

"That would be wonderful." Shannon glanced in the rear view mirror and saw a car come out of nowhere and pull up close behind them.

"I'll leave you my cell number, and you can call me in the morning or early afternoon. Hopefully, I'll have something for you."

Shannon knew Christopher was talking, but she was too focused on the car behind them to pay attention to him. She tried to determine if the vehicle was the black sedan, and although she couldn't tell for sure, she knew it looked an awful lot like it.

He noticed her looking at the car behind them, and examined it in the mirror. "What's this asshole's problem? Why doesn't he just pass me if he's in that big of a rush?"

Christopher slammed the accelerator, and for a moment, put some distance between his Lexus and the car trailing them. Although the car immediately caught up, it gave Shannon a chance to see that it was indeed the same black sedan.

"Christopher, please pull over here."

"What? Why?" He continued to drive, angrily glaring back at the tailgating car.

"It's important that you pull over now."

"For what?" He sped up and seemed annoyed that the black sedan stayed right on his bumper. "We're not near a hotel yet"

"Please, just do it."

"Fine." He abruptly guided his car to the curb. As the black sedan passed he said, "At least I got this idiot off my ass." He didn't speak and watched with a hint of worry as the sedan also pulled to the curb about a hundred feet ahead of them.

"What's the deal with this fucking car?" he muttered, staring ahead in disbelief.

"Thank you, Christopher. You've been wonderful."

She put her hand on the door latch as he said, "What are you doing?"

She started to open the door, paused, looked back at him, and said, "Saving you."

Before he could respond she was out the door, disappearing into the darkness of a nearby alley.

CHAPTER FIFTY-FIVE

Randolph heard the knocking and moved toward the door with all the speed he could muster. As he pulled the door open, he leaned on the doorknob as if it were a crutch, his lungs wheezing.

The Aryan guard stood in the doorway with his muscular arms crossed. "What do you need?" he barked, his annoyed scowl aimed at Randolph's eyes.

"Thank you for coming, my friend." Randolph extended his hand, his fingers—bony as a hawk's talons—clutching an envelope.

The guard snatched it out his hand and angrily glanced at the writing on it. "Dr. Kuhn? Why don't you bring it to her yourself?"

"If I was in the position to do that, then I wouldn't require your assistance, would I, young man?"

"Yeah. Whatever." The guard slipped the envelope into his pocket and turned away.

"Please deliver it promptly. It is of the utmost importance."

"All right," he shot back. "I'll bring it to her."

The guard angrily stormed away as Randolph violently coughed for a minute. After regaining his composure, he moved slowly toward the center of the room. He staggered for a few steps and collapsed to the floor. Staring up at the large portrait of Hitler, he choked on the lack of air.

But after a moment, he pulled himself up by the arm of the couch. Once standing, he gazed at the towering painting watching over him. "I'm coming, my Fuhrer." He turned, and with a great deal of choking, gasping, and near falls made his way up the stairs.

Once there, he slowly made his way to the edge of the balcony. His tear-filled eyes looked straight ahead at the portrait as his frail, wraith-like body leaned against the railing. At long last, Randolph knew he had finally reached the end.

Calling upon the last bit of energy in his dying body, he leaned over and grabbed onto the rope. It was as he prepared it earlier in the day—tripled knotted and securely fastened to the base of the railing. Certainly strong enough to hold his eighty-nine pounds.

The noose slipped around his neck like the welcoming hand of a long lost love. His decrepit lungs drew a final labored breath as he raised his right hand in a Nazi salute. "Heil Hitler!" he shouted. "It will be done as you commanded, my Fuhrer."

He leaned over the railing, and in a final determined effort, raised his right leg over it. He teetered there for a moment, and then the rest of his body followed. The rope stopped his fall, snapping him up in the air like a buoy bobbing in the sea.

CHAPTER FIFTY-SIX

When Shannon's eyes finally adjusted to the darkness of the alley, she was able to make out some of her surroundings. She ran between two tall brick buildings, and found nothing in the alley, save a large Dumpster and some garbage cans.

She was convinced that the men in the sedan were from The Power, and knew they were probably done trying to fool her. Now, she believed, they meant business and would apprehend her at any cost.

Although she had a chance to escape with Christopher, she couldn't bear the thought of endangering his life when his family was home waiting for him. This was her mess, and she would get out of it on her own.

She didn't bother to look back, but just ran as fast she could down the alley. She believed her only hope was to keep the pursuit a foot chase, and hope she could outrun them. She thought of Neil and wondered if he was still being held captive in the compound. *Maybe he escaped,* she thought. *Maybe he'll come for me.*

When she reached the end of the alley, she stopped running and stood in front of a huge factory. She looked up at the broken windows and dilapidated walls, and assumed it was abandoned. Deciding what to do, she knew she could run around the massive building, but felt she might be in the open for too long. With no other alleys to duck into, she tried to stay calm and think of a solution.

But the sudden sound of footsteps attacked her from behind. Without thinking, she dashed toward the factory and ran to the closest thing she could find: a wooden door full of splinters and peeling paint. She pulled the door open, but the sound of her name froze her before she could enter.

She started to turn toward the sound of the heavy footsteps, but thought better of it. She jumped inside, and slammed the door shut, leaving her in the unknown darkness of the deserted building. She turned and cautiously moved ahead, occasionally bumping into unidentified obstacles. She rushed forward as fast as she could manage until she found a set of stairs. She paused for a moment and looked around the blackness of the old factory, her eyes straining to see anything. But after hearing the door creak and swing open, she knew she had to climb.

"Shannon, wait!" She thought the voice sounded familiar. She wanted to see who it was, but fear drove her up the stairs. As she climbed, she heard someone rattling their way across the junky floor below. She looked down, struggling to see the identity of her pursuer, but it was too dark.

Then, her right foot fell through the stair beneath her. She couldn't hold back a scream as her leg dropped through the stair, leaving her squirming like a fish snagged on a lure. She desperately clutched the splinter-filled step above her and tried to push herself up. As her leg started to break free from the hole, she heard a loud crack and then felt the stairs crumbling beneath her. Her arms flailed like a drowning victim, frantically grasping for anything. But she had no chance; she was falling.

She closed her eyes, bracing for the impact. God only knew what she would land on. What kind of long-lost piece of factory equipment was waiting to rip into her skin and bone when she landed? With her fists balled and teeth clenched, she hit the ground.

After the shock of impact, she opened her eyes and tried to feel for any injuries. But to her surprise, she felt no pain. With her arms stretched out, she felt the dusty floor underneath her. As far as she could tell, she was perfectly fine. But she didn't understand how she could not be hurt.

Then, she felt something move. She froze, thinking it was her imagination. But then she heard a noise, which sounded like a man groaning. She twitched her body, and pushed on the floor to prop herself up, and she heard a scream directly in her ear.

As she jumped up from the ground, her feet became tangled up with something almost sending her sprawling back down. Again, she heard a man groan. With her eyes now better adjusted to the darkness, she could see something on the floor, something that she had landed on.

"Shannon..." The man was obviously hurt, but managed to extend his arm in her direction. Her first instinct was to run, but as she started to make out his face, she realized who it was.

"They're after you," Christopher said, wincing in pain as he tried to wake. Shannon helped him to stand as she realized what had happened. She looked up and saw the hole in the stairs that she had fallen through. Unfortunately, she knew, she had landed squarely on Christopher, which cushioned her fall but possibly broke a few of his ribs.

"Are you okay?" she asked, as she steadied him on his feet.

"I think so."

"I'm sorry I ran from you. I had no idea it was you."

"It's all right," he replied, looking around anxiously. "But you have to hide. They were right behind me. They're looking for you."

"You mean the men from the car?"

"Yes."

"How many are there?"

"Three men in suits. They were chasing you. Do you know who they are?"

Shannon looked over both shoulders, poised to respond to any noise. "Listen Christopher, you should go back the way you came and get to your car."

"Not unless you come with me."

"I don't have time to explain what's going on. But I don't want you involved. I appreciate your help, but I would feel a lot better if you went home."

"I can't leave you here. Not with those men after you."

"It'll be easier for me to get away if I'm alone. I really want you to go."

He paused and looked around, unsure of what to do. "Are you sure?"

"I'm positive."

"But what are you going to do?"

"Believe it or not, I've gotten out of a lot tougher situations than this in the last few days. Don't worry, I'll lose them."

"I'm sorry, Shannon, but I can't leave you here." He pulled a cell phone out of his pocket. "I'm calling the police."

As he started to flip the phone open, Shannon heard footsteps shuffling past the front of the factory. She knew it was the men chasing her, but they didn't seem to know she was inside the factory. Then, she realized that Christopher was about to announce her presence.

"No," she said in a loud whisper, waving for him to put his phone away. But the tiny silver device made two loud beeps, and Shannon saw the shadows stop.

"What?" he whispered back. But it was too late. In an instant the door opened.

"Let's go," she said, grabbing him by the shirt. He groaned in pain as she dragged him with her, his injuries from her fall now making themselves known. They ran deeper into the pitch-dark factory with no idea what was ahead of them.

She heard the area behind them break into a loud clamor of footsteps and clanking metal. Whoever was chasing her seemed to be crashing into everything that lay about the factory. But still, they kept coming.

Shannon let go of Christopher's shirt and now led him by the hand. They ran side by side, desperately looking for any means of escape. Then, they saw something. They didn't need to communicate to know that the door in the distance was their destination. They ran straight for it, occasionally bumping into unknown factory equipment in their path.

The men had similar trouble moving across the dark room, and Shannon and Christopher were able to reach the door before the men could catch them. The relief of getting out of the factory didn't last long, as they found themselves in another alley. With no time to contemplate which way to run, they went right. But after running a few yards, they realized they had made the wrong decision.

The alley ended with a collection of Dumpsters up against a fence. Shannon could see that the fence had swinging doors, but could also see the chains and padlocks that kept them from opening. As they ran closer, they knew they had made a mistake.

Shannon stopped running about fifty feet in front of the Dumpsters and Christopher stopped with her. "We can't get out this way," she said, out of breath.

"Let's go back," he said. But as they turned in the opposite direction, they saw the door they had exited open. Three middle-aged men in suits spilled into the alley.

Shannon froze for a moment as she watched the men gain their footing and resume their pursuit. She knew her only hope was to go up and over the fence. And climbing the Dumpsters was her only chance. As she started to run, she reached behind her and once again pulled Christopher with her.

They scampered down the rest of the alley as Shannon yelled, "We're going over." He seemed to understand and burst a few strides ahead of her. He jumped on top of one of the Dumpsters, and extended his hand to her. She grabbed him as her feet hit the side of the metal receptacle. After a quick tug, she joined him on top.

They had a perfect view of the men and could see they were only few a few yards behind them. They both turned to look over the fence, and saw the dirt road that led around the corner of another building. She knew it didn't matter where the road led; they had no choice but to follow it.

"We have to jump over," she said.

"Let's go," he said and put one foot on top of the fence.

As she took his hand and also put her foot on top of the fence, she heard one of the men yell. "Shannon. No. Wait."

She turned with surprise and saw the three men gasping for breath at the base of the Dumpster. Christopher looked at her with wide eyes, shocked that she was hesitating. "Let's jump, Shannon."

As she looked at Christopher, she heard another one of the men call out. "Come down from there. We're here to help you." Now, they both looked down at the three men. "We're from the New England Law Center."

Shannon's mouth hung open as she examined the men. "They're lying," Christopher whispered.

"Bullshit!" Shannon yelled, and put her foot on top of the fence again, ready to jump over.

"No, Shannon. Wait!" one of them yelled. He pulled something out of his wallet and extended his arm, showing her the laminated identification card. "Look at my ID. We're here to help you."

Shannon tried to look at the ID without moving much from her position near the fence. She noticed Christopher leaning close to it. "That could be a fake," he yelled.

"I'm telling the truth," the man replied as one of his colleagues furiously pulled out his wallet, while the other man pulled a cell phone out of his pocket, turned, and stepped away.

The man who pulled out his wallet threw it on top of the Dumpster, landing a few inches from Shannon's feet. "Look for yourself. We have nothing to hide." Christopher cautiously picked up the wallet. But before he had the chance to examine the contents, he saw the man with the cell phone climbing the Dumpster.

"What are you doing?" Christopher yelled. "Back off, or we're going over." Shannon draped one leg over the fence, and was convinced she was going over in a matter of seconds.

When the man reached the top of the Dumpster, he extended his cell phone, keeping his feet planted at the edge of the metal bin. "Shannon, please. Just take the phone."

"Why?" she shouted back.

"It's the only way you'll believe us," the man replied.

Shannon moved toward him, one small step at a time. She was poised to leap back at any moment, but she desperately wanted to know who was on the phone. When she reached him, he gently handed it to her.

Still ready to disappear over the fence, she carefully took the phone out of the stranger's hand. She put the phone up to her ear, her hand slightly shaking. Her body tensed into a tight ball as she listened to the voice.

"Shannon, are you there? It's Neil."

CHAPTER FIFTY-SEVEN

The black sedan crawled down the dark Boston street until it eventually stopped in front of a towering stone church. "The NELC office is in a church?" Shannon asked from the backseat, her shoulder brushing against the wide body of the suited man next to her.

"No," the driver answered. He turned toward Shannon and said, "It's near here, but you have to tell your friend to get lost."

Shannon glanced out the back window and saw that Christopher's Lexus was still following. "He just wants to make sure that I'm okay."

"That's real nice, but he can't know where our office is. This is as far as he follows us."

"You spoke with Neil," the man next to her said. "Don't you trust us?"

Shannon swallowed the lump in her throat. Trust was a difficult concept for her after learning that Neil had lied about his name, and who knew what else. But now, she had no other choice.

"Give me a minute," she said, putting her hand on the door latch. "I'll get rid of him."

"Make it quick," the driver shot back.

Shannon exited the black sedan, and walked over to Christopher's vehicle. He lowered his window and said, "Are you okay?"

"Yes. And it's time for you to go home. They won't take me to the office with you following, and Neil will be there soon."

"You're a hundred percent sure you can trust Neil and these guys?"

"Yes. A hundred percent," she lied and feigned a smile.

"Okay…if you're that sure." He handed her his business card. "My cell number is on there. If you get in trouble again, make sure you call me."

She gave him a firm handshake. "You're very kind. Thank you for everything." They waved to each other as he pulled away.

Shannon got back into the black sedan, and they were off without a word. They drove for a few blocks and parked in an underground garage. The three men whisked her down a dimly-lit, concrete hallway, and then down two flights of a fetid stairwell. After a quick walk down another hallway, one of the men jangled a set of keys in front of a steel door.

Where the hell are we? she thought and wanted to ask, but instead said, "This is a law office?"

The man pushed open the heavy door as his two accomplices guided Shannon inside. They stood in an average-sized room with some simple living room furniture and a desk. Now, in the better light, she could make out the faces of the suited men.

The driver was a burly man with salt-and-pepper hair and a crooked nose. The other two looked similar—maybe a little younger—and wore matching black suits with Italian loafers.

These guys look more like mobsters than lawyers, she worried.

The driver popped a cigarette out of his jacket pocket and flipped it into his mouth. Before he lit it, he said, "This is one of our locations. We have a few. We thought this would be the best place to bring you because there's a bed in the other room."

A bed? Did they bring me here to rape me? She took a step back as her muscles tightened. A terrifying thought entered her mind. What if The Power tortured Neil into telling her to go with these men? Or worse, what if it was his idea?

The cigarette smoke spiraled around the driver's head as he took a step toward her. His weathered face looked almost demonic as his small black eyes focused on her. Panic overwhelmed her, and she started to choke on her own salvia. She turned toward the door, and although the other two men were stationed squarely in front of it, she ran toward it.

The men looked stunned as they threw their hands up to block her. To her surprise, they didn't slam her onto to the ground and drag her off to the bed, but gently deflected her away from the door. "What are you doing?" they both took turns saying as they continued to push her away from the door.

"You guys aren't lawyers!" she yelled. The two men looked puzzled as their pudgy faces crinkled in confusion. The driver stepped forward and flicked his smoke to the ground, crushing it beneath his shiny black shoe.

"Who said we were lawyers?" the driver asked in a deep voice.

"You did," Shannon answered, now slowly backpedaling from the three hulking men.

"We said we worked for the New England Law Center. We never said we were lawyers."

"Then what are you?"

"We work security."

Her head toggled between the three men as she tried to make sense of the situation. "I don't understand," she managed to say and stood still.

"Listen," the driver began, "I'm sorry if this place is spooking you. I know it don't look like a lawyer's office. And it ain't really an office; it's just a couple of rooms that the firm rents. But Neil thought this would be the best place to bring you because you can get some sleep here."

"What?" Her body relaxed.

"He said you would probably need sleep. He thought you would want to crash in the bedroom."

"He said he would meet me at the law office."

"Yeah, but he's in a plane. He's still got at least four hours before he gets here. He figured you'd want to get a little shut-eye. He asked us to stay with you until he got here."

Shannon's mouth opened but she did not speak. Her head spun, confused, unsure of what to believe.

"What's the problem, anyway?" the driver said and glanced at his watch. "It's almost two in the morning. Aren't you tired?"

"Yes…it's just that…I thought…" She saw concern oozing out of their normally tough faces. She couldn't bring herself to share what she was actually thinking. "I'm sorry. I'm just a little freaked out."

"Is there anything we can do?" the driver asked.

"No. Nothing. I don't mean to seem ungrateful. I appreciate your help."

"So do you want to get some sleep then?"

"I guess so."

"The bedroom's right through that door." He pointed to a wooden door on the other side of the room. "We'll wait out here until Neil shows up."

"Thanks, guys." Shannon felt stupid for letting the moment of panic overtake her as she made her way through the door. What she found on the other side was not really a bedroom, but a storage room with a small twin bed tucked in the corner—behind a couple of metal filing cabinets.

She kicked off her shoes, squeezed herself between the metal cabinets, and climbed over some boxes before sprawling across the bed. The mattress was as comfortable as a medieval torture rack, but the dust that kicked up from it bothered her more, tickling her throat and making her cough. But still, she was tired enough to sleep on it.

As she drifted off, she thought of only one thing: the fact that when she woke, Neil would be here. *Did he betray me or not?*

In her last moment of consciousness she saw his eyes—perfectly blue as the center of a flame—and she knew in there she would find her answer.

CHAPTER FIFTY-EIGHT

Her lips curled at the edges when she saw her mother's face. The whiteness of her cheeks glowed like the moon as her sun-pinkened nose twitched with happiness. When her mother held the cool cloth against her forehead, she felt the pain in her head slowly drift away.

"You'll be okay, honey," her mother said, and ran her fingers down her daughter's face. The touch electrified her, bouncing from the top of her head to the tips of her toes.

"Mommy," she said. When her mother leaned close—her fawn-like eyes melting over her like a pad of butter—it made her feel safe.

Shannon felt the mattress sink, and this caused her to sit up. "I'm sorry," a voice anxiously said. "I didn't mean to wake you."

When she opened her eyes he was there, sitting next to her like nothing had happened. Like everything was normal. Like he belonged there. A surge of emotions consumed her, constricting her throat and stabbing her gut. She ignored the cramp that was trying to cripple her and sat up.

"What's wrong?" Neil asked. "You look like you've seen a ghost."

Her blood beat thick, accentuating the pain shooting throughout her body. Then, without thinking, she asked a question. "Who are you?"

A look of worry overtook his face. "What do you mean, Shannon? It's me...are you okay?"

She hopped out of bed, and winced in a struggle to ignore the pain of her naked, cut-up feet. "I know your last name's not Henry." The color left Neil's face as he stared back at her, impassively.

"Wait...Shannon—"

"But what I don't know is what other lies you've told me."

"Please let me explain." They were silent as they studied each other, their heavy breathing the only sound. "You caught me off guard when we met. I didn't know if you would believe the truth, so I told you that Mr. Henry was my Grandfather. It was stupid, I know. But given the circumstances, I didn't think you would believe the truth."

"What is the truth?"

"He was my colleague. A former colleague, I mean. He was retired. But we were very close. Everything else I told you is the truth."

"You mean about being there because he wasn't answering his

phone?"

"Yes. Everything else was true. And he was like a grandfather to me. I guess that's why I told you that."

"So your last name is Franklin?"

Neil's bottom lip dropped as a quiet gasp passed over his lips. "How do you know that?"

"I've got to catch you up on a lot."

"The same here."

"How did you get out of the compound?"

"I earned their trust."

Shannon remembered the pathetic DJ and became angry. "I can't believe you kidnapped that DJ. He was an innocent man. How could you do that?"

"How do you know we kidnapped the DJ?"

"Like we said, we've got to catch each other up on a lot."

"All right then, let's do it in the car. We have to get to the funeral home."

"Funeral home? What for?"

"They have Efram's body."

"Efram?"

"I'm sorry...I mean Mr. Henry."

"Oh..." Shannon's knees buckled, taken back by the idea of seeing the corpse of her former neighbor. "They haven't buried him yet?"

"They need me to identify him. He kept a low profile in recent years. No one currently in the firm knows what he looks like. So...I guess it's up to you and me."

A half-hour later, Shannon walked out of a discount shoe shop with a cheap pair of sneakers on her feet. She hopped back into Neil's rented BMW, and they were off to the funeral home.

"So where did you lose your shoes?" Neil asked as he guided the car through the insane traffic bustling around them.

"I didn't lose them. I left them in that guy Brad's apartment that I told you about."

"I can't believe he had you in his place. I can't tell you how much that angers me."

"You didn't tell me how you know him."

"He's part of The Power, but is sort of a renegade member. They don't always endorse what he does, and have kicked him out many times. I'm guessing he's out now, and tried to use getting you as a way to get back in their good graces. But with The Power or not, he's bad news. A real dangerous guy."

"Oh my God," Shannon gasped, her eyes bulging out of her head. "If he was trying to get back in The Power, then he must have returned the DJ to them."

Neil forced down the lump in his dry throat as he said, "I told you not to worry about the DJ. Peter has a plan to rescue him when he makes his escape."

"But it's my fault he's back there. I had him out of the compound. I can't believe I fell for Brad's bullshit. I should have known he wasn't with the FBI."

Neil stopped the car in front of the funeral home. "I told you the DJ will be all right. And some day we'll nab Brad and he'll get what's coming to him." Shannon looked at him, confused. "I mean prison, Shannon. We're not the mob. In fact, our firm has made a living fighting people who do that sort of thing."

Shannon nodded her head. "I know."

"Do you?" Neil looked deep into her eyes. "I need you to trust me again. We have to finish what we started. And we can only do it together. So…do you trust me?"

Her heart dribbled like a basketball as her eyes ran up and down his face. She knew she had to make up her mind. Either she would trust him—or not. And now she had to decide. She remembered the papers that Brad showed her that linked Neil with The Power. They looked real…but…she couldn't be sure. There was too much information for her brain to decipher. So she relied on her heart.

"I trust you," she said, fighting back tears.

"Okay then. Let's get this over with so we can give a proper farewell to our friend." Shannon nodded in agreement, and they were on their way into the funeral home.

The thick wooden door creaked as Neil pushed it open, and Shannon noticed some of the white peeling paint spilling onto his sleeve. The striking green rug stung her eyes as they stepped into the large foyer, and it took her a moment to realize the numerous green plants that now surrounded her were plastic.

A tall skinny man in a black suit appeared out of nowhere and stood in front of them. His pale skin looked like chalk against his dark clothing, and Shannon thought his abnormally long neck looked like a fifth limb.

"I am Albert," the man said, gently folding his long bony fingers in front of his crotch. "How may I help you?"

"We're from the NELC. We're here to identify the body you have," Neil said.

"Very good, sir," Albert replied. "I'm very happy to see you. He's been here for some time. Your colleagues delivered him here and were fairly sure of his identity, but could not confirm it with absolute certainty."

"That's right. A former member of our firm was kidnapped and taken to South America. The body you have was found there, and matches the description of the man kidnapped. They assumed it was him, but we can identify him for sure."

"I'm sorry for your loss. Is he a relative?"

Shannon and Neil shared a quick, uncomfortable look. "No. He's not. But he's a good friend."

"Of course, sir. Please follow me."

Shannon and Neil followed Albert's lanky body, listening to his heavy black shoes swishing against the carpet. Albert stopped behind a table at the end of the hall, which was next to a large empty room.

"My assistant, Dennis, will bring the body up in just a moment. Please have a seat."

Shannon and Neil sat in the metal folding chairs in front of the table as Albert sat in the cushioned chair behind it. He dialed a phone, mumbled something into it, quickly hung it up, and spread some paperwork out on the table. "There's much we have to discuss," he said, as he took a long yellow pencil out of the desk drawer. "What is the deceased's name?"

Again, Shannon and Neil shot each other an awkward look. "Funny you should ask," Neil began. "You see, he changed his name when he came to America. But I'm not sure if he went to the trouble to legally change it or not."

"What was his original name?"

"Efram Heinman."

"And what did he change it to?"

"He changed his last name to Henry."

Albert scribbled the information on a form and asked, "Are there any family members we can contact to verify his legal name?"

"I'm afraid not," Neil replied. "His family was wiped out in the Holocaust. If he has any blood relatives, I don't know of them."

Shannon's eyes diverted to the room next to them. There, she saw a man in his mid-twenties wheeling a gurney. The man stopped in the center of the room, and turned his gaze toward Albert.

Shannon focused on the body. It was enclosed in a bag, and she knew it contained the body of Mr. Henry. She remembered his kind face. His gentle touch. The handpicked flowers he had personally delivered when she first moved in to her home. *What a horrible way to die,* she thought. *To be taken from your home, brought to a strange country, and shot like an animal.* He deserved better, she knew. Especially for a man who dedicated his life to helping others.

"I need to inform the city coroner of his legal name for his death certificate," Shannon heard Albert say.

She knew Neil responded to him, but didn't register what he said. Without realizing it, she was walking into the room, moving quickly toward the body.

Dennis perched on the balls of his feet as he stood next to the gurney like a guard. He flashed an awkward smile as he said, "Can I help you, ma'am?"

Shannon stopped about a foot before the gurney. With her eyes fixed on the body bag, she said, "I'm here to identify my friend."

Dennis looked back toward the desk and saw Albert and Neil still talking. He looked back to Shannon, and said, "Yes, ma'am. Should I wait for your husband?"

"Oh...he's not my husband. We're mutual friends of the deceased."

"I see. You'd like to see the deceased now?"

Shannon glanced over her shoulder, and after seeing that Neil and Albert we're still discussing details, she said, "Yes. Please."

Without a word, Dennis unzipped the bag. Shannon felt her heart crawl up her esophagus as he peeled away the plastic covering. She looked at the face, ready to cry—maybe scream. Normally she was okay at wakes and funerals, but she had such a soft spot in her heart for Mr. Henry that this was almost unbearable.

Still, she knew she had to identify him. She leaned close, recognizing the familiar white hair. Dennis stood motionless as she focused on his face. As she examined him, something unexpected took over her. She stumbled backward, out of control. She heard herself gasp loudly as she struggled to keep her balance.

Dennis stepped toward her with a concerned look on his face, but before he reached her, she turned and ran. She fell into Neil's arms, and he gently held her up straight.

"What is it?" Neil asked with a panicked face.

Shannon saw the shocked face of Albert and heard the footsteps of Dennis behind her. Neil's warm breath poured over her as she said, "It's not him."

CHAPTER FIFTY-NINE

During the last few days, Shannon had become convinced she would never see New Haven, Connecticut, again. But now, after the three-hour drive from Boston, she admired the familiar sights of her neighborhood from the BMW.

When he pulled the car down her unpaved road, she wondered if he intended to just drop her off, or talk in the car, or come inside. She had not spoken since she insisted that he drive her home immediately, and Neil apparently respected her need to process what she had seen, remaining silent during the trip.

But as they passed Mr. Henry's house, she finally spoke. "Do you even care that we still have no idea what happened to him?"

"Of course I care," he shot back as he guided the car over the bumpy road. "I've been quiet to give you some space since you were so freaked out."

"And you're not bothered that wasn't Mr. Henry?"

"Not only am I bothered that it wasn't Mr. Henry, but I know who the dead man is."

"You're kidding?"

"I wish I was. He's another former colleague." Neil stopped the car in Shannon's driveway. "He was never as important in our firm as Mr. Henry was. And to tell you the truth, I didn't think he knew anything about the location of the boy. He had been retired for years, and last I knew was living in Southern California. But if The Power kidnapped him and took him to Ecuador, then he must have known something."

"But what about Mr. Henry? Where is he?"

"I wish I knew." Neil shut off the car and they both stared out the window, lost in thought.

Shannon's eyes darted toward him, "If he's still alive, then he must be in that compound somewhere."

"We don't know that for sure."

"Where else would they take him?"

"I have no idea."

"Then we have to go back and look for him."

Neil's eyes widened. "Then you're willing to keep helping me?"

"Well," she hesitated, "I really wanted to end this, but I don't know now. Maybe."

"You don't know how happy I am to hear you say that." He patted her leg and draped his arm over her shoulder. She recoiled as if she had burned. She might be ready to help him again, but trusting him to the point of being intimate would take some time.

"Hold on. I said I'm not sure. I'll need some time to think about it."

"I understand, and totally respect your need to do that. But you should know that we're running out of time. The longer we wait, the closer it is until The Power begins their plans."

"All right," she replied with an impatient sigh. "Let's go inside. Can you wait while I think about it in the shower?"

Neil smiled. "I'd be happy to do that." As they walked inside, Neil flipped his cell phone open and said, "I'm going to arrange for the plane to pick me up in Hartford. Hopefully, you'll be getting on it with me."

"We'll see," Shannon replied as she took a long, comfortable stride into her living room. She pointed to her couch. "Make yourself comfortable. I won't be long."

"Thanks. Listen, before you get in the shower, I just wanted to say something." He swallowed hard and cleared his throat. "I know the last few days have been crazy, and dangerous, and totally insane. But I don't think I would have survived it if you weren't with me."

He swallowed again and continued, "I'm so sorry that I hurt you with the lies that I told. But I want you to know that I've developed very strong feelings for you."

"Neil, wait...don't say this now. I have too much going on in my head right now."

"Okay, I'll stop. But I just want you to know that I really need you to get through the rest of this."

Shannon let out a heavy sigh and bit her lower lip. She looked him in the eye and said, "I'm assuming the plane would take us back to Idaho, where we could try and find Mr. Henry."

"Yes...umm...I mean eventually it will take us back there. But we'll need to make a little pit stop first," Neil said as he returned her intense gaze.

"A pit stop? Where?"

Neil pulled a vial of blood out of his coat pocket and showed it to her. "Ruhpolding, Germany."

CHAPTER SIXTY

The leather belt struck Peter's back with the ferocity of a hundred wasps stinging him at once. The pain made his body quiver and his head vibrate. He moaned without meaning to, and flopped over like a snagged bluefish on the deck of a fishing boat.

When he opened his eyes, her foot was inches from his face. Her black stockings and pointy high heel were wrapped around her foot tighter than the casing of a sausage. He tried to speak, but could only release a gasp of air.

He didn't see her foot lift off the ground, but felt the impact of it striking him on the side of his face. It took him a moment to realize the warm fluid in his mouth was his own blood, and the rattle he heard was his front tooth ricocheting off the hardwood floor.

Now, on his back, he felt the sharp end of her heel dig into his chest like a dagger. He lifted his chin, and for the first time, saw Dr. Kuhn's face. The goons who had brought him here stood behind her, burly arms crossed and faces smirking with a sick satisfaction.

Finally, she spoke. "I understand you intercepted a package that was meant for me. This could be a very long night for you if you don't immediately divulge what it is you took and your reasons."

"I can explain...but—"

Her heel pressed harder into his chest, causing him to squirm. "I don't want to hear the word 'but.' You will tell me now or suffer pain that you've never imagined."

She smacked the belt against the cement floor, inches from his face. The noise made his body convulse, expecting the pain. When it didn't come, he stared up at her, slightly shaking.

"You haven't felt pain yet," she said as she took her foot off of him and gestured toward one of the guards. "Bring me my bag," She glared at him, her eyes dancing with delight. "Now, if you still won't talk, you'll feel real pain."

One of the guards handed her a small black handbag that looked like an ordinary purse. But Peter knew that Kuhn didn't keep money or makeup inside of it. His fear was confirmed when she pulled out a small metal instrument.

Before he could focus enough to identify the object, her knees planted squarely on his chest. Now, she held the shiny scissors inches from his face. Her breath poured over his face as she spoke. "Know what I can do with this?"

He stared at her, his upper lip quivering. Before he could reply, she continued, "I'll use this to cut off your balls and shove them up your nose. Then I'll cut off your cock and shove it down your throat."

Again, he tried to speak but only released a nervous gasp of air. Dr. Kuhn reached into the bag and pulled out a long, sharp knife. She pressed it against his cheek as she said, "Have anything to say, or should I begin?"

"I'll talk," Peter gasped, her knees crushing his ribs.

She held the knife against his throat. "You better hope I like what I hear, or these words will be your last."

CHAPTER SIXTY-ONE

With her face just inches from the showerhead, she took delight in the warm water beating off her forehead and rolling down her tired, battered body. Her first shower in days was not a disappointment, but, unfortunately, she knew she would have to cut it short. Neil needed an answer soon, and she either had to set off with him toward the airport or say goodbye.

Changing into clean clothes—after days of wearing the same thing—was almost as pleasurable as the shower. As she wrapped a towel around her wet hair, she thought of Ruhpolding and the humble village that Neil described. Supposedly, the daughter of Hitler and Eva Braun lived there.

Neil had explained that somehow Peter managed to acquire a vial of blood from the boy. The plan was to travel to Ruhpolding, find Braun's daughter, convince her to give up some of her blood, and have a DNA test conducted to match the two samples.

If the boy is indeed the grandchild of Hitler and Braun, then the DNA test will show that this woman is the boy's mother. If, however, the test shows that Braun's daughter and the boy are not related, then this information will be used to enlighten the leaders of The Power that they have the wrong boy. And, ultimately, halt their imminent plans to take over the country.

Amazing. Exciting. Challenging. Yet the more she pictured herself flying with Neil to Germany, the more she longed to sit on her porch and watch the sunset. *Does he really need me? What good will I do anyway?*

Not having to dry her short, stubbly hair, she plopped a baseball cap over her head and made her way downstairs. There, she found Neil waiting on the couch.

"Ready to go?" he popped up with a hopeful smile.

"I'm sorry, Neil, but I'm not."

His smile sank away in an instant. "But, Shannon..."

"It's not that I don't want to be with you. But after the last few days I need some time to chill out here."

"But I need you."

"I don't understand why. You're going to Germany to get some blood from an old woman. After what we just did the last few days, that should be a piece of cake."

"Remember that this woman has no idea who I am or that I'm coming to see her. Would you expect her to just give a complete stranger her blood? This is going to take some work. Not to mention the fact that I have to find her. I'm sure she's not listed in the phone book under the name Braun or Hitler."

"You can handle it." She opened the door to her deck and walked outside.

Neil followed. "Why did you change your mind? It seemed like you were ready to go when we got here."

"I really want to find Mr. Henry. If he's alive, I want to try and save him."

"But what we'll do in Germany could save thousands, if not millions of people."

"I know you think that. It's just hard for me to grasp that concept. Mr. Henry, I know. With him it's personal."

"Helping me isn't personal?"

"Of course it is." She paced her deck. "But even if we're just talking about our relationship, I still think it would be better for us if I had some time to think."

"I won't argue that. But there are other reasons why I want you with me."

"Why don't you come get me after you get back from Germany? I'll probably go to Idaho with you after I have some time to myself."

"I don't want to leave you here alone."

"We're back to that line now," she said as leaned over the deck railing, shaking her head in frustration.

"It's not a line, Shannon. It's the truth."

"Even if they are interested in me, they're getting ready to launch their master plan to take over the country. They don't have time to come to Connecticut and bother with me."

"I don't think that's true."

"I know it was dangerous running around their compound. And that weird woman really freaked me out when she knew my name, but that's not enough to make me worry in my own home."

Neil walked away, biting his lip in frustration.

"What is it, Neil? Why don't you just tell me exactly what you're worried about?"

He spun toward with a start. "I won't let them kill you too!"

Shannon froze as she studied his face, red as an apple. A look of regret quickly consumed him as he took a step back. "Kill me too?" she said with curiosity as she took a step toward him. "Who else did they kill?"

He sat in a lounge chair, avoiding eye contact. She leaned close to him and repeated, "Who did they kill?" When he didn't respond, she stood and began an irritated stroll around his chair. "I thought you said that you didn't know if Mr. Henry was dead or alive."

"I don't know," he shot back.

She glared at him, waiting for more, but he was silent. "Then what are you talking about?"

His red face turned to her. "It wasn't a coincidence that you ended up on the same street as Mr. Henry."

"What?"

"We put you here."

"Put me here?"

"To protect you."

"Are you insane? No one put me here. Derek and I found this place on our own."

"Completely on your own?"

"More or less. The real estate agent we were working with at the time found it."

"Pretty good deal, wasn't it?" he said with a raised eyebrow.

"What's that supposed to mean?"

"You bought this house in 2005, correct?"

"That's right."

"And what did you pay for it?"

"One hundred and fifty."

"So just two years ago you purchased this property for a hundred and fifty thousand. *This* house, which happens to be a new construction, built on the Connecticut shoreline with the beach as your backyard. This four bedroom, 2500-square-foot house only cost you a hundred and fifty thousand."

"We were told the people selling needed to get rid of it in a hurry."

"They could have listed it for a half million and got rid of it in a hurry. We made the arrangements to put you here for what you could afford."

"Why would you do that?"

"Like I said, we were trying to protect you and Mr. Henry. This is a secluded spot that was easy to watch. We thought we could protect all of you here. But, obviously, it didn't work."

At first, Shannon assumed he said this because Mr. Henry had disappeared, but then, a more terrifying thought entered her mind. She cast him a look, which shouted her thoughts. "Who else did they kill?" she asked between trembling lips.

He looked at her, his face pale and downtrodden. "I'm sorry to tell you this, but Derek's death wasn't an accident."

CHAPTER SIXTY-TWO

As the work crew put some finishing touches on the stage, the Supreme Leader and the boy looked on. The structure was no less extravagant than what a touring rock band would require. It was ten feet off the ground, a hundred feet wide, and two hundred feet deep. There was scaffolding stretched above it, and hanging lights, which seemed to be aimed at one spot on the stage.

When the boy saw what was on the stage, his heart sank. Despite the elaborate setup, the huge area had only one object: a simple podium. The boy knew it was there for him. As he watched a worker secure a microphone into a stand on the podium, his palms became sweaty.

He looked over his shoulder and saw the gigantic empty field. There was enough room to hold a million people, he thought. He pictured all of them standing in the field, looking at him, listening to him.

"Check one, two. Check one, two." The voice boomed from above, and the boy almost jumped out of his shoes. He whirled in a fright, looking around.

The Supreme Leader saw his reaction and gently patted his shoulder. "That's just the sound system, young man. Once you start to speak into it, you'll get used to it in no time."

"I don't know if I can do this," he said, fighting back tears.

"There's no need to worry. The people here will hang on your every word. They'll cheer for you like you are a god."

"I'll be too nervous to talk."

"Nonsense, young man. You'll do fine. I brought you here to rehearse your speech. After you practice it a few times, your fear will go away."

A worker, holding a clipboard, approached the Leader, and he turned his attention away from the boy. The boy watched the two men talk as they pointed to various spots on the stage.

A flicker of light caught his eye, and he noticed a platform behind him full of spotlights. Technicians scrambled across it, running cables and bolting down instruments. The butterflies in his stomach turned into angry hermit crabs, and he almost doubled over in pain.

When he regained his composure, he turned and saw that the

Leader had not even noticed his distress. The Leader took his hand and said, "Now let's practice your speech. The sound board operator needs to adjust his levels for the volume of your voice."

The Leader led him up the stairs onto the stage. There, he hoped his fear would subside and he would be able to make the speech. When he stood in front of the podium, two technicians appeared and began adjusting the height of the pedestal and the microphone stand.

When the workers were done, they immediately disappeared as if they crawled into underground tunnels beneath the stage. Suddenly, the boy was alone, staring at the field of shiny green grass, which seemed to shake in anticipation of the thunder of feet that would soon be upon it.

With the microphone almost touching his lips, he thought he could hear his breathing coming from the sky. He looked around in confusion and then heard an unmistakable voice behind him. "Talk," the Leader said. He looked over his shoulder and saw the old man scowling at him. "Say the speech."

He reached into his pocket and pulled out the folded piece of notebook paper that contained the words the Leader wanted him to say. It was true he had practiced it a few times, but that was in the house. This was different.

He felt the Leader's hand on his shoulder. "Don't be afraid, boy. You'll feel better after you read it a few times. Go ahead."

The boy looked at the paper. But his hand was shaking so violently he couldn't read a word. He felt the Leader's fingers tighten more on his collarbone as each silent second passed. Finally, he slammed the paper on the ground as if he were a spiking a football and ran off the stage.

Two security guards appeared out of nowhere and closely shadowed him as he stumbled away from the complex. They didn't touch him, but he knew they wouldn't allow him to wander far.

He walked for a while and then fell on the hard ground. He fought off the urge to cry until he saw a shadow cross his face. He knew it was the Leader. "I can't do it!" he screamed as some tears welled up in his eyes.

The Leader released a disgusted sigh as he watched the boy squirm in distress. He turned to one of his guards and said, "Call Kuhn. There's obviously much more work to be done."

CHAPTER SIXTY-THREE

As Shannon thumbed through the selection of DVDs, the feeling of Déjà vu was too much too ignore. Here she was again on the same plane, with the same pilot, and once again trying to find a decent movie to watch. Neil slumped on the same couch across from her, and as he did when they traveled to South America, was starting to doze.

Only this time she wasn't going to allow him to sleep. At least not until he delivered the explanation he had promised her. She knocked his feet off the couch and sat next to him. "Okay," she said purposely loud. "You said you would tell me more once we got in the air. Well, here we are."

She didn't react emotionally to Neil's statement about Derek's death. Maybe it was because she was having trouble bringing herself to believe it. It was enough to get her on the plane to Germany, but she didn't understand how it could be true. Who? Why? How?

None of it made sense to her, and she refused to get worked up over something that couldn't possibly be true. But still, there was something eating at her. Something that was telling her there's more than she's able to see. She remembered the eyes of the Bald Man when he focused on her face. She remembered the chill she felt when Kuhn said her name. For some reason those people knew her. But that didn't mean that The Power murdered Derek. Did it?

If Neil knew the answers, then she wouldn't accept anything other than a full disclosure. And she wanted it now. "I'm waiting," she said as Neil rubbed the sleep out of his eyes.

"I see that," he mumbled and sat upright. "Okay, Shannon, I'm going to be completely honest with you."

"It's about time."

"I know you probably think I'm a jerk for not telling you what I know."

"You could say that."

"But I had my reasons for not telling you. And unfortunately, I still do."

"What does that mean? You're still not going to tell me how these people know who I am?" They stared at each other in silence for a moment until Shannon continued. "You can tell me that you think they killed my fiancé, but you can't tell me why?"

"It's not that I can't tell you. It's just that it's better that you don't know everything right now."

"That's bullshit!" She stood up in anger.

"I'm doing this for your own good."

"What the hell does that mean?"

"It means that if you know everything now, it may put you in greater danger."

"That makes no sense."

"It may not make sense now, but it will."

"When do you plan on telling me everything?"

"Very soon. But I may not need to tell you."

"Someone else is going to tell me?"

"No. I think you may come to realize it on your own."

She studied his face, trying to interpret his meaning. After a minute she gave up and dropped into the couch across from him, the hum of the plane the only sound. "I believe that Derek's death was an accident, and I'm going to continue to believe that. I need more than a few cryptic statements from you to change my mind."

"I understand."

"But I do know that some of the people in The Power know who I am. And I want to know why. I don't understand how knowing that could put me in more danger, but I guess, for now, I'll have to trust you."

"That means a lot to me. I want you to know that I have your best interests in mind."

"I hope that's true."

"You have my word." He tapped his chest and his smile pulled at her heart. She wanted to kiss him again, but wouldn't dare move near him.

"Why don't you put one of those movies in?" He gestured to the stack of DVDs she had been looking through. He sprawled back on the couch. "Let's relax and hopefully get some sleep. We still have a long flight."

CHAPTER SIXTY-FOUR

April 18th, 2007

To Shannon's surprise, the plane didn't land in Germany, but Salzburg, Austria. Neil explained that the airport in Salzburg was by far the closest to Ruhpolding, only being about a thirty-minute car ride away. This meant that they had to go through customs both at the airport and again at the German border, but once there, they had a mere twenty-minute cab ride.

They found a cab at the border instantly, and Shannon was surprised and impressed that the driver spoke some English. "American?" the young blonde man asked.

"Yes," she answered. "We're from America."

"Urlaub?" he asked with a wide smile. After giving him a blank stare, he shook his head and said, "Sorry. Vacation?"

"Yes. We're here on vacation," Shannon lied.

"Ski?" The cab driver pantomimed a skier pushing ski poles down a slope.

"That's right," Neil said as he suddenly stepped forward. "We've come to ski." He turned to Shannon and whispered, "Ruhpolding is a ski resort. We'll tell people that's why we've come here."

"Okay," Shannon whispered back. She noticed the driver opening the trunk. He then turned toward them.

"Gepack?" he asked, still smiling. He then realized his mistake and corrected himself. "Luggage?" he said, pronouncing the two syllables separately.

Oh Shit, Shannon thought. She took the small backpack off her shoulder, which contained a few essential items she had quickly thrown together before leaving. She handed it to the driver, who took it but held it awkwardly, waiting for more.

She looked at Neil, who puckered his lips as he tried to think of something. "The airline lost our bags. They'll send them to our hotel."

The driver looked at them confused as Neil pulled a small leather book out of his back pocket. "I just bought this in the airport," he said to Shannon. "As you can see, we're going to need it on this trip."

He started flipping through the book as she realized it was an English to German dictionary. He stopped on a page. With his finger holding a place, he said, "Verloven." He pointed back in the direction of the airport and said, "Flugzeug. Lost on the plane."

The driver shook his head knowingly, tossed the backpack in the trunk, and slammed it closed. He opened the back door and waved them inside. Once they were seated, he turned back to them and asked, "Hotel?"

Shannon and Neil looked at each other, once again caught off guard. Shannon tried to think of an appropriate response when Neil said, "Whatever hotel you recommend, my friend. Take us to the best hotel in Ruhpolding."

The driver cast a confused glare back at them. After a moment he said, "Reservation?"

"No," Neil replied. "We have no reservations. You take us to a hotel."

The driver didn't change his confused expression. "No reservations?"

"No," Neil said again. "Please take us to the best hotel."

"Yes," he said as he nodded his head and started to drive.

After a few minutes of driving, Shannon asked, "Do you have any idea where the woman that we're looking for lives?"

"Unfortunately, no."

"How big is this town?"

"About fifty square miles with a population a little over six thousand."

"Are you sure that she's still alive and lives here?"

"Our intelligence is limited, but we know The Power has remained very interested in this little village."

"So basically we're on a wild goose chase?"

"That's why I need your help."

After suddenly pulling off the highway, the driver asked, "Steinbach?"

"I'm sorry," Neil replied, "I don't know what that means."

"Hotel. Hotel Steinbach."

"Yes. Of course," Neil replied as if he knew of the hotel. "The Hotel Steinbach would be just fine."

The driver seemed pleased and proceeded speedily around several sharp corners. Then, after climbing up a tall hill, a great green landscape opened before them. "Ruhpolding," he said in an excited voice. And for the first time, Shannon and Neil set their eyes on the town.

It was a bright green valley, surrounded by towering mountains. Tiny orange and brown rooftops filled the perfectly green land, and gray lines sliced through the area like a spider's web. As they continued their descent, Shannon could now see the houses, hotels, and roads. From their high perch, she thought they looked like plastic toys on a child's train set. But when the taxi hit the dirt road leading into town, she realized that this place was real.

The vast mountains dominated the area as their white tops

reminded Shannon that they were supposed to be on a skiing trip. *If the driver only knew we were here to find the daughter of Adolph Hitler and Eva Braun.*

They drove along dirt roads, and occasionally came across paved streets when they passed more crowded areas. But there were no highways, no busy traffic, and only stop signs at rare intersections. They passed simple homes—most of them with pitched roofs and with some sort of balcony—and small businesses, which only differentiated themselves from the houses by small wooden signs hanging above their doors.

Shannon eagerly absorbed every inch of the beautiful land. This was the type of place she had only dreamt about. So peaceful. So quiet. So green. This little village, hidden away in the Bavarian Alps, was the type of place a person might never want to leave.

After a few quick turns, the taxi stopped, and Shannon saw a church steeple protruding above a thick patch of trees and shrubbery. The driver popped out and quickly opened her door. She stepped out, trying to determine if the church was on the top of a hill or was incredibly tall.

She wandered toward the impressive structure until she heard Neil. "Shannon! Where are you going?" She turned toward him. "Our hotel is over here."

Shannon turned and saw the Hotel Steinbach. There were three white buildings with brown trim, each three stories high. The middle building had the word "Hotel" above the doorway, which Shannon now realized must be the same word in German as it is in English.

As she walked to the front of the building, the driver was there, holding the door open with her backpack draped over his arm. She took her bag and strolled into the lobby. Her feet sank into the soft carpet as she admired the plush yellow furniture and long marble reception desk. She turned to see Neil pay the driver, shake his hand, and wave goodbye.

She waited for him before they approached the desk, and after finding a smiling young woman behind it, Neil asked the most important question he could think of. "Do you speak English?"

"Yes, sir. Welcome to Ruhpolding."

Shannon could see Neil's body relax as he breathed a sigh of relief. "We'd like a room, please."

"A room for two?" she asked, her permanent smile toggling between the two of them.

"With two beds, if possible," Shannon added.

The woman tapped a keyboard for a moment and then said, "Of course, ma'am." She reached for a set of keys behind her and placed them on the counter. "You have room 212, right up the stairs," she said, pointing to a hall behind them.

Neil handed her a credit card and she tapped some more on the keyboard. "How many nights?" she asked, her eyes fixed on the computer.

"Umm..." Neil glanced at Shannon, who shrugged her shoulders. "We're not sure. Just one night for now, but we may need more. Is that okay?"

"That won't be a problem. Our busy season is over," she replied. "Are you here to ski?"

"Yes," Neil answered as he slipped the credit card back into his wallet. "We love to ski." He turned slightly toward Shannon, fighting off a smirk.

"Do you know that the ski season is almost over and there are only a few trails open?"

"Huh?" Neil replied, his smirk now gone.

"There is limited skiing now. If you like, I will arrange a guide for you. He'll bring you to the few mountains where there are still open trails."

Before Neil or Shannon could respond, she turned and dialed the phone. A moment later she was talking in German into it. "We have to stop her," Shannon whispered. "We can't waste time driving up mountains with some guide."

"What should I tell her?"

"Let's tell her the truth...well, maybe not the whole truth. But we can say we're doing research for a book. Maybe she can help us find who we're looking for."

"Excuse me, Miss," Neil said loudly.

The young woman pulled the phone away from her ear and looked at him. "Yes, sir?"

"We won't be skiing."

"I'm sorry. I thought you said—"

"I did say that, but it's not true. But we could use your help with something else."

The woman hung up the phone and stepped closer to them. "What can I do for you?"

"I'm writing a book about Eva Braun." Neil paused, watching the woman's smile sink away. "She was Adolph Hitler's mistress."

"I know who Eva Braun is, sir. How can I help you?"

"I was told her family lived here in Ruhpolding—"

"Eva Braun was from Munich. Not here," she interrupted.

"I know that," Neil quickly replied. "But I believe her family lived here after the war. Do you know if any of her family members still reside here?"

"No family of Eva Braun has ever lived here," she replied coldly.

"But I've read that—"

"I'm sorry, sir. I can't help you." She jotted something on a piece of a paper and handed it to Neil. "This is the address of our tourism office. They can provide you any information about the town that you may desire. Enjoy your stay at the Hotel Steinbach."

She quickly disappeared into a back office, leaving Neil and Shannon leaning on the marble counter. They looked at each other, momentarily lost for words. "So what do you think?" Shannon asked.

"As I suspected," Neil replied with a sigh, "this isn't going to be easy."

CHAPTER SIXTY-FIVE

After dropping the backpack into the room and taking a quick glimpse of the hotel's pool and restaurant, Shannon and Neil found a street map of Ruhpolding. They realized the location of the tourism office was only a mile walk into town, and were on their way.

Despite the urgent nature of their purpose in Ruhpolding, the trek over the hilly countryside soothed Shannon's nerves. They walked in silence, the fresh air invigorating her lungs as her feet sunk in the cushy green grass. But it was the mountains that mesmerized her more than anything. Their long curvy slopes. Their bright green sides, leading to their snowy tops. They surrounded the village like they were there to protect it. A security force to preserve the simplicity of the place, and keep away the evils of the outside world. For some reason she found their presence comforting, like they were there to protect her too.

They reached the small center of the village faster than they expected. They found just a few official buildings, and located the tourism office with little effort. "Let's see if we have better luck in here," Neil commented as he held the door open for Shannon.

Inside, they found an office with two desks, a few chairs, and numerous brochures displayed on a large table. They saw no one at first, and glanced at the brochures, which advertised the various activities Ruhpolding had to offer: skiing, golf, tennis, hiking, mountain biking, and the plethora of hotels in the small town.

"Too bad we don't have more time," Neil joked as they hovered above the table. Before Shannon could respond, they heard footsteps from a backroom, and a woman—also blonde and smiling but a bit older than the woman from the hotel—appeared.

"Good day," she said with a heavy accent. "How may I assist you?"

"Hello, ma'am," Neil said, clearing his throat. "I'm looking for some information. I'm working on a book—"

"Oh," the woman interrupted. "You must be the Americans asking about Eva Braun."

Neil's eyes almost popped out of their sockets as Shannon's jaw fell open. "Excuse me for asking, but how do you know who we are?"

"We may not be as technically savvy as an American city, but we do have telephones."

The population of this town is only 6,000. Everyone must know each other.

"I see," Neil said. "So can you help us?"

"I'm sorry to tell you that Eva Braun has no connection to the town of Ruhpolding."

"It's well known that her mother and perhaps some other family members lived here after the war," Neil responded.

The woman rolled her eyes and sighed with disgust. "That's a rumor. There's no truth to it. If you're looking for Eva Braun's history, you should go to Munich. We can't help you."

"Thank you, ma'am. Have a nice day."

Neil abruptly walked out of the office. Shannon followed him into the street and asked, "Why did you give up so easy?"

"She's lying," Neil replied.

"What?"

"I don't know why, but I can tell she's not being truthful. There's no sense in wasting our time on a dead end."

"So what do we do now?"

"We need to talk to some regular people. Not hotel or town employees."

"Where do you want to go?"

Neil pointed across the street. Shannon turned and saw a small shop with a neon beer mug in the window. "I don't know about you," Neil said as he took a step into the street, "but I'm thirsty."

She followed Neil into the building and noticed a sign above the door that read "Freunde und Speise." She found herself in a dimly lit room with a long wooden bar and a few small tables scattered around. Neil confidently strode to the bar and leaned against it. The dozen or so people in the establishment went silent and locked stares on them as if they fell out of the ceiling.

"Beer," Neil said loudly as he slapped his hand on the bar. Shannon meekly slid next to him as she noticed the pale faces of the interested patrons had still not left them. He turned to her and again said, "beer." After once again slapping his hand on the bar, Shannon covered it with hers.

"What are you doing?" she whispered.

"What do you mean?" he whispered back. "I'm ordering us beer. Don't you like beer?"

"No, I don't. You know I prefer Scotch."

"We're in Germany, Shannon. Have a beer, for God's sake."

The bartender, a tall man with short, stubbly blonde hair, approached them. Neil held up two fingers and said, "Two beers, please."

"What kind would you like, sir?"

"Oh," Neil said, surprised. "You speak English?"

"Yes, sir. We have some American and Canadian beer, if you like."

"No. We'd like German beer. Whatever is customary here." The bartender nodded and turned to fill two mugs. Neil looked at Shannon. "So should we start talking to the people?"

"I don't know, Neil." Shannon glanced around the tavern again and saw the same bewildered faces staring at her. "These people look like they're afraid of us. Maybe we should take it slow."

"I'd like to, but we don't have time." The bartender plopped the mugs of beer in front of them. Neil took a hearty sip and turned toward the other patrons. "Greetings, friends." Shannon almost spit up her beer as she heard his stentorian voice bouncing of the walls of the small tavern. "I am an American writer. I have come here to do research on a book. I am researching the life of Eva Braun."

Shannon was convinced that not one person in the tavern spoke a word of English as they watched Neil with confused expressions. Until he said the name Eva Braun. Then, a mixed look of horror and anger consumed their faces. But before she could share her observation, he continued.

"I know that Eva Braun's family lived here in Ruhpolding after the war. I'd like to know any information anyone has to offer. I'm particularly interested if any of her relatives are still alive and living here. I'm also interested in where her family lives or lived. If anyone has any information, we are very eager for you to share it with us."

"Sir!" The bartender's voice erupted behind them. "That's enough!"

"What's wrong?" Neil asked like a scolded child to his father.

"No one here can help you with information about Eva Braun. She never lived here."

"I know that," Neil replied with the tavern patrons leaning close to hear. "But her family lived here after the war, and maybe some of them still live here."

"That's not true," the bartender fired back. "Eva Braun's family never lived here. That was just a rumor."

"How can you be certain? Maybe the rumor is true," Neil offered with a smile.

But the bartender did not return the friendly gesture. He placed his hand over the top of Neil's mug, and slid it away. "Listen, friend, you're welcome to stay here and drink. But if you insist on talking to my customers about Eva Braun, then I'll ask you to leave."

"Very well then," Neil said, stepping away from the bar. "We'll take our business elsewhere."

"Have a nice day, sir." The bartender dumped both beers into the sink and turned away. Neil quietly strolled out of the tavern. Shannon followed after a final glimpse at the still rapt pub patrons.

They stood in the street and looked at each other, their eyes glowing with frustration. Neil shook his head with disgust as he said, "What's wrong with these people? Why are they trying to deny that some of the Braun family lived here?"

"Can you blame them?" Shannon replied. "This town obviously relies on tourism as its main source of income. I don't think they want to be associated with a Nazi."

"Actually, Eva Braun never joined the Nazi party. They say she knew almost nothing about Hitler's politics."

"She married him. It doesn't matter what she knew."

"I don't agree with that, but I won't argue with you now."

"I suppose I should be thankful for that."

As Neil prepared an answer, the tavern door swung open. Shannon and Neil watched in silence as a short woman in her sixties slowly stepped off the curb. Shannon recognized her from inside, and was surprised to see that she was heading toward them.

"You ask von Eva Braun," the woman said, speaking each word awkwardly.

"Yes, ma'am," Neil answered, turning toward her.

She stopped walking as she faced them and said, "I say English. Wenig." She held her index finger and thumb an inch apart to indicate a small amount.

Neil pulled out his translation dictionary and said, "Go ahead, ma'am. I can look up words that I don't understand."

The woman looked confused until Shannon said, "Please. Tell us."

"My enkelin at universitat."

"A university. A college," Shannon said, and the woman nodded her head yes. "What's the other word mean?"

"I'm looking," Neil said as he furiously flipped through the dictionary.

The woman began to speak in German rapidly until Shannon slowed her by gently waving her hands. "We don't understand. Please talk slow."

The woman stopped talking and looked confusion. "Granddaughter," Neil almost yelled. The word is granddaughter."

"Your granddaughter goes to a university. Is that what you're trying to tell us?"

"Ja," the woman replied with a wide smile. "In Klasse. Sie project. Here sie forschung Eva Braun."

"Got anything?" Shannon asked as Neil continued to flip the pages of the dictionary like a speed reader overloaded with caffeine.

"I think she said her granddaughter had a class and needed to do a project. I'm not sure of the word before she said Eva Braun. Try to get her to say it again."

"A project? In college that would be a paper. Maybe she wrote a paper about Eva Braun."

"Here sie forschung Eva Braun," the old woman repeated.

"Wait!" Neil yelled with excitement. "I got the word. Forschung.

That means research. She's saying her granddaughter did research on Eva Braun."

"And she said here. She means she did her research here," Shannon said, her face bursting with exhilaration. The old woman shook her head yes, as if she understood everything they were saying.

"Where can we find your granddaughter?" Neil asked.

The woman continued to smile, not answering Neil. "What's the German word for where?" Shannon asked.

"Hold on," Neil said, flipping through his book. "Wo."

"Wo enkelin," Shannon said slowly, over pronouncing each syllable.

"Here," the woman said.

"Here?" Shannon asked, surprised. "In Ruhpolding?" The woman nodded her head yes.

"Can you take us to her?" Neil asked, finally putting the book down. "Wo enkelin jetzt?"

The woman nodded her head again and said, "Mein haus."

"Translation?" Shannon asked, nudging Neil to look in the dictionary again.

Once again, he madly flipped pages. When he stopped, he focused on something, and then a wide smile came across his face.

"What is it? What did she say?"

He closed the book, still smiling, and said, "My house."

CHAPTER SIXTY-SIX

Even though it was two days before the President would be in New Haven, certain streets in the downtown area were already closed. The block surrounding Woolsey Hall was abuzz with activity. Inside the historic building, technicians worked on transforming the stage to suit the President's needs. And outside, secret service agents were busy inspecting nearby buildings and barricading roads and alleyways.

The Bald Man sat across the street on a bench. He was dressed in a blue jogging suit, and was unarmed. Various secret service agents examined him as they passed, but on the surface he was no one to fear. Just a local guy on his lunch break, hanging out on a bench.

When George Winfield walked by, he paused by the Bald Man and put his foot on his bench, pretending to tie his shoe. "Three blocks down on your right in ten minutes. Clark's Dairy. Sit at the counter."

The Bald Man nodded his head without looking at George, and as quick as he came, the Secret Service agent vanished. The Bald Man eyeballed the side of Woolsey Hall. He was about to find out the details of what his team would need to do, but he knew the side door was their point of entry. In just two days, his team would barrel through the door and add another chapter to a history book that began with John Wilkes Booth at Ford Theatre—the assassinations of U.S. presidents.

The Bald Man stared at the side door, thinking. In two days the hand of Adolph Hitler will reach up from the grave and grab the United States by its throat. Then the world will know that the Third Reich did not fail, but was just waiting for their opportunity. Now, it was time for the Fuhrer's vision to come to fruition. And the assassination of this president would begin it all.

He stood up and walked down the street, trying to hide his smirk at the sight of the busy agents in the area. If they only knew. He walked into Clark's Dairy and sat the counter. The diner was hopping and a stocky bald man in a jogging suit drew no attention at all. So little, in fact, that he sat there for several minutes before a waitress approached him.

As he ordered a cheeseburger and a strawberry milkshake, George plopped next to him. Without looking at the Bald Man, George said, "I'll have the grilled cheese and the beef barley soup." The waitress jotted down their order and flew away to another customer.

George looked forward, acting as if he didn't know the Bald Man. He spoke under his breath. "Your team knows what to do?"

"We'll wait across the street for a signal from you. When we see it, we'll move forward on the door."

"I hope your men are good shots."

"The best."

"Because when I open that door, your men will have a second, a second and a half at best, to set, aim, and fire. It's not an easy assignment."

"They've been training for months. This team is good. And if given the opportunity set up by you, the target is dead."

George smiled, and nodded his head in approval at the Bald Man. "I like your style. But just so you know, I've been undercover for years. You don't get to guard the president overnight. So when I pop out that side door and signal you, my cover is blown. And in order to make my years of work worthwhile, your team had better take the target out."

George swiveled in his stool and looked directly at the Bald Man. "Listen, friend, I know your reputation. I know how tough you're supposed to be. But I want you to know that if you fuck this up, I'll personally tear your fat fucking head off, and shove it up your fat fucking ass."

The Bald Man chuckled, holding back a larger laugh. George was still facing him, and the Bald Man took the opportunity to glare in his eyes. "You listen too, friend, I want this just as bad as you. I've been working for this day just as hard as you. So if I fuck up, you won't have to fight me to rip my head off. I'll serve it up to you on a platter."

George turned away, once again acting as if he didn't know the Bald Man. "When you see me step out that door, that's your signal. After that, you'll have about two seconds."

"Consider it done."

CHAPTER SIXTY-SEVEN

The weathered tires of the ancient Mercedes rolled over the bumpy road, scattering rocks and pebbles in its wake. As Shannon glanced out the side window, she wondered if they could move faster on foot. The old woman's husband was the driver, and Shannon assumed he was at least ten years older than his wife. The man sat so close to the windshield that Shannon thought his nose could have been glued to it.

They were heading away from the center of Ruhpolding to wherever these people lived. But since the village was only fifty square miles, Shannon knew it couldn't be too long of a drive. And since they hadn't seen another vehicle since they pulled away, it seemed unlikely that the old man could cause too bad of an accident.

They were all silent now as the car picked up a little speed—maybe twenty miles an hour. But there had been a considerable amount of chatter up until this point. Using the dictionary and a lot of gesturing, Shannon and Neil were able to learn a few things about the couple's granddaughter.

They knew she was in her twenties and was an art student at New York University. Shannon assumed she was on a break from school, and chose to spend it with her grandparents in this quiet little sanctuary.

They knew she did some sort of paper that involved information about Eva Braun. She had done research on the paper. Research here in Ruhpolding. They didn't know if it involved contact with any living relatives of Braun—the language barrier wouldn't allow the conversation to get that complex.

But why else would she do the research here? What does this village have to offer, except, possibly, relatives of Eva Braun?

As they drove farther away from the center, only a few houses now dotted the landscape. They passed an occasional farm, but nothing that looked too busy. Shannon was not accustomed to this type of peace. This village moved in slow motion even compared to the most serene New England town.

The screeching of a belt and rattling of something loose under the hood blasted across the still countryside as the old man wrestled with the steering wheel, guiding the rusted hunk of metal into a driveway. At the end of the driveway, Shannon saw the little house that this couple called home.

Before Shannon could even open the door, a young woman appeared in the doorway and bounced over to the car. Shannon and Neil climbed out of the enormous vehicle and stood on the lawn as the girl and the old couple spoke in German.

Shannon assumed she couldn't be older than twenty-one or twenty-two. In just shorts and a tee shirt, she was able to admire the girl's toned legs that supported her skinny five-foot-nine frame. As their conversation continued, the girl's eyes darted between Shannon and Neil. After a while she stopped talking, and listened to the hurried speech of her grandparents.

Then, the talk ended abruptly and the couple was on their way up the walkway. The girl's face broke into a wide smile as she took a few steps toward Shannon and Neil. She extended her hand and spoke with an accent. "Welcome. It's nice to meet you. I'm Berlin."

"Berlin," Neil shot back. "Like the city?"

"Yes...well, that's not my real name. That's where I'm from. But everyone at school calls me that. So, I guess it's like my name now."

"It's very nice to meet you, Berlin. I'm Shannon and this is Neil."

They shook hands as Berlin said, "It's nice to meet you too. My grandparents said you're here to do research on Eva Braun."

"Yes," Neil said, trying to curb his excitement. "We're hoping you can help us."

"I should be able to point you in the right direction. I did research on her for a history paper last year. Some history books mention that her family lived in Ruhpolding after the war. But none of them go into any detail. So I thought it would be cool to write a paper about it since my grandparents live here."

"How did it work out for you?" Shannon asked.

"It was tough at first. People in this town don't like to talk about it. I don't think they want to be known for that. But, anyway, I eventually found the right people and the paper came out great. I got an A plus."

"Congratulations," Neil said, feigning a smile. "So you can set us up with some of these people that you talked with?"

"Sure. But why don't you come inside first."

"We don't mind talking out here," Neil said.

"Actually, it's my grandparents that want you to come inside."

"Oh really?" Neil replied with a raised eyebrow.

"They said that you two really like beer. He brews his own in the basement and he wants you to drink some."

Shannon had to paralyze the muscles in her face to hide her disgust. She hated beer to begin with, and the thought of drinking some old man's homemade swill made her stomach turn.

"That would be wonderful," Neil said, his grin aimed at Shannon. "We do love beer."

"Great. Come inside then." They followed her to the front door. She turned to face them, her hand poised to push open the door. "I should mention one thing. My grandfather's beer is not like American beer. But if you really like beer, you might think it's okay. But I should warn you that my grandmother makes her own schnapps. She may offer you some, but I strongly advise that you do not drink it."

Berlin pushed open the door, leaving Shannon to ponder the warning. Neil happily strolled inside, and clasped Shannon's hand, gently pulling her with him. The house was small, dusty, and cluttered with books and boxes. Berlin swiped off an area on the couch and kicked the debris under it. They couldn't see the couple, but could faintly hear their chatter not far off.

"Have a seat," she said, her baby face flashing a smile. "I'll be right back. I have to get some warmer clothes on. I guess I'm a little too anxious for spring to come. Did you know people are still coming here to ski?"

"So we've heard," Neil said and watched Berlin sashay out of the room.

"You know I hate beer," Shannon angrily whispered.

"We're in a mountainside village in the Bavarian Alps, and a native man is kindly offering some of his beer that he probably lovingly made after years of practice. What could be better than this?"

"I could think of a thousand things."

"Just smile and force it down. He'll probably only offer us one each, anyway."

A wooden door suddenly burst open, and the old man appeared, backing his way into the room. After several steps, Shannon could see that he was struggling with something. Then, his wife appeared behind them, and she could clearly see what they were carrying.

The hard plastic crate contained a dozen two-liter soda bottles. As Neil jumped to his feet and helped the couple guide the crate onto to the coffee table, Shannon could see that the bottles did not contain soda but a yellow liquid that she knew could only be one thing.

The woman disappeared into the kitchen and was back in an instant with four tall beer steins before Shannon could force down the lump in her throat. Berlin returned, now wearing a sweatshirt and jeans, and smiled when she saw the crate of beer. The old man handed Shannon a stein and immediately filled it. Now that Shannon was holding the brew, her worst fear was confirmed: the beer was warm.

"Getrank! Getrank!" the old man yelled as he waved his arm at Shannon.

"He wants you to drink," Berlin interjected.

The couple exchanged some words as Shannon realized everyone had a full stein, except Berlin who held bottled water. "They want to toast," Berlin said, raising her water. They all lifted their beers and paused as the old man said something that Shannon and Neil could not understand.

They tapped their drinks together and took a big sip, save Shannon who held the rim of the mug against her lips. Then, with eyes closed, she forced some of the warm liquid into her mouth and down her throat. Although she had never consumed warm rusty water before, she thought that this is what it must taste like.

She sat down, flashing dagger eyes at Neil, who offered a fake smile back at her. "So, Berlin," Neil began, "what can you tell us?"

They all sat except the woman who once again dashed into the other room. As they watched her go, Berlin said, "My grandparents want you to watch slides of their summer vacation to Greece."

Oh God, Shannon thought as she pretended to take another sip.

The woman carried a projector into the room and placed it next to the crate of beer. "You know," Neil said, still smiling, "normally we would love to see slides of Greece, but we're in a bit of a rush."

The couple talked furiously as they manipulated the projector, aiming it at the wall. "I'm sorry," Berlin said, "but they're very persistent. I think it would just be easier if you sat through the slides, and then I'll tell you everything I know."

"Okay then," Neil said, relaxing against the couch. "That's what we'll do." He looked at Shannon and raised his stein. "All we need now is some popcorn."

CHAPTER SIXTY-EIGHT

She never imagined that she would be able to do such a thing. But somehow—due to the constant pressure from the old couple— Shannon was nearing the end of her third stein of beer. The others were probably on their sixth, so her drinking ability didn't impress anyone. But she was proud of the effort she made to swallow the putrid, foul-tasting ale.

When she placed the mug on the end table, she expected one of them to charge over, plastic bottle in hand, and insist that she have yet another. But to her surprise she was left on the couch, unaccosted. When she looked around the room—through her increasingly blurry vision—she saw the old couple putting away the projector.

Thank God! It's over.

To make matters better, Berlin pulled her chair over, positioning herself in front of Shannon and Neil. "Thank you for humoring them. They don't get many visitors."

"No problem," Neil said as a belch slipped out of his mouth. "The beer went down pretty smooth after the first couple. Don't you think?" He glanced at Shannon, who once again shot dagger eyes at him.

"Well, I appreciate it anyway. Now, I'll tell you how I went about my research."

Before she could continue, the old woman reappeared, this time holding a tray of shot glasses. Shannon focused on the glasses and saw that they were filled with green liquid.

The schnapps!

She recoiled against the back of her seat, a tsunami in her gut at the thought of more foreign liquor invading her. She remembered the warning from Berlin, and declined the repeated offers to take a glass. Finally, Neil snatched a glass off the try and placed it in Shannon's hand. She saw that he had his own glass when he said, "Aw, come on. You survived the beer."

He flipped his head back and tossed the shot into his mouth, the muscles in his throat constricting as he swallowed. Rather than argue more with the old woman, Shannon did the same. Her taste buds exploded in chaos as the evil fluid, which reminded her of gasoline, slid down her throat. She thought once it was down that the worst was over, but this was not true. Her throat burned like the worst case of strep she ever had, and then she gagged, but managed to hold off any unwanted regurgitation.

Berlin persuaded the old woman to leave the room, taking the rest of the schnapps with her. She extended a bottle of water to Shannon and said, "Sorry. Don't worry. I'll keep them out of here for a while."

Shannon gulped several mouthfuls of water. The pain subsided a bit, and she said, "Thank you. We really want to hear about your research." She thought she spoke her words slightly slurred, and noticed Neil's eyes rolling back in his head. Shannon gave him a soft kick to his ankle and Neil perked up, immediately focusing on Berlin's young pretty face.

"I started off by walking around town, asking people what they knew about Eva Braun's family living here—probably like you've already done."

"You're right. But no one would tell us anything," Shannon replied.

"I didn't have any luck at first either. But my grandparents knew of the rumors, and after I complained that no one would talk to me, they put me in touch with a friend of theirs. I'm not supposed to say too much about this because their friend was a part of the Nazi party. He isn't a bad man or anything; he was just a soldier who was lucky enough to survive the war."

"He lives here now?" Neil asked.

"Yes. And he's the one who knew about the old farmhouse."

"Farmhouse?" Shannon asked.

"That's right. The Braun family owned a plot of farming land with a house on it here in Ruhpolding. There was even a rumor that Hitler himself purchased the home, so Eva's parents would have a quiet place to live during the war. We don't know if that part is true, but I was able to confirm through town records that the land was owned by Fritz and Franziska Braun, Eva's parents."

"Do you know where this farmhouse is?" Neil asked, almost falling off his chair.

"I know exactly where it is."

Shannon and Neil shared an eager look. "What happened to Eva's parents?" Shannon asked.

"Her father died in the sixties, and her mother died in 1976. But they didn't live here alone. They had another daughter, who was a couple of years younger than Eva. Her name was Gretl."

"I've read about her," Neil interrupted. "Wasn't she married to one of Hitler's lieutenants?"

"Yes, she was. His name was George Otto Hermann Fegelein. There's a famous picture of Hitler and Eva together at Gretl and George's wedding. But unfortunately, things didn't turn out too well for Gretl and George. He tried to flee the country near the end of the war, but Hitler's men caught and killed him."

"He had his own brother-in-law killed?" Shannon asked, surprised.

"What do you expect?" Berlin said as she flipped the hair off her face. "He was Adolph Hitler."

"Tough family to marry into," Neil commented. "So did Gretl live here in the farmhouse with her parents?"

"Yes. After her husband was killed and the war ended, she and her daughter moved in with them."

"She had a daughter? With George?" Shannon asked.

"She gave birth to her in 1945. Just a short time before her husband was killed."

"That's very sad," Shannon added.

"She named her Eva," Berlin said.

"Eva?" Neil said, surprised. "She named her daughter after her sister?"

"That's right," Berlin began. "Gretl named her daughter after Eva, and there was a rumor that Eva named her daughter after Gretl."

"What did you say?" Shannon asked, her mouth hanging open. "Did you say that Eva Braun had a daughter?"

"It was just a rumor," Berlin clarified. "Supposedly, Eva had a daughter near the same time as her sister. The rumor says that they named their daughters after each other; Gretl naming her daughter Eva, and Eva naming her daughter Gretl."

"Impossible to know if it's true or not, though," Neil commented, sneaking a look at Shannon.

"Actually, I was able to confirm at least half the rumor," Berlin said.

"What do you mean?" Shannon asked.

"I met Eva Braun."

"What?" Neil said as Shannon joined his shocked expression.

"Of course I mean Gretl's daughter, not the Eva Braun."

"Oh," Neil replied, understanding now. "She used the surname Braun instead of her husband's name."

"That's what Eva told me. But it gets complicated. Her father's name was Fegelein, but Gretl refused to use that name, and wanted her to use the name Braun. But then the whole family was forced to change their name because of how famous Eva became after the war."

"After the war?" Shannon said. "Wasn't Eva also famous before and during the war?"

"Believe it or not, no. Even though she was Hitler's mistress since 1932, he kept their affair a secret. There are many theories on why he chose to do that, but their relationship didn't become common knowledge until they died together in April of 1945. Then, slowly, she became a household name, and her poor family had to deal with it."

"So what did the family change their name to?" Neil asked.

"Wolfenhaus," Berlin said and took a big chug of water.

"Why Wolfenhaus?" Shannon asked.

"Eva didn't tell me. But I have my own theory. Hitler's favorite animal was the wolf. In fact, in some circles, that was his nickname. And, as you probably know, *haus* in German is house."

"So it means house of the wolf?" Shannon said.

"That's right. But the word 'house' is also an old interpretation for your family. What house you were from meant what family you were a part of."

"So it means the family of the wolf?" Shannon said.

"Or, since that was Hitler's nickname, it could mean the family of Hitler."

"That's kind of creepy," Shannon said.

"A lot of this is creepy," Berlin said. "But Eva Wolfenhaus is a very nice sixty-year-old woman who lives in a suburb outside of Munich. In her heart, as it was in her mother's heart, she is Eva Braun, named after her aunt."

Neil straightened up, trying to shake off his buzz and said, "So Eva Wolfenhaus grew up here in Ruhpolding? In that farmhouse?"

"That's what she told me. After her grandmother died she lived there with her mother and a cousin."

Shannon almost jumped out of her skin as she saw Neil's face turn white as a sheet. "Cousin?" Neil said, suppressing his shock.

"Yes. She said she grew up with her cousin. I tried to find out how they were related, but she wouldn't talk about it."

"And what about now?" Neil said, almost falling into Berlin's lap. "Who lives in the farmhouse now?"

"I looked that up in the town records. The deed was transferred to Eva Wolfenhaus as part of her inheritance. When I asked her about it, she confirmed that she owns the property. She said that someday she'll sell it, but right now she has a cousin who lives there."

"A cousin?" Shannon asked. "Is it the same cousin she grew up with?"

"I asked her that, but she wouldn't give me a straight answer. In fact, she avoided most questions about the farmhouse, and wouldn't say much about her cousin."

"I wonder if the cousin is still living there," Shannon said.

"I went there to find out."

Shannon and Neil both sat back in their seats, trying to hide the hurricane in their stomachs. "You went to the farmhouse?" Shannon managed to spit out.

"Yes, I did. There's a woman in her sixties living there. I tried to talk to her, but she shooed me away. I have no idea if she's Eva's cousin or not."

"We need to go to this house and talk to this woman," Neil said. "Is there any possibility you can take us there?"

"Well...maybe, but it's getting dark out, and...you guys seem a little drunk to go now."

"You're right," Shannon replied as she glanced out the window and saw the setting sun. "What about tomorrow?"

"I'm not sure. I'd like to help you, but I have some things I need to do."

Neil leaned forward. "I'll give you two-hundred American to take us there and assist with translation."

"Make it two-fifty and it's a deal."

"You got it." Neil and Berlin shook hands.

"Would you mind dropping us off at our hotel?" Shannon asked. "I think we're too drunk to walk."

"No problem. What time do you want me to pick you up tomorrow?"

"In the morning," Neil said and they all started toward the door.

"How long will you need me for?"

Neil and Shannon met eyes, searching for an answer. "I don't know," Neil slurred as he stumbled into the door. "I'm sure we'll have to spend a good amount of time with her before she'll give us her blood."

The silence wrapped around them like a blanket as the young girl's eyes widened.

Drunken idiot, Shannon wanted to scream as she fired the angriest look she could muster at Neil's red face.

"You need her blood?" Berlin finally managed to say.

"Listen," Shannon put her hand on Berlin's shoulder, "if you're going to translate for us tomorrow, then there's a lot we have to tell you."

CHAPTER SIXTY-NINE

When the telephone rang, Shannon rolled over, dragging a tangled mess of sheets and blankets with her. She picked up the phone and said hello in a sleepy, mumbled voice. After listening to the message from the front desk, she bounced out of bed and looked around for Neil.

When she didn't see him she assumed he had left the room, but then she saw a sliver of light seeping through the crack in the bathroom door. She pushed it open, but it stopped halfway—like it hit something.

"Ahh," Neil cried from behind the door. Shannon poked her head inside, and saw him stretched across the white linoleum floor. She slammed the door into him again, and this time he rolled over. "What are you doing?" he garbled.

"She's here." She slid her skinny body through the small opening.

"Who's here?"

"Who do you think? She's in the lobby waiting for us. If she leaves, we're screwed. So let's get down there now." Shannon abruptly left the bathroom, and heard him scramble to his feet.

In a matter of seconds they were on their way down the stairs, both cringing from the hammers pounding inside their skulls. "What the hell was in that beer?" Neil muttered as they traipsed down the steps.

"It was the shot that did us in. Berlin warned us not to do that shot."

"From now on we listen to Berlin."

After taking a few steps into the lobby, their young guide popped up from a couch. They exchanged a quick greeting and then found themselves squeezing into her Volkswagen. Shannon vaguely remembered the vehicle from their ride home last night. She also remembered explaining their reasons for being in Ruhpolding, but her drunken haze prevented her from recalling the exact details of what they shared.

As the Volkswagen puttered down the road, Berlin said, "You two were a little drunk last night."

"I know. We're very sorry," Shannon replied from the passenger's seat as Neil crouched in the back.

"I'm the one that should apologize. My grandparents can get a little carried away."

"They're very nice people," Shannon said, smiling. "The two of us drank too much and that's our own fault. I hope we didn't do or say anything to offend you."

"Not at all. You were both very nice. But I'm not sure if you remember hiring me to bring you to a woman who lives here."

"Of course we remember that," Shannon replied. "Neil has your money."

"So you still want to see the cousin of the woman I interviewed for my paper?"

"Absolutely," Neil said, perking up from the back seat. "Last night we agreed to hire you to bring us to her and translate for us."

"Okay. Good," Berlin said as she navigated the Volkswagen around a corner. "Then I'll take you to the farmhouse. But you two also told me a lot of weird stuff during the ride back to your hotel last night."

"What do you mean?" Shannon replied.

"Well...you said that this woman that I'm taking you to see is the daughter of Adolph Hitler and Eva Braun. And you also said that there's a Neo-Nazi Aryan group in America that thinks they have this woman's son. And you need her blood in order to prove that this boy is not really her son, so this group won't launch an attack against the American government and eventually the whole world."

Berlin chuckled as she shook her head. "I've known my grandmother's schnapps to sometimes make people hallucinate and stuff, but no one's ever come with a story like that."

Shannon looked at her somberly as she said, "I know the story sounds crazy, Berlin. But...it's all true. We have to ask this woman questions about her past and her son. So while you're interpreting, we don't want you to be shocked by our questions."

"Oh," Berlin replied with a far-off look.

"We know this is bizarre, but we swear it's all true," Shannon said.

"So you're serious about this? I mean about everything you told me?"

"Believe me," Neil began, "I wish it was your grandmother's schnapps that made us tell you that story last night. But unfortunately, that's not the case. And we have very little time left to stop this Neo-Nazi group in America. As far fetched as it may seem, talking to this woman and getting her blood could save many lives."

"I believe you," Berlin said, her eyes fixed on the road. "I know it's a wild story, but it struck me as odd that Eva was avoiding talking about her cousin. And this explains why."

"I'm glad you believe us," Shannon said. "And we really appreciate your help."

"I don't know how much help I'm going to be once we get there. I told you that this woman wouldn't talk to me."

"We'll keep trying until she does," Neil said.

The road straightened out and they could see the flat, green, farmland all around them. "The road is somewhere around here," Berlin said, quietly. "I'm trying to remember exactly where." She slowed down as they passed each intersecting road and studied the area.

They came upon an intersection with a small white house with green shutters on the corner. The house was run down, with peeling paint and an overgrown lawn. The sight struck Shannon, and although she didn't know why, she thought this was the road where they should turn.

"Is that the road?" she said as they flew past it.

Berlin glanced over her shoulder, taking a long look at the road. "You know...that might be it." She stopped the car and took a better look. "Yeah, I think the farmhouse might be at the end of that road."

Shannon looked at the road again. She searched her brain for an explanation of why she recognized it, but found nothing.

There was silence in the car as they all examined the intersection. "Shannon," Neil said, his voice surprising them from the backseat, "how did you know this is the right road?"

"I don't know. Let's just go down it and see."

Before Shannon could spit out her last syllable, Berlin had the car turned around and they were off down the side road. They passed more farmland, and then entered an area with a broken, moss-covered, spilt-rail fence. The land behind it was unkempt, with overgrown grass. Then, as they passed a tall, dilapidated barn, Shannon began to think they were in the right place.

Berlin slowed the car and a red farmhouse came into view. The house had a pitched roof with light brown shingles, and the shutters hung unevenly next to the windows with broken and missing slots. The wide wooden door had a pile of firewood next to it. Behind the house was an area penned in with a wire fence. The grass was low in it, and in some parts there was bare dirt. But the rest of the land was growing wild, like no one had tended to it in years.

Berlin parked the car next to the barn, and shut off the ignition. "This is it," she said as she leaned her palms on the steering wheel.

"You're sure?" Neil asked.

"I'm sure that this is the land that the Brauns owned. But I can't make any promises about who we'll find inside."

"But this is where you found that woman you told us about?" Shannon said.

"That's right. She answered the front door of that house, but like I said, she wouldn't talk to me."

"Well, let's try again," Neil said and opened the car door.

"Hold on a minute," Shannon said. "If Eva Braun really did have a daughter, then maybe that rumor is true about naming her daughter after her sister."

"That's right," Berlin interrupted, "we know that Gretl Braun named her daughter Eva. And the rumor is that Eva named her daughter after Gretl."

"So if this woman is Braun's daughter, then her name might be Gretl," Shannon said. "If we can call her by her name, maybe she'll be more willing to talk to us."

"We don't just have the first name, but the last name too," Neil added.

"True," Shannon said. "So we'll assume this woman's name is Gretl Wolfenhaus, and see if that gets us anywhere."

They nodded in agreement and got out of the car. They walked alongside the tall wooden barn. Shannon eyed the weathered boards and jagged splinters protruding out of it. As they approached the front of it, she found the two swinging doors wide open, leaving a perfect view of the inside.

"Oh," she said with surprise as the three of them peered inside. "This was a dairy farm."

"How do you know that?" Berlin asked.

"The stalls inside are for housing cows," Shannon said, pointing to the long row of stalls. "And there's a trough where the cows would feed. And look over here…" Shannon walked into the barn as Neil and Berlin followed.

"Look at this old thing." Shannon kicked a dirty, stainless steel jug that stood as high as her hips. "This is an old milk container. Now they have machines that pump the milk out of the cows, but back in the day when this farm was operational, it was all done by hand." She walked a few steps and picked up an ancient metal pail. "The workers would milk the cows into buckets like these. When the bucket was full, they would dump it into the larger container. And then someone strong enough would carry it onto a cart, where it would be hauled away."

"There are a lot of stalls in here," Berlin said as she strolled back outside, glancing around the land. "They must have produced a good amount of milk. But what about the rest of the land? Didn't they grow vegetables and stuff?"

Shannon and Neil followed her out. "Actually, I don't think they did," Shannon answered.

"Really? Why?" Berlin asked.

"I know it looks like a lot of land, but for a farm it's pretty small. They probably used the land they had to grow cattle corn for the cows," Shannon said.

"Cattle corn?" Berlin said.

"Yeah, it's cheap corn that they would use to feed the cows in the winter. They stored it in the silo," Shannon said.

"Silo?" Berlin said, looking around. "Where's there a silo?"

"Behind the house," Shannon said, pointing.

They all looked but saw no silo. Shannon took a few steps farther into the property and pointed again. There, the silo could be seen in the distance, about a quarter mile behind the house.

"Oh," Berlin said. "Yeah, I see it."

"How do you know so much about farms? Did you grow up on one?" Berlin asked.

"No," Shannon answered. Her mouth hung open as if more words were about to come out, but she was silent.

Berlin stood poised on the balls of her feet, waiting for her to continue until Neil stepped between them. "I don't mean to interrupt," Neil said. "The history lesson about the farming is interesting and all, but we don't have a lot of time."

"Okay," Shannon nodded her head and focused on the house.

As they approached it, they saw a goat and a few chickens moving about in the pen. "It looks like someone's still living here," Neil commented as they stepped over the loose gravel that made up the front walkway. A moment later, they found themselves inches in front of the thick wooden door.

Neil looked at Berlin, whose eyes were now as wide as headlights. "When she comes to the door," he began, "tell her that we're friends from America. Tell her that we would like to talk to her about her son. Tell her that he's in trouble, and we're trying to help him."

"Okay," Berlin said, swallowing a lump in her throat.

Neil rapped on the door, and they all stood, nervously rigid as boards. They waited a moment and heard nothing. He knocked again and it sounded like thunder against the silence of the countryside.

Again, there was nothing. Their eyes shifted back and forth between the door and each other, wordlessly asking if they should leave or try again. But then there was a sound. Shannon didn't recognize it, but when she heard it again she realized it was the sound of floorboards creaking.

The door rattled and slowly swung open. Appearing in the doorway was the figure of a woman. At first she was just a shadow—like a mysterious specter from another world—but then the light crept over her face. Her steely blue eyes struck Shannon first as they darted between the three strangers, exposing her fear.

Shannon looked down at the woman's tattered dress and noticed the leathery skin encasing her arms. Berlin took a small step forward and cleared her throat, preparing to speak. As Shannon looked at the woman's face again—now seeing her uncombed gray hair—she became convinced. This was the right woman.

CHAPTER SEVENTY

Dr. Kuhn's high heels clicked against the polished hardwood floor, announcing her presence in the Supreme Leader's private chamber. With her silk robe just skimming the tops of her ankles, she halted her promenade, now standing next to the Leader's leather chair.

He turned his attention away from the television monitor, and swiveled the chair to face her. "Oh my," he said, his eyes lighting up at the sight of her red robe. "I hope I didn't wake you."

She smirked as she said, "Hardly, Your Excellency. I wore something suitable for the occasion, but prefer that your guards don't partake in the view."

"Excellent, Doctor. As you can see, the boy is waiting for you." The Leader gestured to the monitor.

Kuhn focused on the screen as her eyes widened with surprise at the sight of the boy sitting in the living room of the Fuhrer's house. "So this is your surveillance that you told me about."

"Yes indeed, my dear." The Leader clicked a remote, switching the monitor to various rooms. "I can watch him wherever he goes in the house. He's far too valuable to entrust his security entirely on the guards. We were lucky to have the cameras in place when Randolph decided to pull his stunt."

"You watched him hang himself?"

"I didn't see the act itself. But when I turned on the monitor I saw that sorry soul dangling off the balcony like a dried smoked fish. Fortunately, I was able to alert the guards in time to get his carcass down before the boy saw him."

"What a fool. We have enough problems with the boy. We don't need to traumatize him with a sight like that."

"This is true, my dear. Which brings us to the topic at hand. You're aware of the recent difficulties with the boy making the speech?"

"Yes, Your Excellency, I was informed."

"Do you think you can fix the problem? We only have two days until we need him to make this speech."

"Oh yes, Your Excellency. I will have the boy ready for his big moment—one way or the other."

She flashed him a sadistic smile as the Leader returned a worried look. "Dr. Kuhn, you are aware of the mandate that we not harm the boy."

She chortled quietly as she unfastened the sash of her robe. "Why would I need to harm the boy? I have more effective ways to influence him." She threw open her robe, exposing the black lingerie that clung to her shapely frame like a shadow.

"Good God!" the Leader cried. He clutched the arm of his chair to prevent from toppling over as he almost choked on his own saliva. She closed her robe and refastened the sash as the Leader pulled himself to an upright position.

"Don't worry, Your Excellency, the boy will do exactly what I tell him to do."

"Thank you, Dr. Kuhn," he replied now fully recovered. "I didn't mean to doubt your...ahh...abilities."

"No offense taken, sir. But I do have one small request before I visit the boy."

"Of course, Doctor. What can I do?"

She stepped to the television and shut it off. Then, she reached behind the monitor and detached a cable. She pulled the other end of the cable out of the wall and draped it over her neck. "If you don't mind, I'd rather handle this without an audience."

"I understand, my dear."

"I'll return this when I'm finished," she said, gesturing to the cable.

"Very good, my dear. I have every confidence that you'll handle this matter sufficiently."

"You should," she said, and sauntered away.

CHAPTER SEVENTY-ONE

Shannon felt like time was standing still as she examined the wrinkles and lines on the woman's face. Like a traveler studying a road map, her eyes pored over every dimple, every crevice of her face. She knew she had never met this woman before, but still, there was something about her. When they had discussed the woman yesterday with Berlin, Shannon pictured her. And to her surprise, this is the face she had seen.

She realized that Berlin was talking, but her daze from the woman's familiarity kept her from concentrating. When she heard the woman's voice, she suddenly snapped out of it. Although Shannon couldn't understand a word the woman was saying, it was obvious that she wasn't happy. Then, without warning, the door slammed shut.

Berlin turned to them, her face sagging with disappointment. "Sorry. She wants us off her property."

"Why?" Neil asked.

"She said that she's had enough, and to leave her alone."

"Had enough?" Neil replied with surprise. "We've never seen this woman before. Do you know what she means?"

"No. I told her what you wanted me to say—that you're from America and want to help her son. But it just seemed to get her angry."

"You have to try again," Neil said. "Please tell her that we've never bothered her before. Tell her we just want to help."

"Okay," Berlin said as she unenthusiastically turned back toward the door.

"Maybe you should try her name," Shannon offered.

Berlin nodded her head in agreement and called out the name, Gretl Wolfenhaus. She waited and after hearing nothing, repeated the name. Then, after another moment of silence, spoke German loudly for a few minutes.

They waited a minute that seemed like an hour and once again heard the floorboards creaking. The door swung open, and the woman and Berlin broke into a fast verbal exchange.

Shannon noticed that the woman's face was no longer angry, but was curious as her eyes softened with each word that came out of Berlin's mouth. Berlin turned toward them and said, "She wants to know how you know her." Berlin's eyes widened and she continued, "Do you realize that if she's admitting that her name is what we called her then she's—"

"I know," Neil interrupted. "But let's play this cool. I don't want to freak her out. Just tell her that we are trying to stop some bad people who may have taken her son. And we want to talk to her about it."

Berlin nodded and turned back toward the woman. After another verbal exchange, the woman backed away from the door and Berlin turned around. "She said that she thinks we're mistaken about her son, but we can come inside."

Shannon's gut swirled like a tornado as she stepped through the threshold of the doorway. She moved cautiously, once again hearing the now familiar sounds of the floorboards. When she looked down, she saw the dusty bare wood boards, and had to step around one that was jutting up from the floor.

The room, which she guessed was used as a living room, was larger than she expected and had the biggest fireplace she had ever seen. But there was no furniture, save a wooden rocking chair and beat-up table with some dusty books on it. There were a few closed doors that Shannon assumed led to other rooms, but the only room she could see into looked like a kitchen.

Shannon could see Gretl standing in there, too shy or uncomfortable to invite everyone inside and offer them seats. Shannon could tell from the old woman's eyes that she wanted to do this, but didn't know how. So she stepped toward the kitchen and looked back at Neil and Berlin. "Let's join Gretl in the kitchen."

When she entered the kitchen she noticed that it was almost as large as the living room, but there was not a modern appliance to be found. In fact, Shannon didn't even see a refrigerator. Through the window, she saw two sheds in the backyard, and thought one was an icehouse and the other an outhouse.

Gretl said something and Berlin stepped forward and nodded her head that she understood. Berlin turned toward Shannon and said, "She's inviting us to sit down and wants to know if we would like tea."

Shannon saw the weathered farm table as Gretl moved near it. "Tell her to not bother with the tea. But please let her know that we appreciate being allowed into her home, and her kind hospitality."

They all sat at the table as Berlin and Gretl spoke. After a few minutes of calm, apparently friendly conversation, Berlin said, "Gretl welcomes you here, but would like to know what you want."

"Tell her that we are seeking information about her family," Neil said.

After a brief exchange, Berlin said, "She said she has no family."

"Tell her that we know she has at least one child," Neil said.

Berlin spoke to Gretl and then said, "She would rather not talk about that."

Neil leaned forward and said, "Tell her that we also want to talk about her past. Specifically her parents."

Berlin looked uneasy as she stared back at Neil. "Are you sure? We just sat down. I don't want to scare her."

"Neither do I, but we don't have a lot of time. We have to get this done as soon as we possibly can."

"Okay," Berlin said with a sigh. She spoke with Gretl and then looked back at Neil. "She wants to know why you care about her parents."

"Tell her that we know who her parents are," Neil said.

Once again, Berlin stared at Neil. "But Neil—"

"Please, Berlin, just tell her what I say. I would love to take our time and handle this delicately, but we have to get to Idaho in two days to stop a ceremony that will begin a killing spree of many innocent people. We have no time to spare."

"All right," Berlin said, stunned by Neil's words. "I'll just repeat whatever you say." Berlin spoke slowly to the woman and then hung on the end of her chair, waiting for her reaction.

Gretl's face reddened as her eyes were overtaken with wetness. Her head snapped toward Shannon and Neil as she gasped in shock. She jumped up from her chair and ran out the door, loudly sobbing.

Berlin flashed an angry look at Neil as she sat back against her chair and folded her arms. Neil watched Gretl through the window for a moment, and then hung his head, massaging his temples with a slight groan seeping out of his mouth.

Shannon abruptly stood. "Don't take this wrong way, Neil, but I'd like to take over."

"What?" He looked at her with a dazed expression.

"I want to talk with her." Neil opened his mouth to reply, but Shannon cut him off. "I'm fully aware of everything at stake. But I think a different approach will get us what we need."

"Go for it," he said and leaned back against the chair. Shannon stood, waved for Berlin to follow, and made her way toward the door. Outside, they saw Gretl standing in the far corner of the yard, leaning against a fence post.

Shannon walked toward her—stepping around the chickens and goats— with Berlin a step behind. When they reached her, Shannon took Gretl by the hand, pulled her to her, and hugged her. The old woman cried softly on her shoulder as Shannon held her tightly.

She gestured at Berlin to come closer. When she did, Shannon said, "Tell her that I'm very sorry for her. Tell her that I know it must be awful to have parents that are so well known. And ones that so many people hate."

Berlin translated the words, and Gretl nodded at Shannon, acknowledging what she said. Shannon continued, "Tell her that we know she is not a bad person. Your father was a misguided soul, but that doesn't mean you're like him. And we know that your mother knew nothing about what your father was doing. Your mother was a good person, who must have loved you very much."

Berlin repeated the words, and Gretl cried harder for a moment, but then suddenly stopped. She made eye contact with Shannon as she spoke, and Berlin translated as quickly as she could. "Thank you for your kind words. The only people who know about my parents have been mean to me. No one understands who I am. My parents died when I was a baby, and I was raised here by my aunt and grandparents. But now, I am the only one left."

Shannon spoke and Berlin translated. "You are a strong woman for surviving all the adversity you were forced to face. I admire you very much. But now, I must ask you about your son. He's in trouble and we have to help him. So, please, answer our questions."

When Berlin finished speaking, Gretl broke into tears. As Shannon held her hands, her crying subsided and she spoke. "I did a terrible thing." Before Berlin could speak the last word, Gretl was hysterically sobbing. Shannon held her, and looked at Berlin, wondering what to do. Berlin patted Gretl's back as she and Shannon shared a confused stare, neither knowing what to do.

After her crying calmed, Gretl sat on the ground as Shannon and Berlin flanked either side of her, grasping her hands. Shannon had Berlin ask, "Please tell us what you had to do."

"I know about my father's final testament. His group has watched me my whole life. The testament says that they cannot harm me or even interfere with my life, but they have always been there—watching. They wanted my child to fulfill my father's crazed vision.

"Although I knew they would not harm me, I worried for my child. These people thought the future of the world depended on my child." Her eyes welled with tears as she looked away. "I did a terrible thing."

"It's okay," Shannon said and Berlin translated. "We understand that you had some tough choices to make. We want to help. So please tell us what you did."

"I took the orphan." She cried into Shannon's shoulder harder than she had before.

"What do you mean?" Shannon asked.

After a deep breath, Gretl said, "When I became pregnant, I had to hide because of my father's testament, and I knew they were watching me. After I gave birth, I hid the baby in the basement. A friend of mine snuck it away and raised it. But they would visit here almost every day. I pretended the baby was hers when I knew they might be able to see. This went on for years, and then, I heard about the orphan."

"The orphan?" Shannon asked.

Gretl sobbed as she spoke, "There was an orphan infant boy that was left in town. No one knew what to do with him. And I did a terrible thing."

Shannon almost lost her breath as she realized what Gretl was telling her. "You faked being pregnant and then pretended you gave birth to the orphan boy?" After Berlin translated, Gretl nodded her head yes. "But what about your own child?"

Gretl spoke quietly, and Berlin squeezed the woman's hand as she slowly translated her words. "They never knew about my real child. And after they took the orphan, I arranged for an adoption to take place for my child. I wanted to know my baby would be okay. I knew they would never stop watching me—and they haven't."

"That's incredible," Shannon said as she hugged Gretl. "I'm so sorry you had to live through that. I know that must have nearly killed you."

Gretl shook her head in agreement when Berlin translated. Tears rolled down Berlin's cheeks as she spoke Gretl's words. "My heart died when my baby had to leave. And I will never forgive myself for what I did to that poor orphan. I pray to God everyday that both of them are safe."

"We don't know anything about your child," Shannon began, "but I think we know where the orphan is."

Gretl looked at her, her eyes begging for positive news. "The people who follow your father's testament have him, and are about to anoint him as their leader."

Gretl moaned in pain when Berlin finished. Shannon continued, "They will have a ceremony in two days, which will make this young man their leader in principle. But the people who really run the group plan to launch the worst part of your father's testament. That's why we're here; we're trying to stop them."

"I know of the testament," Gretl said somberly. "They plan to launch an attack on the world—starting with America."

"That's right," Shannon replied.

"I hope that you can stop them. But how can I help?"

"You're aware that the testament says they need the first male descendent of Hitler before they can begin."

"Yes. Of course."

"Well, the boy they have is not related to you or your father. If we can prove that to them, then we hope they'll stop their plans."

"How can you prove this?"

"We can do a blood test, and show the results to the people who are in charge of this group. If they see that the boy they have is not related to your father, then we hope they'll call off the attacks they have planned."

"Blood test?" Gretl looked worried as Berlin spoke her words.

"Yes. Neil has a syringe and can take some of your blood. Hopefully, if we're not too late, we can get the results of the test to the people who run the Nazi group, and prove that the boy is not your child."

"I don't understand," Gretl said. There was silence as Shannon and Berlin stared at the woman.

"What don't you understand?"

"They already took my blood."

Shannon froze, her stomach tightening in a knot. "Who took your blood?"

"The men who watch me."

Shannon and Berlin locked eyes as Gretl's words melted over them. Finally, Shannon spoke to Berlin. "We need to get Neil."

CHAPTER SEVENTY-TWO

Neil moved so quickly back to the car that Shannon and Berlin could barely keep up. He held the vial of blood in front of his face, the red liquid shaking violently in its container as he eyeballed it. When he reached the car he looked back at the girls, anxiously waiting to go.

"Neil," Shannon began, "don't you think we should try and find out who else took this poor woman's blood? And why they did?"

"I'd love to, Shannon. But I should share our itinerary with you. Hopefully, Berlin will be kind enough to accept some more money and drive us to the airport in Salzburg. Then, we fly back to Boston, where we go to my law office and have a DNA test done for these two blood samples. After we get the results, we fly to Idaho. Then, we sneak back into the Aryan compound and with some luck, find Peter. He then helps us to get the DNA results to the right people, who will then halt the plans that The Power has had in place for years.

"All this will obviously take some time, especially if you take into account the distance we have to fly and the time it will take to complete the DNA test. So, as much as I would like to know who else took Gretl's blood and why they did, we have absolutely no time."

"All right," Shannon said as she opened the car door, "let's just go. But when this is over, we have to come back here and help this poor woman. She's terrified that those men may come back."

"I give you my absolute promise," Neil began with his hand over his heart, "when this is over, I will bring you back here. And we'll give this woman whatever help you think she needs."

"I'll hold you to that."

"You can count on it. Now let's get going." Shannon climbed into the backseat as Neil looked for Berlin, who was still strolling toward the car. Neil took out his wallet and flipped through some bills. "Berlin, I've got your money. If I throw in another fifty, will you drive us to Salzburg?"

"Sorry. I can't do that."

"Jesus Christ, you drive a hard bargain for a college student. I hope you're studying business." Neil pulled out a wad of cash. "I can give you an extra hundred for the ride. That's all I have on me."

"It's not the money, Neil." Berlin said as she stopped walking a few feet in front of him. "I heard you talking, and I don't think your plan is going to work."

"I know. I know," Neil said, shaking his head in frustration. "You're thinking there's no way we can get to Idaho in time, but we have a private jet. So we might be able to just make it."

"Actually, that's not what I was thinking." She flashed a strange grin, one that Neil had not seen on her face before.

"What do you mean?"

"I don't think your plan will work, because I'm not going to let it work." Before Neil could move a muscle, Berlin pulled a small, black semi-automatic pistol out of her pants, and jammed it into his neck.

CHAPTER SEVENTY-THREE

They came a day early, but were prepared for the wait. Tents popped up all over the massive field, and the Aryan guards even allowed some RVs on the property. Propane grills were assembled, kegs of beer were tapped, and Nazi flags were unfurled. Skinheads, Klansmen, and other devoted followers of The Power buzzed with excitement, eagerly anticipating the weekend's activities.

The Supreme Leader watched them from his balcony. Seated comfortably in the chaise lounge with a martini in his hand—which he had to make himself with Randolph no longer around—he smiled with satisfaction at the sight below him.

They looked like ants, slowly crawling their way toward their mound of dirt, he thought. But they were his ants—his followers. And he would lead them to a future they never imagined. After the ceremony tomorrow, The Power will begin their reign as the most powerful group on the planet, he thought.

He knew all the people now occupying his field were here because they were told a new Supreme Leader would be inducted. He chuckled at the thought of it, and was glad that Dr. Kuhn suggested such a brilliant idea. What better way to call the followers of The Power to the compound without revealing the true nature of the ceremony?

And what a joy it will be to see the faces of so many loyal followers when the truth is revealed. The moment when the boy is introduced and gives his speech will excite the crowd beyond belief. They will know that the time for The Power has finally arrived.

But the Leader could not help but worry about the boy's speech. He still didn't know the result of Dr. Kuhn's meeting with the young man. Now that he knew the Bald Man had the two assassination teams set in Connecticut and northern California, there was nothing else to be concerned about, save the boy himself.

As his lips made contact with the fine crystal of his martini glass, he heard the now familiar clicking of shoes. In the past, he would rely on Randolph to announce all his guests, but now he relied only on his guards to restrict visitors. But he knew they would always allow entry to Dr. Kuhn.

When he turned, he was happy to see her. No longer dressed in the robe or lingerie, her white summer dress covered about as much of her body as a dinner napkin. He took pleasure in watching her long, smooth legs as she stopped just a few feet in front of his chair.

"It is done, Your Excellency."

"You mean the boy?"

"Of course."

"He will make the speech?"

"He will do whatever I tell him to do."

"Has he rehearsed on the stage? It's too late for him to practice on it now, as you can see." He gestured to the crowd below.

"You don't need to worry, Your Excellency." Dr. Kuhn tossed the cable to the Leader's monitor on the ground under his chair. "Everything will be just fine. But I wanted to let you know that he prefers to stay in my cottage with me until it's time for his speech."

"What? But we don't have security assigned there. I have no surveillance set up for your cottage. How will I keep track of him?"

"You're going to have to trust me."

"Of course, I trust you. But there's so much at stake here. We can't take any chances."

"This is not a chance, Your Excellency. This is a sure thing. Just let me handle him for the next day, and when you need him, he'll give you what you want."

"Very well, Doctor. I will leave him in your very capable hands."

She leaned close to him and squeezed his hand. "You're a very wise man, Your Excellency." She gently kissed his forehead, and flashed a devilish smile before confidently strutting away.

CHAPTER SEVENTY-FOUR

Shannon couldn't believe that she was, once again, in a private airplane. But with her hands cuffed behind her back and a leather strap restraining her to her seat, the ride wasn't quite as comfortable. She felt the heat radiating out of Neil's body—who was similarly restrained in the seat next to her—and knew he was furious.

Berlin walked by again, and this time Neil snapped at her. "Why bother with the handcuffs and the strap? You have a gun. What do you think we're gonna do?"

"Shut the fuck up," she fired back, "or I'll gag you."

"Why don't you just shoot us then? I don't understand what you need from us," he said.

"My orders were to bring you back to the Aryan compound. Which is where you wanted to go anyway, so you really shouldn't complain. Especially since I'll have you there in time for the ceremony."

"Oh yes," Neil sarcastically replied, "we're so appreciative."

"Let me ask you something, Neil." She sat in the seat in front of them, her angry eyes poring over them. "How can you be so stupid? Did you think you could just show up in Ruhpolding and start asking the questions that you did? Didn't you think we'd be watching her?"

"To be honest with you, I was looking for anyone from The Power who might be watching. I never expected that they would trust that assignment to a young girl like you."

"I may be young, but I know what I'm doing."

As Shannon studied Berlin's face, the young girl's eyes seemed to change as she spoke. It was a look that seemed familiar to Shannon. Like she had just seen this face recently. And then it came to her.

"Kuhn!" Shannon blurted. Neil and Berlin interrupted their argument and stared at Shannon. Shannon noticed Berlin's lower lip hanging low like a guppy's.

"How do you know my name?"

Neil's head snapped toward Shannon. "You look like Dr. Kuhn," she said.

"What did you say?" Berlin shifted her body toward Shannon.

"You look like Dr. Kuhn."

"How do you know my mother?"

"Your mother?" It was Shannon's turn to flash a shocked face.

"Yes. My mother."

"Who's Dr. Kuhn?" Neil interjected.

"She's a psychologist who's working for The Power," Shannon replied. "But it's obvious that her involvement is a lot deeper than that."

"Shut up, bitch!" Berlin angrily jumped to her feet. "You don't know anything about my mother or The Power, so stop pretending that you do. Who the hell are you, anyway?"

"You know," Shannon said with a sigh, "lately, I'm not sure if I know."

"That's your problem, bitch," Berlin said as she stood up and moved across the plane.

"Listen, Berlin," Neil called out, "if your mother is really a ranking member in The Power, then you're obligated to tell her everything that Gretl said."

"You don't tell me what to do, asshole."

"She confessed that she faked a pregnancy and led people to believe that the boy was her child. This is the same boy that your group is exalting as their leader. You can reveal the truth."

"Maybe I will. Maybe I won't."

"I don't understand why you brought us there and translated our conversation. If you were there to protect her from us, why did you help us meet her and talk to her?" Neil asked.

"Maybe we wanted to see what you would ask her, and what she would say."

"Then you should tell your mother that they have the wrong boy," Neil said.

Berlin suddenly lunged toward Neil and stuffed a rag in his mouth, which she then tied around the back of his head. She looked at Shannon and said, "I don't care if you know my mother. I need to get some sleep, and you two won't shut up." She stuffed a similar gag in Shannon's mouth and also tied it behind her head.

"There," Berlin said, satisfied with her work. "Now I can get some sleep. And if you have any more questions about my mother, then you can ask her yourself. Because she's the one that gave me the orders to bring you back to the compound. And she told me that she has a big surprise for both of you."

CHAPTER SEVENTY-FIVE

April 20th, 2007

Shannon and Neil were escorted from the plane to the idling van like prisoners—hands cuffed behind their backs with ankle bracelets limiting their gait to tiny steps. During the slow walk, it was obvious that Berlin was not joking. Four beefy security guards circled them like vultures, sneering like they welcomed a chance to get violent.

No one spoke during the ride to the compound. Berlin's face beamed with pride at her impressive catch. Shannon and Neil recognized the landscape of the compound as they drove through the front entrance. Only this time, something was different.

The area was littered with tents, campfires, RVs, and groups of people drinking beer and hoisting Nazi flags. Shannon couldn't stop staring at the now busy grounds that she and Neil covertly passed through just a few days ago. As they drove past a large field, they saw the impressive stage with light towers surrounding it.

Shannon wanted to ask Neil about what they were seeing, but didn't dare break the unnerving silence. The van stopped in front of a small house. The security guards and Berlin filed out, leaving Shannon and Neil in the van. Shannon and Neil watched the group talk outside as one of the guards and Berlin vanished into the house.

"What the hell are all these people doing here?" Shannon asked Neil.

"This is the day."

"What? What day?" Shannon leaned forward in her seat.

"It's April twentieth. Hitler's birthday. Now that they think they have Hitler's male heir of age, this is the day to launch their plan."

"And what, exactly, will they do today?"

"The boy will give a speech and that will allow the members of The Power to believe that the plan should begin. And they'll begin with trying to assassinate some very high ranking U.S. officials."

"What U.S. officials?"

"I'd rather not speculate."

"You don't mean the pres—"

"I don't know for sure, Shannon. But we have to assume the worst."

"So how can we stop them?"

Neil nodded toward their handcuffs. "It doesn't seem like we can do much now."

The van door slid open, and Berlin stuck her head inside. "Ready to get off the van, kids?"

"So you're real proud of yourself?" Neil said, his nostrils flaring in anger.

"Why shouldn't I be?"

"Are you as proud about betraying your organization?"

"What the hell are you talking about?"

"So I guess your mother must be the one who's making this revolution start before its real time."

"Real time?"

"We know what the testament says. The Power has been around in one form or another for sixty years. And through that whole time the various leaders have remained true to Hitler's vision. And now your mother is taking it upon herself to change things."

"She's not changing anything."

"She's letting this revolution start when she knows the boy is not the true male heir of Hitler. You know it too, Berlin. Sixty years of loyalty to one cause ended by a mother and daughter team."

"Nice theory, asshole. Too bad you're dead wrong. Now let's go. Off the van." Berlin waved them forward. Neil sneered at the blonde girl as Shannon stumbled out of the van.

She looked Berlin in the eye, their faces almost touching. "At least tell your mother what Gretl told us."

"Shut up, bitch." Berlin shoved Shannon forward into the waiting arms of a security guard. "Bring her inside and strap her to a chair next to the other one."

The other one? Shannon knew they wouldn't answer if she asked, but realized she was about to find out who was inside as the security guard roughly pushed her into the house. She almost fell, her ankle cuffs limiting her ability to stride long enough to keep up with the pace that was being forced upon her. But every time she started to go down, the guard would pull her up by the back of her shirt and propel her forward.

They barged through the door, and the guard pushed her even faster before spinning her into a seat. As they strapped her to the chair, she saw something in the corner of her eye. It looked like someone in the same predicament as her. She turned and saw Peter tied to the chair next to her.

She was about to call his name, but stopped when she saw the bruises on his face. He looked half-dead, like a man whose soul had long abandoned his beaten body. After a minute, his head slowly turned toward her, his small black eyes flickering aimlessly.

"Peter." There was no reply. "Peter, it's me." She thought he looked at her, but still, he did not respond. Neil was placed next to her and also strapped to a chair. Shannon watched him look toward his friend, and saw his eyes dart away in a mix of sadness and disgust.

The door flung open and Dr Kuhn made a dramatic entrance, her short skirt sliding high up her hip. She kissed Berlin on the cheek, and then moved straight toward Peter. To Shannon's horror, she lifted her pointy high heel and planted it in Peter's groin.

Peter screamed and squirmed in his restraints as Kuhn smiled, her leg muscles flexing close to Shannon's face. Kuhn leaned toward Peter and said, "So would you like to tell your friends, or should I?"

CHAPTER SEVENTY-SIX

The Supreme Leader couldn't be more pleased. He sat atop his deck, vodka martini in hand, and couldn't hold back a smile after seeing the sight below. They had traveled from all over the country—and in some cases from all over the world. As he watched them frolic around the open field, the pleasure rose inside of him like an ocean wave.

Mt life's work finally has meaning. All these people are here to worship the Fuhrer's vision.

He heard a noise behind him, and once again cursed that stupid Randolph. Now he would have to turn and see for himself who was approaching. When he saw the Bald Man, his expression quickly changed as a smile curled his lips.

"So good to see you, my friend," the Leader said. "I hear the kill teams are in place in Connecticut and California."

"They're prepared to take down their targets, sir. They only await the order from you."

The Leader glanced at his watch. "And they will have it in less than an hour. Why don't you sit?" The Leader gestured toward an open chair. "We'll have a drink before the war."

"Actually, Your Excellency, Dr. Kuhn would like to see you."

"That's fine. Have her come in. We can all have a drink."

"No, Your Excellency, she wants you to come to her cottage."

"To her cottage?" The Leader raised his eyebrows. "What for? Is everything all right with the boy?"

"As far as I know, the boy is fine. But she said it's important that she sees you right now."

"Very well then. I'll have to notify my guards."

"You don't need to bother with that." The Bald Man put his arm around the Leader's shoulder and guided him toward the door. He jangled his keys in his other hand as he said, "I'll drive you over."

CHAPTER SEVENTY-SEVEN

"The Supreme Leader's house servant, a man named Randolph, took a blood sample from the boy." Peter spoke cautiously, his eyes on Dr. Kuhn's heel that rested against his testicles. "He gave it to a guard, who was supposed to deliver it to Dr. Kuhn."

Peter stopped talking, as if he was done. Kuhn shifted her leg, causing Peter to squirm in pain. He continued, "I was friendly with the guard, and when I heard about what he had, I took it from him. I sent it back to our law firm with instructions to get it to you."

Once again Peter paused, and Kuhn put pressure on his groin. She slapped Peter's face and said, "Tell them the rest."

"But she found out what I did. And they've kept me prisoner here in this house ever since. They knew what Randolph was trying to do."

He paused, and Neil asked, "What was he trying to do?"

Peter looked up at Dr. Kuhn as if he was asking permission to finish. When she didn't speak, he said, "Randolph must have suspected that the boy was not the true heir of Hitler. He wrote a note to Dr. Kuhn that said she should check the DNA of the boy compared to the woman who they knew was Hitler's daughter." He glared up at Kuhn, who sneered down at him.

"Then what happened?" Neil asked.

"Well," Peter said and cleared his throat. But before he could utter his next syllable, the door rattled. Kuhn removed her foot from his groin and turned toward the door.

"It looks as if your surprise is here," Kuhn said with a wide smile.

"Surprise?" Neil said. "What surprise?"

"You lucky three get to meet the Supreme Leader," she said, taking a step toward the door.

Shannon thought of the injustice of the situation as anger rose up inside of her like bile creping up her esophagus. *What about all the innocent people who were hurt? The poor boy who was nothing but a pawn in this sick scenario. What about Mr. Henry, who is likely dead because he devoted his life to fighting this evil organization?*

She wanted to scream at Kuhn and the others, but controlled her temper. Her eyes focused on the door as she awaited the arrival of the

Supreme Leader. She knew this was the man that was responsible for it all. He was in charge of this evil operation, and ultimately, he was the one to blame.

Kuhn smiled as the door broke away from its frame. Shannon saw a leg poke into the room as Kuhn said, "Ladies and gentlemen, the Supreme Leader."

Shannon flashed a look of hate at the doorway. And then, the Leader entered. At first, Shannon saw nothing but the long white rope that nearly brushed the floor as he walked. Her eyes scanned upward until she saw his face.

She blinked once, and then closed her eyes for a moment, thinking she was hallucinating. She looked at him again, leaning forward to focus better. Then she realized that she was not seeing things. This was real.

She was looking at the face of Mr. Henry.

CHAPTER SEVENTY-EIGHT

When the truck lurched forward the milk cans clanked together, almost tipping over. As it pulled away, Shannon chased it, tears rolling down her face. "Come back. Come back!" she shouted.

She stumbled and fell on the dirt road. She sobbed so hard that a violent case of the hiccups consumed her. The cloud of dust stung her eyes and made her cough. She lifted her tear-filled face as her dirty hands spread sand and pebbles into her sweaty hair.

Then, his warm embrace engulfed her. "It's okay, baby," he whispered. "The truck has to leave so it can deliver the milk. It will be back for more in the morning." He carried her inside, gently brushing the dirt off her clothes.

She looked at his face and smiled.

"Take the handcuffs off of her," the Leader said, his nostrils flaring in anger. "Let her up from the chair. She is not to be restrained." He shot an angry look at Kuhn and her guards.

"I'm sorry, Your Excellency." She bowed her head, submissively. Nodding at her men, she ordered them to release Shannon. "It was just a precaution. She doesn't understand everything yet."

"I don't care," the Leader looked at Kuhn with disgust as the Bald Man slid into the room. "This is not acceptable."

As the guards freed Shannon, Kuhn said, "I accept responsibility for this, Your Excellency. It's just that she still doesn't know."

Once free, Shannon jumped to her feet and looked in his eyes. Still breathing heavily, she muttered, "Mr. Henry, what are you doing?"

The guards and Kuhn squinted their eyes in confusion as they watched Shannon approach the Leader. "I'm so sorry, my dear. I know you must be terribly confused."

"You two know each other?" Kuhn asked as the Bald Man now stood next to her.

Shannon turned away from him, her beet-red face broadcasting her anger. "I never knew him as this." She took a step away, a plethora of thoughts invading her brain. But then, one thought stood out amongst the others and demanded attention.

He had Derek killed!

"Why?" She screamed, whirling toward him.

"I'm sorry, dear?"

"Why did you have Derek killed?"

"Listen, Shannon, there is much you need to know. I know it's painful to lose a loved one, but once you understand everything that's at stake—"

She lunged at him and connected with a right cross to his chin. He fell back into the wall and toppled over. The guards pounced on Shannon in an instant, and held her firmly against the floor. Kuhn stepped forward and said, "Get her back in the chair. Put the cuffs back on her." Kuhn turned toward the Leader, who was being helped up by the Bald Man.

"That, Your Excellency, is the reason we thought it best to keep her restrained," Kuhn said, pointing at Shannon who was now once again secured to the chair.

"Very well," the Leader said, carefully stroking his sore chin. "But just for now. I'll explain everything to her. And when we leave to begin the ceremony, we'll release her."

"Release her before the ceremony?" Kuhn asked.

"She is not a prisoner here. Once she knows the truth, she's free to do what she wants."

"What is the truth?" Shannon screamed. "Why will you let me go, but not my friends?"

"Your friends," the Leader stepped closer to her, "are part of the ceremony."

"What are you talking about?"

"Today's ceremony will launch the final phase of the Fuhrer's plan, when our organization will rise up and begin our conquest of the civilized world. When the first male heir of the Great One has come of age, and will lead us back to glory.

"Included in the ceremony is a sacrifice of one of our enemies. We had some stupid disk jockey here that we were going to use, but we let him go. Your friends make a much better sacrifice, as they have been formidable enemies."

"But what about me?" Shannon said. "Why are you letting me go? I'm your enemy too."

"Oh no," the Leader said, moving even closer now. "You are not our enemy. Nothing could be further from the truth."

"How can that be? I don't even know you."

"Shannon, my dear, I've known you your whole life."

"No you haven't." She choked back some tears.

"I've been watching and protecting you from the day you were born."

"You're lying. I wasn't even born here. I was born in Russia. I was adopted by an American family when I was three years old."

"I understand that they had to tell you that. The truth would have been too confusing for a small child to understand."

"What truth?"

"The truth about you, Shannon."

She stared at him, her pale face trembling. Her moist eyes widened as he started to speak.

"I'm sorry you weren't told this earlier in your life, my dear. But the truth is—"

Suddenly there was a blast, as if a bolt of lightning ripped into the house. At first, Shannon saw nothing, as something burned her eyes. When she struggled to reopen them, Mr. Henry was gone. But when she looked down, she saw him lying by her feet, the top of his head now gone.

She looked up to see the Bald Man standing over him. He smirked at her, and then placed his gun back in its holster.

CHAPTER SEVENTY-NINE

Dr. Kuhn stepped over the body as the Bald Man moved out of her way. Shannon saw the evil woman's cold blue eyes examine the lifeless lump beneath her, and then she turned her gaze toward her. "Sorry about that, Shannon."

Kuhn knelt over the body and ripped away a piece of cloth from the dead Leader's robe. She handed it to one of her guards and said, "Clean her up."

Shannon didn't realize that she had blood and bits of brain splattered on her until the guard began to wipe the mess off of her. "I never really liked that stupid robe, anyway," Kuhn said as she stepped in front of Neil and Peter.

"I don't think I'll wear one," Kuhn said with a wide smile as she glared down at the two restrained men. "I've never been much of a traditionalist. Besides, it would be a shame to cover up some of my best assets." She gestured at her body. "Don't you think?"

"So you're the new Supreme Leader?" Neil said, glaring at her with disgust.

"Right after I'm inducted in today's ceremony."

"So you're the one that's deceiving everyone about the boy," Neil said, tightening his muscles in anger. "You know that boy is not the real heir of Hitler. You've orchestrated this whole thing so you can have the glory of leading this insane revolution."

"Not exactly," she said and moved in front of Peter. "Me and your friend here got to spend some quality time together the other day. He didn't want to talk to me at first." Once again, she planted her heel into Peter's groin as he winced in pain. "But you know I have ways of making men talk."

"So what?" Neil said.

"You should be thankful that your friend here told me what you and Shannon were trying to do."

"You mean in Ruhpolding?"

"That's right." Neil looked at Peter, his eyes squinting in anger. "Don't be mad at him." Kuhn interrupted his gaze. "If he didn't tell us what you were up to, then we wouldn't have done what we did."

"I should be thankful that you sent your daughter out there to kidnap us?"

"Actually, she happened to be there, and wanted the chance to prove herself." Kuhn met eyes with Berlin, who was standing just a few feet away. "But that's not what I mean."

Shannon and Neil looked at each other, their faces lost in confusion. When they turned their attention back to Kuhn, she continued, "Even though I thought Randolph was a pathetic fool, I decided to share the information with my colleague here." She gestured toward the Bald Man.

"He told me that there was a rumor that our former Supreme Leader had some type of cancer. We started to wonder if he knew he only had a limited amount of time, and perhaps wanted to advance the start of the revolution. So—"

"You had your men in Ruhpolding take a blood sample from Hitler's daughter," Neil interrupted.

Kuhn nodded her head. "That's correct."

"And you took blood from the boy and ran a DNA test."

"Very good, Neil."

Shannon, Neil, and Peter toggled their heads back and forth between each other and Kuhn's smiling face. Finally, Shannon blurted out, "Do you have the results?"

"Oh, yes," Kuhn said as she motioned to the Bald Man. He stepped forward, and pulled a piece of paper out of his back pocket. Kuhn snatched the document from him without taking her eyes off of her prisoners.

She stuck the paper in front of Neil's face and said, "They're not a match."

She dropped the paper, and as it glided to the floor, Neil and Shannon almost busted out of their restraints. Neil spoke first, "So what does this mean?"

"It means that today's ceremony will be what we told our members it would be for. The induction of a new Supreme Leader."

"Then there will be no revolution?" Shannon asked.

"There most certainly will be a revolution. But it will not start today. I will wait until we can do it the proper way. The way the Fuhrer instructed us to do it in his final testament."

"So what about us?" Shannon asked.

"You, my dear, are free to go." Kuhn looked at her guards. "Please release her."

As the guards untied her Shannon said, "What about my friends? I'm not leaving without them."

"Interesting you should bring that up." Kuhn moved between Neil and Peter, and looked down at both of them. "Even though your interference inadvertently helped us stay true to the Fuhrer's testament, you are both sworn enemies of The Power. And because of that, I should kill you both."

Shannon took a sudden, violent step toward her until Kuhn held her hand up, stopping Shannon in mid-step. "Let me finish," Kuhn said calmly, and Shannon took a step back. "I will allow you two to leave here alive for one reason."

They all stared at her, their mouths agape. "I want you to help Shannon get him home."

"Him?" Shannon asked softly.

Then, from the shadows in the far end of the room, emerged the boy. He approached slowly and stopped next to Dr. Kuhn. "This is the boy?" Shannon muttered out of her dry throat.

"Indeed he is," Kuhn answered. "Allow me to introduce John Keller, a young man who we now know has nothing to do with our cause. He lives in Houlton, Maine. And I trust that you three will return him to his parents."

"Of course we will," Shannon replied as she smiled at the young man.

The Bald Man released Neil and Peter from their chairs. As the men stood up, the Bald Man stepped on their feet and glared at both of them, his beady, soulless eyes cutting into them. "You may be able to walk out of here today, but if we ever meet again, I promise my face will be the last thing you ever see."

"Yeah, thanks, pal," Neil said and yanked his foot away. The Bald man took a step back, but kept his hateful stare on them. Neil and Peter moved toward the door, and saw that Shannon was shaking hands with John. Then, all four walked toward the exit.

Once outside, it took them a moment to figure out where they were. But soon, they realized the direction they needed to walk to get out of the compound. They strolled down the dirt road and awkwardly made conversation with John, who they knew must have been scared to death.

As Shannon fell behind a step, the chatter of small talk and the crunching of pebbles under her shoes mixed with the gentle rustling of leaves high above her. She stopped for a moment as her three companions continued, unaware that she was no longer behind them.

She watched Dr. Kuhn, the Bald Man, and the rest of their entourage making their way toward the huge field that was now filled with excited members of The Power. The sky loomed over them—gray as cigar ashes—and a gentle breeze tickled her cheek as she watched them get smaller in the distance.

She thought about the words of Mr. Henry. *He said he's known me my whole life.* Faded memories and vague dreams darted through her brain faster than she could absorb. But some of it was starting to make sense. Some of it fell perfectly into place.

She looked ahead and saw that Neil, Peter, and John were now about a hundred feet ahead of her. Although she knew she should catch up with them, she couldn't bring herself to move yet—her feet planted into the ground as if they were rooted there. When the noise of the sound system and the blast of the cheering crowd erupted in the distance, her companions stopped. Their heads shot back, and she knew they saw her. It was then that it finally came clear.

I know who I am.

CHAPTER EIGHTY

The hum of the plane was mesmerizing. Peter and John had been sound asleep for over an hour, and Shannon knew that Neil was fading. As tempting as it was to drift off to sleep, her mind couldn't relax. Until now there was no opportunity to talk with Neil privately, but now that the other two were sleeping, she decided to do it.

"I think I finally know who I am."

"Excuse me?" Neil said, leaning forward, shaking the cobwebs out of his brain.

"I know who I am."

"What do you mean by that?"

"I think I remember Mr. Henry. I've had dreams about him, but I never realized it was him."

"You've dreamt about him?"

"I think he may be my biological father."

"Why do think that?"

"I was told that I was adopted from Russia, but that idea never felt right. I always felt more German than Russian, and I think that's what Mr. Henry was trying to tell me before they killed him.

"He was going to tell me that he is my biological father. That must be why Kuhn and the Bald Man recognized me. They knew I was his daughter and weren't allowed to hurt me."

She looked at him, waiting for confirmation that her theory was correct. After a long pause, he finally spoke. "You're partly correct. I think it's possible that Efram—or Mr. Henry—is your biological father. But that's not the reason they decided not to hurt you."

"What do you mean? Why else would they not hurt me?"

"You say that you don't think you were raised in Russia, but in Germany?"

"That's right." She leaned forward on the couch, the plane's engine providing the perfect background noise.

"What do you remember about your childhood?"

"I've told you before that I have some memories of living on a farm."

"A dairy farm?" Neil also leaned forward on the couch.

"Yes," she mumbled quietly. "I think so. How do you know that?"

"I agree that Mr. Henry may be your father, but that's much less important than the identity of your mother."

"My mother? What does she have to with anything?"

"Everything."

Shannon looked at him with a confused face. "What are you saying?"

"Didn't you recognize it, Shannon?"

She stood perfectly still as the blood drained out of her face. Then, she realized what Neil was saying. "Are you trying to say that the farm in Ruhpolding is the place where I grew up?"

Neil nodded yes, his eyes glued on the floor of the plane. Shannon opened her mouth to speak, but then suddenly stopped and gasped as if a bee flew in her mouth and stung her tongue. Then, she jumped to her feet, her face as white as a bed sheet.

"Are you saying that woman is my mother?"

Neil nodded, and then rose his moist eyes to meet hers. "Neil," she muttered through trembling lips, "that would mean that I'm..."

"We know, Shannon. Believe me, we all know. And The Power knows. Hitler's Testament specifies that any of his direct ancestors are not to be harmed, or their life altered by The Power."

"I am not a descendent of Hitler!" she yelled, and then covered her mouth, realizing her volume. Their sleeping companions stirred but did not wake. Shannon and Neil were silent, anxiously watching them squirm on the couches where they slept. After a few minutes, they were motionless again.

"Listen to me, Shannon. That woman we visited is your biological mother. And as crazy as it may sound, she is the daughter of Adolph Hitler and Eva Braun." They stared at each other, the silence crushing them. "For what it's worth," Neil added, "she had no idea who you were."

"I don't understand how you know this."

"Do you remember when Gretl told us that she hid her real child for years and then pretended that John was her child to fool The Power?"

"Yes, but—"

"That child was you. That's why you remember growing up on a dairy farm. You spent the first three years of your life on that farm, when it was active and busy. She managed for you to be adopted by your parents here in the States."

"If that's true, how do they know who I am? If she had me secretly adopted, then no one should know where I came from."

"You're right, Shannon. But you have to remember that for that last thirty years my group and The Power have been in a battle for information. We've each had spies, gathering as much knowledge as we could get. It's been a war of intelligence."

"What does that have to do with me and where I came from?"

"People have been watching you—us and them. We suspected that you might be linked to the Braun family because of where you came from and the mystery about your background. Obviously, The Power knew as well. Efram had us fooled, and if he was your biological father and knew you your whole life, then he really tricked us. We had no idea."

"But you thought he was on your side, right? That's why you were at his house. Is that all true?"

"It's absolutely true. He was working as a double agent. No one was more shocked than I was when he walked into that room today. I thought he was my friend."

"I can't believe this," she said, staring at the floor and shaking her head. "I have to get out of my house. I have to hide and change my name. I have to—"

"Shannon," Neil interrupted. "You're thinking too far ahead. You should just go home and try and live your normal life."

"Are you crazy? They'll be watching me. I have to get out of sight. Go underground. Disappear."

"Listen to me, Shannon. You're in no immediate danger. They're not allowed to hurt you. In fact, they're not supposed to even interfere with your life."

"They've already interfered with my life. I don't know what they'll do next."

"The worst thing that you could do is let them know that you figured everything out."

"What do you mean?"

"They don't want you to know the truth. That's why they had Brad Palmer send you that e-mail when you were researching the Nazis. They were obviously monitoring your online activity and wanted to scare you from learning too much about Nazi history.

"Right now, I think they'll just have a couple of guys watching you. Nothing more. If you go about your regular life, they won't do a thing. But if you get crazy and take off or something, you may force their hand."

"Force their hand?"

"I'm not sure what their plan is. But they obviously will stay very interested in you. They're going to be on high alert for the next week because they're not sure if you know the truth. So the worst thing you could do is pack up and run away. That would force them to do something."

"I know what you're saying, but there's a thousand different things going through my head right now. How can I go back to my normal life?"

"You have to, Shannon. Go home and water your garden. Sweep your deck. Do your laundry. Rent a movie. And make sure you go to work."

"Then what? I mean, how long before I do something."

"I'll come see you in a month."

"A month?"

"I know it seems like a long time. But we have to give things a chance to cool down. Then we'll consider making a move."

"A move?" Her wet eyes poured over him. "What kind of move?"

"I don't want to talk about it now. Just go home. And be normal."

Shannon nodded her head and laughed. "Yeah, I'm normal."

CHAPTER EIGHTY-ONE

May 20th, 2007

Shannon rested in the chaise lounge, her neck slightly angled to the left so she could watch the seagulls devour the bread that she had left on her back lawn. Her joints ached as her body slowly relaxed into the plush cushion. It felt strange to be tired from work and the other mundane responsibilities that had so consumed her over the last month. She didn't think it would ever be possible, but she felt normal again.

But now, it was Sunday, the agreed upon day of his visit. Something was telling her that the feeling of normalcy would be over soon. Right on cue, she heard his car rolling over her loose-gravel driveway. She didn't move as she listened to the engine shut off and the door swing open. *He'll figure out that I'm back here.*

A moment later a shadow covered her face, and she opened her eyes to find that the object blocking her sun was indeed Neil. "Are you asleep?" he asked, jangling his keys inside his front pocket.

"Not anymore," she replied with a grin.

"It's good to see you so relaxed." He sat in a chair next to her.

"Actually, I only look relaxed. Inside, I'm boiling over with anxiety. Now that you're here, that is."

"I'm sorry if I'm making you nervous."

"It's not you exactly. It's just that I was able to get absorbed back into my boring life these past few weeks. But you being here reminds me that I still have some pretty big problems to deal with."

"So things have been quiet?"

"Very. How about with you? Have the Aryans done anything worth talking about?"

"They're laying pretty low, as far as we can tell. But that won't last forever."

"I want to talk to you about two things," she said. She sat up, and leaned close to him.

"Okay," he replied, folding his hands in his lap. "Fire away."

"What about us?"

"Huh?" He looked afraid.

"I want to know about you and me. And if that night we spent together meant anything."

"Oh. Wow. I didn't think that with everything else going on you would want to talk about that."

"Why not?"

"It's just that there are so many other bigger issues at hand."

"I think this is a pretty big issue, and I want you to be brutally honest with me. If you don't feel anything for me, then tell me now and we won't discuss it again."

Neil swallowed hard. "Well...the truth is..." He swallowed again and cleared his throat. "I'm absolutely crazy about you."

A smile took over her face as she said, "Really?"

"Honest."

"Are you just saying that to make me feel good?"

"It was torture staying away and not calling for the last month. I couldn't wait to get here."

"I'm glad to see you too." She squeezed his hand.

"So the feeling is mutual?"

"You bet it is."

"I'm very happy," he said, breathing a sigh of relief. "I wish we could be something close to a normal couple, and go on a date."

"You mean some place other than South America, or northern Idaho, or eastern Europe?"

"Yeah. Maybe the diner or a movie theatre."

"That would be nice." Their eyes got lost in each others until Shannon popped to her feet and started pacing the deck. "Okay, but I have to talk with you about this other thing. It's sort of related to our first topic."

"Go ahead."

"I want to ask you something about my biological mother, Gretl."

"Okay."

"Did she have any other children?"

"No."

Shannon's face cringed. "So I have no siblings?"

"That's right."

"So if they're waiting for a male heir of Hitler to fulfill the testament, how would they go about getting that child?"

There was a pause as Neil's eyes flickered. "I'm sorry to tell you this, but he would have to come from you."

Shannon collapsed back into the chaise lounge. She sighed with disgust and said, "That's what I thought, but I was hoping maybe there was some other relative they could use like a great nephew of Hitler, or something like that."

"I wish there was, Shannon. I hate for you to have this burden. But it's the truth. It's you and only you."

"So I can never have a baby?"

"No one is saying that."

"I should have my tubes tied right away."

"No, Shannon, you don't have to do that."

"But if I have a boy, you know what will happen."

"We'll fight them. We'll be there to protect you and your child."

"How can I take that risk?"

"I know this is very distressing, but we have some time to think about the best way to handle it."

There was silence. Shannon's head was hung low as Neil tried to make eye contact with her. "Shannon, what's wrong?"

She looked at him through teary eyes. "We have a very difficult decision to make."

"We?" Neil said, confused. "What do you mean?"

"My period is late."

"Oh," Neil replied and stood up. "Okay," he nervously circled her chair, "how late?"

"I took a home pregnancy test this morning. It was positive."

"Oh my God!" Neil sat back down and held her hand. "Umm...when...who..."

"You're the father, Neil. No question about it."

Neil's mouth fell open but only a slight gasp of air crossed his lips. "Like I said," Shannon continued, "we have a difficult decision to make."

"No, we don't," Neil said as he jumped to his feet again, snapping out of his temporary daze. "We are having the baby. There are no other options to consider."

"You're sure that's the right thing to do?"

"That's the only thing to do."

They embraced as tears welled up in their eyes. As they pulled away, Shannon said, "I know you said it was okay for me to be here, but I'll be showing soon and..."

"We can't let them know you're pregnant. We have to get out of here."

"When should I plan on leaving?"

"Now."

"Now?" she said, surprised. "But I—"

"Listen, Shannon, we can't give them a chance to figure out that you're pregnant. It's too risky to even stay here a couple of days. We have to go now."

"I know you have to hide me. And I'm sure you have a place somewhere in mind. But I can't stop thinking about Gretl. She seemed so lonely and afraid on that big old farm. It looked like she could barely take care of herself. I want to get her and bring her with us—wherever we go."

"To be honest with you, Shannon, I didn't expect to leave here today without you. And I knew that you wouldn't be able to leave your mother living in that place all alone."

"So what does that mean?"

"It means I already made plans.

"Plans?"

"Yes, and we should get going. The plane is waiting."

Dan has had several short stories published in various mystery magazines, including the U.K. magazine, *The Crime Scene*. He graduated from the creative writing program at the Educational Center of the Arts in New Haven in 1986. Since then, he has seen 18 of his plays produced on various stages in Connecticut. His play, *A Sparkle in The Sky* was the first runner-up in the 2001 ATHE national playwriting competition. Dan has had three short screenplays produced, and currently has two more in production. His feature-length screenplay, *Slip*, was a 2004 Project Greenlight finalist and a 2007 finalist for best screenplay at the International Mystery Writers' Festival. His debut novel, *The Camera Eye* was published in 2006.

Dan lives in Connecticut with his wife and two children. To learn more about Dan and his writing, visit his web site at www.dwsmith.net.

Printed in the United States
93472LV00003B/205-207/A

9 781591 332435